San Camilo, 1936

San Camilo, 1936 The Eve, Feast, and Octave of St. Camillus of the Year 1936 in Madrid

Camilo José Cela Translated by J. H. R. Polt

Duke University Press Durham 1991

Printed in the United States of America
on acid-free paper ∞
This edition has been translated with financial
assistance from the Spanish Dirección General del
Libro y Bibliotecas of the Ministerio de Cultura.
Originally published in Spanish with the title *Vísperas, festividad y octava de San Camilo del año 1936 en Madrid,*

Library of Congress Cataloging-in-Publication Data
appear on the last printed page of this book.

Contents

Translator's Preface xiii

San Camilo, 1936 3

A List of Characters and Other

Matters of Interest 291

Bibliography 301

July 18, St. Camillus de Lelis, heavenly patron of hospitals

To the conscripts of 1937, all of whom lost something: their life, their freedom, their dreams, their hope, their decency. And not to the adventurers from abroad, Fascists and Marxists, who had their fill of killing Spaniards like rabbits and whom no one had invited to take part in our funeral.

Translator's Preface

Unlike many another preface, these pages really are meant as a guide to the reader of *San Camilo, 1936*, supplementing the list of characters that I have placed at the back of the book. I therefore promise not to give away the ending nor to discuss details of the story that no one can understand without having read it. If you, reader, do not need or want any guidance, feel free to skip the preface. Otherwise, read on.

Almost forty years ago, Camilo José Cela wrote, "I consider myself the most important Spanish novelist since the Generation of 1898, and I am shocked at how easy that has been for me. I beg pardon for not having been able to avoid it." Read in its context, a prologue to a collection of the author's short stories, this statement calls for a pinch of salt; yet a commentary on Cela's contemporaries and a note of arrogance and boastfulness lie beneath its irony (also, seen with the benefit of hindsight, an element of prophecy). In 1989 the Swedish Academy consecrated Cela as still the most important Spanish novelist when it awarded him the Nobel Prize for Literature, making him the fifth Spaniard, and the first Spanish novelist, to win that distinction. At the award ceremony in Stockholm, Knut Ahnlund, a member of the academy, called *San Camilo, 1936* "perhaps Cela's masterpiece."[1] Who is Camilo José Cela, what sort of novels does he write, and what sort of book are you now holding in your hands?

Camilo José Cela was born on May 11, 1916, in Iria Flavia, a village in the township of Padrón, province of La Coruña, in Galicia, the northwestern corner of Spain. His father was also named Camilo José Cela; his mother was Camila Trulock Bertorini, whose family names attest to her Anglo-Italian ancestry. Yes, Cela's son is also called Camilo José, and his

1. Knut Ahnlund, "El Premio Nobel de Literatura, 1989," *Insula* 45.518–19 (Feb.–March 1990): 3.

granddaughter, Camila. The author's adolescence was spent in Madrid; at eighteen tuberculosis forced him for a while into a sanatorium. About this time Cela also had his first tentative brush with a university education and began, as many young Spaniards do, or did, to write poetry, which would not be published until after the Spanish Civil War.

The outbreak of that conflict caught Cela in Madrid. In the normal course of events he would have been called the next year, 1937, for the military service expected of all young Spaniards, but because of his history of tuberculosis, he was declared unfit for duty. Still he managed to find his way to the Nationalist zone, to serve in the Nationalist Army, which was evidently less finicky than that of the Republic, and to be wounded. Being a veteran of the winning side had its advantages after the triumph of General Franco; it may also be something that some people will never forgive.

After the war ended in 1939 Cela had another brush with higher education and another with tuberculosis, neither of which produced any lastingly deleterious results. He worked where he could, and he wrote: advice to the lovelorn, children's stories, articles, short stories. From then to the present his pen has produced a steady stream of stories, accounts of travels through different parts of Spain, satirical sketches of manners, poetry, drama, research in taboo words, and, most important for us here, novels.

Cela's first novel, *La familia de Pascual Duarte (The Family of Pascual Duarte)*, appeared in 1942. It is a violent depiction of lower-class life and came as a shock at a time when literature was expected to celebrate the blessings of Christian civilization that the Nationalist victory had supposedly guaranteed. It caught the eye of Spain's intellectual elite and also that of the censors, who confiscated the second printing. *Pabellón de reposo (Rest Home)*, published the next year, is also a horror story, but of a different kind of horror, the quiet desperation of those condemned to die in a tuberculosis sanatorium. Cela next began to write a novel that would reflect Spanish society after the Civil War. That book, *La colmena (The Hive)*, was rejected by the censors, and for good reason, since it shows a Madrid in which every one of the values in whose name the Civil War had supposedly been fought and won has been abandoned or perverted. It was published in Argentina in 1951. Twelve years passed before it could appear in Spain, but since then it has been constantly reprinted and also made into a movie (as has *Pascual Duarte*). *The Hive* was followed by *Mrs. Caldwell habla con su hijo (Mrs. Caldwell Speaks to her Son)*, a series of surrealistic letters addressed to her dead offspring by an Englishwoman who has been out too long in the noonday sun of motherly love. Then the government of Venezuela asked Camilo José Cela to produce a novel set in that country. The result, after a trip to South America, was *La catira* (*The Blonde*, 1955) and also, it seems, a substantial retainer that allowed Cela to move his family from Madrid to Majorca, where he was subsequently to reside.

Although living on an island, Cela in Majorca was hardly isolated. He maintained his connections with the literary circles of Madrid and established contacts with some of the leading figures of the Spanish intellectual world, among them Picasso, Miró, and the great historian of Spanish culture, Américo Castro. He founded a literary review, *Papeles de Son Armadans*, which published important contributions from Spain and abroad. In 1957 he became the youngest member of the Royal Spanish Academy. Books of various kinds kept flowing forth, including collections of stories and, in 1962, *Tobogán de hambrientos* (*A Slide for the Hungry*), a novel consisting of a carefully structured chain of micronarrations; but there was no major new novel until the publication of *San Camilo, 1936* in 1969. Since then three additional ones have appeared: *Oficio de tinieblas 5* (*Tenebrae*, 1973), a nightmarish evocation of the world whose creation was commemorated yearly on April 1, the anniversary of the victory of 1939; *Mazurca para dos muertos* (*Mazurka for Two Dead Men*, 1983), a story of the Civil War in the author's native Galicia; and *Cristo versus Arizona* (*Christ versus Arizona*, 1988), a stylized and deliberately deformed fable of the American Southwest.

Over the years Cela has prospered and become something of an institution. Surveys regularly proclaim him his country's most popular author. His books are instant best-sellers, and two have been made into successful movies. He appears on television and is interviewed by newspapers. After the restoration of democracy in his country, he served for a time as an appointed senator and took part in the drafting of the current Spanish constitution. In 1987 he was awarded the Prince of Asturias Prize for Literature, a major honor; and in 1989, as we know, he won the Nobel. It is worth remembering, however, that in earlier times, when things were a good deal more difficult for Spaniards, and especially for those with something to say, Cela not only dared to speak boldly in his own writings but championed freedom of expression for others. I have myself heard him speak public and courageous words in the Royal Spanish Academy in 1968 in defense of a man unjustly persecuted by the authorities.

Cela's fiction deals with a variety of subjects: murder, life and death in a sanatorium, a mother's abnormal love for her son, the apparently "petty pace" of daily existence, individual lives in the midst of historical cataclysm. There is, however, a constant theme that runs through it, the author's view of man as a pathetically limited creature. In a prefatory note to *The Hive* Cela writes: "The culture and tradition of man, like the culture and tradition of the hyena or the ant, are oriented according to only three cardinal points: nourishment, reproduction, and destruction." Man is thus no different in his essence from other animals, including, deliberately, some of those we least admire. He is not a lion or an eagle. He tries to survive and to find pleasure, and in the process he struggles, often ruthlessly, against others. His actions, his thought, and his morality are dominated by physiological imperatives. As an individual, he does not count for much in the universal equation. The concluding sentence of *Rest Home*, after the death of all the main characters, is: "The universe, unmoved by suffering, keeps on turning through space in obedience to the complicated laws of celestial mechanics."

There is thus little room in Cela's fiction for the "dignity of man." His characters are not heroes; they lack spiritual greatness and the capacity for either good or evil on a grand scale, and even when some of them show themselves to be capable of a certain altruism and elevation, a sordid note is always present. In *The Hive*, for instance, two young women sacrifice for the men they love, but in each case they can do so only by prostituting themselves. There is a touch of nobility there, but it is not unalloyed.

Such a view of man might seem bitter, but in Cela's case it is tempered with irony and compassion. Cervantes, an inevitable point of comparison for any Spanish novelist, showed us how an ironic vision can combine understanding for man's heroic longings with acknowledgment of his pitiful limitations. Unlike Don Quixote, Cela's characters do not usually have heroic longings, but not infrequently, when contempt for them seems to dominate, a small sentimental touch will humanize them for us and show them to be more weak than evil, more to be pitied than scorned. Precisely because they count for so little in the world at large and have so little beyond their poor bodies and not very great minds, the little that they have is all the more precious to them.

What is also evident to the reader of Cela is that sex, one of the "three cardinal points" of man's existence, looms large in his fiction. His characters are constantly busy with sex, obsessed with sex: mercenary, spontaneous, heterosexual, homosexual, incestuous. Sex functions as a medium of exchange in *The Hive*, and prostitution plays a role in most of the novels. Sex is frequently linked to violence, beginning with *The Family of Pascual Duarte*.

Violence, furthermore, permeates Spanish society as it is depicted in these novels, a sick violence born in part of sexual repression, grotesque in the tradition of such earlier Spanish writers as Quevedo, Larra, and Valle-Inclán and of the satirical drawings, particularly the *Caprichos*, of Goya. The modern culmination of this violent streak was the Civil War of 1936–1939, which, in the foreground or in the background, is important in several of the novels as well as in the travel narrative *Viaje a la Alcarria* (*Journey to the Alcarria*, 1948). The author's view of his country is thus another constant theme in his fiction, but the failures and limitations of Cela's individual human beings are not primarily the product of a social context but of the human condition and human nature.

If Cela's novels have a certain thematic unity, they display great formal diversity. From the beginning of his career the author has experimented constantly—and this passion for experimentation is the only constant in this respect—with varieties of narrative situations and temporal structure. The linear but discontinuous narration of a whole life told by its protagonist (*The Family of Pascual Duarte*), an exquisitely balanced juxtaposition of first-person fragments (*Rest Home*), a splintered and temporally distorted third-person narration by an often forgetful narrator (*The Hive*), a single but clearly demented first-person perspective (*Mrs. Caldwell Speaks to her Son*), the nightmarish flow of more than a thousand segments with almost complete elimination of plot and time (*Tenebrae*), the uninterrupted monologue of a not quite reliable narrator in which motifs, themes, and what we could call narrative modules rhythmically reappear (*Christ versus Arizona*): these are some of Cela's principal experiments with novelistic form, and in this respect his next novel will probably be different from all the previous ones, just as each of these has been different from the rest. At this point the English-language reader will be reminded of Joyce, Dos Passos, and Faulkner; this, however, is not the place to speculate about literary influences, but to note the fact that Cela, like his colleagues in other national literatures, has worked constantly at reshaping and expanding the traditional form of the novelistic genre.

One other feature of Cela's novels in general should be mentioned here: his enormously rich and varied language. Our author began his literary career as a surrealistic poet, and poetic prose crops up in the most unlikely places in his novels; the main roots of Cela's language, however, draw their substance from contemporary spoken Spanish, taking in its colloquial syntactic structures and its whole range of vocabulary (including the idiomatic, the trite, the vulgar, the picturesque, the forbidden). He is one of those writers (Leandro de Moratín and Galdós were others in Spanish literature) who have a superb ear for the rhythms and flavor of spoken language, the literary recreation of which is something very different from simple transcription of real speech, as anyone with access to a tape recorder can easily find out.

This, then, is the body of work within which *San Camilo, 1936* appeared. In 1950, in the prologue to an autobiographical volume, Camilo José Cela declared that his memoirs "will not progress beyond St. Camillus' Day of 1936. . . . If God grants me life I shall write my novel about the Civil War within fifteen or twenty years."[2] *San Camilo, 1936* is that novel, and it was published in 1969, just within its author's self-imposed deadline. That is, *San Camilo* is Cela's novel about experiencing the outbreak of the Civil War, and, though it does not follow the war to its conclusion, it is in a sense his commentary on the whole conflict. By now, more than half a century after those events took place, a quick review of them may be in order.

The Spanish monarchy had been progressively losing prestige and moral authority by the time that municipal elections throughout the country were held in the spring of 1931. Those elected were in the overwhelming majority monarchists, but not in the major cities, where elections were believed to be more honest and where leftist and republican sentiment prevailed. Interpreting the results as a plebiscite on his reign, and with his advisers unwilling to take up arms against what was perceived as the popular will, King Alfonso XIII suspended the exercise of his powers and went into exile, where he was to die a decade later. On April 14, 1931, the Spanish Republic was proclaimed, Spain's second experiment with republican government. The Republic was born with wide, but, as it turned out, not very deep support not only on the Left but also among intellectuals and in the middle class; and it set to work trying to solve some of Spain's long-standing problems, including land ownership, the distribution of wealth, the role of the Roman Catholic church in education and family law, and the role of the military. The Republic was also faced from its beginning with hostility from those who, on the Right or on the Left, simply did not want or believe in a liberal parliamentary democracy except perhaps as a means to their own ultimately illiberal and undemocratic ends. This hostility sometimes took violent forms, as in the abortive rightist coup of August 10, 1932, led by General Sanjurjo, and in the more extensive and far more violent leftist rebellion in Asturias in October 1934, ultimately suppressed by Army forces under the command of one of Spain's most brilliant and youngest generals, Francisco

2. *La rosa* (Buenos Aires: Destino, 1979), 20. Translation mine.

Franco. In the first five years after its establishment, the Republic made some progress in its attacks on the country's endemic ailments; but these attacks necessarily threatened the interests and often the beliefs of whole sectors of Spanish society, some of which became increasingly alienated from the new regime.

For the parliamentary elections of February 1936 the parties of the Left joined in a Popular Front, a tactic that with the blessing of Stalin was also being used in other European countries. The Popular Front won those elections, though not by much, and its victory was widely perceived as the prelude to proletarian revolution, hopefully by the Marxist Left, fearfully by the Right. In the meantime Fascist and quasi-fascist groups had also sprung up, as hostile to democracy as the Marxists and quite as willing as they to use violence to subvert the liberal democratic state. In the spring of 1936 disorder spread through Spanish society, with frequent strikes and anticlerical violence, as well as street battles, often deadly, between supporters of different political movements. Less visibly, Army officers, including several that had supported establishment of the Republic, were plotting a coup d'état, counting on the support of monarchist groups, other rightists, and Fascists.

This simmering cauldron of troubles came to a boil in July 1936. Three months before, in fighting over an earlier killing, José Castillo, a young lieutenant of the Assault Guard, an elite organization whose members were chosen for their loyalty to the parties of the Left, had killed Andrés Sáenz de Heredia, cousin of José Antonio Primo de Rivera, founder and leader of the Fascist group Falange Española. On the evening of July 12, he was in turn shot dead on a Madrid street by Falangists. Within hours, before dawn on July 13, a car of the Assault Guard with several troopers, a leftist officer of the Civil Guard, and some civilians went to the home of José Calvo Sotelo, a leading politician of the Right and member of parliament. He was taken from his home and shot, and his body was dumped in the cemetery. A similar expedition was sent after José María Gil Robles, another leader of the Right, who, fortunately for him, was abroad. Faced with this deteriorating situation, the plotters among the military realized that they had to strike now or never.

The military rebellion began on July 17 in the Spanish protectorate in Morocco. The next day General Franco, who had flown from his post in the Canary Islands, issued a proclamation setting forth the aims of the movement, which spread to Spain proper that same day, July 18, subsequently celebrated annually, until Franco's death, as the anniversary of the

Glorious National Uprising. In a sense the coup failed; instead of achieving a neat and rapid seizure of power it turned into a bloody war lasting nearly three years.

July 18 officially marks, then, the outbreak of the Spanish Civil War. It is also St. Camillus' Day, the saint's day of Camilo José Cela and, one might say, of almost his entire family. St. Camillus is, appropriately enough, a patron of hospitals. The novel *San Camilo, 1936* is Cela's attempt to come to grips with his experiences and, by implication and extension, those of all Spaniards. This is not the occasion for an analysis of this work, and I have deliberately left it to the reader to decide to what extent my comments on the author's fiction in general are valid for *San Camilo*, but a few introductory remarks may help.

Historical fiction is no novelty, in Spain or elsewhere. In the nineteenth century Spain's greatest novelist after Cervantes, Benito Pérez Galdós, wrote dozens of *National Episodes* in which he used a mix of fictional and historical characters to try to make sense of critical moments in the modern history of his country. Not coincidentally, these works are mentioned more than once in *San Camilo*. With respect to the Spanish Civil War of 1936–1939, novelistic treatment began almost as soon as the fighting stopped. Cela's book, however, can most profitably be read not as a novel about the war or even about the outbreak of the war but as one about what it felt like to experience that outbreak.

Historical events are important in the narration, but it is a history seen from close up and, as the narrator says, "seen from close up history confuses everyone, both actors and spectators, and is always very tiny and startling, and also very hard to interpret." The question is one of perspective: someone living in the midst of significant historical events does not see them in the ordered, abstracted way in which the historian subsequently and necessarily views them, and he has concerns of his own that within his life may overshadow them. *San Camilo* is an effort to recreate that original experience, in terms that years earlier the critic Jean Onimus explained thus: "History shapes the past, stylizes it once and for all, and stows it away definitively in its archives: this happened thus, that's definitive, let us speak no more about it. Memory, on the other hand, is a living return of the whole being toward its past, or toward the legend of a more remote past."[3]

To evoke that past Cela uses a nameless but not quite faceless narrator. We know that he is a young man of twenty, of the middle class, due to be

3. "L'Expression du temps dans le roman contemporain," *Revue de Littérature Comparée* 28 (1954): 315. Translation mine.

conscripted in 1937, suffering from tuberculosis, studying for a "practical" career but really interested in literature, and much concerned with sex. It is tempting to identify him with Camilo José Cela, and opposite its title page the first edition of the novel carries a photograph of Cela at twenty. The similarities are of course deliberate, but so is the anonymity. The narrator's knowledge of events that on a strictly realistic plane he could not know suggests that he also stands for a collective consciousness, an everyman. The fact that he addresses his narration to himself, that the single subject is thus split into speaking "I" and spoken-to "you," reflects, on the grammatical and narrative levels, the state of civil war, in which the self and the other are in a sense the same.

The play between the self and an other who is in truth that same self is also expressed through the motif of the mirror that runs through the novel, though the mirror also suggests the problem of our perception and recreation of reality. It is an instrument of vision, and its shape and condition affect the image that it reflects. The reader can extrapolate from there to what it may imply for the characters' perceptions of their circumstances and, for that matter, for the novel's reflection of the vast complexity that we blithely subsume under the single word "reality."

San Camilo, 1936 is an essentially complex novel. One strand of this complexity consists of the historical elements: characters, books, texts, events. Another is made up of the fictional personal elements: characters, conversations, events. The presentation of one strand is exactly like that of the other, just as in "real life" a headache or diarrhea is as real as an assassination or a proclamation. Yet another strand, or substrand, of the fictional, consists of dream sequences that are woven into the narration, though these are generally recognizable from their more markedly surrealistic quality and from transitional sentences.

The attempt to reflect the undifferentiated complexity of real experience, as opposed to the a posteriori schematization of history, also explains the linguistic and typographical peculiarity of Cela's book. One kind of language (conversation, news broadcast, narration, advertisement, etc.) flows into another in a great stylistic collage, just as events large and small flow into each other. There are no paragraphs or quotation marks, and only a minimum of other marks of punctuation cuts the text into separate and classifiable segments. The reader, however, quickly learns to supply all that is missing, helped, of course, by a skillful author whose imitation of chaos is only that, an imitation carefully ordered to give the impression of disorder.

Throughout *San Camilo, 1936* readers will find motifs familiar to those who know some of Cela's other works: sex, sometimes grotesque violence, sickness (physical and moral), and death, most of them very appropriate to a moment in history when truth (such as the public desecration of the corpses of nuns or urinating in the emptied eye sockets of a dead enemy) seemed sometimes to be beyond anything that even Goya could imagine. The theme of the nature and role of the individual human being, so important in Cela's fiction in general, is central also to this novel. A relatively new but also important theme is the ritual, liturgical quality of much of the action, a quality already hinted at in the ecclesiastical language of the novel's full title, *The Eve, Feast, and Octave of St. Camillus of the Year 1936 in Madrid*.

This liturgical quality is related to a possible explanation of what is happening in the novel, advanced largely by the narrator's Uncle Jerónimo, who also expresses other ideas about the causes of Spain's troubles. The exact function of this character is something that would bear a good deal of discussion; for now I shall only say that the authority of his voice seems to me by no means unambiguous.

And that brings us to the "lesson" of *San Camilo, 1936*. Is Cela trying to say something about Spain's Civil War? If not, why is he writing about this experience? If so, what is it? I have tried to deal with this question elsewhere, and my views are certainly not the only ones. I think the reader is best advised to form his own after he has finished reading and not to enter the novel with preconceptions shaped by me or by anyone else.

In translating *San Camilo* I have attempted to render as faithfully as I can the stylistic complexity of Cela's work, trying at the same time to make it, as far as possible, as comprehensible within an English-language idiom as it is to the Spanish reader. Thus, to take an extreme example, when I translate *horchata* as 'lemonade,' I do know that an *horchata de chufas* is not a lemonade but a milky drink made from the "edible tuber of a sedge," which in turn is a "cyperaceous plant," and I also now know that the English word *orgeat*, clearly a cognate of the Spanish *horchata*, is a drink made of almonds, sugar, and orange blossoms; but I ask the reader whether he would rather have a character, as a not particularly significant act, consume a lemonade or an orgeat or an *horchata* with an explanatory footnote. In a very few places I have added a word or two that clarifies a meaning for an American reader or suppressed one that makes a distinction which simply does not exist in English. In short, I have tried to be faithful to the original but in another language and with some concessions to the context of another culture. I have not tampered with the typographical form of the novel or its punctuation because I consider them closely linked to its theme.

The reader of *San Camilo* will see that characters weave in and out of the story with very little, if any, warning, but he will come to recognize them and follow their lines of action. He can assume that most of the politicians and military men who appear in the narrative are historical persons and that the characters who take part in scenes of private life, though possibly modeled on real people, are fictional. I believe that with these assumptions and a developing familiarity with the cast of characters, *San Camilo* can be read successfully and profitably by any reader of modern fiction. I have therefore refrained from the academic vice of footnoting except in a handful of what seem to me compelling instances. Those, however, who lose track of a character or who want to know whether he is historical and, if so, who he is, will find at the end of the volume the list of characters and some other matters. The information given there is only of the most thumbnail sort and makes no pretense at fullness. I repeat that I think a reader can make his way through *San Camilo* successfully and, I hope, reasonably happily without ever looking at the list. Anyone who wishes to read more by or about Cela or about *San Camilo, 1936* can consult the bibliography at the end of this volume.

In semiconclusion I wish to thank those who have assisted me in this endeavor. First of all, Don Camilo José Cela, for graciously permitting me to translate his novel. Secondly, those who have helped me with problems of interpretation, including Juan Miguel Godoy Marquet, Ana María Gómez Bravo, Fernando González Corugedo, Luis Monguió, and Carmen Usobiaga. Then there are the many who have written about Cela and whose ideas have often helped to shape my own, even if there is no barrage of footnotes here to bear witness. And, last but for me always first, my wife Beverley, whose keen ear for real English has kept me now, as in the past, from blundering. For whatever defects in my work they have not cured, mine alone is the blame.

And now it only remains for me to express my hope that the reader of this translation may enjoy reading it as much as I enjoyed preparing it.

Oakland, August 1990

San Camilo, 1936

Part One The Eve of St. Camillus' Day

. . . insecurity, the only thing that is fixed among us.

—Pérez Galdós, *Fortunata and Jacinta*, III, 1, 1

I

A man sees himself in the mirror and even feels comfortable addressing himself in a familiar way, the mirror has no frame, it neither begins nor ends, or yes, it does have a splendid frame gilded with patience and with gold leaf but the quality of its pane is not good and the image that it reflects shows bitter and disjointed features, pale and as though one had slept badly, maybe what's happening is that it reflects the astonished face of a dead man still masked with the mask of the fear of death, it's probable that you are dead and don't know it, the dead are also unaware of being dead, they don't know anything at all. A man examines his conscience and nothing becomes any clearer, no, you are not Napoleon Bonaparte, neither are you King Cyril of England whom his courtiers murdered pouring molten lead into his rear as if he were a fairy monkey, you are a nobody, a poor fellow with his head full of gregarious ideas, of redeeming ideas that lead nowhere, to be a hero you have to be humbler and above all not know it, here everything moves on a smaller scale, inside your head and outside your head, here everything is more domestic and ordinary, heroes are very domestic and ordinary until one day without anyone's being able to explain it they become history and their families are fed up, yes, their families, do you remember the flu of '18, which decimated whole families?, the memory of the flu of '18 (of the loss of Cuba, of the Tragic Week of Barcelona, of the strike of '17, of the lost battle of Anual, of the dictatorship of Primo de Rivera, of the flight of the Plus Ultra, of the 14th of April, of the revolution in Asturias) is the refuge of presumptuous men without history, as fierce and vile as presumptuous men with history, you face the problem and naturally you don't solve it. The body of Inmaculada Múgica has a rancid smell, Inmaculada Múgica's real name is Magdalena, she doesn't have any last name, you think the smell wakes you up, your legs, your chest, and your head ache but you also feel good, vaguely good, caressing your penis with your hand, the bedroom has a sour smell, it smells of antiseptic and cold coffee, all smells are good and bad at the same time, it's the same as with sounds, a fly is dying in the coffee cup, at first it flutters violently and kicks, then it gets tired and winds up drowning, it doesn't much matter, there are plenty of flies, the flies of the dead are more playful and light-hearted, you can tell that they're better fed, the flies of lovers, including those of the lusty lovers who wander around near the slaughterhouse, are very prudent and almost always end up drowning in dregs of cold coffee (or hot coffee, you'll never be able to get precise information about that). Yes, you face the problem again and again and you still can't solve it, it probably has a solution but you don't know what it is. To call things by their name, not to call things by their name, to swear off all things human and divine, not to swear off all things human and divine, to go to bed with this woman who smells of grease and cologne, not to go to bed with this woman who smells of grease and cologne, this woman who smells of grease and cologne may be Magdalena, alias Inmaculada Múgica, and maybe not, to take a walk through the park and the vacant lots where couples do their inevitable dirty business, not to take a walk through the park or the vacant lots where couples do their enjoyable and inevitable dirty business that will eventually make them weak, to watch with satisfaction how they beat a child to death, not to watch with satisfaction how they beat a child to death, there are children that take forever to die, to give the finger to the cripple who sells tobacco (maybe he's a hero of some war), not to give the finger to the cripple who sells tobacco (maybe he's a hero of some war), to take your life with gas, not to take your life with gas, to feed the hungry, not to feed the hungry, to give drink to the thirsty, not to give drink to the thirsty, to squeal to the police, not to squeal to the police, to compose sonnets, not to compose sonnets, to play dominoes, not to play dominoes, to murder a schoolmate treacherously, not to murder a schoolmate treacherously, etc. No, it's no use, you are not Napoleon Bonaparte or King Cyril of England, you are fodder for the catechism class, fodder for the brothel, you are cannon fodder, you are the unknown soldier, the man on whose forehead no little star shines, men who are meat for the gallows are usually more self-assured, history gives a lot of confidence, you are among the public—in the catechism class, in the whorehouse, at the front—and although sometimes you think the world revolves around you, you'll never stand out boldly above the other pupils in the class, the other customers of loose women, the other soldiers, no one will ever notice you but that shouldn't make you feel sorry, every man goes as far as he can and as far as the others let him and you're being allowed to live, isn't that something?, and to learn Christian doctrine and to consort with women and to do your military drills, and also to sum things up, above all to sum things up. On the Calle de Mendizábal, on the right as you go down Marqués de Urquijo, lives Domingo Ibarra, the Nicaraguan musician, your classmate and the classmate of Alonso Zamora Vicente, of Gregorio Montes, of Rafael Pérez Delgado, of Camilo José Cela, of Dámaso Rioja, of Julián Marías, and of Luis Enrique Délano in Pedro Salinas' course on contemporary Spanish literature, Délano was secretary of the Chilean consulate under Gabriela Mistral and still is under Pablo Neruda, you, officially and as far as your family is concerned, are studying for the entrance examinations for the customs service but secretly and behind their back you are attending some courses in the College of Philosophy and Letters, the customs classes in the school run by Cela's father, right by the parliament building and by the party headquarters of the Republican Union (maybe it's the Republican Left or maybe it's not that either) and by Azorín's house, begin at 7 A.M., it's a very modern method of fighting the heat, the Ebro with its tributaries the Rudrón, the Oca, the Tirón, the Najerilla, the Iregua, the Leza, the Cidacos, the Alhama, the Queiles, the Huecha, the Jalón, the Huerva, the Martín, the Guadalope, and the Matarraña on the right, and the Bayas, the Zadorra, the Ega, the Aragón, the Arga, the Gállego, the Segre with the Cinca and the Ciurana on the left. On April 14 the speakers addressed the people from the balcony of the Republican Center, the crowd sang the *Marseillaise* but since people didn't know the words they hummed it, it was a pretty odd and dramatic experience to hear two or three thousand people hum the *Marseillaise* full of good intentions and doubts, lots of doubts. On July 18 at 6:30 A.M. a car smashes against a lamppost across from the Bank of Spain, it's a black Dodge coupe and it has bloodstains on the windshield, on the seats, and on the floor, its driver and two passengers die, two rich boys and a prostitute, some workers cover the bodies with tarpaulins that they get out of the night repair trolley (dark grey like a warship) and wait for the authorities to come while they silently smoke with their hands in their pants pockets. You have a girl called Tránsito, you were right to change her name, Tránsito is very good-looking and well-built, with big dark eyes, long hair, well-shaped legs, a small waist, gleaming buttocks (like in a novel), hard breasts, etc., when she's naked Tránsito looks like an art photo from *Crónica*, in her slip Tránsito looks like a drawing from *Muchas gracias*, Tránsito may be more than you can handle but look, you're lucky and enjoy it while you've got it!, you were right to change her name, Toisha is a very pretty name that sounds Japanese, besides it's easier to write poems to your girl if she's called Toisha than if she's called Tránsito even if she's the same girl. The trolley workers look like village gravediggers, you can be sure they drink the alcohol used in the autopsies and then sing pasodobles and throw around farts and stones. Ibarra and you have founded a confusing but pretty religion with echoes of Nietzsche and Buddhism, for the time being you only have one convert, your girl Toisha (on Sundays and without your knowing about it she probably goes to mass before noon, the time when you meet at the San Luis square), there's nothing bad about amusing yourself by founding religions although sometimes people rebel and strangle or burn or crucify the founders of religions. You face the problem but it's no use, you don't know how to solve it, the ideas run away like frogs, jumping like frogs, and suddenly you find your head empty, with not a single frog left in your head, the news is confusing, very confusing, and you don't know how to put it in order, do you suffer from a urinary ailment?, try Boston plant juice and get rid of your worries, avoid unnecessary expenses, ha ha!, you laugh at Boston plant juice because you are young, very young and do not suffer from urinary ailments, acute and chronic bladder infections, inflammation of the prostate, difficulty in urination or frequent and abnormal need to urinate, pain in the kidneys and abdomen, acute and chronic inflammations, narrowing of the urethra, acute or chronic blennorhea, discharges, kidney and bladder stones, cloudy urine, etc., have a little patience, everything will come in due time (if you don't fall by the wayside and they kill you with a bullet in the mouth before you get old and sick), you try to foster ideas of solidarity in your head but you're just a puppet and a busybody who can't solve the problem of talking confidently in front of a mirror, why don't you shut up?, Hemorrhoidol Yer, this wonderful medication, a masterpiece of modern medicine, quickly and thoroughly cures every kind of piles, your watch stopped at 10:10 like the watches in the ads and you don't have money for having it fixed, and then you think you can conquer the world?, weakness, exhaustion, anemia, Deschiens hemoglobin wine and syrup, this woman is rancid, she tastes rancid like bacon that's been forgotten for months under a pile of newspapers, but you have no right to any higher aspirations, be satisfied with what you've got and get your pleasure out of it, it's better than nothing, Maravillas Theatre, sensational debut of Marlene Grey the Blonde Venus, Miss Shapely of 1935 in Trouville, in her exciting nude dances among wild lions, thirty minutes of beauty and courage, you'd like to be a deputy but you're not even a voter, you are a minor, how ridiculous!, and you depend on your father's being willing to give you five pesetas on Sundays, hemorrhoids, varicosities, ulcers, Dr. Illanes, the oldest clinic in the field, the two sisters with TB whom you take for walks in the Retiro park are good-looking, do you remember that afternoon when they got to hitting and biting each other like two bitches in heat?, the famous Losada files magically and painlessly remove corns, bunions, and overgrown toenails, no, the problem does not lie in looking at oneself in the mirror, not even with a certain degree of confidence, and trying to take a certain familiar tone with oneself, probably you are almost dead and almost don't know it, the dead don't know they're dead, I told you that, and those who are dying prefer to smile and utter clever words, no matter how you look at it you are not Napoleon Bonaparte, no matter how vile you pretend to be you aren't King Cyril of England either, try to remember, search your memory and be satisfied with what other people give you, the crumbs from the banquet table, some people are worse off, some people have throat cancer and can't even swallow the crumbs from the banquet table, inventors always have a hard time, look at Isaac Peral, one vacuum calls to another and you still refuse to fill the vacuum, even with dead men, fear is the egg of hope but when you're afraid and do not yet hear the beating of hope, crime begins to decorate the soul like a moss that spreads without leaving any crack open through which the air can administer a healthy bloodletting, why not kill this foul-smelling woman?, we all want to act out our part but you don't know what your part is, it doesn't matter, the same thing happens to a lot of men even though they pretend otherwise, crime is no longer necessary for the dead, don't kill this foul-smelling woman, get back into bed with her and let the next man to come kill her, think of King Cyril of England and get ready once more for the lash of the flesh that is gentler than the deadly scar of burning lead, your arms, your belly, and your ears ache but you feel fine and at peace with your conscience while this diligent woman fulfills her obligation, contribute something, you're being selfish in not contributing anything, not even love, you write and write telling God what's happening on earth, maybe that's not enough. Don León Rioja, the father of your classmate Dámaso Rioja, goes every Saturday to visit his favorite whore La Hebrea, there are several Spanish proverbs about love on Saturdays, one night when father and son met in the brothel they studiously ignored each other. Look at yourself in the mirror, always look at yourself in the mirror to see yourself die a little at a time. Dámaso can forgive his father because his mother, Doña Matilde Brocas, has been sick and paralyzed for more than ten years now, the old man also has a right to life, that's clear enough to you, naturally! Body hair and excess hairs are a true affront to beauty, what do you think of that sentence? Manuel Fernández, the only survivor of the fishing vessel Joven República, had a close call, Manuel Fernández left the sanatorium Valdecilla en route to his hometown, Candás. Villa Milagros is a really elegant house, a refined house where they're very demanding in choosing the merchandise, all the girls seem to have had a convent education and if new visitors don't come recommended by a trusted steady customer they don't even open the door for them, I'm sorry, all the ladies are busy. Dámaso Rioja and you go with the TB sisters to the movies at the Panorama Theatre at 3 P.M. and there you stay till nine or nine-thirty, their father, Señor Asterio Cuevilla, doesn't let the sisters go out at night, not that he's afraid they might catch a cold but because somebody might get them in trouble, these two daughters have turned out to be tramps just like my sister-in-law Rafaela, you can tell it's in their blood, if I don't get them married soon they'll give me nothing but trouble, sometimes you call Señor Asterio Señor Ricardo, it's an unforgivable gaffe, people don't like to have their names mixed up. Don Roque Barcia, who has nothing to do with the other Don Roque Barcia, the Barcia of the *General Etymological Dictionary* and the independent canton of Cartagena, nor with Don Augusto Barcia, the Foreign Minister, is a deputy of the Agrarian Party and a reader of Aparisi Guijarro and Macías Picavea, Don Roque likes fat and powerful women and his breath stinks to high heaven, Don Roque smokes cheap cigars, reads *El Debate* and lets healthy rolling farts that startle any bystanders, Don Roque is a big horny fellow, a little stoop-shouldered, free with his money, with a gold tooth and a jocular and kindly good humor, Don Roque holds a gymnastic concept of love and what he likes is making love in jumps, zap, zap!, like in the horse races, Don Roque does not believe in the sins of the flesh and in his boardinghouse he fondles the maids in the hallway and then gives them a peseta, when Don Roque is in Madrid he lives in a boardinghouse on the Calle del Príncipe, where he pays for a room for the whole year. Pérez de Ayala, who along with Ortega y Gasset and Marañón belongs to the Association of Intellectuals in the Service of the Republic, speaks in *Troteras y danzaderas* of the González Fitoria brothers, "famous authors of comedies" and steady visitors at the house of Socorrito, who "had been the friend of one" of them, Socorrito is an Andalusian, "young, graceful, and lively" with flowers in her knotted hair, who "acts as though she had a monopoly on wit," according to that book "all the jokes and punch lines that the González Fitoria brothers put in their comedies are Socorrito's," *Troteras y danzaderas* is a roman à clef, everybody sees through its disguises and the way it deals with writers has even been the subject of doctoral dissertations (Martha W. O'Cherony, *The Reflection of Contemporary Spain in "Troteras y danzaderas"*, University of Denver, Colorado, 1932; Robert A. Lewald, *Pérez de Ayala, Historian of His Time*, Wayne State University, Detroit, 1934; Anthony M. Baum, *The Writer Between History and Novel*, University of the Pacific, Stockton, 1934; Hans Hesse, *Betrachtungen über die Objektivierung der unmittelbaren Realität im erzählerischen Werk Pérez de Ayalas*, Universität Hamburg, 1935), according to these studies the González Fitoria brothers are the Álvarez Quintero brothers, you don't get involved in this question because anyhow it's all the same to you, what these scholars don't clarify are the nonliterary names and places. There are no women in the house on Espíritu Santo, it's only a house of assignation, in the guidebook *Madrid at Night* by Don Antonio Aullón Gallego the houses of prostitution are called "discreet licensed houses" and the houses of assignation, "maisons meublées," you had an affair with a girl who was a maid in the house on Espíritu Santo whose name is Chonina, don't deny it, afterward, when she decided to go all the way and become a whore herself she told you to go to hell and you lost your free lays, don't deny that either, the maids in the brothels are of only two kinds, old and young, they all earn little and the old ones put up with it, what else can they do?, the old ones are usually retired whores who didn't manage to save anything but did learn resignation, the young ones, on the other hand, are full of dreams and as soon as they get rid of their scruples they go full steam ahead, become whores themselves, and that's the end of that, enjoy it while you've got it. Antonio!, coming!, Antonio is the watchman on the Calle de Alcántara, he also takes care of the villas on the Calle de Naciones, Antonio (don't you remember whether his last name is Collar?) is from San Pedro de las Montañas, in the township of Cangas de Narcea, in Asturias, when he gave up this job he started driving a taxi, then he was a stowaway on a British ship and finally he worked as an overseer of natives in Guinea, maybe he thought of that because of his dealings with Petra la Grillo, the mulatto who turned up with her throat slit on the Dehesa de la Villa without anybody's ever finding out the motives for the crime or the identity of the criminal, Antonio shares his watchman's job (one month one and the next the other) with Enrique, a very reserved fellow who naturally is not especially remembered in history, you are not obliged to speak of anything except what you know or to invent confusing stories, Antonio!, coming!, Don Estanislao Montañés Sainz sometimes gets impatient, where were you?, Antonio smiles his forced smile, keeps quiet, unlocks the door, and pockets his peseta tip. They call the house on the Calle de la Madera the League of Nations because there they've got everything, Moors, Germans, Belgians, Frenchwomen, Portuguese, everything, the waiting room of the League of Nations has a bench running around its four walls, it looks like the third-class waiting room of a railroad station, there are no pictures on the walls but there are two signs in porcelain enamel, white with blue letters, one says Price per visit, 7 pesetas, and the other, No oral sex in this establishment, that's a lie, they'll do oral sex in the League of Nations even if the customer doesn't ask for it, it's simpler for the girls to spit than to be washing themselves, you can spit your soul out through your mouth, the most that can happen is that the devil will carry it off, but you can't wash your heart either at home or at the dry cleaner's, the heart shrinks, water for number nine!, out of the way, you slob!, can't you see I'm in a hurry?, Mireya is a heavy Frenchwoman with a mane of gold-colored hair that hangs down to her waist, she looks like Mary Magdalene but blonde, the women in the Bible were not usually blondes, son of a bitch, what a monumental woman!, men don't last long with Mireya, some don't even have time to get undressed and others, the youngest ones, sometimes don't even get to the room, they shoot their wad in the hallway, what a woman!, what a hell of a woman!, Mireya is a powerful and tireless machine who could lay a whole regiment of hussars at one sitting, Allons, anozer john, one who's more of a man, I like also to make ze love! As it returns from America the dirigible Graf Zeppelin flies over Seville dropping mail with a parachute, the dirigible Hindenburg with fifty passengers on board leaves Germany en route to the United States, a committee of Socialist, Communist, and Anarchist labor leaders visits the governor of Guipúzcoa and complains about the bad quality of the food that they serve the inmates in the prison at Ondarreta, it is feared that the Japanese intend to seat Emperor Kan Te of Manchukuo on the throne of his ancestors in Peking, two licenses for tripe shops are granted, one at 16 Calle Diego de León and the other in the Diego de León market, at the conclusion of the Metz-Belfort stage of the thirtieth Tour de France, the ranking of the Spanish cyclists is as follows, Federico Ezquerra, 36, Mariano Cañardo, 39, Julián Berrendero, 50, Salvador Molina, 58, and Emiliano Álvarez, 62, ladies, you can achieve regular periods with the famous Fortan pills, does your stomach give you trouble?, no matter how long and how stubbornly it's been acting up, genuine old San Bruno herb tea will restore your health and well-being, that's all you can get out of the newspaper, the fact is that for fifteen centimos you can't ask for Galdós' *Episodios Nacionales* either. Go on, tell Isabel to give you some time off, I'm inviting you to supper, the villa on the Calle O'Donnell is a very distinguished house, with luxurious furniture and moiré bedspreads on the beds, each room has its bathroom with two little cakes of fine Heno de Pravia soap, always new ones, and a bottle of Listerine for those who want to gargle, because some people have their obsessions and are scared of everything, Isabel can't deny Don Máximo anything he asks for, he is a good customer and a man with all kinds of connections with whom it's a good idea to be on friendly terms, Don Máximo is a deputy of Martínez Barrio's party and they say he's a Mason, nobody knows that for sure, that's one of those things people never know for sure, Don Máximo wears a rubber girdle and very elegant grey boots that give him a certain air of being an English lord, Isabel, every time that Don Máximo wants to take one of the young ladies out to supper or to the theater or for a drive out on the La Coruña road, tells him yes, delighted, of course, Isabel has a strong political instinct and a fine diplomatic touch, Isabel is the sister of the fellow who takes care of the swords of a top bullfighter, a Gypsy bullfighter famous for his outrageous behavior, for his exquisite artistry, and because once in Villa Rosa he set a whore on fire after dousing her with anise, wow, how fast a whore will burn! At the Golden Grapes about 9 P.M. Victoriano Palomo Valdés, Doña Sacramento's son-in-law, usually has a couple of glasses of red wine and a plate of cracklings, his friend Paquito, who although he's the son of a count never has five centimos in his pocket, not even five lousy centimos, will take whatever he can, it's a lemon fizz for you, what do you say to a lemon fizz?, thank you very much, and a fried bird to go with it?, thank you very much, and a cigarette?, thank you very much, boy, you don't pass up a thing!, no, why should I?, I'll take what my friends offer me, I'll make it up to them when my father dies, Doña Sacramento whom they call Sacra runs the house at 132 Calle de Ayala almost across the street from the playing field of the Unión Soccer Club that became very famous for two reasons, because of the good soccer that's played there and because six or seven months ago it was the scene of a crime of passion that had all the women of the neighborhood, and that's quite a few, in an uproar, what happened was that at the first crack of dawn the garbage men found the corpse of a young woman of about thirty who was literally covered with stab wounds, according to the coroner's report the victim had been dead for several hours when they found her, long enough for the cats to eat her eyes, the deceased's name was Marujita Expósito and she was a prostitute from Villa Rita or the House of One-Hand on the Calle de Montesa corner of Ayala, the corpse's ears and nipples were also missing but the cats weren't responsible for that, the police found the ears in the vest pocket of the murderer who confessed, half cynically and half sadly, that he had eaten the nipples because they were his and because he was fed up with having others eat them, the murderer of Marujita (now you can't remember his name but it doesn't matter, you know it, of course you know it, but now you can't remember) committed suicide in the Model Prison by tearing the veins of his wrists open with his teeth, it was a pretty bloody story that caused a lot of comment, Doña Sacramento has a branch in the Calle de las Naciones, when my father dies you'll all shit with envy and till then what's wrong with my accepting the invitation of a friend? Amanda Ordóñez, who has a scar on her face that even looks cute on her, receives the homage of her admirers in Doña Fe's house on the Calle de la Reina, Amanda had been a waitress in the Bar Moderno on the Calle de la Aduana when you come from Montera on the left opposite the Edén Lounge, but she quarreled with the manager and had to leave because he gave her no peace, Amanda was always one for a row, an inclination that sooner or later you pay for dearly, one night in the little joint they call Maxim's Golfo in San Ginés alley next to the Eslava Theatre she threw a cup of boiling coffee at the wife of a master sergeant of the Customs Guard who'd gone out for a little fun to take advantage of her husband's being away on service in Alcalá de Henares, she hit her in the middle of the face and gave her some fairly serious burns which the sergeant's wife, to avoid explanations, didn't want to have taken care of at the first-aid station. Number 128 Calle de Ayala doesn't have a special name, 128 Ayala is a house full of mystery where they receive only very highly recommended and serious visitors, the manager Doña Cándida, let alone the owner Doña Valentina who is a real lady (she never goes out without a hat and gloves), won't stand for any horseplay and won't let anybody raise his voice either, if you want to make a scene go to a brothel, love has nothing to do with vulgarity and bad manners, shit, what a highfalutin superfine lady we've got here!, doesn't that piss you off?, please sir, we don't allow any swearwords or foul language here, all right, all right, I'm going . . . , excuse me, I didn't know I'd got into the catechism class, this is not a catechism class, sir, but it's not a brothel either, this is a love nest, good night, good night, listen, before I go and just out of curiosity, do the crabs here dance the minuet?, they slammed the door in Miguel Mercader's face, Doña Valentina faced Doña Cándida, I've told you not to let these sonofabitch students in!, I'm up to my ass with students!, let 'em fuck their fathers if they can find 'em! Beyond the Retiro park, the vacant lots that are opposite the Niño Jesús station and back up against the zoo are thick with one-peseta whores, the tired tarts of soldiers and poor students, the bitter sluts of pensioners, chronic invalids, and other second-rate fauna, Paca, yes sir, jack me off, I can't even find it any more, yes sir, Paca is young, that's true, but misshapen and she doesn't have much luck, Paca has a slight curvature of the spine (well, the truth is she's just a plain hunchback), she won't do for a maid, not even a simple one, because people laugh at her, nor for a nanny because she scares the kids, Paca doesn't know how to fry an egg (Paca has never in her life eaten a fried egg) and so naturally she's no good as a cook either, even if she weren't hunchbacked how could she be any good as a cook if she doesn't even know how to fry an egg?, Paca lives in the caves by the Abroñigal creek on the road to the Eastern Cemetery, in the late afternoon she combs her hair a little and goes as far as the walls of the Retiro to see whether once night comes she can earn a peseta or two taking care of night owls of limited means, Paca doesn't want to go to bed with anybody, she doesn't like it, Paca specializes in hand jobs, besides when she came from her village they got her pregnant and she had all kinds of trouble before she managed to abort, Paca doesn't want to go through these calamities again where somebody else is to blame and then takes a powder, Paca is from Puebla de la Mujer Muerta, in the Province of Madrid, Paca didn't know what electric lights or the train are, she didn't know how to read either (she still doesn't), Paca subsists on lamb's lettuce, around the Abroñigal the lamb's lettuce often grows wild and it's very tasty and even nutritious, sometimes when she has some money she buys peanuts and also dried figs, Paca, yes sir, what have you got on your hand, it scratches, nothing, why? Above Los Caracoles on the Calle de los Jardines there is a house where they're all French, Frenchwomen are very refined in bed and not at all squeamish, what's annoying is that they look down on you as though we Spaniards were all bums, Guillermo Zabalegui, who's quite the young gentleman and had a mademoiselle when he was a boy, often goes to the house on Jardines to talk French with the women, that makes a really superior impression and gives a very European air, at home they call Guillermo Zabalegui Willy but he doesn't want it known because he realizes it's pretentious, Guillermo Zabalegui, who went to school at the Instituto Escuela and not with the friars, which is the usual thing, is a real intellectual, very well-bred, he talks without raising his voice, he wears a silk tie and uses cologne, Guillermo Zabalegui comes from a rich family, his father has a bus company in the Basque Provinces and his mother Doña Cristina Ortiz de Amoedo (who, gossip says, was the mistress of Gallito, the bullfighter) owns many acres of olive trees in the Province of Jaén, Guillermo Zabalegui is studying to be an agronomist and is a friend of Dámaso Rioja's, Gregorio Montes', and yours, Guillermo Zabalegui plays billiards like an angel, he's always very well combed and elegant, he's a marvelous dancer and very successful with women, the fact is nobody knows why he goes to the whorehouse, some people have strange tastes!, one of these Frenchwomen gave Guillermo Zabalegui a first-rate case of the clap, a clap that had him sweating blood for almost a year, the medical offices on the Calle de la Luna (blood tests, urine, discharges, etc.) charge two rates, special from 2 to 4 and economy from 6 to 9, Guillermo Zabalegui signed up for the special rate and even so he went through agonies and suffered beyond words when they cauterized him with a platinum-iridium mixture, what luxury!, red hot and with electromagnetic prostate massage (patented) via the anus, it all seems half silly but if you've been through it you know what the worst is like, you wouldn't wish it on your worst enemy!, how horrible!, what a way to see stars! Number 3 of the Calle de Naciones is a dual establishment, something like the two-headed eagle of the Habsburgs, at number 3 Naciones the command is split between Doña María Luisa and Doña Margarita who at least outwardly get along well and operate in harmony, the cattle in this villa is of only middling quality, it's young, not very dangerous cattle good enough for some festival but not for a full-scale bullfight with picadors, the truth is that it's not expensive either, that should also be said. There's a bricklayers' strike in Madrid, a reapers' strike in the whole province, a strike by everybody (bricklayers, stuccoers, tilers, carpenters, plumbers, electricians) in the madhouse of Alcalá de Henares, a strike of shopclerks in Málaga, a strike of typesetters in León, a laborers' strike in Medina del Campo, a fishermen's strike in Vigo, a streetcar strike in Oviedo and in Avilés, a miners' strike in Santibáñez, and a general strike in Dueñas, where are we headed, you tell me!, Don Vicente Parreño doesn't know where we're headed and he doesn't much care, Don Vicente Parreño (you were about to say Parrondo, you've got to watch that memory) only knows where's he's headed tonight, to 3 Naciones to have a nice peaceful lay, you mentioned a proverb before, Saturday, Saturday, nice clean shirt and nice little lay, a custom is a custom and with all these strikes and so many things going on people are half disjointed and forget the custom. Doctor Albiñana gives the Fascist salute in the parliament building, Mr. Bermúdez Cañete, a member of the CEDA, the Autonomous Right, comes to blows, also in the parliament building, with Don Belarmino Tomás, a Socialist, because he didn't like Don Belarmino's calling him a clown, people are all up in arms and here they're not even going to let a man fuck in peace, that's what's happening, look here, Don Lucio, I don't give a fuck about all this strike business, what can I tell you, I mind my own business and don't mess with anybody, well they'll mess with you, don't you worry. Don Leopoldo Garrido Manzanares and his wife Doña Bernardina Pacheco have seven children, four sons and three daughters, Leopoldo, twenty-four, is studying to be a notary, Enrique, twenty-two, is already a doctor, Pepita, twenty-one, holds a teaching certificate, Conchi, nineteen, is studying pharmacy, Berta, seventeen, is studying arts and letters, and Tomás, fifteen, and Manolito, eleven, are in high school, they're all good Catholics who live the way the Church tells them, the only one who's turned out a little shaky in the faith is Enrique. At Madame Teddy's house on the Calle de Gravina almost facing the pharmacy, the gentlemen who regularly visit the owner play cards, drink glasses of Tres Cepas brandy, and pat the girls on the behind in between their tricks, inside Madame Teddy's house you find a very cultured and liberal atmosphere and the owner lets the girls eat with her close friends, a little before you get there and on the same side of the street there is a tavern where they serve good drinks, Casa Benito, where a cousin of Gregorio Montes' works, Julianín, who had a little stroke that left him kind of half-witted, when Madame Teddy's whores pass by Casa Benito they usually stop in for a vermouth and some sardine pie, Madame Teddy's regular circle of friends includes newspapermen, writers, and even librarians, sometimes if you close your eyes you could think you're among the intellectuals at the Ateneo there's that much culture pouring out in the conversation, Landsberg has just pointed it out unequivocally in his second lecture in Santander, the three basic formulas of human knowledge that Scheler defines—technical knowledge or Leistungswissen, cultural knowledge or Bildungswissen, and knowledge of redemption or Lösungswissen—do not exhaust the list of possible and necessary distinctions since juridical knowledge, for example, is not of a purely practical nature in view of its natural ordering when you look at the problem from the perspective of the classical aphorism *sapienti est ordinare*, keep your hands to yourself,

Enriqueta, there's a time for everything, you there, Angustias, bring more brandy for everybody, let's make an occasion of it!, all right, St. Thomas clearly points out the line between philosophy and mysticism, now in spite of St. Thomas can we therefore say that Aristotelian philosophy is not part of the *itinerarium mentis ad Deum?*, obviously not, hold still, dammit, if you don't behave you can go screw your old man! Casa Gayango on the Calle de la Aduana doesn't close all night, Casa Gayango is next door to Merceditas' furnished rooms which is where you take Toisha when the Nicaraguan doesn't give you the keys to his apartment and you have five pesetas in your pocket, Merceditas' place is very discreet and clean, it's not the most luxurious or the most comfortable but it is very discreet and clean, more than good enough for you, Toisha is some woman, I'll say, a hell of a woman, you ought to know, but she's also full of fears and scruples, Toisha is afraid her family might find her out and on Saturdays and Sundays you can't touch her, Toisha is a lay for weekdays (the best days of the week are Tuesday and Wednesday) and for off hours (three-thirty in the afternoon), the girl is right in taking her precautions because if her father finds out that her virginity is nothing but a memory he's liable to kill her, do you suppose anybody's seen us?, no, oh how much I love you, darling!, I never thought I could be so crazy about a man!, what things you make me do, sweetheart!, I'm a slut, a real slut!, no, no, just half-way, one place you couldn't drag Toisha is Casa Gayango, it's easier to romance a woman if her name is Toisha than if it's Tránsito even if it's the same woman, there are amorous names and forensic names, that's indisputably clear, but what can't be done is to get her into Casa Gayango, the TB sisters you can, Lupita and Juani will get into anyplace you tell them except bed, Madrid is very big, it would have to be real bad luck for father to go out for a fling the same time we do! In his book *For My Friends* Silverio Lanza, in those pages he titles *What the Devil Does*, writes some very worrisome words, do you know them?, yes, by heart, you have a very good memory, the memory of a fool, my writings may turn out to be novels but I devote myself only to writing to God and telling him what is happening on earth, it's not enough, maybe it's not enough and what's needed is something else, stop it, your head can't stand being overheated, right away it starts to rave and to see beetles and scorpions crawling down the electric wires, memory has its appointed tasks and one of them, perhaps one of the most painful, is the one that empties your head of shadows and of proper names and draws you very grey, almost imperceptible silhouettes of animals on a shiny white backdrop. It's been a number of years since Mahogany was one of the girls at 17 Ventura de la Vega from where the prime minister himself took her out, this was still in the time of the monarchy and there's no reason for you to give further details because Mahogany lives—and very properly to be sure—respected by all and lulled by golden memories, Mahogany was beautiful like the Callipygian Venus which means the Venus with the beautiful buttocks (thanks, Jesualdo) and her skin was on the dark side and like porcelain, you can well understand that a prime minister would not settle for any old thing, of course!, that's what undersecretaries are for, and from there on down!, a prime minister needs a top-notch woman, people wouldn't forgive him if he took up with a dog, before her promotion Mahogany already had a very good clientele, bankers and aristocrats, which allowed her to eat at Los Burgaleses and even at Lhardy if she felt like it and to stand rounds of drinks like a well-to-do cattle baron or the manager of a star bullfighter at Villa Rosa, at Concha's place, and at Los Gabrieles, you had to be somebody to treat Mahogany, you keep your dough to buy your wife a pair of stockings because she sure can use it, when Mahogany is on the scene not even God Almighty gets to pay, do you understand?, and even less a clerk of the Interior Ministry and anybody who doesn't like it can get out, because I haven't asked anybody to come, excuse me Mahogany I didn't mean to offend you, I swear, well just in case! Don León is employed in a notary's office and is a republican of Alcalá Zamora's party, Don León speaks very well and is very patriotic, what annoys him most is disorder and a lack of authority, it's no yearning for adventures believe me my friend Asenjo, just face it, it's a desire, which all of us good republicans ought to reward with hearty approval, a desire to save the country and to pull our chestnuts out of the fire although we Spaniards maybe don't even deserve it, we're going to face a question of life or death here, either somebody with authority stands up here or we're going to wind up hunting each other down like wild animals (it's possible that these words were not spoken on the night of Saturday the 11th but on that of the next Saturday, the 18th, or never, but it's all the same). At Villa Paca on the Calle de Alcántara La Hebrea does twenty-odd or thirty men every Saturday night, one of them is Don León Rioja who treats her with a lot of respect and doesn't ask for anything kinky and always gives her a three-peseta tip, you know the houses on that block well, the one formed by Alcántara, Ayala, Montesa, and Naciones, when you were a boy you lived at 9 Alcántara at the corner of Ayala, in the same house where the Maroto Press was which is where Juan Ramón Jiménez had his magazine *Índice* printed, the entry was marble and one day you fell when you were playing with your hoop and broke an arm, do you remember?, they took you to the Encarnación Hospital that was right across the street, on Ayala, and Dr. Blanc straightened it out and put it in a cast. In the Panorama Theatre you can lift the arm rests, it's very comfortable and costs 1.50, will you buy me some potato chips?, didn't you bring your sandwich?, yes, but to go with it, *Thunder Over Mexico* by Eisenstein is a very intellectual movie, Dámaso Rioja, the sisters, and you already know it by heart, we were better off in the park, here the usher could catch us, don't be silly, you just be quiet and go on, all right, Dámaso Rioja recites verses to Lupita, Dámaso Rioja usually attacks by way of sentiment, the movies are healthier than dances, people usually leave a dance with their balls swollen and aching, from getting so heated up of course, on the other hand you leave the movies fresh as a rose and rested, very rested, neither Lupita nor Juani let Dámaso Rioja and you go all the way, they both dream of getting married and their cherry is their price, still it wouldn't be fair to say that they're a couple of cockteasers, I'll do anything you want for you honey, anything except that, don't ask me to do that!, Tránsito is something else, Tránsito is freer (maybe she's less temperamental) and is three years older, in three years Lupita and Juani will also have swallowed their cherry, nobody can resist forever, go on, sweetheart, go on . . . , are you enjoying it, you old pig?, am I ever, Juani . . . , take out your handkerchief . . . , all right. Margot is chubby, blonde, and very affectionate, Margot has a scar on her neck, she covers it with a silk scarf, scrofula?, no, a stab wound, a stab wound her husband gave her, Margot is married to the owner of a second-hand store on the Calle del Prado, a very demanding and dignified man capable of stabbing his own father on the slightest provocation, dealing in second-hand goods is usually an occupation for quiet cautious people but Margot's husband is an exception, Margot's husband is Joaquín del Burgo, Don Joaquín del Burgo del Maestre y López-Artaza, and he wears bold sideburns and an aggressive mustachio, Don Joaquín is more of a man than anybody and even though he can't see the hand in front of his face he hardly ever puts on his glasses because he thinks being near-sighted is something for faggots, Margot is separated from her husband who sometimes, two or three times a year or maybe more, gets all dressed up and goes over to Villa Milagros to go to bed with his wife, the manager doesn't know they're husband and wife and Margot just to avoid trouble keeps it quiet and smiles, Margot's name is not Margot but Paquita, Don Joaquín is a better john than he is a husband, he treats Margot better than he treated Paquita, he cut Paquita's throat, any more and he would have killed her, and he licks Margot's scar like a lap dog, how're things going?, can't complain, and you?, well, you know, I'm getting along, day before yesterday I sold a pair of old-style high-backed armchairs and I said to myself I'm going to go over to Villa Milagros, maybe I'll be lucky and Margot won't be busy, Margot doesn't hate Don Joaquín, she's forgotten all about the stabbing, time heals all things, and the kids?, fine, they're fine, the girl's turned into a real little woman, Don Joaquín smiles while he strokes Margot's hair, let's hope she turns out a little less of a slut than her mother!, Margot doesn't smile, she's on the verge of tears, hush!, whatever you say. Maruja la Valvanera is the owner of 10 Alcántara (and also of 130 Ayala), Don Roque is Maruja's oracle, what's going to happen here, Don Roque?, things are going from bad to worse, nothing, honey, absolutely nothing's going to happen here, you'll see, from your mouth to God's ear Don Roque!, I'm more scared every day, forget it, get rid of those bad thoughts!, Don Roque changes the subject, Don Roque hasn't gone to the Calle de Alcántara to talk about politics, let's see, what have you got there?, Maruja smiles, I've got a new girl from Santander that you're going to like better than candy Don Roque, what breasts, Don Roque!, what a fanny, what hips!, well, you'll see her and you can judge for yourself, you'll see how you come back for more, she's busy now but she'll be out soon, are you in a hurry?, well, not to leave, but to hit that gal for a couple of pieces of ass if she's the way you say . . . , just relax a little Don Roque, she can't be long, men don't last much with this girl, Consuelito is a lot of woman for these modern lovers! Don Leopoldo Garrido is a public employee, he works in the Bureau of Agriculture, Forestry, and Livestock, Section 7, Forest Ownership and Appeals, his superiors appreciate him because he is punctual and does his duty. Socorrito's place, "a twenty-five peseta house," is at 7 San Marcos, it's very luxurious and there is no other one in Madrid with "a dining room equipped with walnut furniture with gilded ironwork," Socorrito's name is not Socorrito but Milagritos, Milagritos Moreno, and she lives on the Calle de Amor de Dios away from her business and surrounded by many Virgins and saints, Milagritos has no connection whatsoever with Villa Milagros, they are two separate firms, if a general railway strike is called the first to suffer the consequences will be the government, the editorial in *ABC* is right, the problems that burden the government all come from the same source, they are created by its allies, Milagritos give me another glass of brandy, the government has no other problems, would you like another glass of brandy too?, Milagritos make that two brandies, this separatist business has really boiled up too, Fuentes Pila hit the nail on the head, three hockey teams have entered the People's Olympics in Barcelona, Spanish, Catalonian, and Basque, that's just looking for complications, Don Cesáreo Murciego wears a green hat (the color VERDE means "Viva El Rey De España," long live the king of Spain) and a pearl tie pin, if we're all Spaniards, what's all this about Spanish, Catalonian, and Basque?, in spite of what these separatists have done Spain is still a single legal entity in the League of Nations, yes, you can't argue with that, of course not!, that's as incomprehensible as if they said French, Norman, and Béarnais, the United States even though it's a federation doesn't send three teams, United States, California, and Kentucky. You used to bed down with Chonina over by the canal, the place wasn't comfortable but it was cheap, sometimes you rolled around on top of a dried or half-dried turd, that comes with the territory, but since you're both young and hot you even laughed about it, on your birthday—twenty years old already!—Chonina gave you a tie decorated with little brass stars, it was horrible that's for sure and you threw it into the toilet at the Pleyel Theatre, what do you suppose the plumber said when he had to clean it out!, look at that, a sky-blue tie studded with gold-colored metal and dipped in shit!, maybe he washed it and ironed it carefully and gave it to a cousin of his who had to pay a formal call, the toilets of movie houses are very mysterious if you kept digging in them they might cough up all sorts of things, excrement of both kinds, sanitary napkins, semen from shopclerks and corporals of artillery and students, menstrual blood or blood from the lungs, handkerchiefs, neckties, cigarette butts, razor blades, advertising flyers, fetuses, etc., in the toilet of the Pleyel Theatre the patrons have been amusing themselves by covering the walls with inscriptions, Luisito's girl is the world's biggest slut, Long Live the King, Shit in peace, shit with calm soul, but son of a bitch, shit in the bowl, Whoever reads this eats it, Whoever wrote it eats more, Long Live United Socialist Youth, The king must shit, so does the pope, I learn, and in this shitty world of ours, each one of us must shit in turn, This is a place to shit, this is a place to pee, this is a place where if you've got time you can jack yourself off for free, Don't shit on the lid you asshole, Long Live Falange Española, José Sacristán Gutiérrez shit here February 12, 1936, long live the Republic!, La Mascota Contraceptives 4 Calle del Gato, Don't pull the chain, everything for our leader, In this most holy place where so many people sit, the laziest man will strain and the bravest lose his shit, Your sister's pussy, Long live the draftees of '35, etc. At 13 Naciones is the establishment of Doña Patro the Lacemaker, which advertises in the neighborhood movie houses, if you're here to see Chelo don't even come in, she drank a whole bottle of lye and they took her to the first-aid station more dead than alive, Don Estanislao is thunderstruck, to the Calle de Castelló?, yes, I think so, at the first-aid station, amidst the quiet and the smell of filth and medicine, there is only a medic with dirty fingernails reading *La Tierra*, on a gurney you can see a plate with leftover meatballs and also two books, *A Woman Made to Measure* by Pedro Mata and *An Easy Woman* by Alberto Insúa both of them very worn and with bloodstains, good evening, the medic doesn't answer the greeting, what do you want?, Don Estanislao swallows, you could have smothered him with a feather, excuse me, is there a young woman here who swallowed lye?, the medic doesn't even look at Don Estanislao and turns the page of his newspaper, you mean the whore from the Calle de Naciones?, Don Estanislao gets a lump in his throat, when things get tough a man either gets a lump in his throat or the blood rushes to his head, nobody has any control over it and you never know what's going to happen, whether it's going to be a lump in the throat or the blood rushing to the head, when they get a lump in the throat people cower and shrink, when the blood rushes to their head people, even those who seem the most peaceful, are capable of killing their own father, it depends on how it hits you, Don Estanislao got a lump in his throat, yes, that's the one, the medic doesn't take the butt out of his mouth to talk, she's gone to the morgue, Don Estanislao's ears ring, but . . . ?, the medic looks at Don Estanislao over the top of his glasses, what do you think they go to the morgue for, vacations? It was your fault that the Frenchwoman at the League of Nations almost killed Gregorio Montes one day, the two of you had bet five pesetas that he couldn't hold out inside her for three minutes and he almost croaked right there, me, not last three minutes inside?, that's what I say and what's more I'll bet you five, let's see about that!, Gregorio Montes asked for a string and tied a good tight knot on his scrotum, okay?, anything's okay except chickening out, the women were splitting with laughter and so were two or three customers that were in the waiting room, poor little boy, *certainement* 'e will die wiz 'is balls burst!, voulez vous faire la criquette avec moi, mon petit?, oh, what a big *polard* for ze *laque* of 'is little Frenshy!, Mireya said it as a joke but if we'd been a little less careful Gregorio Montes would have died with his testicles straining and ready to burst, it was awful what happened to them!, like melons!, the manager cut the string with a razor blade and taking good care not to ruin him (first we tried it with a pair of nail scissors but the string was so tight that there was no way to get under it) and then with bowls of cold water he got a little better and we were able to take him home, first we gave him a good strong coffee and a glass of brandy because he'd turned a little pale, to try to make him feel a little better Mireya masturbated him very tenderly and delicately, she was a changed woman, so maternal, it was nice to see her, the other women were quiet, because of the impression it all made on them, you could tell, and the two or three customers in the waiting room left very discreetly without saying a word, will you forget about the five?, of course, who'd have the nerve to collect it from you after what you've been through! Until recently Isabel had a faggot from Cadiz whom they called Pepito la Zubiela employed in her house, she had to kick him out, there was no way around it because he was foolish and a troublemaker, when he got excited he didn't think and you can't have that when you work for the public, it's just not possible, it seems that one night and for no good reason he patted Don Máximo's butt and on top of that he called him my little republican pigeon, Don Máximo went wild and laid into him so hard that he knocked him right through a wardrobe mirror, God what a row!, Don Máximo wanted to kill him, in the ass, I'll kick his ass till he kicks the bucket, doesn't he like to take it in the ass?, well he'll get what he likes, he'll get what's coming to him!, to calm him down Isabel offered Don Máximo a nice cup of linden tea, linden tea my ass!, bring me a double brandy!, to avoid more trouble Isabel had them hide Pepito in a trunk, after several hours when Don Máximo left in a calmer and more peaceful mood Isabel got Pepito out of his trunk half suffocated but at least alive, she settled her account with him and threw him out, look Pepito, I don't care if you're a faggot, you know that, for making the beds here I'm not going to be hiring General Prim, after all, but insulting my customers, that's something I won't allow, so out you go, away with you!, I don't ever want to see you again!, Pepito didn't take being fired at all well, I may be a faggot but what about you, you whore!, you're the biggest whore in all of Spain!, I'm telling you, if come was colored your kids would be like peacocks, Isabel had two children, Ismaelito who became a Marist brother and Isabelita who married an aristocrat. They call Victoriano Palomo Valdés "Gonococcus" because of his mother-in-law's business, well, they call him that but they don't really say it to him, you've got to be a brave man to call somebody Gonococcus right to his face!, Victoriano is a chiropodist and according to him he has studied medicine for two years, nobody knows whether it's true but most people don't believe it, on Saturdays Victoriano goes for an extramarital lay to the house that's above the Golden

Grapes on San Marcos, this house belongs to Paquita Pineda the owner of the house of assignation on Augusto Figueroa, one of the regulars at the Golden Grapes is Don Leoncio Romero, a clerk in the Finance Ministry, a Saturday john who builds up his energy stuffing himself with cracklings, if there were a contest for crackling stuffers Don Leoncio would take the first prize, one of Don Leoncio Romero's legs is shriveled up and shorter than the other which obliges him to wear some heavy complicated hardware for stability and a sole almost eight inches thick on one shoe in order to keep his balance, whenever the others allow it Don Leoncio picks out Donata, who is not young any more and never was pretty but who has a good body and above all a lot of patience for taking off and putting on his straps and screws, what's up, Don Leoncio, time to give your straps and screws a workout?, well yes, you've got to keep them from rusting from lack of use, every month or month and a half Don Leoncio pays for a lay for Paquito, neither you nor I is rolling in money that's for sure and I even less than you, but I can't tell you what it makes me feel to leave this kid just longing for it while you and I are fucking away happily upstairs, I get sort of a twinge of conscience!, Victoriano Palomo's sentiments are less charitable, let him long!, Paquito is a social parasite, a drone, that's what Paquito is, he can fuck when his father dies!, well, you do as you like, I wasn't saying it so you'd chip in, when Don Leoncio invites him to a lay Paquito's little eyes sparkle with joy and he even looks handsome, thank you Don Leoncio, God bless you, when my father dies I'll make it up to you, forget it son, I hope it does you good. The man who was with the wife of the master sergeant of the Customs Guard, who was a corporal, also of the Customs Guard, who was dressed in civilian clothes because he was off duty, broke a bench on Amanda's ribs and if they hadn't held him down in time (you also helped to hold him down, he was mad as a hyena) he would have killed her right there, the sergeant's wife told her husband that the alcohol burner had blown up on her and of course her husband believed her, why shouldn't he have believed her?, don't alcohol burners sometimes blow up?, Amanda is from Alcázar de San Juan, where she had to leave when she was still very young because she took a stone and cracked the head of a boyfriend of hers who got her pregnant and didn't want to recognize the child, the picador Tomás, Honoria's Tomás, marked Amanda's face in the town of Don Benito during a rough party that almost wound up in disaster, that was when she came to Madrid where she found work as a maid at 5 Barbieri in the house of Angelita, Old Tricky's Angelita the successor of Enriqueta Clavijo, because of her bad character and especially because of her scar she couldn't be one of the girls at Barbieri and had to settle for making beds and washing sheets and washcloths, flashy living has its price and at the end the one who's lived it winds up quite subdued and doing menial labor, it's all a matter of time because sooner or later it always happens that way, is Amanda in?, yes but she's with an all-nighter, all right I'll come back next week, give her regards from Matías from the commissary, I'll do that. Doña Bernardina and her husband say the rosary every afternoon, Pepita and the three little ones usually accompany them, of course they sometimes get distracted but that doesn't matter, something will stick. Doña Fe is a good housekeeper and super-clean, you can say what you want of her house but not that it's not clean with everything in its place and in order, Doña Fe has a daughter studying in a convent, I'm bringing her up to be lady, it's not the girl's fault that her mother has had to make her living working like a slave, Doña Fe's daughter was very carefully brought up, shortly after she left the convent she got married and when her mother died she didn't want even to hear about the business and gave it to the managers, who were three, Petra Soto Coscoja, Sabina Burguete González, and Baldomera Hidalgo Ibáñez, a typesetter at Rivadeneyra's whose name is Floreal Mingo and who belongs to an Anarchist union says that the house at 23 Calle de la Reina was turned into a cooperative of pleasure, the first in the history of Spain, now that we have a Republic and there is no queen the Calle de la Reina is called Calle de Gómez de Baquero, the only thing they still have to do is to give the workers of sex, the selfless servants of the sack, a share in the business, a dawn of hope appears on the horizon! The name of the watchman of the Calle de Ayala is Saturnino and he is from Santiago de Sierra also in the township of Cangas de Narcea, Saturnino eventually gave it up because he came down with rheumatism which is the hoof-and-mouth disease of watchmen, their professional ailment, following in the footsteps of his colleague Antonio Collar, Saturnino, when he hung up his nightstick and handed over the neighborhood keys, spent some time driving a taxi but since his rheumatism also bothered him in this new profession he turned to something more sedentary, married the daughter of a flunky at the Mint and opened a tavern on the Paseo de las Delicias, later he moved his establishment to an alley in the University district, behind the Calle del Noviciado, Saturnino!, coming!, Saturnino, limping like a leaking skiff, doesn't let a single tip get away, some customers at 128 Ayala even give two pesetas, Saturnino is a friend of yours and of Dámaso Rioja's, Saturnino is a cultured man who reads *Rocambole* by Ponson du Terrail and

The Count of Montecristo by Alexander Dumas père, this house is as sluttish as any or worse, it's just that Doña Valen likes to play the lady and so naturally she has maintained the proprieties, if I could talk!, you could say that I can't talk because in this business we have to be blind and deaf and dumb, but if I talked! On the days when there is a bullfight Paca makes a few pesetas tending the fire and washing dishes at some chicken-tripe stand near the bullring, nice hot chicken-tripe is delicious and very comforting, on the way back from leaving a dead relative or friend in the graveyard, people who attend second- or third-class funerals (not first-class) generally stop for some chicken-tripe at the stands by the bullring, poor Damián, how he liked chicken-tripe!, do you remember?, well, may he rest in peace!, Paca is obedient and shy like a village dog, obedient because she has to be and shy in spite of herself, Paca is like a village dog, just like one of those mixed-up mongrels that skulk around the slaughterhouse with their tails between their legs, an evasive look in their eyes and their backs ready to receive the blow of the bored bumpkin, on Paca's back, maybe so you can see it better, shines the hump of ridicule and of hope, Paca, yes sir, I'll give you half a peseta if you let me rub my prick on your hump, they say that brings luck, yes sir. Guillermo Zabalegui, after he'd learned his lesson about going in bare and coming out burned, took his precautions and ever since that memorable gonorrhea never again went to the whorehouse without a condom, Zabalegui buys his condoms by the dozen at La Ideal, 23 Calle de Jardines, a mysterious little shop that has a half-deaf and half-fairy clerk, or rather a complete fairy, who had been a brother of the Congregation of Christian Doctrine and with whom it's not easy to communicate, Matiítas?, that's the one, do you know him?, sure I know him!, my Uncle Esteban the blind one has hired him to read him novels every night, from ten or ten-thirty till twelve-thirty or one, my Uncle Esteban says he has the voice of a cricket but he can't find anybody else, Matiítas is obedient and humble and when my Uncle Esteban insults him and even says foul things about his mother he lowers his eyes and keeps quiet while he gives him the finger with impunity, a finger that my uncle doesn't even see, Matiítas really likes the novel *For Love and Virtue* by M. W. Hungerford that's appearing in the *Blanco y Negro*, the young woman knelt before her mother-in-law, moved and frightened by her own daring, and tried to draw Lady Rodney's hands away from her face, when Matiítas is through reading Don Esteban his nightly ration he takes a turn around the Botanical Garden to see how the cheap whores masturbate transient johns, the street belongs to everybody, sir!, I'm not doing any harm to anybody sitting here on a bench!, yeah, but I'm the one who's going to do harm with the punch I'm going to lay on you if you don't beat it! Two or three nights ago there were some words at Los Caracoles between some Andalusian workers from the Socialist union and a group of Falangists, the police didn't get there before they came to blows but they did make it before they killed each other, that's something at least, the French girls were very excited and happy looking out the window and applauding. Don Vicente Parreño and Don Lucio Martínez Morales are both of them customers of the same female, María Inés la Cordobesita who was a model for famous painters and the mistress of big bullfighters and who still preserves a few remains of her former vigor and greatness, every Saturday Don Vicente and Don Lucio toss a coin to see who goes first just like soccer players who toss for the side of the field and the start of play, luck usually favors Don Lucio although not always, when he has to wait Don Lucio keeps busy reading the papers, when Don Vicente is the one who has to be patient for a bit the newspaper stays in its place without anyone's touching it, Don Vicente prefers to turn up his eyes and imagine La Cordobesita naked in bed, sometimes Don Vicente gets distracted and thinks of something else, of his wife's asthma that's a little better now thank God, of his daughter's boyfriend who's just gotten a job in the post office and who seems to have honorable intentions, of his second son who has to be enrolled in the business school, etc., one night when luck had as usual favored Don Lucio, Don Vicente told him, I respect the outcome of the toss, naturally, but I'd like to ask you a favor, to let me go ahead of you, my wife's asthma is worse and I don't want to get home too late, by all means!, I'm in no hurry, you go ahead, thank you very much Don Lucio old friend, I'll try not to take too long, you're welcome, you're very welcome, you just go enjoy yourself in peace and quiet because I'm in no hurry, thank you, you're welcome, and I hope your wife is better soon, I sure hope so too, she really isn't well. At Madame Teddy's place the women are usually tall and heavy, you can't understand why but that's the way it is, at Madame Teddy's place there are no short women even though they're so affectionate, Jesualdo Villegas, a reporter for *El Sol* and before that, a few years ago, an avant-garde poet, is wild about Enriqueta (a hundred seventy pounds of woman, very well distributed) and the only thing he doesn't let her do is interrupt him, I'm telling you, be still, didn't you hear me?, Roque Zamora comes in like a flash, do you know what happened at Las Navas, the coffeeshop?, well Sánchez Somoza, the deputy, found his wife having a snack there with

Taboada, not with Raúl Taboada the one from *El Liberal* but with the other Taboada, the younger one, that slim fellow who does the local news in *El Debate*, and he got so furious that he almost killed them, he pulled out his gun, had them close the place and made his wife and the guy with her drink two big bottles of milk and eat twelve buns apiece, didn't you want a snack?, he told them, well here's your snack!, bums!, fools!, didn't you want a snack?, Sánchez Somoza was going wild, he had everybody scared and nobody there dared to raise his eyes or even breathe, then he had them bring two kettles, big ones, of boiling chocolate, pulled the pants off Taboada, lifted up his wife's skirt and gave them both a hip-bath, what a brute!, after that he left slamming the door and breaking all the glass in it and now, just try to catch him!, what a row this is going to become!, and when was this?, this evening about seven, once Cánovas Cervantes finds out about this!, Enriqueta finds it perfectly reasonable for a man to burn his faithless wife's bottom with chocolate, hush Enriqueta, don't be a brute!, Landsberg's ideas about human knowledge seem very opportune and up-to-date to Jesualdo Villegas, Roque Zamora cares less about them, Roque Zamora writes for *El Heraldo* but he's not on the staff and lives from day to day, which always distracts a man from philosophical speculation. On Tuesdays and Wednesdays Toisha ties up her hair, doesn't put on any perfume or much makeup, wears a medium heel and walks with her eyes on the pavement, on Tuesdays and Wednesdays Toisha acts like a female who's going to play around but for love and in a decent way, the sisters in spite of their cherry are bigger and bolder sluts, more given to flings and teasing, Toisha never asks for anything except love, she accepts an ice cream if it's offered to her or some other refreshment but she never asks for anything, with the sisters on the other hand you'd think a friar had made their mouth and they spend the whole day asking, now a sandwich, now a beer and potato chips, now a popsicle . . . , the sisters would be very expensive if they got their way, the good thing about them is that you tell them no and they settle for that, will you buy me a strawberry ice cream?, no, all right, at Los Corales a little farther on and on the other side of the street they have very good fried fish, two fish and four beers!, Dámaso Rioja thinks half an order of fish per person is more than enough and furthermore if you eat fast you get more than half, Lupita and Juani don't even notice. Don Leopoldo and Doña Bernardina are Paquito's aunt and uncle, Paquito's mother is Doña Bernardina's sister, it's true she married a count but still you couldn't say she made a good marriage, Paquito's father is full of crazy ideas and useless for any work, it's probably syphilis. At 6 Chinchilla there aren't any women, you've got to take your own, at 6 Chinchilla they supply the bed and the decorations, discretion and hygiene (such as it is), tolerance and a condom (if you ask for it and pay for it separately), but not the woman, you've got to bring her from the outside with the arrangements all made, at the Miami Bar, two doors farther down, the women wait patiently for someone to pay attention to them, Ginesa the Murcian is like a guardsman and according to those in the know she has hair between her tits and in her navel, the cigarette man at the Miami Bar is cross-eyed and only has one tooth, a gray one as big as a donkey's, the cigarette man at the Miami Bar is called Senén and boasts of having the most enormous prick in all Madrid, Ginesa the Murcian says it's true, that she's never in her life seen a prick like that, Don Gerardo Sanemeterio (he himself explained to you that it's written Sanemeterio, all as one word) is a rich man from Cáceres with more money than Croesus and a worse disposition than a Miura bull, when Don Gerardo comes to Madrid he treats Senén to one visit a day to the Murcian but he limits his time, the first day fifteen minutes, the second fourteen, the third thirteen, and so on until Senén comes back with his tongue hanging out and buttoning his fly on the street, Senén's record is seven minutes, he can't get it any lower than that, the day you get done in five minutes I'll give you five pesetas as a present on top of everything I do for you, but if you try to fool me and not come, you'd better make your peace with God!, no cigarette vendor is man enough to fool me!, do you get it?, yes sir, I get it, and thank you very much for what you do for me. You read Juan Ramón at the university and with your classmates, Juan Ramón is a great poet (that's the official version), maybe a little hysterical and prim, Dámaso Rioja claims that Juan Ramón has never been to a whorehouse, women don't interest him, only his poetry, Don León Rioja, Dámaso's father, doesn't know who Juan Ramón is and doesn't care, look Mr. Rioja what I say is that nothing's going to happen here, there's talk and more talk but then what?, not a blessed thing, not a soul's about to open his mouth here, people just don't want to get into a scrape, I doubt that but, well, I hope you're right!, of course I am, you'll see, nothing ever happens here, a few strikes . . . , a couple of arrests . . . , somebody gets beaten up on the Calle de Alcalá . . . , I'm telling you, not a blessed thing, maybe, how about a cigarette?, thanks a lot Mr. Rioja, I won't turn you down, Doña Encarna runs her business with a lot of tact or with a heavy hand, whatever is called for, Doña Encarna doesn't let the young men talk about politics, the older gentlemen are something else and you've got to treat them with more respect, look here young man you can't talk politics here and certainly not shout, here you know it's get laid or get out, excuse me, the older gentlemen are something else, they're more polite and speak very seriously, while they're waiting for their turn, about Mr. Lerroux's statements to the press, about the award of the gold medal of the City of Madrid to the ex-Minister of Public Works Don Indalecio Prieto or the Manila-Madrid flight that the Philippine airmen Calvo and Arnáiz have just made (successfully), Don León, yes Doña Encarna, you can go in, La Hebrea is available now. When Don Joaquín goes to Villa Milagros he always goes to spend the night, he talks to Margot a little, lays her a couple of times, and goes to sleep, the next morning he has his breakfast served in bed, reads the papers, and goes away quietly, without shaving and almost without saying good-bye, one night when Margot was busy he went to bed with Petra la Grillo a Guinean mulatto with loose habits, is it better with me than with your wife, you bum?, Don Joaquín's voice clouded over, he could hardly talk, if you say that again I'll kill you, you black bitch, Petra la Grillo didn't take what Don Joaquín told her seriously and a few days later she showed up dead on a picnic ground in the Dehesa de la Villa with a slash across her throat that cut her jugular in two, one thing piled on another and the authorities (it's quite understandable) could never get anything clear, Paquita, my name is Margot, what do you want?, nothing, just, don't they know who killed the black one?, Margot looks her husband in the eye in such an expressionless way that it's scary, I do but nobody else, I swear it, Margot prefers to defuse the situation, it's no big loss!, she was a bad whore!, the next day Don Joaquín sent his wife a bouquet of carnations, her johns went off wearing them in their lapels. Don Roque likes change and one by one he tries every fat woman that Maruja la Valvanera serves up, what's become of that girl from La Mancha, the one from Villarrobledo who was so ticklish?, you mean Rómula?, yes that one, she's not here any more, she left three or four months ago, her parents started feeling old and sent for her, Don Roque's expression turns nostalgic, what a cheerful bitch she was!, what a damned lot of fun she was in bed!, do you remember the day when we broke your bed, Maruja?, ha ha, at first you were mad as a wet hen, but Don Roque, I didn't really know you yet!, I understand . . . , Rómula was a lot of fun!, would you believe she laughed even when she was fucking?, yes, that's what other gentlemen have told me too, some of them didn't like it, well you mustn't be surprised at that, some people are always in a bad mood, Rómula is not in her village taking care of her parents as Maruja la Valvanera says but in San

Juan de Dios Hospital scratching away at a case of the clap. Don Cesáreo usually wears a little religious medal attached to his shirt collar but when he goes to the whorehouse he puts it in his vest pocket, Milagritos, yes Don Cesáreo, do you think Miss Eyes is going to be here soon?, no, she ought to be here now, she had a date at the Palace Hotel but she ought to be here now, why don't you take her sister who is also very affectionate?, no forget it, I'll wait a while longer, if she's not back by eight-thirty send me the sister, that way we keep it all in the family, Don Román Navarro laughs at Don Cesáreo's joke, Don Cesáreo is the one who usually pays for the brandy, and what do you say about this business of tearing poor helpless girls from the arms and the protection of selfless holy women like the Sisters of Charity?, please, Don Cesáreo, don't even talk about that! Chonina is on the Calle de Hileras now in Leonor Bustillo's place and is getting to have a steady clientele that allows her to spend a good five pesetas when she feels like it, she has Tuesdays off and since she likes to save and thank God is strong and healthy she tries not to waste her time and instead of going to the movies to spend her money she drops by the Café Aquarium to try to keep on earning some, at the Café Aquarium there's always some gentleman from the provinces who feels like living it up and shelling it out, these johns that Chonina picks up on her own time she takes to the Calle Augusto Figueroa to Paquita Pineda's place or to the house of Mari Pepa the Copper, some people know this place as the Granadan's after its former owner, you had an affair with Chonina, don't deny it, it doesn't do you much good now because the girl won't even give you a glance, Pepe the Dog-Man the one who turned up murdered on the road from Húmera to Pozuelo was a friend of a brother of Chonina's who had to make a statement to the authorities, what the hell do you care if the construction workers are on strike?, are you a construction worker?, no, so . . . ?, sometimes just for the fun of it (or rather as a deed of charity) Chonina goes to bed with Don Olegario Murciego who is an inventor, his brother Don Cesáreo won't hear of him and although he is well off he does nothing to help him, Don Olegario is dirt-poor and not quite right in the head, Don Olegario has invented a stationary balloon for the prevention of hailstorms and a urinal that by means of a very delicate mechanism plays *La Madelon* as soon as you piss into it, every time he went to see some capitalist to explain his devices to him he got kicked down the stairs, the great Edison also had to put up with this kind of unpleasantness!, so he thinks in order to encourage or at least console himself, from time to time Chonina lays him for the hell of it and then she gives him a peseta so he can get himself a drink, thank you dear, don't mention it Mr. Murciego, you know you've got a friend in me, you didn't take Chonina's defection very well, don't deny it. Mahogany, besides being very beautiful, was very temperamental and capricious, at the Restaurant Cartagena where you can hear the singing of the best canaries in the world there was a bit of a row one night because she ordered fried birds and they told her they didn't have any, and what about those?, those are not for sale, ma'am, those are singing canaries, well they might as well be fiddling thrushes, you idiot, charge whatever you want, you don't scare me, let's go, fry me half a dozen of your virtuosos!, Mahogany didn't take kindly to a no and the blood was starting to rise to her head and the owner of the Cartagena, smelling trouble, phoned for help from Manene Chico, a *banderillero* with the bullfighter Rafael el Gallo and a man whom Mahogany was wild about, and he came by right away and was able to distract her, thanks, Manene, you're very welcome, man, what's a friend for?, but listen, what would you have done if you hadn't found me?, what do I know!, when this woman gets going it's not easy to stop her, if I hadn't watched out she'd have fried my whole chorus here, it would have ruined me!, at 17 Ventura de la Vega they remember Mahogany fondly, she was the finest woman in Spain, she was like a queen, when she was naked she looked like one of those statues they have on fountains, 17 Ventura de la Vega is still a distinguished place, now, besides bankers and aristocrats, some deputies from the Radical Party or Alcalá Zamora's party go too, this whorehouse business can put up with a certain degree of mingling, at least that's what Jesualdo Villegas claims, as Max Aub used to say, one man one vote, one woman one cunt, if that's not democracy I'd like to know what the hell is, but listen, everybody eating from the same plate like that!, my friend, it's the times.

II

Look at yourself in the mirror and don't break out crying, it's hardly worth while for you to break out crying because your soul is already more than damned, be respectfully still as though you were in the presence of someone who had died of hunger and don't think of suicide, nobody would believe you, you are a nobody, you are a nobody, you are a nobody . . . , that is the only truth, you don't have the courage to turn on the gas jet, to take a whole bottle of pills, or to put a bullet in your temple, you are a nobody, you are a nobody, you are a camouflaged nobody, with your skull full of gregarious ideas, of redeeming ideas, of other people's ideas, why won't you admit it?, you are a nobody, you are a nobody, you are a nobody made of the stuff of fear of everything around you, no, you are not Saint Paul who saw the light on the road to Damascus, neither are you King Cyril of England who died . . . you know how, you live nourished by fears, just like a rat, but you're not brave enough to fight biting in the dark like a rat, what's it to you that the body of Magdalena known as Inmaculada Múgica smells rancid if it's not yours?, the rancid smell of Magdalena's body matters to no one and least of all to you who are afraid of the rancid smell that rises from the body of Magdalena Inmaculada Múgica, you'd like to keep a lock of Magdalena Inmaculada Múgica's hair in the drawer of your night-table but you're not brave enough to ask her for it, to steal it from her, to buy it from her, you'd like to keep some item of Magdalena Inmaculada Múgica's underwear (used and unwashed) in your closet among the shirts but you're not brave enough to ask her for it, to steal it from her, to buy it from her, you're afraid of smothering her with the pillow if she won't give it to you which is what most likely would happen, or if she discovers your intentions, you live with your family but you don't dare to ask for a cup of coffee between meals, if you lived alone you would already have died from fear of being alone, the dead don't drink coffee, nobody asks them whether they want some coffee to fight the cold of the cemetery and the loneliness, you'd like to be a fly in a brothel, a witnessing fly, a lascivious fly on sheets crushed by fear of fellowman, but you're afraid to tempt God with your humble requests, your abject and domestic requests, around the village slaughterhouses the guts of the dead cattle rot in the sun while the insatiable blue flies of a gorgeous metallic blue buzz, devour, and make love amidst strident laughter, some flies have a red belly with flashes of green or a green belly with flashes of red, these are the very devil, you cannot stand the glorious spectacle of murdering a woman with a soup spoon, no, you are not Saint Paul nor Buffalo Bill, you are fodder for the catechism class capable of killing for a smile from those in command, fodder for the gallows capable of hanging your brother for fear that someone might think you are afraid, fodder for the common grave capable of wishing yourself already dead to avoid the moment of death, you go for walks in the darkest and most humid corners of the night while your heart trembles with fear of darkness, of humidity, Magdalena Inmaculada Múgica's body smells rancid but the smell does not awaken you, you're used to it, the dead owe nothing to anybody, debts expire with death and sleepers even if they smell rancid (especially if they smell rancid) hardly owe anything to anybody, at the most a little room in the bed to let them keep on dying slowly and to their heart's content, Magdalena's pulse is strong and healthy, rhythmic and almost noisy, but you do not hear the pulse of Magdalena Inmaculada Múgica who at that moment is dreaming that she is walking barefoot in the Holy Week procession, in Magdalena Inmaculada Múgica's guts the gurgle of digestion rises and falls in challenging scales (like those the cornet in the band plays in rehearsals) but you don't listen to the gurgling in Magdalena's belly because at that moment you are dreaming that you're flying like an angel above the acacias at second-story level, Magdalena's breathing whistles a little in her lungs, hardly at all, it's not odd that you shouldn't hear the whistling of Magdalena Inmaculada Múgica's lungs, turn your face to the wall and drive away bad thoughts, it's not worth while to kill this woman, it wouldn't be hard, it's easy to kill a woman, easier even than it seems, you cover her nose and her mouth with your hand, you hold her down firmly, she kicks a little and that's it, what's bad is if she looks you in the eye because then maybe you let her go and you have to run out of there and never stop and keep running and running all your life, but, like I said, it's not really worth while to kill this woman, no, don't kill this foul-smelling woman, you could bring about your ruin for a few moments of pleasure, cover her with kisses, get back in bed with her and let the next man kill her, somebody will kill her, don't worry, you are not the Cid and why would you want to be, neither are you King Cyril of England who had a solution for everything till luck turned her back on him and his own knights killed him, look at yourself in the mirror and escape from the mirror, it's like a gymnastic exercise, look at yourself in the mirror, escape from the mirror, look at yourself in the mirror, escape from the mirror and so on until you can't take it any more, Magdalena Inmaculada Múgica is sleeping unaware of your thoughts, that is her duty, she pulls the covers up to her head and under the blankets she sweats a sticky, pitiless sweat, Magdalena is probably a loathsome woman but you shouldn't be troubled by that, loathsome women also have a right to life, we can practice charity with our hands and our heart, caressing and loving, and we can also feed avarice with our hands and our heart, slapping and forgetting, take refuge in hatred for Magdalena Inmaculada Múgica and for her greasy smell, that's probably your only way of avoiding jail, will pay surprising prices for gentlemen's suits, overcoats, furniture, objets d'art, antiques, china, watches, medals, table service, silverware, glassware, knick-knacks, Casto, phone 51752, too bad there are no secondhand dealers for consciences or dead women, the brave matador Daniel Luca de Tena has appointed the former banderillero José Riaño, "Riañito," his agent, everything has a connection with everything else except the stench of Magdalena, don't pump the well of memory, the well of memory, the well of memory, the well, run away, you can still run away, maybe tomorrow it will be too late to run away and you will have no choice but to give yourself up to have your hands tied behind your back, Dorothy Gray's Beauty Mask gives your face a serene beauty, it wipes out every trace of fatigue and leaves your skin as tight as alabaster, something like that is what you need to keep on living, to let others keep on living, Magdalena Inmaculada Múgica, keep at it, Magdalena Inmaculada Múgica!, and again, Magdalena!!, what do you want, nothing, just wanted to know if you're all right, yes, right as rain, let me sleep, death of the publisher forces sale of *El Eco Taurino* with complete files, 26 years' worth of photographs, complete collections, information at 2 Juan de Mena, ground floor in the printing shop, from 4 to 9 P.M., Magdalena, aren't you going to let me sleep, what do you want?, nothing, I have a little headache, and what do you want me to do about it, does it hurt a lot?, no, just a little, come on, go to sleep, Magdalena, what?, I'm going to kill you, don't be silly, come on, go to sleep, it's still night, some women put a lot of value on night, more than anybody, Magdalena Inmaculada Múgica, what?, nothing, Magdalena turns on the light, come on, squirt it out again, isn't that what you want?, and let me sleep in peace, no, that isn't what you want but it's not a bad idea either, Magdalena smells like lamb and you are not Napoleon Bonaparte but neither are you King Cyril of England, Magdalena Inmaculada Múgica is so sleepy she doesn't even wash herself out, through the half-open window you can hear the watchman's club hitting against the sidewalk and from time to time some taxi that stops in front of the whorehouse with fresh customers, no, don't kill this woman even though she smells like the dead, Toisha, even when she doesn't wear perfume smells clean and of perfumed soap on Tuesdays and Wednesdays, sometimes it's a little shock for the conscience to notice how good she smells, you be patient, always be patient and everything will come in due time, unlike what happens to most people you don't envy what you touch but what you smell, it's confusing but that's the way it is, you're not to blame either, women do not want to inspire love but pity so that afterward they can spit love in your face, Magdalena Inmaculada Múgica smells too much of dead grease not to be an exception to the rule, Magdalena, what, I've got a headache, and what do you want me to do about it? Enrique Garrido works in the first-aid station of the Chamberí district on the Calle de Eloy Gonzalo, he doesn't earn much but he can stay more or less afloat without having to go to a village, that's like death, you can have the villages, Enrique is no longer a burden to his parents, what with this and that he at least earns enough for cigarette money. Dámaso Rioja goes to noon mass at Christ church on Ayala, Dámaso does not believe in God, or rather he tries not to believe in God, but he goes to mass every Sunday because in a minimal and almost contemptuous way he's chasing Maripi Fuentes the youngest daughter of the Count and Countess Casa Redruello who is a real doll who lets herself be petted without any particular demands or obligations, after the noon mass on the sidewalk by the Café Roma you can usually see people coming to politically inspired blows, nothing important, Maripi likes a highball with a sprig of mint before dinner and dancing the tango and a slow foxtrot very close, later on Maripi lets herself be kissed on the lips and on her décolletage and petted in a refined way, that is, silently and as though absentmindedly, Maripi has no regular boyfriend, she's had several but none of them lasted her long, what are you going to do this evening?, I'm going to a party at the Aguados,' why don't you come too?, I don't know them, will there be any food?, boy, I guess you're hungry!, Dámaso Rioja doesn't know whether to go to the party at the Aguados' or to the movies with the sisters, one on his right and one on his left, I don't know, I'll go if I can, try to, I'd like it if you went, it's at 13 Núñez de Balboa almost across the street from the Immaculate Conception. Look at yourself in the mirror and do what you can not to run away, stand firm, let no one say you've shit in the pants of your soul, you are so poor that all you have is time but any day now they might rob your time and then you'll be as defenseless as a newborn pigeon, you are surprised by the truth and by the name (unpronounceable) of the truth, you are surprised by the obvious and the odd name of the obvious (this woman who smells of grease or any other woman), you are surprised by everything and you don't know what to call your surprise, sometimes whistling can be very consoling, there are some very distinguished people who when they have the mange say I have a slight itch, yes, sure, an itch!, what you have is a world-class mange!, you ought to go confess as soon as possible, you ought to make sure the mange doesn't start to eat at your conscience, once that happens everything is harder to fix, you too ought to make sure you're not stuck with this woman dead in bed even if it's not you who kills her, explanations are always troublesome and often nobody, absolutely nobody, believes them, in every family there is an older brother who talks endlessly at the dinner table and speaks despotically to the family, his wife is fat and on the way to being fatter still, it's better to have than to want and the fact is there are lots of women who are dirt poor and many who are plain sluts, will you buy me a glass of wine?, I can't, I'm flat broke, and what did you spend the two pesetas on?, none of your damned business, sorry, it's all nonsense, bulls yes, cats no, dogs yes, parrots no, horses yes, lambs no, get this idea into your head, it's not prudent for you to kill this loathsome stinking woman. So then Don Gerardo he says listen, he says, listen girl, if you go after that priest who looks like a canon from the cathedral I'll give you fifty shining pesetas, all your own!, and what did she say?, nothing, she didn't say a thing, Conchita isn't any too bright, you know, she's only half there, boy, if he'd tried it with Ginesa!, you're telling me!, what a shame!, it's hard to believe how some of them blow their chances!, well, it's their lookout, Conchita is a maid in Maripi's house and she only goes whoring on Sunday afternoons and to make a little extra, just to make a little extra, to buy a little purse or a pair of stockings or a little bottle of Maderas de Oriente which is a very voluptuous and delicate perfume, etc., Conchita didn't like the joke with the priest, enough is enough, Conchita is not very proper nobody says she's very proper but religious and respectful she is, you have to keep things straight! At 7 A.M. the Northern Railway Station is swarming with people heading for an outing to breathe the clean mountain air, the young men and women of the parties of the far Left, Socialists and Communists, wear white shirts and red kerchiefs around their necks and sing the *Chíbiri*, people call them "chíbiris," on Sundays in the country the chíbiris do exercises, eat potato omelette and drink red wine, sing till they are hoarse and finally fuck a while discreetly, some of them do military drills, study the classic Marxist texts, and vaguely feel themselves to be the depositaries of revolutionary essences, isn't Engracia coming?, no, they've arrested her father, Señor Ramón?, yes, that's an outrage, arresting a lifelong republican and a decent hardworking man!, Engracia works in the packing department of a mattress factory and is an active member of the United Socialist Youth, Engracia is young and graceful, healthy and romantic, not very good-looking (not ugly either) but full of dreams and selfless, Engracia has the makings of a heroine, in Spain there are many heroines of the siege of Saragossa, many Agustinas de Aragón, it's just that you can't recognize them, Engracia dreams of a Spain of strong and chubby children, of a Spain without illiterates or unemployed workers or exploiters, I know very well that we'll have to sacrifice many things and at least a generation or two but the revolution is well worth trying for, our people cannot live without horizons! The gurgling in Magdalena Inmaculada Múgica's gut has become alarming, Magdalena Inmaculada Múgica is probably letting some gas even though she doesn't want to, that's the limit!, you shake Magdalena by the shoulder to awaken her, what's up?, nothing, let's just see whether your gut will lay off that racket, boy, can't you leave me in peace, why don't you just let me sleep in peace and quiet?, no, don't kill her, hit her on the mouth but don't kill her, hit her just hard enough, no more than that, measuring your blow and trying not to let it get out of hand, Magdalena Inmaculada Múgica has a friend from Tangier who has some words tattooed all around her navel like the face of a clock, *Vivre libre ou mourir*, what an idea!, Magdalena has no tattoos but she does have scars, sores, and bruises, scars from two Caesareans and various boils, rose-colored sores with greenish flecks, bruises from the bites of whoregobblers, the point is to be able to recognize corpses easily, they ought to tattoo a number on people's backs so they could never get away, look at yourself in the mirror if you feel like it, do whatever you want but without making faces, you can't paint a mustache and horns on the soul the way you can on the saints in *Mundo Gráfico* and *Blanco y Negro*, on Merle Oberon, General Graziani, Peter Lorre, the students in the arts and crafts school for natives in Tetuan, etc., yes, look at yourself in the mirror but in a natural way, in a very natural way, it wouldn't do you any good to make faces in front of the mirror, to disguise your face as the face of another, the face of a Chinaman, the face of an alligator, the face of a dead man, it's been many years since treason moved judges to compassion, the animals in the zoo are like sad, resigned prisoners, just like sick prisoners without much hope, the lion has a cast in one eye and bald spots in his mane, the camel is covered with sores, it has even more sores than Magdalena Inmaculada Múgica, it looks as though they hit it with sticks and stones once people have left, the wolf spends his time lying in a corner looking sidewise, the elephant doesn't leave his hut much maybe he's bored with the spectacle, the tiger is as swaybacked as an old mule, the monkeys masturbate without a letup they're going to wind up exhausted, the llama has dirty yellowish-gray fur especially on its belly, the only animals that seem to be enjoying themselves are the chickens in their little pens and the cats that stroll among the flowers and on top of the walls and the roofs, the cats at the zoo are very deserving and brave and steal food even from the lion as soon as he gets a bit distracted, these cats do not live at the zoo they're only visiting, these fierce wild cats live in communities like monks in the ruins of the chapel of San Isidro de Ávila right next to the fence at the Calle O'Donnell and they are a good-sized group of maybe two or three hundred, in the body of a vagabond cat there often lives the soul of a woman who was vexed to death bit by bit without respite day after day night after night without letting her breathe hour after hour minute after minute smiling at her so she'd have some confidence second after second and so on until she bursts like a boil just like a boil and the pus rises to her head and she dies maybe smiling too, women who are going to be vexed to death have very odd habits and wash their soul with lye before giving it to some vagabond cat, some shy cat capable of eating the lion's food or the bear's. On Sunday mornings Don Vicente Parreño goes to mass at Our Lady of Mount Carmel with his wife and afterward he takes her for a little walk in the Parque del Oeste, the air that comes from the mountains and from the Pardo woods is good for sufferers from asthma, colds, bronchitis, pleurisy, tuberculosis, and other respiratory ailments, Mrs. Parreño, poor woman, has no respite the fact is she's going from bad to worse, Don Vicente doesn't know what to do with her, Mr. Parreño's wife is Doña Eduvigis Olmedillo and she has the little face of a hungry rat with sunken eyes and a mustache, every kind of treatment failed with Mrs. Parreño, they gave her Abbé Hamón's cure number fifteen and she still couldn't breathe, she took Salud, a hypophosphite—

and even granulated Vitefosfor which they say is stronger—and her appetite still didn't come back and her legs kept on aching, for a whole month they were putting two large tablespoons of Dr. Valdés García's meat extract in her soup and she didn't gain an ounce, Vial wine doesn't tone her up and Dr. Andreu's pills don't get rid of her cough, maybe she'd get a little better if they took her to the spa at Panticosa but probably not, most likely Doña Eduvigis is just a hopeless case and besides a spa costs an arm and a leg, who could even think of that, Don Vicente is poor, anyone who lives on a salary is poor, and he's already making quite an effort in buying her her medicines, which, to be sure, she always gets, Don Vicente treats Doña Eduvigis very affectionately and considerately and even buys her comic books and plays parcheesi with her to entertain her, Vicente, what, I'm not going to last much longer, oh yes, you'll see you will, Doña Eduvigis' mustache trembles ever so slightly, Vicente, what, will you swear to me that once I'm dead you won't give your love to any other woman?, of course I swear. It's hot and a little ray of light slips through the partly open blind and in it the floating dust draws subtle and poetic pictures, you blow and the dust turns and dances, slowly at first, then quickly, the shadows of passersby are reflected on the wall, long and fragile, very mysterious and rapid, as though they were escaping from the sour smell of this woman, the shadows of the passersby don't cross the room with their feet on the floor but with their feet on the ceiling as though they were very thin giant grasshoppers, you are alarmed, it's worse to die than to be already dead forever and buried in the vast desert of peace, Magdalena washes her face sitting on a chair, Magdalena Inmaculada Múgica is so poor that she is on the edge of vileness, she doesn't know it but it's true, Magdalena, what, how did you sleep?, fine, and you?, badly, I slept very badly, throughout the house you begin to hear women moving around taking their showers and men singing *Katiuska* while they shave, some order coffee and a roll and while they have breakfast read the papers, nothing's happening, nothing's really happening, well, the usual, have you seen *A Ball at the Savoy*?, if you like I'll take you, flies always wind up drowning in the coffee cups, that's well known, Sundays at noon you usually go for lunch with your Uncle Jerónimo, an old liberal who lives by himself surrounded by books and photos of Krause, Sanz del Río, and the worthies of the Free Educational Institute, all of them under the protection of a fairly well done copy of Goya's portrait of Jovellanos, your Uncle Jerónimo maintained a voluminous correspondence with Joaquín Costa and Manuel Bartolomé Cossío whose letters he has kept in very careful order, he also has the manuscripts of Costa's *Agrarian Collectivism* and Giner de los Ríos' *Studies on Art and Literature*, beautifully bound in leather, your Uncle Jerónimo was married many years ago to a German student of philosophy whose name was Uta Greiner, they were married in a civil ceremony in Zurich in 1907, a lot of water has gone over the dam since then!, after a bit Uta caught typhus and your Uncle Jerónimo who is very apprehensive and sees germs everywhere left her in the hospital and never heard from her again, he's probably a widower but maybe he's still married and doesn't know it, the fact is he doesn't much care. Pepita Garrido didn't ask for assignment to a school because they would have sent her away from Madrid and she doesn't want to be separated from her parents, Pepita is very modest in her dress, she doesn't use makeup and always wears long sleeves, now she gives some classes, they don't pay much but since she has few needs she gets along and can even help out a little at home. You are not Saint Paul, why should you be Saint Paul?, but you are not Pepito la Zubiela either, you are just one man in the herd a little below the midpoint of the herd and you intend not to strangle Magdalena come what may, Magdalena isn't good for much but she is good for something, we're all good for something we just don't usually know it, the bold are not good for any more than those who aren't bold but on the other hand they know it and go straight ahead like a flash and without looking to left or to right, perhaps you should not spare the life of Magdalena Inmaculada Múgica who is like a vengeful toad, you ought to think this over very calmly and not make any rash decisions, mange is an ailment that appears only on the outside, so they say, on the skin, it would be awful to have the mange inside, on your palate, in the head, or in the lungs!, Magdalena washes sitting down and almost dressed, Magdalena Inmaculada Múgica washes almost contemptuously, maybe mange is starting to break out on Magdalena. On Sundays they eat paella at the sisters' house, Señor Asterio, their father, faithfully respects tradition, stew on Mondays, breaded cutlets on Tuesdays, meatballs on Wednesdays, beans and sausage on Thursdays, cod on Fridays, tripe on Saturdays, and paella on Sundays, Señor Asterio is a master plumber and has an important and well thought of shop, the sisters' mother, Señora Lupe, worked in an ironing shop on Serrano at the corner of Marqués de Villamejor before she was married and she is still lively and good-looking, nothing can stop Señora Lupe, Señor Asterio is a Socialist, a follower of Pablo Iglesias, and a very solid man with some education and who has done some reading, Señor Asterio does not go to mass, Señora Lupe does, the sisters say they will so their mother won't scold them or insult them but the fact is they don't go either, when Señora Lupe finds out that her daughters have not gone to mass she doesn't call them atheists or heretics or freethinkers but pigs, whores, and hairy apes, everybody speaks Spanish the way he wants, that's why it belongs to everyone, Señora Lupe usually puts mussels and even shrimp in the paella, the fact is the family lives well and even has a little money in a postal savings account, for whatever might happen, an operation, the girls' weddings, a time with less work, etc., Señor Asterio, Señora Lupe and their two daughters live on the Calle de la Libertad next to the Arrumbambaya, where actors and writers eat, in an old and not very comfortable apartment but one that's cheap and suits them very well and above all is more than big enough for them, Señor Asterio and Señora Lupe had a son, Asterín (they called him Emilito, nobody knows why), older than the sisters, who drowned in the Tajuña when he was six or seven years old one bad day when they had the ill-fated idea of going for a picnic in the country, Señor Asterio and Señora Lupe don't speak of their dead son but they can't forget him either, some afternoons when she's at home alone Señora Lupe even cries, taking advantage of the fact that nobody can see her, Señor Asterio does not cry but sometimes, when he is in his shop, he can't avoid being troubled by bitter thoughts and overcome by sadness, Emilito would be twenty-one or twenty-two now, a grown man, his sisters don't remember him, that's natural because they were just two and three when it happened, sometimes you call Señor Asterio Señor Ricardo, what a crazy habit of mixing up people's names!, have you gone to mass?, yes mother, let's see, what color were the priest's vestments?, his vestments?, well yes, his vestments, I'm not going to be asking you about his undershirt!, come on, what color were they?, white mother, all right, now come take your medicine, I'm about to serve the paella, Lupita and Juani take Tricalcine and Bisleri Ferroquinine but it doesn't show, they get skinnier by the day with bigger rings around their eyes, Lupita and Juani, without their family knowing about it, also take Pilules Orientales, they'd like their tits to be a little bigger, but not too much, come on, time to eat, you look like two dried herrings!, yes mother, after dinner Lupita and Juani rest for an hour and when they get up they fix their face a little, get themselves as clean as they can (they put on lipstick and a little eyeshadow on the stairs or in the doorway) and out they go for some necking and petting till suppertime, with you or anyone else fond of those sports, on Sundays they go to Stambul or Ideal Rosales to dance a little and, if they're lucky, to get treated to some refreshments. Anybody's palate itches and anybody can have something like vicious gaps in his memory, observe yourself well (you can say to anybody), the need to commit a murder is felt in the palate as a hot sticky little itch that alights on the palate and then spreads to the tongue, the gums, and the whole mouth, gaps in memory cannot be stopped with recollections because recollections flee to give way to the blood that you are going to spill, to the blood that will be a balsam for your itch, you think you are confused but no, you are not confused, anybody can be confused but not you, it could be that you are confused but no, you are not confused, you need luck for that, lots of luck, and you've already noticed that itch more than once although not as strongly as now, perhaps you are not yet ripe (neither historic nor messianic, it's all the same), all the better, if those in command guess that you have that itch there's no way around it, they call you aside they put a hand on your shoulder they look at you fixedly they talk to you with a very dark conspiratorial voice they smile a fatherly or confidential smile at you (both kinds are effective) and that's it, in a few hours you have become a murderer (historic or messianic, it's all the same), you couldn't help it and you're even proud of it, the little itch is now like a rusty coin, your temples throb, and your penis goes through all its states one by one from pointless flaccidity to pointless erection, you want to urinate but you are afraid to go as far as the urinal, stupor comes later, after you piss for the first time, and finally fear shakes you and makes you flee and keep on killing (or wanting to kill) wherever you go. All right now, at a quarter to ten on Augusto Figueroa between Fuencarral and Hortaleza, at a quarter to ten?, yes, you ought to be at the Café Gran Vía at nine-thirty, don't go in, wait outside, our three friends will be in the Café Gran Vía at nine-thirty, don't greet them, there's no need, Lt. Castillo will leave his house at ten to ten, give or take a minute, it's all got to go very fast, you've got to shoot him in the small of the back, from behind, you and N-2 shoot him, both at the same time, N-1 and Perico will cover you as you get away, you've got to run downhill and scatter right away, when you get to the corner keep going at a normal pace and completely calm, and at ten-thirty, be here, get it?, got it, all right, get to work, and good luck!, thanks. It is easy to turn a young man into a murderer, it is also easy to make him into a good torturer, a good cop, all that's needed is for someone stronger to smile at him at the right time as though leading him to feel himself mature (or historic or messianic, it's all the same), it's desirable first to empty his head through the hole made by the little itch, which is like a coin, the little itch can (should) spread rapidly over the whole body, it's the same as a mange that starts on the roof of the mouth and then spreads to the tongue and the gums and even reaches the toes, then we have a murderer ready to obey, it is not advisable to let him drink wine or other drinks, it is better for him to be a little thirsty. Sunday mornings you take Toisha for a walk as your steady girlfriend, you meet her on the street at the San Luis square and then you go to the Prado Museum or stroll a little on the Castellana or in the rose gardens of the Retiro depending on the season and the weather, Recoletos is more ordinary, Recoletos is full of shop clerks and vulgarians, on Sunday mornings it is very correct to walk around a bit with your steady girl, to try to polish her a little taking her to museums and to have a beer, before dinner, at one of the stands on the Castellana, on the left-hand side, Sunday mornings are a time for a lot of farce and propriety, of course no one will believe it but they're a time for a lot of farce and propriety, what's the matter with you?, you seem kind of odd, with me?, what should be the matter with me?, nothing, nothing's the matter with me, on Sunday mornings your girl Toisha puts on perfume and dresses to the nines in an elegant suit with very high-heeled shoes and her hair well combed and gathered a little on the nape of her neck, it's a pleasure to see her. Don Roque takes the two maids from the boardinghouse to the bullfight that is being held in honor of the airmen Arnáiz and Calvo, Don Roque is very gallant with the ladies, his hands tend to wander a bit but he is very gallant, both of you have to look your best, you can't go to a bullfight just dressed any old way, don't you worry, Don Roque, you'll see that you won't have to be ashamed of us, I hope not, I hope not . . . , the program for the bullfight is not very brilliant—the airmen Arnáiz and Calvo would have deserved something better—but that's all there is, José Neila, Pedro Ramírez, and Pedro Barrera, with bulls bred by González Camino, and then they rejected two of them that were replaced by two from Don Juan Terrones but one of these turned out to be too tame and its place was taken by an ox from Don Gabriel González that needed banderillas with fire to get it going, a real bargain-basement bullfight!, the airmen Arnáiz and Calvo and the public deserved something else, Don Roque sat with Paulina on one side and Javiera on the other, Paulina is more obliging but Javiera is better-looking and showier, Paulina is hotter but Javiera is no prude either, Paulina is jealous and Javiera on the other hand just wants to get taken for a snack and to the bullfights, Pedro Ramírez known as "the Triana Kid" was awarded an ear for his second bull, the two other matadors were just in there trying, when the Triana Kid saluted from the middle of the ring Don

Roque asked Paulina, would you lay him?, hush there, Don Roque, what a way of talking!, well, I know you would, Don Roque turned to Javiera, and how about you?, what about me?, would you lay him?, Lord, what an idea! María Zambrano lives on the Plaza del Conde de Barajas and is the friend and high counselor of young poets and painters, you owe a great deal to the friendship and the wise and generous support María Zambrano gives you and without having any real reason to pay attention to you since you are nobody and count for nothing, Miguel Hernández shaves his head and has very good coloring, healthy and like a tan, Maruja Mallo talks a lot and paints vignettes for the *Revista de Occidente*, Ildefonso Manolo Gil accepts some of your poems for his magazine *Literatura*, Camilo José Cela also writes poetry but up to now he hasn't been able to publish it, Arturo Serrano Plaja is serious and looks as though he is meditating, and Luis Felipe Vivanco who publishes in *Cruz y Raya*, what a guy!, is thin and even more serious, more as though he's meditating, than Arturo, more than anybody, you went to María Zambrano's Sunday gathering, you were taken by your doctor, Carlos Díaz Fernández, María's brother-in-law, who treats your tuberculosis and cheers you up and lends you some expensive or hard-to-find books, María Zambrano serves tea with cookies or a cold drink, whichever you like, her sister Araceli, Carlos Díaz's wife, is very beautiful and spectacular, tall, with a good figure and glasses, she looks like a foreign intellectual, you read your poetry to María and María puts up with it patiently and even shows a generous interest in it, you don't dare to take Toisha to María Zambrano's house, Toisha is something else and for the time being wouldn't know her proper role, later on we'll see. Doña Matilde Brocas, the mother of your friend Dámaso Rioja, hears mass on a phonograph because she can't get out of her chair, it's too bad they don't broadcast mass for the sick even if it were at 7 or 8 A.M., her spiritual director Father Ramírez, a Salesian, gave Doña Matilde a record of the mass, it's not the same as being present at the holy sacrifice but in the eyes of the Lord it is a special devotion very worthy of being borne in mind, thank you Don Vicente, God bless you, you're always so good, no my dear, we are all sinners, Doña Matilde sure isn't much of a sinner, Doña Matilde has no spirit left even for virtue, let alone sin, from her chair Doña Matilde sees death coming little by little and prays for everyone. At the Águila, on the other side of the Calle de Serrano, the young gentlemen of Renovación Española drink their beer, they seem a bit stupid but they're brave, very brave, with a rowdy and a little old-fashioned bravery, part chivalric, part sporting and part boasting, they wear green hats (we already know why), gold rings with their family crests cut in dark stones, and a properly trimmed mustache, they don't fool anybody, there are some Falangists too and an occasional student from the Carlist student group, did you break up with Maripi?, yes, more than a month ago, now she's going with an odd guy, I think he must be some kind of atheist or socialist, who reads *El Sol*, imagine!, and writes poetry, the kind that doesn't rhyme, poor kid!, no, why?, as long as she gets squeezed at parties and somebody swears eternal love to her, that's all Maripi asks. The Falangists act in politics as though they were playing rugby, the Carlist boys seem like crusaders and talk about the Cause, with a capital C, some of them believe, you bet!, and some just go along to see whether they wind up believing. Conchita is servicing José Carlos, Mr. José Carlos, Maripi's older brother, he began patting her butt as though by accident if he met her in the hallway, or in the pantry when he went for a glass of water or a box of matches, and he wound up getting into her bed on Thursday afternoons when the other maid, Sabina, was off, one Thursday afternoon José Carlos came to Conchita's room a little earlier than usual and found her in bed going at it with his sister Maripi, the three of them pretended nothing had happened and at supper-time Maripi didn't even dare to raise her eyes, Conchita had a boyfriend, a baker who left her because she was a whore and who furthermore told her so, Conchita is no whore, well, not much of a whore but she is young and sexy, Don Carlos, the father of José Carlos and Maripi, looks sideways at her legs when she serves at table and imagines her naked or better yet in her slip, a nice very short black slip with lace all around the edges, what's the matter, Carlos?, you seem off in the clouds, no dear, I'm worried about what's happening, God only knows what's to become of our poor Spain!, the countess still looks good, with a white décolletage and powerful hips and her little mouth painted into a heart shape, Don Carlos wrote a little note to the maid, typed it so as not to compromise himself, Sunday at 6 go to La Gran Peña, go in by the back door, the one from the Calle de la Reina, and ask for me, you'll get a little present, Don Carlos gave the note to the maid on the sly and Sunday at six he took off her clothes in a private room of La Gran Peña, would you like a vermouth?, no thank you, your lordship, it makes me dizzy. Engracia has a boyfriend who repairs radios, Agustín Úbeda Martínez, who can't quite see what his purpose in this life might be, with some savings he had managed to make, Agustín wanted to open a tavern with private rooms and a little flamenco dancing and singing, it wasn't easy for Engracia especially at first but she finally got that idea out of his skull. Agustín joined the United Socialist

Youth and now on Sundays he too goes out in the country to drink in life and get in touch with nature, can't you see that this is much more natural?, yes, maybe, don't you feel more complete, more responsible?, yes, yes, I told you yes, the two young people are husband and wife in their own eyes, which is what matters, even if not in the eyes of the law (neither the law of God nor the other, that of the courts), the two young people go to bed together every day, they're at the age for it, but they don't live under the same roof, his parents are very conservative, almost reactionaries, and hers, though they're more progressive, wouldn't understand it, it's a matter of generations, why cause them an annoyance like that?, that's what I say, why?, Engracia and Agustín avoid having children because the revolution that is impending, that is on its way, that you can already breathe like the air itself, does not allow such concessions, there will be time enough for having children, Engracia is very loyal to Agustín, ever since they have had these relations she has not allowed anyone else the slightest liberty, you couldn't say that of Agustín, do you think Agustín has bourgeois ideas about love, no, neither bourgeois ideas nor the other ones, well, I mean Marxist ones, the thing about Agustín is he just wants to live it up, Engracia's going to have a big job reeducating him!, well, I suppose she knows what she's doing, the fact is Engracia would have deserved a better partner. On Sundays as the local trains leave you can also hear political punches in the Northern Railway Station, it doesn't amount to much, it's worse when they come back, when people come back tired and excited. Leopoldo, the oldest son of Don Leopoldo, already knows almost the whole law of mortgages by heart, we have to pray a lot for this boy, his mother always says, we have to pray he doesn't lose his mind from so much studying. At the entrance to the zoo, the vendors of cookies and of pinwheels wait for the capricious child whom his parents gave twenty-five céntimos, in the afternoon you can also see soldiers drawn by the sharp and amorous aroma of the nannies and the cooks, miss, let me introduce you, one of my girlfriends, a corporal from Segovia, pleased to meet you. The cats on the roofs and the empty lots mew in the month of January, now we're in summer but it's all the same, bitches, even the elegant bitches that are bathed and perfumed and even wear a ribbon and a bell, rub against the pavement every six months when they're in heat, they want to screw, there's just no getting away from it, the owners of these fancy dogs, who if they were more decent would also rub against the pavement instead of thinking dirty thoughts, take them to the veterinarian, my doggie isn't feeling right, you know, poor Betty, she wants to get married, the classic veterinarians, country veterinarians, who wear a sash and a billed cap and who prescribe enemas and exercise for mules, are plain ordinary men who play cards, drink vermouth, fart, etc., city veterinarians are something quite different, they specialize in purebred dogs and are something quite different, city veterinarians are younger, are well dressed and have clean nails, speak very correctly, smile elegantly, and as for dogs they can take care of anything, they vaccinate them, they operate on them (castrate them), they wash and comb them, they find them a mate . . . city veterinarians are more psychotherapeutic and they also flirt with the doggies' owners and if it comes to that lay them, you are the woman of my life, I'd rather not have told you!, oh Raúl, don't ruin me, I'm an honest woman!, when the doggie's owner says that you know what has to be done with her, get her into bed. Mr. Simón Tendero is a park guard in the Retiro and a wounded veteran of the Melilla campaign in Morocco, where he made the rank of sergeant in exchange for losing three fingers. The monastery of Lebanza is comfortable and quiet, it's a little far off, in Cervera de Pisuerga, in the province of Palencia, but it's very comfortable, it's worth the trip, in the monastery of Lebanza for twelve pesetas they give you a room with hot and cold water, laundry service, five meals a day and all the milk and eggs you want and can eat, the monastery of Lebanza is almost five thousand feet above sea level, more than twice as high as Madrid, with a clear fog-free climate where you breathe a very thin purifying air, it was Guillermo Zabalegui who told you about the monastery of Lebanza, he discovered it by chance back when his Aunt Mimí had the affair with that picador who wound up running off with her jewelry. Since your Uncle Jerónimo has no servants and eats raw eggs, vegetables, milk, and honey, he takes you to the Casino de Madrid where you can eat à la carte and whatever you want, your Uncle Jerónimo makes no converts, how are your studies going?, the customs studies, bad, well, worse than bad, the literary studies, a little better. All right, and your love life?, I don't have any love life, I don't have a girl. All right, let's reword the question, have you solved the sex problem?, well yes, I manage. Good, in suitably hygienic conditions?, well yes, I think so. Good, what would you like to eat?, your Uncle Jerónimo never gives advice to anybody, he asks questions and is interested in things but he gives no opinions or advice, he doesn't seem Spanish in this respect, your Uncle Jerónimo does not deviate an inch from the route he has laid out for himself but he lets everyone else go wherever it suits him, all roads lead to freedom, that is a law of the philosophy of history which a people cannot escape in spite of all the efforts of reaction, of course. At night Don Joaquín del Burgo drops by the Paseo de Rosales to hear the concert of the municipal band, lonely people tend to listen to band music whose noise is also very lonely, Maestro Sorozábal is a great conductor and the program is good and varied, Don Joaquín del Burgo would have liked to go with Paquita, well, even with Margot, but he doesn't dare to suggest it to her, the pasodoble *Las provincias* is sonorous and moving and *La dolorosa* has some very familiar measures, the ones from the duet in which Rafael says my poor Dolores, oh please tell me why I can't do something so you won't cry, etc., and Dolores answers him, my poor Rafael, you still suffer for me, though it's my crazy doings that have brought this to be, etc., let's hope they've picked that part for the medley, they probably have because it's very typical, the music in the middle, Beethoven's *Fifth Symphony*, a selection from *La Bohème* by Puccini, and Schubert's *Serenade*, is easy to take, the good thing about music is it lets you think about something else and even empty your head like a little pitcher that's overflowing, Don Joaquín del Burgo doesn't know what to do so Paquita, well, Margot, won't cry, Margot never cried and Paquita stopped crying some time ago but Don Joaquín doesn't know that, Don Joaquín hardly knows anything except what a face the mulatto Petra la Grillo made in her last moments, a face like that of an old sheep in the slaughterhouse, that is a memory he cannot wipe from his head even while he's listening to the music, what a bother!, Don Joaquín goes to the concert of the municipal band alone, it's a beautiful night, not too hot, and people listen to the blowing of the musicians respectfully, the panting of locomotives drifts up from the Northern Railway Station and sometimes the travelers coming back from the mountains trade punches coming up the Paseo de San Vicente. The name of Sacra's daughter, the one who's married to Gonococcus, is Virtudes and a year ago, when she was still single, she was chosen Miss Carabanchel in a highly competitive contest in which some really beautiful women took part, Gonococcus, that is, Victoriano Palomo, takes his wife to the movies on Sunday afternoons, they're expecting their first child, Virtudes is already overdue, the baby can come any time now and Victoriano is very affectionate with his wife, at the Pardiñas they're showing *Mamá* with Catalina Bárcena which is very sentimental, Virtudes and her husband watch the film holding hands, when Victoriano notices that his hand is sweating he lets go and blows on it a little or dries it on his pants or with his handkerchief, Virtudes is a refined girl with good manners who depilates her armpits with Taky Water and then applies Axilol so she won't sweat. Yes, look at yourself in the mirror, why don't you look at yourself in the mirror?, are you scared to look at yourself in the mirror?, yes, you're scared to look at yourself in the mirror, are you afraid of finding the mark of the murderer on your forehead or on your cheeks?, yes, you're afraid of finding the mark of the murderer on your forehead or on your cheeks, above your eyes, in front of your eyes on top of them there crosses the mark of the murderer, a zebra playing the guitar with a kerchief on its head like an Aragonese peasant, it's all simplified with six or seven little points forming a constellation, there are obtuse murderers who never get to see their mark but there are also murderers who are not yet murderers although the dance of the mark won't let them sleep, yes, it's easy to be a murderer, all men carry in their breast a little bulb of very fragile glass in which lurks the egg of murder, at the slightest slip this bulb breaks very easily, the rest comes naturally and in due time, it's like an infection, yes, look at yourself in the mirror and, if you dare, smile at the mirror, don't make a dreadful face, it's not worth while, you'll get one gradually and without being able to help it, the nearly true falsehood is the most poisonous and dangerous of all falsehoods and the crime that you have just committed or that you are committing or that you are going to commit at any moment is a plain fact, truth and falsehood are blended in the fact of murder and then you can never again look at yourself in the mirror, trust in little hopes and don't let yourself be smiled at or applauded by the man in charge who may also be the first to be hanged, the first to be spat upon, good-looking young widow would accept protection serious gentleman prefer priest or government employee, the young pigeon of murder sometimes nests in the classified section of the paper, weak at first and featherless but turbulent and deadly as soon as it grows a little, don't run away, look at yourself in the mirror every morning and try to stand fast like the bullfighter or the gladiator, death does not respect those who flee, death does not respect anyone and spreads itself around very equitably don't you forget it. Gregorio Montes likes greyhound races, when he has five pesetas he goes to the greyhound races to try his luck, Don Olegario Murciego, Don Cesáreo's poor brother, takes great pains to sneak into the greyhound races, Don Olegario looks very respectable which always helps, bet on Red Arab, he's some greyhound, he'll win hands down, and if you don't want to bet lend me a peseta and I'll bet, we'll split the winnings, you don't risk a thing, all right, Gregorio Montes and Don Olegario are good friends and they usually win two or three pesetas a night, that's better than nothing. Conchita Garrido is now engaged to Gumersindo López Lahoz, a young fellow who was studying for the priesthood and gave it up to become a mailman, just as soon as Conchita gets her degree in pharmacy and the two are husband and wife, Gumersindo plans to open a drugstore in his home town, he takes things as they come and doesn't ask for much. Mr. Simón Tendero has two worries, the couples in the park, who start getting out of hand as soon as the sun sets, and his daughter Emilita, who doesn't look as though she'll ever get married, he no longer worries about his son Raúl, his son Raúl is a veterinarian and has a good clientele of very distinguished and wealthy people, this poor daughter is the one I lose sleep over!, what a piece of bad luck that that lousy truck killed Alfonsito, her boyfriend!, now that he'd recognized the kids and wanted to get married!, Gregorio Montes is sort of a friend of Raúl's, or rather an acquaintance, Raúl no longer goes by Raúl Tendero (who wants to be called "shopkeeper"?) but by Raúl T. Ortiz de Ojuel, Ortiz is his late mother's maiden name and Ojuel is a hamlet in the township of Cabrejas del Campo, in the province of Soria, where his maternal family come from, his regular clients call him Dr. Ojuel, and when he hears it he practically bursts with pride, one afternoon when Rioja had to shepherd a relative from the provinces around Madrid Gregorio Montes went with you and the sisters, whom he didn't know except by reputation, to visit the zoo, in front of the monkey cage Lupita was splitting with laughter, good Lord!, what a way of jacking off!, now I see why they say hornier than a monkey, Gregorio was kind of rattled but when night came and the sisters brought their tits out over their décolletage before anybody had even asked them to he started to feel a little more confident, damn, what a pair of sluts they've turned out to be!, was his comment to you the next day, what a couple of Traviatas you've pulled out of your sleeve, my handsome friend! In the monastery of Lebanza people rest, love, and conspire, but all of it very hush-hush and without setting any tongues wagging, Guillermo Zabalegui wound up laying his Aunt Mimí, his mother's younger sister, who suffers from nerves and tries to cure her nervousness cheating on her husband with the first man to turn up, the chauffeur, a brother-in-law, the boy from the fish store, the telegram messenger, a picador from the bullring, her dear nephew Willy, anybody, they'll all do and they all serve the same purpose, the picador was a wild brute who wanted to kill Guillermo and his aunt Mimí with a knife, at the monastery of Lebanza they don't remember another scandal like that, it was shameful for all concerned that the Civil Guard had to be called, Don Teófilo Sacristán, a deputy from the Agrarian Party, went to the monastery of Lebanza to talk to Major Martínez Paudel, one of General Mola's trusted aides, Don Teófilo always travels with a secretary, a very cute and proper girl who probably isn't good for anything but to take letters in shorthand and then type them very carefully and with the left-hand margin always in the same place, Don Teófilo goes to bed with her but with the light out and without taking off her nightgown, behind the tennis courts a farmhand uncouples an amorous and astonished pair of dogs with the edge of his knife, everybody laughs a lot, when you think about it it's something to make you split your sides laughing, sometimes some joker separates wandering dogs, it's all the same whether they're city dogs or country dogs, with a knife or with a shoemaker's awl, you'd die laughing!, the dog gets the scent of a bitch in heat, he comes up to her, he sniffs her a little, he halfway courts her and, wham, down to business, the guy with the knife caresses his weapon in his pocket and notices a kind of fever, the guy with the knife is feeling sexy too, as sexy as the dog who doesn't even suspect the danger he's in or even sexier, there are two different techniques, both of them good, for separating coupled dogs with a knife, getting straight to the point or waiting till they finish, the first is more exciting but the stroke can miss, the second is surer, when God made the world he could not figure that knives would be opened to bring the loving of animals to a sudden dead end, the guy with the knife comes up on them as though nothing were happening and if he's skilled and has a steady hand, zap, he uncouples the dog from the bitch with a single stroke of the knife, you'd wet your pants laughing if you could see the expression on the face of the animal who runs off howling and staining the lavender bushes with blood, Guillermo Zabalegui did not laugh, the others did, the others laughed a lot and with a very healthy and sporting laugh. Your Uncle Jerónimo lives off a little income that your grandfather left him but since he has no big expenses or vices he manages, he dresses properly, he can buy an occasional book and, something important to his conscience, he doesn't owe a single peseta to anybody, your Uncle Jerónimo is rather short and thin, he wears a beard and glasses and takes a cold shower every morning, his sister, your Aunt Octavia, who has her own peculiar idea of heaven and hell, is determined to save his soul and frequently goes to visit him to see whether he wants her to introduce him to a very well-read and modern priest who is a friend of hers, your Uncle Jerónimo listens to her very calmly and instead of kicking her out as a busybody and a bore just changes the subject, your Uncle Jerónimo is especially fond of you, do you get any exercise?, well, not much, really. All right, do you smoke too much?, well yes, I rather do. All right, would you like a cigar?, thanks a lot, uncle, according to your Uncle Horacio, your Aunt Octavia's husband, your Uncle Jerónimo, because of his wife's typhus, lived with another German woman, Miss Lieselotte Vonderhinten, also a philosophy student, who ran away from him with Mauricio, the youngest of the Pleyelhoff brothers, the famous international clowns, your Uncle Horacio is not very trustworthy and anyhow these details of family history are always hard to verify. People talk about a coming military coup, idle chatter!, at this stage of civilization it's just talk for talk's sake to think about an army revolt, look how Sanjurjo's rebellion ended, and that was Sanjurjo!, what do the young people think?, bah, I think everybody has his own ideas, that's bad, bad!, when young people are in disarray humanity does not move forward on its path, nor does it when young people blindly follow the route laid out for them by their parents, this business of analyzing why humanity moves and marches forward is very complicated! It's not that in the monastery of Lebanza they give asylum to criminals, they just don't ask any questions, N-2, an hour and a half after shooting Lt. Castillo, leaves for the monastery of Lebanza in a Fiat Balilla provided for him, so as not to raise suspicion he travels with Marta, the sister of Miss Eyes, whom he introduces as his lawful wife, Marta is a well-bred presentable girl and both of them have their papers in order, falsified but in order, they've been preparing for the trip for almost a month and Marta had more than enough time to buy herself a very discreet outfit suitable for a girl from a good family, I'll give you half an hour's warning, have everything ready because I'll give you half an hour's warning, as soon as my father goes to Cordova, I don't know when it will be because he always travels on the spur of the moment, don't worry, I'll be ready, Marta hardly wears any makeup and plays her role as a newlywed very naturally and with aplomb, maybe her real calling is to be a wife or a dramatic actress and she doesn't know it, that happens sometimes, on this decent and happy occasion Marta is María del Pilar Romero López, that's what her ID says, born in Madrid, province same, September 10, 1917, daughter of Ildefonso Romero and María del Pilar López, single (the paper they gave her at the courthouse remedies that), occupation housewife, place of residence Madrid, 68 Príncipe de Vergara, when Marta gets under way there are two things she doesn't know about, the death of the lieutenant and the connection that N-2 might have with the death of the lieutenant or of anybody else, at night you can travel well and calmly, the highway is a joy at night, the young couple spends the night at Olmedo, near Valladolid, that night N-2 is more loving than ever. Don Gerardo Sanemeterio invites

Ginesa the Murcian and the cigarette man Senén to supper and then takes them to La Cigale Parisién, formerly Maipú Pigalls, to dance a little and have a good time, no cheek-to-cheek with Ginesa, do you understand?, for today you've got enough with a deluxe supper, you dance with her so she can digest her sweetbreads and as soon as I make you a signal you beat it and that's that, do you get it?, yes sir, I get it, all right, what do you say?, thank you, Don Gerardo, God bless you, all right, and no cheek-to-cheek with Ginesa, do you hear?, yes sir, yes I hear you, Senén is a veritable fashion plate in his brown Sunday suit and a green and yellow striped tie that Don Gerardo gave him, can I order more sweetbreads?, yes, you order whatever you want, let's live it up, at Eladio's they serve great sweetbreads and Ginesa the Murcian stuffed herself to bursting with sweetbreads, what a woman, what a way to gobble sweetbreads!, Don Gerardo eats sea bream for his fish course and then leg of lamb and Senén eats hake (there was only one serving of bream left) and also leg of lamb. Turquoise works at the Cigale, she's an internationally famous light chanteuse and the Murcian's cousin, how come you're here?, well, I'm with this gentleman and this old friend, well, I'm delighted!, Turquoise's big hit is called *The Babydoll* and makes the audience roar, the words begin in that babydoll nightie you're really a treat, even prettier than in your pajamas my sweet! Things aren't going well for Miguel Mercader, last night they threw him out of Doña Valentina's for not behaving properly, that's what Doña Valentina says, and this evening a little before suppertime, maybe about nine-thirty or a quarter to ten, he got his skull cracked in the row that broke out on the Plaza de Santa Ana and what's worse without his having anything to do with it, I'd like to know how I got into that mess, it's an outrage!, I was walking quietly down the street when these two little groups ran into each other, they started punching at each other and obviously I got caught in the middle and got the hell beat out of me, what a bunch of brutes, what a way of kicking they had!, what I'd like to know is how I got into that mess, when they take Miguel Mercader to the emergency room nobody pays any attention to him, there's a lot of hubbub and police and civilians coming in and out and they don't pay any attention to him, people are nervous and with all the jabbering nobody understands anyone else, sitting on a bench Miguel Mercader tries to stop his bleeding with a handkerchief, I am a reporter from *El Heraldo*, can you tell me what the assassination was like?, assassination?, well yes, assassination, what would you call it?, well, well . . . I'll tell you, I was walking peacefully down the street when these two little groups ran into each other . . . , two little groups?, yes sir, two little groups, ten or twelve persons apiece, all right, go on, well that's it, I was walking peacefully down the street when these two little groups ran into each other, they started punching at each other and obviously I got caught in the middle and got the hell beat out of me, what a bunch of brutes, what a way of kicking they had!, but let's see now, did you hear the shots?, what shots?, what shots he asks, well not any shots from the Spanish-American War!, well no sir, I didn't hear any shots, all there was was punches, lots of punches for sure, all right now, tell me, where did this happen?, well in the Plaza de Santa Ana, isn't that what I told you?, where else should it have happened?, the reporter from *El Heraldo* turns his back on Miguel Mercader, can anybody understand this?, it's not a question of understanding things but of believing them and when your skull is cracked and you're trying to stop your bleeding with a handkerchief you believe almost anything, another reporter talks to another wounded man, to Mr. Fernán Cruz or Fernández Cruz, there's no first name and the family name isn't quite clear, I'm from *La Voz*, what can you tell us about the crime?, well I'll tell you, it must have been 9 P.M., that's it, 9 or 9:10 P.M. when I got on a number 18 at the Glorieta de Bilbao, a number 18, the Obelisco-Sol line, which to be sure took quite a while to get to the corner of Fuencarral and Augusto Figueroa, it took a long time, and that's where I got off, as I was walking past the chapel I took off my hat, I'm in the habit of taking off my hat when I walk by a church, and I stopped to look hard at an old man whose behavior surprised me because he was kneeling in the middle of the street crossing himself and making some very grotesque and exaggerated gestures, maybe he wasn't quite right in the head, have you got a light?, yes, thanks a lot, well as I was saying, as I was heading into Augusto Figueroa just as you turn the corner of the chapel I saw a lieutenant of the Assault Guard coming, a young man with glasses and a little mustache who crossed the street, and he hadn't got halfway when four or five individuals jumped him, I can't say just how many, and one shouted, that's him, that's him, shoot!, then an awful shooting started, bang, bang, bullets everywhere, and the lieutenant stumbled and fell on top of me and knocked me down too, I hurt my elbow, now they've given me first aid, I tried to get up and when I noticed I'd lost my glasses I looked for them and found a pair right next to the dead man, I mean the dying man, I put them on, and what a scare!, I couldn't see a thing!, I thought the shock had made me dizzy but no, what happened was that those weren't my glasses, a man on the street gave me another pair and those were mine, I put them on and then a young man,

Don Félix Terán, came up to me, he was wounded too, and between the two of us we got the victim into a car that was driving by there and we brought him to the emergency room, have you got a light?, my cigarette's gone out, I can't remember what the attackers looked like, whether they were well dressed or not, whether they were young or old, I was very nervous and it all happened so fast, and I'm terribly sorry about it because this killing people in the middle of the street is a real outrage, that's a sight I won't forget so easily!, the reporter from *La Voz* sticks his notes in his pocket and dashes out, in the emergency room they take care of a fourth wounded man, José Luis Álvarez, age 18, address 29 Malasaña, pharmacy clerk, with entrance wound due to firearm in the rear of the left thigh, with comminuted fracture of the femur, without exit wound, serious condition, they wash Miguel Mercader's wound with antiseptic give him three stitches and put a bandage all around his head, you were lucky, well yes I can see I was, the lieutenant died on the way, he was dead on arrival at the emergency room, he spoke his last words to Fernández Cruz and Terán as he was lying in the car, take me home to my wife, Lt. Castillo had married a month before, Drs. Moreno Butragueño and Tamames found him already dead, the body of Lt. Castillo showed an entrance wound from a firearm on the rear side of the left arm, lower third, and an exit wound on the front side, with comminuted fracture of the humerus, and another entrance wound, also from firearm, in the fifth intercostal space and without exit wound, necessarily mortal, while the doctors examined the body the Director General of Public Safety Mr. Alonso Mallol, Colonel Sánchez Plaza commander of the Assault Guard, the Commissioner of Police Don Antonio Lino, and several comrades of the unfortunate officer appeared at the emergency room, you ran into Miguel Mercader on the Calle de Preciados, what happened to you?, nothing, they just beat the hell out of me, can't you see?, but did you get into some kind of mess?, no, I didn't get into it, they got me into it, that's not the same thing, I was walking quietly down the street on the Plaza de Santa Ana not messing with anybody when these two little groups ran into each other, they started punching at each other and obviously I got caught in the middle and got the hell beat out of me, you can see that, they've sewn me up in the emergency room, that's some pandemonium in that emergency room!, they killed a lieutenant of the Assault Guard and in the process wounded half a dozen passersby, in the Plaza de Santa Ana?, no, it seems it was in the Calle de Fuencarral, this is getting to be like Mexico!, no, worse, like Chicago, really awful, anyhow, I'll buy you a brandy to help you over the scare, after all you were lucky, that depends on how you look at it, man, you were luckier!, yes, that's true enough, Miguel Mercader and you go into the Café de Levante, right next door there they shot José Canalejas, well, neither you nor I had been born then, people look at you but not too much, you thought they'd look at you more, how's Toisha?, fine, I just dropped her off at her house, as beautiful as ever?, well yes, she won't get over that anytime soon. On Sundays the sisters play around on their own, the sisters are very independent and don't want to get tied down to anybody maybe they're right. I'm going through a season of bad luck, fuck it, what a time it's been!, what'll it be?, two brandies, pour two grand reserve!, the waiters call the bulk brandy grand reserve, yesterday they kicked me out of a whorehouse, I'll be damned!, which one?, Doña Valentina's, this morning my father read me the riot act because he says I'm a bum who never cracks a book, how does he know that when the makeup exams aren't till September?, and he wouldn't give me one peseta, my mother did, my mother gave me five, this afternoon when I thought I'd take the sisters dancing I couldn't find them, and tonight when I was on my way to supper they split my skull, what a life! The sisters are back home already, they were at the Forteen and had a good time drinking highballs and eating stuffed olives and letting themselves be petted by their admirers, Paquito and Alfonso, two boys from Salamanca who are spending a few days in Madrid. Every day of the week Don Máximo invites a different whore out to supper except for Fridays when he doesn't leave the house and keeps a diet of fruit and vegetables, Don Máximo, who is very well organized, has a different whore for each day, a total of six, and the next week he punctually starts the roll over again, Don Máximo usually takes them to supper at Riesgo or on the La Coruña highway depending on whether it's winter or summer and gives them bonbons and toffee and even pairs of stockings, Don Máximo goes to bed with the women of his harem three times a week, on Tuesdays with Rafaela and on Thursdays with Angelines, those are his two favorites, and usually another day by turn among them, whether or not he lays them Don Máximo is always generous with women, Don Máximo is a real gentleman, gallant, well-bred, and openhanded, a pleasure to deal with, on Don Máximo's calendar Sunday is assigned to Miss Dulce, one of Milagritos' girls, Don Máximo and Dulce are having supper in a private room at Casa Mariano on the La Coruña highway, Dulce is a platinum blonde and paints her lips in a heart shape, Dulce is luxuriously dressed in a dark red sleeveless silk suit with a plunging neckline and a very showy little fur cape. Toward 11 P.M. and by order of Mr. Alonso Mallol the body of Lt. Castillo was moved to the offices of the Public Safety Commission. It's not like it used to be, Máximo, you've changed a lot, you don't love me any more, don't be silly, what a way to talk!, why shouldn't I love you?, what do I know!, it's been at least two months since you've taken me to bed, well dear, remember that I'm no boy any more, no you're not a boy but you're very strong, thanks, and better looking all the time, thanks, what have Rafaela and Angelines got that I couldn't give you?, not love, that I swear to you, neither of them loves you more than I do, darling!, sure kid sure I know . . . don't call me kid!, all right dear, it's just a way of talking. The body of Lt. Castillo, in a mahogany casket, was placed in the red room, his uniform jacket is on display in the lieutenant colonel's office. When he gets back to Madrid Don Máximo goes to bed with Dulce, when you think about it the girl is cute, as cute as any, that's for sure, and well-bred, more than anybody, that's also for sure, Don Máximo gets back to his house after two, on his pillow he finds a note that the maid has left him, Don Diego says to phone him whenever you get back, what could be the matter? At Milagritos' place Dulce is in bed with N-1, what's the matter with you?, you seem kind of nervous, have you been drinking?, no, well yes, the usual, Perico is already in Toledo at his parents' place, Perico made the trip by motorcycle, he has a big Indian that goes like lightning, N-1 feels as though a rusty coin were coming off his palate and for the first time in his life he misfires, Dulce talks while she combs herself in front of the mirror, don't be silly, that happens to the best of them, if I started telling you, you can tell you're half drunk I think you're half drunk, sleep a little and it'll come when you wake up, Dulce turns out the light and N-1 drops off and sleeps like a log, with his knees bent his hands between his thighs his chin resting on his chest and his whole body very curled up, you never dreamed it would be so easy to take good photos, for every age, for every taste, a complete range of quality Kodaks from 50 pesetas, and Brownies for the kids from 12.90, the illustration in the ad shows a very smiling family looking at pictures, the caption says, this one's really good of Pepito! No one knows whether it is better to remember or to forget, memory is often sad and forgetting on the other hand usually repairs and heals, drive away bad thoughts, you won't have to kill Magdalena, that woman who smelled worse than any other, she's already dead, the fact is that it's no great loss but then, it's sad, too, the fact is that the poor woman was heading for death, those who are heading for death can't be saved by peace nor by charity they are predestined and they cannot escape their fate even if they hide beneath the stones, the subway killed Magdalena

Inmaculada Múgica in the Manuel Becerra station, nobody really knows how it happened evidently she was pushed accidentally or maybe on purpose, as a joke, but the fact is she fell between two cars and the wheels ran over her head and left it like a bloody wafer, with her brains scattered on the tracks and one eye at least five yards away, she couldn't even have felt it, poor smelly Magdalena, stinking Magdalena, with your smell of grease and fried oil, what a wretched death you ended up with!, now nobody will be able to wish you dead, Magdalena, rest in peace, and you, you coward, who do not rest in peace nor in war, look at yourself in the mirror even if it's with bowed head and make yourself smile while you think of the sisters' tits or the glorious nakedness of Toisha, that woman whom you deserve neither naked nor clothed, come on, speak up, why don't you go to the morgue to take some flowers to Magdalena and at the same time to steal her panties or her bra or some other piece of her underwear?, it will be your last chance and besides theft is always more difficult in the cemetery, you who commit almost every sin so timidly do not usually believe in the existence of the great sins you do not commit, that is the clearest sign of your weakness, come on, speak up, why don't you go to the morgue to pray an Our Father for Magdalena and to smell her for the last time?, no, go to bed in your parents' house and sleep quietly or restlessly but at least comfortably, drive away bad thoughts, Magdalena will never again smell bad to you, Magdalena Inmaculada Múgica is dead, the subway killed her in the Manuel Becerra station, you know that, the whores and you have a topic for conversation for a couple of weeks. Don Máximo does not phone Don Diego, it's too late and besides Don Diego is in Valencia, now he remembers, that maid is always mixing up the messages, Don Máximo takes some bicarbonate, pisses, brushes his teeth, goes to bed, and doesn't find out about the death of Lt. Castillo until Monday morning, together with other deaths, at dawn the Undersecretary of the Ministry of the Interior Mr. Ossorio y Tafall receives the press and announces what has happened, Miguel Mercader goes home to sleep, he's sore, his head hurts, and his mother gets up and gives him an aspirin and some coffee, his father gets up too, when will you stop getting in trouble?, this is no time to fool around, son, you could get killed before you know it, Miguel Mercader doesn't even try to protest that they cracked his skull without his having anything to do with it, that they cracked his skull the way he might have been hit by a taxi. As soon as Don Gerardo makes him a sign the cigarette man Senén says good night and takes off, leaving Don Gerardo with the Murcian, since he's eaten well he's happy and he goes for a stroll up to the Plaza de España, this is the life!, fuck yes, this is the life!, you're a poor shit, Senén, but today you've eaten like a duke, if the monks and priests knew the beating they'll get they'd be chanting the praises of freedom I bet, the cigarette man Senén usually expresses his cheerfulness by singing the republican hymn and kicking the light poles, do you know why the band's playing so much today?, do you know why?, 'cause they're paid to play!, Senén is radiant, he feels like the happiest man in the world, the lamb was super!, that Don Gerardo is some guy!, imagine, he invites me to supper so I'll dance with Ginesa for him!, at La Cigale they're starting to flick the lights on and off so people will go, at the end of the day the waiters show their tiredness and bad humor, Turquoise has it bad for the manager Gabriel Seseña who was a banderillero in Nicanor Villalta's troupe and had to abandon the bullring because he developed a hernia, Gabriel Seseña treats everyone very despotically and at every opportunity haggles about their pay or doesn't pay them or pays less than he owes, some night somebody will stick him, some waiter has already thought about it, Turquoise gets sad and sick when she drinks and the trouble is she drinks more than she can hold, Turquoise lives on Pernod and Neosalvarsan but in spite of her depressions and resignations she's good at heart, more than once she pulled the chestnuts out of the fire for her cousin the Murcian, all right, let's go!, Turquoise is very submissive, she gives the impression of being a real fire-eater but she's very submissive, aren't you going to close up?, no, Matías can do it, I'm kind of sick, I don't know what's the matter with me. You are like Gabriel Seseña, you don't know what's the matter with you either, the city is like a dog, it turns around and around before getting to sleep, and also like a hare that sleeps with its eyes open to see whether it's got to run away, sometimes you think cities can run away and obliterate themselves, where's the city?, who knows!, it was here yesterday in this open space, it must have run away, no man, no, cities don't run away, they burn, they rot, they fall apart, but they don't run away, cities can't run away, if they could they would have done it long ago. Turquoise can't run away either, Turquoise burns, rots, falls apart, but she doesn't run away, more than once her cousin the Murcian asked her, Turquoise, why don't you run off without a trace?, it's all the same, Turquoise knows that she can't run away, where to?, it's very easy to say that, come on, where to?, the world isn't as big as people think and besides the world is full of snares and poachers.

III

Blood calls to blood, blood is the echo of blood, the shadow of blood and the trail of blood, there has never been a criminal who has felt satisfied with a single crime and sometimes in the air we breathe there floats something like a perfume of crime that intoxicates more than one man, no, you do not necessarily have to be a criminal but it is very probable that you will be unable to elude the ancient pleasures, ask about the taste of blood, no one will answer you, the taste of blood is a sensation that is as jealously guarded as a secret of the bedchamber, almost no one speaks of his dirty deeds of the bedchamber but almost no one is exempt from his own dirty deeds of the bedchamber, almost no one is capable of strangling them, man fears truth but takes refuge not in lies but in farce, it is easier for a man to poison a woman who asks for a glass of water than to convince her that she is not thirsty, the pain of others, our neighbor's stupor, is the medicine of those unconfessed domestic swine at whom those in command smile for a few moments, it is easy to make murderers all it takes is to empty their heads of memories and fill them with the air of dreams, the air of history, the coin on the palate soon takes shape by itself and faster than we think, the ripening of the coin also comes by itself it needs neither hothouse nor manure, Magdalena is dead that does not matter to anyone but just the same, she is dead, Magdalena was killed by the subway in the Manuel Becerra station, some passengers looked the other way, compulsion breeds necessity which bears three children, displeasure, deceit, and disgust, carefully study the last moments of the fly from the time that it falls into the coffee dregs until its struggles finally end in death, if you could photograph all its death rattles you would see that with its ever weaker little legs it draws delicate Chinese characters that are not easy to interpret, if the fly that is going to die lays its last eggs in a soul all the flowers in the neighborhood die also, all the flowers of a thousand colors (real or not), strangled by the worms that are born, crime is a beast that reproduces itself through parthenogenesis and from a single crime a whole cacophony of crimes can spring. While Senén takes his walk and Don Gerardo frolics with the Murcian, while Miguel Mercader takes his aspirin and his coffee, while Paquito and Alfonso, the two fellows from Salamanca who are spending a few days in Madrid, masturbate while thinking of the sisters, while Don Máximo pisses, takes bicarbonate and brushes his teeth, while at the morgue Magdalena awaits the approaching hour of the common grave, while Turquoise smiles with perhaps a trace of bitterness and keeps on falling apart, rotting, burning, while Toisha dreams inside her transparent nightgown and you, unable to sleep, mull over the fact that you don't understand anything of what is going on, some very different events (come to think of it, not all that different) are taking place in the world, on the Calle de Toledo a truck crushes a drunk who was vomiting quietly in the middle of the street without bothering anybody, on the Calle de Mesón de Paredes a housemaid who got herself pregnant in her village miscarries, on the Glorieta de Bilbao a child is dying of croup, in a private room at a restaurant on the Calle de Arlabán they're singing away until suddenly, wham, a gentleman dies of a heart attack, at the first-aid station on the Calle de la Encomienda they treat two men who came to blows on the street, on the Calle de Velázquez they kidnap a deputy whom they're going to murder, on the Calle de Tudescos they stab a whore to death, they stab her at least twenty times, this case of the whore is less important, there are plenty of whores and besides crimes of passion don't count or don't count for much, people usually like them but they tend to be very monotonous, repetitious, and ordinary, Ducal, gets rid of bedbugs without fail, 1.55 a bottle, seen from close up history confuses everyone, both actors and spectators, and is always very tiny and startling, and also very hard to interpret. The room where Lt. Castillo's body lies in state is swarming with visitors who come and go. In his office Mr. Alonso Mallol tells Don Andrés Amado that the Public Safety Commission has not issued any orders for the arrest of Calvo Sotelo, a short while earlier Doña Enriqueta, Calvo Sotelo's wife, had telephoned Don Andrés. As you turn in your bed you don't think about what you don't know and finally you fall asleep, you are not Napoleon Bonaparte, nor Julius Caesar, nor Saint Paul, nor are you King Cyril of England, almost no one is King Cyril of England, poor sad King Cyril who works with his back turned and whom his servants, his murderers, used to bite in the nape of the neck as though he were a porcupine, do you want to grow three inches?, you can do it quickly at any age with the magnificent Ratio-Grow, write to Don Joaquín Lloris, successor to Professor Albert, 36 Pi y Margall, Valencia, Spain, it is not the dream of justice, no, nor the dream of adventure, that wins the submission of cities, it is no dream, cities yield to insomnia, to hatred, and even to tedium, insomnia is like arsenic, hatred is like arsenic, tedium is like arsenic, in proper doses they can act as stimulants but if their distributor overdoes it they become most active poisons, a sleeping man is like an innocent mineral, the sleepless one is a swarm or nest of scorpions. Gregorio Montes never again asked for a string in a whorehouse but his cousin Julianín drools when he serves vermouth or sarsaparilla drinks to women and stands there staring at their necklines, the rise of her breasts is a very mysterious zone in a woman, Julianín pays a lot of attention to it, Julianín sleeps in the kitchen at Casa Benito on a sack of wood shavings that he lays between the sink and the pantry door, Julianín sleeps a lot, all they let him, and uninterruptedly and peacefully because his conscience is clear, Julianín sleeping is like pyrite or pitchblende, in school they talked to you a lot about pitchblende, Brother Bruno was an enthusiastic promoter of pitchblende, a uranium mineral that contains metals of very rare properties, the rise of the breasts of Marlene Grey the star of the Maravillas Theatre is very rounded and soft, it must be very enjoyable to run your whole finger over it from one side to the other, abundant love, health, and wealth through cosmic rays, for information write P. O. Box 159, Vigo, Spain, no, don't dream in vain, don't dream dreams that are too fantastic. Don León Rioja sleeps like a child and doesn't even hear the moans of Doña Matilde his wife who has been sick for more than ten years, she doesn't get well and she doesn't die, Doña Matilde prefers to moan quietly so as not to interrupt the sleep of her husband who has to go to work the next day. Hatred is like arsenic, that's it, just like arsenic and also like a repressed moan, we do not hate when we despise but when we envy, singing out loud can be a good antidote to hatred. Don Diego, who is back from Valencia, finds out about the kidnapping of Calvo Sotelo at 9:30 A.M. but he doesn't know where he is, nobody knows where he is, Calvo Sotelo has already been lying dead for six hours in the Eastern Cemetery but nobody in the whole country knows about the murder except the murderers, the situation is confused, very confused and rumors filter through people's nerves, Moles the Minister of the Interior does not learn the news until midday. It is not yet known when Lt. Castillo will be buried. People talk to hear themselves talking and some are also still just to be still, more of a balance would be preferable, but that's more difficult, Higinio Cascón & Co., textiles, Béjar, Salamanca, cloth for capes and billiard tables, blue material for uniforms, criminals are usually silent the chatterers are the ones who applaud the criminals, the ones who say you're a worse one and the ones who say it's time to show what you're made of, no, nobody's worse, we're all too much whatever it is, and what we're made of doesn't have to be shown. Don Máximo finds out about Calvo Sotelo at Don Diego's house, we're sitting on a powder keg, Don Diego, I guess you know what we ought to do but I say we're sitting on a powder keg. La Hebrea wakes up around one or one-thirty and has breakfast in bed, that's a luxury that costs more than just wanting it, La Hebrea spends more than an hour primping and reading the *ABC*, on Mondays since the *ABC* doesn't come out she reads Sunday's over again, Zárraga put Abásolo in seventeenth place, that Zárraga is some ballplayer!, the Philippine airmen have finally arrived, I'm sure glad they didn't end up like Barberán and Collar!, Germany and Austria come to an agreement, why won't they just keep nice and still?, La Hebrea is merry and she sings, the happiest mortal's the Pekinese, his merry life is just a breeze. Before lunch Don Roque usually has a beer at La Granja El Henar, sometimes he uses the occasion to have his shoes shined and maybe to write a letter, your usual beer, Don Roque, thank you Gutiérrez, would you get me some paper and pen and ink?, yes sir, I'll get it for you right away, shoeshine, some paper and pen and ink for Don Roque!, Don Roque takes a sip of his beer and reaches for his tobacco pouch and package of cigarette paper, Don Roque uses Indio Rosa, big sheets of paper that let you roll robust man-sized cigarettes, real cigarettes and not those syphilitic little strawlike things that people smoke, Gutiérrez stands there looking at Don Roque, haven't you heard about Calvo Sotelo?, what happened to him?, well they arrested him at his home early this morning and he hasn't turned up anywhere dead or alive, how's that?, you heard me, everybody's talking about it, Don Roque downs his beer in one gulp and tears out of there heading for Cid's house, Don José María Cid's, the former minister and leader of the Agrarian Party, whom he does not find at home, and don't you know where he might have gone?, I don't know, I think he went to parliament, look for him there, all right thank you very much, if I don't find him I'll be back after lunch. Joaquín and Serafín Álvarez Quintero spend the summer at El Escorial, they probably use the time to write some comedy because that's what they live off, writing comedies. Chonina is in luck yesterday a gentleman from Badajoz gave her a hundred twenty-five pesetas inside a purse from Ubrique. On the other hand Paca has been living on lamb's-lettuce for two days, she can't find a customer, her neighbor Fidel Ternera, a dirt-poor fellow they call Vicar because he's pretty well educated, thinks Paca will wind up having to eat her hump like the camels in caravans, Vicar knows a bitter little song that drives away hunger, that makes fun of hunger, go ahead, don't eat, you fool, tomorrow morning just watch your stool, gourmets, do you want to put on weight no matter how thin and emaciated you are?, want to know how?, by eating at Pensión Mercedes, 5 Conde de Aranda, Saragossa, Paca, yes sir Señor Fidel, go to Eulalia's tripe shop and ask for half a pound of lungs, tell them it's for me, I'll invite you for lunch, yes sir Señor Fidel. The magistrate of the third district, Don Ursicino Gómez Carbajosa, begins his preliminary investigation and on the Plaza de Pontejos the police find the Assault Guard van no. 17 with which the kidnapping was carried out, it's said that the driver and several of the passengers have been arrested. Rafaela, Señor Asterio's sister-in-law, is a slut to end all sluts (that's what they say, you haven't been able to confirm the degree), Rafaela does everything well, she plays the piano, she dances the tango, she can make clothes, she's a first-rate cook, etc., Sisinia, retired midwife, 12 Corredera Alta, formerly, it's been a few years, Señor Asterio used to pat his sister-in-law Rafaela's butt now and then, it never got to be anything serious, he patted her butt to entertain himself and also because there it was within reach and there was no way to avoid it and no real reason to try, the sisters greatly admire their aunt Rafaela and try to imitate her in their walk and their style of dress, these daughters of mine have turned out as hot as my sister-in-law, Señor Asterio keeps saying, they're chips off the old block, a fine mess I'll have on my hands if I don't get them married soon. At a quarter to three the judge arrives at the cemetery, several friends of the victim are there, the Marquis de las Marismas, the Count Casa Redruello, Dr. Albiñana, Don Romualdo de Toledo, Don Jorge Vigón, the Bold Knight, and several others. Don Estanislao Montañés still feels the shock produced in him by the death of Chelo, the whore from the Calle de las Naciones, what a brute that medic at the first-aid station was!, Don Estanislao runs into Pepito la Zubiela who is sitting on a bench on the Paseo de Recoletos sucking on a popsicle, hello there, Don Estanis, hello Pepito, what are you doing here?, well not much, getting a little fresh air, all right, I'm glad, and I'm glad to see you, you know you have a friend in me, Don Estanislao walks on, he plans to drop by La Tropical to see whether he finds some friend with whom to chat a while, Don Leoncio Romero, the one with the dried-up leg and the hardware full of hinges and screws, goes every afternoon to have his coffee at La Tropical with his regular circle of friends, among them jewelers, orthopedists, and an occasional government employee, Don Leoncio's lungs are not quite in order and he takes Radiopectoralina Zamit, a medication that suppresses or at least softens his cough, in his circle they're all talking about the two murders, well the brawl's started and now off we go all the way to the end, this is a country full of madmen here every man makes war on his own, what the government should have done was to catch the murderers of Lt. Castillo and those of Calvo Sotelo and hang them all together on the Plaza Mayor as a lesson for those who want to be above the law and so people could breathe easy, right you are, well said, you're as right as you can be, well I don't know, but I think it's just common sense to protect honest citizens, well of course it is, what the majority in the country wants is to live in peace and free of the whims of hired gunmen, why don't they disarm the country, but really disarm it?, why don't they crack down on the boys who spend Sundays drilling?, why don't they lock them all up, all of them?, ah, my friend, I don't know about that, what I do know is that we'll wind up on fire and with our hands on our heads and our butts out in the fresh air to add insult to injury, on Sundays the mountains are like a barracks courtyard, Don Nicolás Mañes, licensed orthopedist, agrees with everything he hears, room and board in the mountains for two ladies must be in good health, telephone 25973, the French Croix de Feu has declared itself a political party, a tea in honor of the airmen Arnáiz and Calvo is being held at the Casa de Campo Park, the municipal band plays a select program and ends with the Philippine national anthem, our sources assure us that the Emperor of Ethiopia will spend some time at Mas Juny at the kind invitation of the painter Sert, the newspapers *La Epoca* and *Ya* are banned until further notice, in Lorca one Francisco Javier Poveda, 19, rejected in his suit by the fair María Rodríguez Mula, 17, inflicts a fatal beating on his successor in the young woman's affections, one Francisco Cervantes Pagán, 19, in Bembibre a raging fire destroys a slipcover factory, the electric train of Buñol, Valencia, strikes and kills Francisco Carboneres Dalmau, 62, at the conclusion of the Belfort-Evian stage of the Tour de France, the ranking of the Spanish cyclists is as follows, Mariano Cañardo, 31, Federico Ezquerra, 44, Julián Berrendero, 48, Emiliano Álvarez, 55, and Salvador Molina, 60, the situation is about the same as before. Don Manuel García Morente says that the tragedy of man does not lie in his not knowing what it means to live but in his not knowing what it means to die, well that's all the same, you live and you die the same and what people would like is to keep on living and not die.

According to the coroner's preliminary report, the body of Calvo Sotelo shows an entrance wound from firearm at the left eye with a necessarily fatal ejection of brain tissue. Paquito the young man who is wishing for his father's death so he can repay the kindnesses of his friends takes a stroll along the Paseo del Prado, sits down at the Fountain of the Four Seasons and reads adventure novels that he trades at a stand on the Calle de Fuencarral, Paquito does the same thing every afternoon, in winter he goes into the Post Office where it's warm and where they don't throw anybody out. Suddenly you remember the name of the murderer of Marujita!, his name was Leonardo Álvarez Maderero and he was from Ávila, well, from a village in the province of Ávila, *The Lives of a Bengal Lancer*, at the Callao Theatre, a film that interests, moves, entertains, this is the film that everyone loves and that you can't afford to miss! Don Máximo speaks sensibly, in politics, he always says, the many pay for the mistakes of the few, lies cost even more than mistakes, people take a while to find out but finally they discover the mistake before they do the lie which often goes to the grave with the liar, the lie is the cover for the mistake, and what with mistakes and lies this is going to lead to blows and if you don't believe it just wait and see. Yes, look at yourself in the mirror and, if you can, smile at yourself almost disgustedly, turn a deaf ear to the siren songs, to the whisperings of the apocalyptic messiahs, and look at yourself in the mirror, we Spaniards should all spend hours and hours in front of the mirror, auction off everything they tell you so deceitfully and look at yourself in the mirror time and again without rest and without closing your eyes, you are guilty, we Spaniards are all guilty, the living, the dead, and those of us who are going to die, do not disguise your pain as anger or as fear, no, not as fear either, anger and fear are stronger than you, they will grip you without your going to look for them, without your watering them with your wild rabbit's tears, spit words out of your mouth, strip yourself of words, wash yourself of words, which all mean the same thing, blood and stupidity, insomnia, hatred and tedium, words are like arsenic and the soul of the dead man turns into an innocent mineral, an innocent aerolite from a meteor that flies without a compass and strikes with no bad intentions, forgive yourself the few words that you pronounce and keep silence, you know that the word calls to blood, it is the fuse of blood. Amanda Ordóñez in spite of her temperament and the scar on her face is standing in line at the San Joaquín Clinic, intimate ailments, venereal diseases, syphilis, gonorrhea, for some time now Amanda has been paying for her glorious old memories in installments, the patients in the waiting room are in favor of drastic measures, they all vote for the garrote and for setting it up on the Plaza Mayor, some prefer the Puerta del Sol and a young woman with a birdlike face suggests the lake in the Retiro with a floating platform in the middle and the audience placed on the walkways and the pier, Amanda joins the ranks of the conservatives, in all probability the Plaza Mayor is really the most suitable place for an execution. The coroners' preliminary report has been revised, instead of the entrance wound being through the left eye and the exit wound in the occipital area it's the other way around, the entrance wound in the occipital area and the exit wound through the left eye. Doña Eduvigis Olmedillo de Parreño believes that all that is happening is God's punishment for men's pride perhaps she's not so far off, Doña Eduvigis' cook is called Generosa Seoane and she is a Galician from Valga, hometown of La Bella Otero, feminine hygiene, preventive and curative medical treatments, tonic and germicide, a complete antiseptic, all in the Green Envelope, oxygenated vaginal douche, price 30 centimos, sold in all pharmacies, what's bad is that no one has as yet invented a Green Envelope for the gonorrhea of the soul, shit calls to shit, shit transforms all that it touches into shit, and this country, let no one forget it, suffers delusions of grandeur, here everybody wants to create the world anew every morning. Do you think there's any hope for us?, this is a country of madmen!, Don Leoncio thinks that yes, this is a country of madmen for which there's not much hope, and the worst of it is that we'll keep on killing each other till not even the prompter is left to tell the tale, it's the way it always is with a brawl, once it's started, off we go all the way to the end, we Spaniards are very nervous and stubborn and always want to be in the right even when we're in the wrong, and if we're in the wrong so much the worse because then we attack our neighbor and if they let us we crack his skull, people here have little education and bad attitudes, the rich know how to hold their forks very properly but they won't read a book to save their lives, those halfway don't hold their forks as well and read a book now and then, they just don't understand anything, and the poor eat with their fingers, when they eat at all, and don't even know how to read, you tell me, what can we expect?, this country is backward because it didn't have a revolution at the right time like France, the fact is nobody wants to make a revolution because they're afraid of getting killed, I can understand that, a revolution here always ends up as slaughter, they kill priests, they kill Andalusian peasants or they kill schoolteachers, it depends on who's doing the killing, but finally nothing is revolutionized, everything stays the same only with more people dead, what's needed here is schools, Joaquín Costa already said that and nobody paid any attention to him, and also to make anyone who gets out of hand shape up, until we do that we'll always stay the same, Don Leoncio, evidently because of the excitement, feels heartburn, bicarbonate, damn it!, haven't I told you I want the bicarbonate on the table?, right away, Don Leoncio, you'll have it right away. They say there is going to be a military coup to guarantee law and order and to save the Republic, perhaps there is no other solution nor any possible formula for a settlement. Lt. Castillo was killed by the Falangists, they say he had killed Andrés Sáenz de Heredia, José Antonio's cousin, at the funeral of the lieutenant of the Civil Guard whom the Assault Guards killed on the Paseo de la Castellana during the parade commemorating the fifth anniversary of the establishment of the Republic, ten or twelve other people died at that funeral, no sir, Lt. Castillo was killed by the Communists so they can put the blame on the Falangists, you are both mistaken, Lt. Castillo wasn't killed by either side, it was a crime of passion, oh no, it had something to do with faggots, listen, couldn't he have been hit by a taxi as he was crossing the street?, no, maybe he died of some disease and they don't want to say so, Lt. Castillo's mother was in a village in the province of Jaén, now she's at the headquarters of the Security Commission keeping watch over the body of her son, Engracia and her boyfriend Agustín Úbeda stand in line to walk past the body, there are many people but everything is progressing in a rather normal way, Lt. Castillo's widow is very young and she seems dazed with her eyes wide open and her face pale and haggard, she looks as though she can't take any more. The message that Martínez Barrio, as speaker of the parliament, sent to the cabinet demanding that Calvo Sotelo be released immediately does no good because Calvo Sotelo is dead, it's an established custom here to lock the barn door, as they say, after the horse is gone, the Assault Guards killed Calvo Sotelo to avenge the death of the lieutenant, but listen, what did Calvo Sotelo have to do with the death of the lieutenant?, ah, that I don't know, ask the Guards. The cabinet appoints the judge of the Supreme Court Mr. Sánchez Orbeta as a special magistrate to investigate the murder of Lt. Castillo. Calvo Sotelo was not killed by the Guards but by a group of Communists disguised as Guards, and how do you know that?, I don't know it, I just think that's the way it was, who could believe that the Guards would take the risk of doing something like that?, who can tell?, the situation is very confused right now and people are capable of the craziest things, even the Guards, if only at least one garrison would rise up and promise to maintain law and order until new elections are called!, you're dreaming, Romero my friend, there's no solution for this even if twenty garrisons were to rise up, well, I don't know about that!, Sanjurjo is an energetic and very patriotic man, no it's too late, I tell you it's too late, the most contradictory and groundless conjectures go bouncing from one table of the café to another, sticks and fists can come into play at any moment, Calvo Sotelo was killed by the Army to justify a coup, don't be silly, why don't you just come out and say that Goicoechea killed him?, well now, maybe Goicoechea has his finger in this pie, for heaven's sake, the things you have to hear!, Calvo Sotelo leaves a widow and four children, but tempers are very agitated and no one has time to remember a widow or her four children, the cabinet appoints the judge of the Supreme Court Mr. Iglesias Portal as a special magistrate to investigate the murder of Calvo Sotelo, the widow cannot watch over the body of her husband until the coroners make their official report on the autopsy, it is expected that this proceeding might be completed tomorrow Tuesday at 6 A.M. A delegation from the Socialist and Communist Parties calls on the Prime Minister Mr. Casares Quiroga to offer him their support in case it should be needed in the face of any possible movement against the Republic, the Governor of the Bank of Spain and former minister Don Luis Nicolau d'Olwer is the victim of an automobile accident in the province of Gerona, fortunately his condition is satisfactory after his resuscitation from the heart attack that he suffered immediately after the crash, the Civil Governor of Madrid publishes an edict reminding all citizens that we are in a state of emergency and that consequently (1) any person who attempts to breach public order will be arrested and his residence may be searched, (2) all gatherings of persons who appear in public with weapons or other means of violent action will be dispersed by the police if they do not immediately obey a first warning, (3) the facilities of any associations whose operations are deemed dangerous to the maintenance of public order will be closed, (4) gatherings, demonstrations, and meetings outdoors are hereby prohibited, and (5) prior censorship applies to all printed matter intended for circulation, for fifty centimos a day you can acquire a Nesco heavy oil range (diesel), for only thirty centimos a day you will prepare your family's meals. Javiera, the maid at Don Roque's boardinghouse, would like to take better advantage of her charms and get more benefit from her pretty face and her youth, she's urged on by Paulina, who has less good looks but more courage and spirit, Paulina knows two confidential addresses, Cupid Enterprises, on the Calle de Jardines, about halfway, and the registered theatrical agency

Pepe Rubio, on the Calle de Juanelo, on the left-hand side as you enter the street, she doesn't know the number but she does know which house it is, you can't miss it, both of them hire performers, tango dancers, and waitresses, and both are serious and financially sound, this is a business like any other and as proper as any, there's no reason to be scared, they won't eat you alive, right now there's not much demand miss, unless you want to work outside Madrid, there are more opportunities in Barcelona than in Madrid, all right I'll think about it, thank you very much, don't mention it miss, you know where to find us, always in the service of art, Paulina doesn't quite trust that much refinement, you'd better stay here, I don't trust that guy, there'll be another chance, all right, and besides you're not exactly starving to death, neither of us is starving to death, true enough! Sit in the café and you'll see the body of your enemy pass by, all men are your enemies and the parade of funeral processions bathes your heart in beatific peace, it's also comforting to read the death notices with their clear beautiful prose, pray to God in charity for the soul of, R.I.P., may he rest in peace, comforted with the sacraments and the benediction of His Holiness, his disconsolate widow, beg that his friends and all pious persons would commend his soul to God (or to God our Lord or remember him in their prayers) and attend the conveyance of his body to its last resting place, the masses to be celebrated in such-and-such a church and at such-and-such hours will be applied for his eternal rest, various eminent prelates have granted indulgences in the usual manner, no flowers please, no announcements will be distributed, etc., anniversaries of a death are less poignant, less gratifying, when someone commits suicide the family does not include the part about comforted with the sacraments, atheists compose more sober announcements and usually ask that the deceased be remembered rather than that there be prayers for his soul, it's all liturgy and we Spaniards cannot escape liturgy, we obviously carry it in our blood, sit in the café and wait, almost all of Spain is sitting in the café and waiting, in Spain the living are as though they were dying and only the presence of death and the memory of death wakes them up, the dead and death and the amphitheater for their proper contemplation, the café, weigh heavily in Spain. Ah, if only Salmerón were alive!, what's needed here is another General Narváez!, the heroic people of Madrid set a magnificent example on the Second of May!, let us follow in the footsteps of the Comuneros!, as Balmes said so well, what are called political passions are usually common passions!, Ferdinand VII was a traitor! Don Román Navarro has no ideas of his own, why should he have them when Don Cesáreo can think for both of them?, tell me if I'm not right, Don Cesáreo, everything that's happening in Spain is a consequence of the crisis of authority that we are going through, very well said!, if the principle of authority is in crisis, how will we ever get on our feet?, Milagritos (Pérez de Ayala calls her Socorrito) admires Don Cesáreo with all her heart, that's the kind of men we need in Spain!, Don Cesáreo is a gentleman of the old school, clever, well-mannered, respectful, it's a pleasure to hear him talk, for Don Román on the other hand Milagritos does not feel so much respect, he is a different case, there's nothing with which to reproach Don Román, but he is a different case, Don Cesáreo learns at the Casino de Madrid what is going on, the members gather in little groups and speak loudly and gesticulate contrary to their custom, Don Cesáreo did not vote for Calvo Sotelo in the elections, he voted for Gil Robles, but he is strongly affected by the news of his murder, nobody at the Casino doubts that the Army will sooner or later rise up, whether we want it or not, whether we like it or not, and I do like it at least as the lesser evil, there's no other solution for Spain, the Republic has let go of the reins and not even its own adherents obey it any longer, if the Army does not rise up the Bolsheviks will slaughter us all, gentlemen, the time for decisive action has come!, Spain or Russia!, us or them!, the situation that has been created is one of life or death!, a democratic order works in England but you can see what it leads to here, murder and chaos! Don Máximo does not applaud such extreme solutions, Don Máximo would like to see the law enforced, yes, but without violating the legal norms of the Republic, Don Máximo has the vague suspicion that in life-or-death situations everyone ends up dying, what he does not know is how to express his thoughts more precisely, Don Máximo is tired and probably also afraid. Politics is not the science of pounding your enemy like a clove of garlic in a mortar and then hanging him out to dry in the sun, but the art of soothing the nerves of all, friends and enemies, so that life can go on without too many afflictions and with no more ailments than necessary, politics is a very humble art that nervous men make proud. The country is nervous, the spark can fly at any moment, maybe it has already flown with these stupid deaths, and the fire, if it breaks out, will be hard to contain, very hard, when a fire is not put out before it acquires consistency and becomes violent then there is no other way of extinguishing it than with its own last ruined ashes. When people get nervous they care less about being right than about having their way, no matter how absurd it is, and people are nervous and are on the way to not caring about being right. Stop a moment and sum things up, I know it's hard. Don Máximo also knows it's hard because events crowd in upon each other in people's heads even more than on the streets. The deputy Sánchez Somoza, the one who burned his wife's butt and Taboada's with chocolate, lays into Don Olegario Murciego with a cane on the sidewalk in front of the Negresco, when they finally free Don Olegario from the clutches of his attacker, the deputy stares at him, shit, excuse me, I mistook you for someone else, Don Olegario wipes his head with his handkerchief to see whether he is bleeding, no, you're not bleeding, just a couple of bumps, that's nothing, nothing at all, as I was saying, I confused you with somebody else, may I buy you a brandy?, all right, yes sir, but next time try to see what you're doing before you go off like that, you're quite right, as I was saying, I confused you with somebody else, the son of a bitch!, Sánchez Somoza treats Don Olegario to a cup of coffee, two glasses of brandy, and a cigar, what do you say to what's going on?, Don Olegario shudders, I?, I don't say anything, what should I say?, Don Olegario thinks that what's going on is madness, total folly, but he doesn't say so, Don Olegario does not want to get another thrashing, he has enough with the one he already got, what's going on?, a provocation, a gross coarse provocation, well said, yes sir, you said it!, that's what I think too, would you like another brandy?, no, thank you very much, I'm not used to it, are you going to turn me down?, no, no sir, it's just that it gives me heartburn, oh, all right, Sánchez Somoza looks at him like Hernán Cortés, most probably Hernán Cortés had a look like that, and Don Olegario feels intimidated. The reporter from *El Heraldo* who found Miguel Mercader in the emergency room has a lemonade with his girl, the reporter's name is Juanito Mateo and among the young women of his neighborhood he is very famous, well, somewhat famous for his vision of the future, his Jacobin orations, and his wandering hands, especially his wandering hands, what has to be done here is to open the prison gates and let the people execute justice on the heads of the leaders of the bourgeoisie, keep your hands to yourself!, his girl admires his gift of gab but won't let herself be felt up in broad daylight, at the movies or in the dark, that's another story, but not in broad daylight, that's the limit!, and once the rule of liberty is established we shall sweep our minds clean of preconceived ideas, we shall move on to a just distribution of wealth, we shall impose land reform, we shall expel the clergy from within our borders and we shall fight for the improvement of our race, the Spaniards of the future must be taller and heavier!, his girl's name is Leonorcita and she is impressed, truly impressed, Juan, get your hand out of there, hold still, good Lord, can't you wait for it to get dark?, sometimes Juanito thinks he is misunderstood, that not even Leonor, his girl, understands him, wait, wait!, that's easily said, humanity has been waiting for one thousand nine hundred thirty-six years, well, even longer than that, wait, wait!, how easy it is to say that!, there are some things that can't wait, the demolition of Spain's obsolete social structure and the love I feel for you, sweetheart!, Juanito Mateo gets up suddenly as though he'd received a kick in the rear, hello there, Don Wifredo!, Don Wifredo is the managing editor of the paper, he really could have thought of taking his walk somewhere else, Madrid is certainly big enough!, who is Don Wifredo, Juan?, nobody, honey, a friend of the family, what a name, Juan!, yes, there really are some pretty odd names. Gil Robles arrives at supper time, a little before supper time, he's coming from Biarritz, the secretary of the CEDA, Mr. Carrascal, got the news to him, they had gone to Gil Robles' house to look for him at the same time that they went for Calvo Sotelo (with other people and in another vehicle), he was lucky because they didn't find him. Your Uncle Jerónimo is much saddened by what is happening in the country, that's not the way, you can be sure of that, that's not the way, you cannot fight crime with crime but only with calm and inexorable justice, you cannot commit acts in the name of liberty that contradict the very essence of liberty, a rivalry in crime can only lead to the liquidation of society, would you like an apricot juice?, no thanks, uncle, how about a glass of wine?, that's another story, I don't want to turn down everything, your Uncle Jerónimo does not have much faith in his contemporaries, what Spain needs now is a decent upright man a Ruiz Zorrilla for example or a decent upright woman, woman has the same rights and obligations as man, a Concepción Arenal for example, in Spain there is a dearth of eminent personalities, it's different in France, your Uncle Jerónimo speaks sadly and faster than usual, democracy is very hard, my boy, democracy cannot leave crime unpunished no matter where it may occur, because if it does not stop it with the full weight of the law, it dies itself or what is worse it becomes debased and deformed, Spain has more than enough redeemers and magicians, what Spain needs are jurists and teachers, believe me. The dead woman Magdalena's friend from Tangier who has a lovely romantic motto tattooed around her navel is called Aixa the Moor and she works around the Plaza de Antón Martín and the Bar Zaragoza, Aixa is already old, she's at least forty, but she still looks good, tall with deep dreamy eyes and a shock of greasy and aromatic black hair, Aixa the Moor is a friend of the Nicaraguan, sometimes they spend the whole afternoon sitting outside a café, talking. Do you remember that business about the fly drowning in some coffee dregs?, well remember it at every moment and come what may, the Moor and the Nicaraguan had never had a fly drown in their coffee, how disgusting, a fly has fallen in my coffee!, don't worry, just order another, Aixa the Moor was married in her country but she put the sea between herself and her husband because he turned out to be cruel and a faggot, he treated her badly and despotically and didn't go to bed with her, the only one to believe this story is the Nicaraguan, Aixa is very grateful to him and never asks him for money or bothers him, Aixa is a simple woman, malicious and cowed, she thinks like a village dog, when the Nicaraguan receives the money his family sends him he always gives her some packages of Capstan or Gold Flake, Capstans come in a very attractive little metal box, inside they have a picture of a locomotive, a waterfall, a ship, or a wild animal, Capstans are very aromatic, they smell better than they taste, but they make you cough because their smoke sticks to the throat, order another cup of coffee, have them take away the one with the fly, no, it's not worth the bother, I'll just fish out the fly. You were probably not any one of the men who murdered Calvo Sotelo but you could have been, neither are you among those who did in Lt. Castillo but you also could have been, some of you Spaniards, perhaps quite a few, reject the notion of murder as a political weapon, the only flaw in your position is that at the end (no, not at the end, rather at the beginning) you usually get murdered, by one side because you defended their victim, by the other because you defended theirs, what they will not forgive is the condemnation of certain methods because when man begins to stumble at the edge of a precipice politics tends to be based on excessively elementary and immediate assumptions, yes, it's true, no one is a murderer until he has committed murder, but the man who is going to be a murderer develops, before he murders, an odd itching on the roof of his mouth, his sight is clouded, his ears begin to ring, and he goes blind but not completely, no one is exempt from having a murky coin form on his palate, there are two kinds of murderers, the kind that kills like a man drinking a glass of water, which is the worst kind, and the kind that kills like a man going to bed with a woman, without being able to help it, yes, you are Captain S., Captain P., executioner F., gunman A., or guard H. who is obedient and blind as a guard should be, all of them obedient and blind, night, the yearning for adventures, the messianic urge, reluctance to let anyone notice your fear, discipline as a mask for the most confused inclinations, and talking too much, these are the best stimuli for crime, afterward when the shot is heard and a body falls it is too late for repentance and undoing, you have to keep going, there is no longer any way but to keep going without looking back, no one would let you stop or turn your head, no one, neither your friends nor your enemies, neither the enemies of the man you killed nor the friends of the man you killed, for a few seconds you plan to kill yourself, you don't see any other way out, then you don't kill yourself or you kill yourself in due time if your enemies (or your friends) haven't killed you first and you cannot sleep or forget and your mouth is always dry and you go blind or are afraid you're going blind and you are startled by the howling of a dog or the patient gnawing of the worm in the legs of your bed, the murderers who kill like a man drinking a glass of water usually kill themselves in due time perhaps after many long years when no one thinks any more that they might finally kill themselves. All the nobles who killed King Cyril of England, who burned to death inside, killed themselves with their own weapons ten or fifteen or twenty years later except for two who were murdered, one by the king's friends and the other by his own accomplices. Aixa the Moor does not know the history of England and does not know where England is whether in the north or in the south, it's all the same to her, Aixa the Moor is ignorant like an angel and not even sin gives her wisdom. Captain S., the one who had gone for Gil Robles, is arrested with some guards H., the ones who went for Calvo Sotelo, Captain P. and his men, are lost in the crowd, nobody can find them and nobody knows where they are, that's because they're not looking for them, don't tell me, that's because the Guard itself hides them, yes, maybe you're right. A little before midnight Prieto requests of Casares Quiroga that the government arm the people, but Casares refuses. No one feels sleepy and no one understands anything about anything but there are two dead men as yet unburied. In the last three or four weeks there have been more than seventy political assassinations, people do know that but don't quite believe it. Don Roque has supper in his boardinghouse and dashes off again to Don José María's house (Cid's, not Gil Robles'), the situation is red hot and the government can't cope with it, the Republic is finished, through, and between the two sides they'll kill it off, you wait and see, did you know they also went after Gil Robles?, yes, I just found out. Close your eyes and do not look at yourself in the mirror at least for a few hours, General Agency, 4 Calle Mayor, permits for firearms. At Maruja la Valvanera's there is not a single customer, the women entertain themselves playing parcheesi and reading old issues of *La Linterna*, Mondays are bad days and this one, with everything that's happening in Madrid, is worse, General Agency, 4 Calle Mayor, hunting permits. People work their own ruin without knowing it, without thinking almost. Maruja telephones Don Roque's boardinghouse but Don Roque is out, he's gone out, who's calling?, never mind, just a friend, I am his secretary, do you know where I might find him?, well no, I couldn't say, Don Roque prefers not to go back to the boardinghouse and heads for Maruja's, while Maruja is phoning him he is already on his way, General Agency, 4 Calle Mayor, registration of documents, what's going to happen here, Don Roque?, things couldn't be any worse, nothing, dear, nothing's going to happen here, you'll see, it's all a question of getting through the first days, General Agency, 4 Calle Mayor, fishing licenses, I hope to God you're right, Don Roque, my nerves are all on edge, Don Roque stays at Maruja's, Don Roque thinks he is not important enough for them to go after him but just in case he does not go back to the boardinghouse, wake me up tomorrow at eight, Maruja, and send out for the *ABC*, General Agency, 4 Calle Mayor, last wills and testaments. After standing in line for two hours Señor Asterio gets to the red room of the Public Safety Commission headquarters, Lt. Castillo, dead and in a very solemn casket, is surrounded by friends, officers of the Assault Guard and flags of the United Socialist Youth and the Communist Party, it is very hot and the windows are open to drive out the smell of the flowers and let people breathe, no one speaks and those accompanying the body smoke one cigarette after another, but not those in the line, those in the line do not smoke and are satisfied with walking by in an orderly way, a little intimidated, General Agency, 4 Calle Mayor, birth certificates, Señor Asterio finds himself out on the street and feels a little confused, perhaps he is a little dizzy and has a headache, a tiny but very steady headache, General Agency, 4 Calle Mayor, death certificates. Anger and remorse are like the duet of the tenor and the soprano in an operetta, which both of them sing without any need for it, anger which is comforting and remorse which is also comforting, General Agency, 4 Calle Mayor, certificates of good conduct. The best thing is to get some fresh air, the best thing is to take a walk and get some fresh air, the best thing is to drink a glass of white wine, the best thing is to go into the first tavern and drink a glass of white wine, the best thing is to go to the whorehouse and forget, the best thing is to go to the whorehouse and forget everything while you screw a good-looking whore, no, a whore neither good- nor bad-looking, no, a cross-eyed whore, what a joke!, and pregnant, no, the best thing is not to go to the whorehouse, the best thing is to close your eyes and grope your way home being careful while crossing the streets, trying not to bump into anyone, long live the Republic!, and when you get home go to bed with your clothes on and without even untying your shoelaces and shit in your pants and then hold your breath, most likely some rich boy has already screwed both of my girls, their health is not good and that's the main thing, and all their mother thinks about is going to mass, and our Emilito is dead, that's life!, General Agency, 4 Calle Mayor, all kinds of official business. It's easy to kill a woman, you poison her and that's it, it's also easy to kill a man, you wait for him at the door or you go up to his apartment and say to him come with us it's just a few formalities, and you shoot him in the head aiming carefully, General Agency, 4 Calle Mayor, real estate registration. No, the best thing is to breathe the air, to take a little stroll as far as the Paseo de Rosales and the Parque del Oeste and breathe the air, General Agency, 4 Calle Mayor, real estate transfers, Señor Asterio takes a little stroll along Rosales and the Parque del Oeste to breathe the air, at the other end of Madrid, toward Vallecas, members of the Socialist and Anarchist unions exchange a few shots, General Agency, 4 Calle Mayor, letters requisitorial, the Fascists seem to have been swallowed by the earth, we'll see tomorrow at the cemetery, General Agency, 4 Calle Mayor, competitive state examinations. It's Pastorita's turn to go out for supper with Don Máximo, look honey, you stuff yourself, eat whatever you want, I just don't have any appetite, after coffee you'll excuse me if I leave you, another woman?, no, silly, I wish it were another woman!, General Agency, 4 Calle Mayor, pharmaceutical register, Don Máximo is in constant contact with Don Diego, between one side and the other they're going to ruin the country, sometimes I think that the only thing Spaniards like is uncertainty, they'll get their fill of that!, you, Máximo, don't you go to either funeral, furnished rooms Paquita Pineda, from five pesetas, hot and cold running water in every room. Magdalena is killed by the subway in the Manuel Becerra station, by now that seems like news of the Spanish-American War, if this were winter Magdalena's body would have wound up in pieces in the dissection room, now they'll most likely throw her into a common grave, the gravediggers are bastards who throw cigarette butts onto the bodies in a common grave, maybe a used-up butt will fall on one of Magdalena's eyes and will stay there till the worms push it aside, Gerardo, tailor, 5 Concepción Arenal, uniforms, formal and sports clothes, the gravediggers generally get a good laugh out of the corpses of the poor, though they are also poor and are headed for death. The gentleman who died in the private room of a restaurant on the Calle de Arlabán while listening to flamenco singing left a rather large bequest to his mistress, he left her more than two hundred thousand pesetas on condition that she marry in the Church and not just live with anyone, La Francesa Prophylactics, 15 Abada, we ship collect to the provinces, you're not going to cheat on my ghost, do you understand, Hipólita?, if you want a little action you get yourself properly married, no shacking up with my dough, while Hipólita weeps over her dead protector and the authorities order the removal of the body, Chato Getafe, a flamenco singer with few peers, pats her butt without much consideration, second-hand jewelry, Cristino Hernández, 23–25 Carretas, why are you wearing a girdle, damn you?, well look, who could have expected this to happen?, Rogelia Santos, midwife, residence for expectant mothers, 3 Glorieta de San Bernardo. The drunk on the Calle de Toledo went to a better world without knowing what had happened, the man was vomiting to his heart's content in the middle of the street without bothering anybody when suddenly, wham, there's the truck and leaves him flat as a wafer, at home his family say, boy, how late father is! They're going to have to enlarge the morgue unless they pile the bodies one on top of the other, Kursaal Pelikan, 68 Atocha, telephone 70903, the fashionable club, always select attractions, magnificent orchestras, beautiful and accommodating women. Napoleon Bonaparte was a great admirer of beautiful and accommodating women, that's what the books say, less so King Cyril of England, King Cyril was at least as much of a fairy as Pepito, Isabel's Pepito, Pepito la Zubiela, who lost his job for laying his hand on Don Máximo. What's needed here is a revolution of the Right or of the Left, you don't quite know which, nobody quite knows which, and then a dictatorship, of Sanjurjo or of the proletariat, that remains to be seen and when you think about it it's all the same, people are out of control and here nobody will obey, not a soul will obey, they all want to do just as they please, whatever gets into their head, what they fucking well feel like doing, pardon my language, the bad thing about revolutions of the Right is that they're not really revolutions but the opposite, that's it, counterrevolutions, the most they dare to do is to reform something so everything will go on as usual, a counterrevolution is a mustard plaster and a revolution of the Right is a paradox, those on top don't want to move anything for fear of winding up on the bottom, they're not very sure of their courage, they're afraid and they're right to be afraid and naturally they try to stay nice and quiet and not to have anybody make a fuss or a row, great evils call for drastic remedies, Don Diego might be the one to fire the last counterrevolutionary cartridge but they won't let him you'll see, you know, my dear nephew, that I am repelled by practical politics, if I speak to you about all this it's because you're asking me, what people want to do is go to the soccer game to see the enemy team lose, what people like is to see others lose, formerly, when there were public executions, you can't remember that but I do, people crowded in to see the garroted man lose and they clapped when his tongue hung out, politicians are usually very chattery and romantic, their head is confused, very confused, the head of a scientist can be confused, that doesn't matter for the work he does because that's also confused, but politicians and artists need a clear head in which everything is in order, Velázquez and Quevedo were marvels of order and clearheadedness, but you can see our politicians, making speeches and urging their followers to hunt each other down with guns, physically man is still in the Upper Paleolithic, thirty thousand years ago, the same is true of rats, they're just the way they've always been, before the Paleolithic man was not a man, he was an ape, and who knows what rats were, man learned to speak and later to write and then he discovered that no two men are alike, no two think alike, maybe rats speak too but what's sure is that they don't write, that's why they are more alike inside, they all think alike and can govern themselves better, rats also kill each other but certainly less than men do, there are men, there have always been some, who dream of turning men into rats and at some points in history they've been on the verge of achieving it, there have also been men, a few, to be sure, but some, who wanted rather to turn rats into men, they were called madmen and heretics and were locked up, run along now, I'm going to bed to read a while till I get sleepy, don't think that turning rats into men is some naive utopia, utopia means no place and what I'm telling you can happen on earth within however-many years, what does it matter how many, not all men have the same aspirations but it is neither tolerable nor sensible to allow certain men to dream of converting man into a rat, according to the Orientals man's possible attitudes are three, devotion (love and hate), action (business and travel), and comprehension (contemplation and speculation), we Spaniards have not got beyond devotion and our action and comprehension, when they appear, are always conditioned by it, and that's why we're in such a mess, well my boy, I'm going to bed, your Uncle Jerónimo is a tireless reader, he is always reading and profiting from what he reads. At the sidewalk cafés on Recoletos and the Calle de Alcalá people drink coffee and talk about Calvo Sotelo, they tend to forget Lt. Castillo, Spain is a very rank-conscious country and the only officers Spaniards know are the generals. Raúl T. Ortiz de Ojuel, that is, Raúl Tendero, speaks very foolishly, Raúl is a bumpkin who talks only nonsense, it gives him good results in his profession and after all it's all the same to you, you're even glad about it, Raúl is full of curiosity and anticipation, Sanjurjo can sweep all of this clean whenever he wants to in five or six hours, just in the time it takes him to show up in Madrid and say, here I am, that's enough civil strife, let us all join in a concerted effort to build a greater Spain, I don't know man, it seems to me you make it sound too easy, well, I don't go for discussions, time will tell whether I'm right. By now Magdalena has probably begun to smell like the dead, before she had the smell of the living who smell dead which although it is quite similar is not exactly the same, it's sweeter and more repulsive, it moves more quickly and naturally is also more disgusting, as soon as a fly bites Magdalena she'll start to rot like cheese, probably a hundred flies have already bitten her, and then she'll start to smell like a goat killed by a cart and stretched out in the sun with its belly bloated in a ditch by the side of a path, next to a yellow or white flower. Men do not have a very sharp sense of smell, any animal has a better sense of smell than man, if odors, like light, had infrared rays and man, just as he does not see the infrared rays of light, could smell those of an odor, the coffee drinkers at the sidewalk cafés on Recoletos and Alcalá would have noticed that the city was beginning to be invaded by the odor of death, what does it smell of?, death, don't you notice it?, but how can it smell of death?, how should I know?, but I say it smells of death, it sure smells of death, Turquoise smells of Crepe de Chine, the perfume that enfolds you like silk, an admirer gave her a little flask of Crepe de Chine, the perfume that enfolds you like silk, and also of stale sweat and wine, Toisha, in her chiffon nightgown, smells of toothpaste and fresh sweat, it must be a pleasure to smell Toisha as she sleeps in her chiffon nightgown, you don't know that, the drunk killed in the Calle de Toledo smells of wine and small change, the servant who miscarries smells of fried oil and silk worms, the mother of the child who died of the croup smells of cologne, she doesn't know it, the gentleman who left Hipólita a bequest of two hundred thousand pesetas smells of tobacco, that's normal, the two who fought in the middle of the street smell of onions, one more than the other, the whore who was stabbed to death smells of Ozonopino, odors are very different and everyone smells of what he can, the city smells of death, that is a very tenuous smell and almost no one notices it, but it smells of death, among the trees on Recoletos neither the nightingale nor the owl, the two birds of night, fly, all that happens in the branches of the trees on Recoletos which may be five thousand or more is too monotonous, the owl seems painted with antiseptic powder and ashes, maybe it's made of antiseptic powder and ashes, the nightingale on the other hand is made of cigar ash with a little soil, it's like a little ghost that sings better than anybody, at the outdoor tables of the Café Recoletos and the Café Gijón people talk about Calvo Sotelo, about the Philippine airmen, about summer, about women, about literature, and about things that happen, some credible and others incredible, there are also those who don't talk and just look distractedly at the rest. Julianín, sleeping in the tavern kitchen, does not even suspect that people might go about the streets at night, he'll find out these and other things when he's older, there's no hurry. Fidel Ternera, Vicar, finds five pesetas at the foot of a tree and says to Paca, Paca, today is a great day, I'm inviting you to a supper of tripe and oranges just like the elite's, Paca is delighted and does not go to the zoo wall to ply her trade, tonight I wouldn't jack off my own father!, well said, girl, you tell 'em, it's not going to be the end of the world either, Paca is radiant and her hump even seems to weigh less and almost to shine, it's delicious, Señor Fidel!, do you like it?, I'll say!, didn't I have a good idea about the tripe?, I should say so, couldn't be better!, well mop it up with your bread, we deserve to celebrate, today we're not poor, Paca, no sir. The Somalian troops under the command of the Italian General Gallina, what a joke for him to be called Gallina, "Chicken"!, are carrying out energetic mopping-up operations between Addis Ababa and Djibouti with the aim of subduing the Ethiopian guerrillas. En route to Berlin Don Porfirio Rubirosa, first secretary of the Dominican legation in Germany, and his wife Doña Flor de Oro Trujillo de Rubirosa, daughter of the president of the Dominican Republic, are visiting this capital, we wish them a pleasant stay among us, don't you?, yes I do too, what do I care? The National Union of Railway Workers believes that there should be no strike and asks for the nationalization of the railways. María Fernanda Ladrón de Guevara is presenting *Our Natacha* at the Pavón Theatre, orchestra two pesetas, a hit. Engracia thinks it's time to stand up and be counted, that the hour of the revolution has struck and that the seizure of power must be attempted with all its consequences, death before slavery!, her boyfriend Agustín is not so sure but keeps it to himself, Agustín has more domestic aspirations, what he'd like is to open a tavern with good *tapas* for people to snack on and a little flamenco singing but naturally he doesn't say so, that would go over like a lead balloon!, you can't talk to Engracia about certain things, the fact is that you can hardly talk to

Engracia about anything, as they were leaving the wake for Lt. Castillo, Agustín suggested to Engracia that they go for some coffee, you could do that under these circumstances?, no dear, I just thought it would pep us up. Jesualdo Villegas, since he has nobody to talk to, look how odd people are, where can they all have gone?, explains to Enriqueta and Angustias that this is the centenary of the Bohemian poet (Bohemian from Bohemia, not because he wears a floppy tie) Karel Hynek Mácha, a powerful voice of Romanticism in his country and a man unjustly underrated by the critics of his time, since Enriqueta and Angustias could not care less about this poet business they both yawn quietly and surreptitiously, it's not that there is no one at Madame Teddy's, some people are there but fewer than usual, when Jesualdo finishes telling about the Bohemian poet (Bohemia Bohemian, not dirty bohemian, it has nothing to do with that), he quickly and almost as though fulfilling an obligation lays Enriqueta and says good-night, I still have to write my article, so long, see you tomorrow. The master sergeant of the Customs Guard whose wife got her face scorched the other night receives orders to report to his unit urgently and without delay, his wife tells him that her alcohol burner blew up, horrors!, why didn't you let me know?, no, what was the sense of frightening you?, after the first moments I could tell it wasn't serious, I didn't even have to go to the first-aid station, well so much the better, you never know where you'll find danger, does it hurt you now?, no, it doesn't hurt any more. On the other hand Amanda's ribs hurt from when the corporal smashed them with a bench, what an ass, what an inconsiderate way of pounding a body!, Matías from the commissary doesn't know that Amanda took a beating, he won't know it till Saturday, Matías has to get up very early, at 4:30 A.M. he's already up, and he can only go out at night on Saturdays, it's the most natural thing in the world, it's the same with a lot of people, Matiítas is somebody else, he has nothing to do with Matías Suárez from the commissary or with Matías Tajuelo the man who shuts the door at La Cigale when he's told to, Matiítas' name is Matías Serrano, what happens is that names repeat themselves nobody can prevent that, Matiítas is a clerk in the condom shop where Guillermo Zabalegui gets his supply, his Uncle Esteban, the blind one, pays him to read novels to him, some of them very spicy, woman is a delicious instrument of pleasure, but one must know her delicate strings, thoroughly study her capricious and volatile keys, Pilar was like a goddess by Rubens, what abundance of flesh!, what saturated white skin!, what does saturated skin mean?, ah, that I don't know, maybe the novelist wrote satiny skin and the printers made a mistake, the novel Matiítas likes best is *For Love and Virtue* but of course he reads what he's told to, Guillermo's uncle is very horny especially for a blind man, you would think the blind ought to be more respectable, you can go take a walk, I'm in no mood for reading today, take your two pesetas and beat it, whatever you say, Don Esteban, shall I come tomorrow?, you come every day, damn it, till I kick you out as a lazy bum!, now leave me in peace, good-bye, Don Esteban, have a good rest, good-bye, son, see you tomorrow, Matiítas takes his usual stroll along the fence of the Botanical Gardens, it's earlier than other nights and the women who usually offer the services of their expert hands must still be chatting with their families or with some neighbor, they'll come later, a group of workers walks by talking loudly, they shout a lot but as they all shout at the same time you can't understand what they're saying, Matiítas hides behind a tree and lets them go by, he never messes with anybody but sometimes they mess with him, especially groups of people, and call him a fairy and a queer. Taboada, not Raúl Taboada of *El Liberal* but the other one, Virgilio Taboada of *El Debate*, the one who was with Sánchez Somoza's wife, is in bed with a fever, he has a bad indigestion that gives him a fever and cramps and on top of that his butt is raw like a monkey's, chocolate burns something fierce, even more than coffee, Taboada's landlady and his fellow boarders can't understand what could have happened to him, but come now, how is it possible for anyone to burn his rear with chocolate?, Taboada has told them over and over but they won't believe him, well, Doña Ramona, it's this way, it burns when you sit in it, but for heaven's sake, man, why didn't you stand up?, because I couldn't, Doña Ramona, do you think I wouldn't rather have stood up and beat it out of there?, the doctor prescribes Carabaña water for his indigestion and compresses of picric acid for his buttocks, you were lucky, my friend, that it didn't affect the scrotum or the tissue of the testicles, yes, very lucky, Taboada tries to lie face down in the bed and when he is alone he takes off the covers and lies there with his butt exposed, even rubbing against the sheets hurts him, Clarita, Sánchez Somoza's wife, who also has an indigestion and a skinned butt, is cared for in her parents' house, offer it to Our Lord, dear, as a sacrifice for the conversion of the infidels, your husband is your cross, we all go through life bearing our cross!, yes Mama, tempting lips all day long, morning, noon, and night, authentic Michel indelible lipstick in four tones, glossy orange, glossy red, bright red, and long-lasting dark red. Matiítas also likes to read aloud from *The Lord of Bembibre* by Enrique Gil y Carrasco, while this was happening in Salamanca, Doña Beatriz, suspended between hope and fear, saw one day pass after another with her eyes fixed on the road from Ponferrada, the groups that are coming from Atocha and Vallecas keep on insulting Matiítas and since he finds everything a little odd he heads home, when people start acting up the best thing is to get out of the way, tomorrow is another day. What Engracia says about death before slavery is neither Socialist nor Communist, it's Anarchist, it's in the anthem *Sons of the People*, sons of the people, you suffer in chains, against such injustice we raise our cry, if life is but sorrow, a world full of pains, rather than slavery prefer to die. Some Anarchists pass in front of the walls of the Botanical Gardens, rise up, oh you true people, rise up with resolution, the call, the call is sounding of social revolution, Matiítas sees them from a distance, from the Calle de las Huertas, he feels a little dizzy, maybe it's fear, and he goes to bed, do you suppose that Matiítas' soul is irredeemably damned?, do not look at yourself in the mirror or break out in tears, it's not worth while, Matiítas' soul is irredeemably damned, there is no way any more to save it from the eternal fire, you do not know why the soul of Matiítas is damned, irredeemably damned, the poor fellow does no harm to anyone, he is a faggot, yes, but what does that matter?, there are lots of faggots and not all of them are damned, some must be saved, well at least one can suppose that some will finally be saved, when Matiítas gets to hell he is in for a big surprise, Matiítas would have liked to be a fly that buzzes around a crotch, a rhythmic fly on the rear of a stallion ass, a cautious fly on a sick man who can no longer move his hands to chase it away, there are callings that are never fulfilled in this life and that are paid for in the next to the chagrin of both offenders and offended, theology is only a quarrel among men, something that does not worry the gods, no, do not look at yourself in the mirror lest you should have to spit at yourself in the mirror, keep your saliva for more pressing needs, for example when you are seized by panic and your throat, tongue, and palate turn dry, and on your palate there springs forth a rusty coin that you will only be able to remove by emptying the magazine of your pistol into your neighbor's back, silence the voice of your conscience when it tells you that Matiítas' soul is already irredeemably damned, alcoholics, guaranteed cure for the habit, they do not notice it and it will not harm them, information available confidentially and without cost. Mimí Ortiz de Amoedo, Willy's aunt, has no strong class prejudices in bed, she's rather democratic, very democratic, the way to see men is in the altogether, I don't ask them their name, I look at their prick, for heaven's sake, Mimí, don't be so vulgar, you sound like a cook!, no silly, a cook would right away ask the name, what she can't forgive the picador is his wanting to run off with her jewels, that was too much!, the man was something of a brute, but you couldn't expect more from him, and that's the least of it because he had real abilities, Mimí's lovers don't usually last long, she's good-looking, yes, and sluttier than anybody, but she's also capricious and despotic and after the first moments that's hard to take. Your father is a man of good judgment, although he is less brilliant his judgment may be as good as your Uncle Jerónimo's, no son, these savages who kill each other on the street are not wolves, they are meek sacrificial lambs dressed in wolves' skins, the wolves are the ones who push them on and fill their heads with wind so they can't think, you can't think well with wind in your head, believe me, not at all well, because the wind drives out the smoke of ideas and makes the brain sick, makes it useless, if things are settled between these two extremist factions these savage lambs will have a very uncertain future, or less uncertain but very grey or painful, it all depends, if their side wins, a little job so they can eat as long as they don't complain, if their side loses, they are subject to the law, that's normal and that's how it has always happened the thing is the savage lambs don't know it, a fighting bull is bred to die with full honors in the bullring, what happens in the bullring means nothing to the bull, if he stood still there would be no use for bullrings, but he charges at the horses, chases the helpers, and dashes at the matador and if he can hooks him and tears out his guts, at the end they kill him and if he behaved bravely and knew how to die with dignity they applaud him as he is dragged off, when the bull is not true to type or is not fierce enough they castrate him and make him into an ox, that's an affront, yes, depending on how you look at it, it's an affront to what the bull thinks a bull ought to be, but it is also life insurance, a leading ox is tame and castrated, no one denies that, but it is he and others like him who rule over the bulls, they tell them here and the bulls go here, they tell them there and the bulls go there, the reason why oxen rule over bulls is very mysterious, maybe it's not all that mysterious but simple, very simple, but the fact is that history is full of examples, the bulls are also savage lambs with wind in their heads, that's why they die young and bloody, no, you are not Saint Paul or Buffalo Bill and your father's words leave you pensive, neither are you the Cid Campeador or Pepito la Zubiela (nor Matiítas), if you were everything would be more orderly and foreseen, nor are you Napoleon Bonaparte or King Cyril of England who died lulled by the belly laughs of moralizing traitors, the enemies of the soul are three, the world, the flesh, and the devil, there is flesh of different kinds and one single substance, gallows flesh and cannon flesh, prison flesh and dead man's flesh (dead from violence, from disease, from disgust), catechism class flesh and brothel flesh, flesh for the common grave and flesh that blows away in the wind like a little cloud, the best thing will be for you to flee like an ox, terrified, the future holds very lofty plans for you and it is not advisable for you to face them, turn your butt to them, but wait till they ask you to, never present your butt for nothing, flee from Tránsito and never again call her Toisha, flee from Lupita and Juani, the accommodating sisters, flee from all women and think of your future, you know it will take an effort but you must try, Spain is a country of oxen who do not forgive the youthful fucker, nor the savage sacrificial lamb that kills because they emptied his skull, nor the wild young bull who does not seek blood but licks his own blood with deep amazement, piss on all advice!, the sisters cling to you like barnacles when they dance and in the Retiro and at the movies they pull their tits out over their neckline, Toisha is a monumental woman, naked she looks like an art photo in *Crónica*, yes, the enemies of the soul are three but the worst of all is the devil who disguised as a coin installs himself on men's palates and lets loose the appetites of death, there is also joyful and loving and sexy flesh that does not move to the rhythm of death what happens is that men usually forget that, Toisha in her nightgown dreams that she is flying softly, lightly, over a meadow with many flowers and a spring of singing water whose stream never stops, outside are heard some shots, running and shouting, no doubt it is the savage lambs that have not yet gone to bed.

IV

The first light of dawn hesitantly breaks over cemetery walls and two unburied corpses await orders, regulations, and policies, is death so wretched?, Vergil asked himself in the *Aeneid*, there are niches in which the rough yellow hedge mustard blooms, tombs adorned with fuzzy red poppies, and sepulchers on which the wine-colored bellflower climbs, yes, with the flowers in the cemetery one could paint every flag, the red, the red and yellow, the red and yellow and purple, the red and yellow and purple and black, the red and yellow and purple and black and green and white and blue, it is no use being too enthusiastic when melancholy nests in the heart, long live the Republic!, be still a bit, long live Spain!, be still a bit, no one should distract the gravedigger. In his garret Matiítas is restless and thinks, sometimes bad lonely thoughts assail him, sad imaginings that fill his mind with sorrow, with some frequency Matiítas dreams that he gouges out the eyes of a blind man, Guillermo turns his head, my Uncle Esteban's?, no, just a blind man, no special one, your Uncle Esteban or some other one, Matiítas does not like women, he stops short of being a perverted pervert, a lesbian fairy, he does not take it that far, but he'd like it if he liked women the way men like women or at least the way dykes like women, the cracks in the plaster on the walls make very whimsical silhouettes, an old man sticking out his tongue, a boy pissing, a horse, a half-moon, a bird, look, this is the beak, these are the wings, a tree with a cloud above, the cracks in Matiítas' little hole make the same figures as the ones on the niches in the cemetery, there's little variety there, Matiítas likes men, the way women like them or rather the way faggots like them, but he'd like it if he did not like men, the way men and dykes and perverted perverts don't like them, beneath the window there is a spot that looks like the globe, here's America, here's Africa, here's Asia Minor, and next to it there is a leaping ballerina, you can see her very clearly, some nights Matiítas is assailed by odd thoughts that fill his memory with fright, Matiítas is a respectable fairy, he is responsible for his respectability, being a fairy came to him all by itself like the mustache that starts to grow on a boy, a bitter fairy without any real conviction, a fairy by obligation and against his grain, a poor devil who one evil day found himself with nothing to do but smile at pricks, he was ashamed but he also enjoyed smiling at pricks, winking at pricks, caressing pricks and storing up scars for a whole lifetime, things go the way they want to go and happen because they have to happen, nobody can stop them, a man goes to work every morning, you know, always along the same streets on the same sidewalk in front of the same store windows hearing the same sounds the passing vendor the girl practicing the piano the maid singing a popular song the streetcar ringing its bell smelling the same smells the dairy stable the fritter shop the market the sewer, a man goes to work for the same reasons that he puts up with a woman till death, she never dies always the same domestic cunt the same domestic tears the same sharp and foul-mouthed domestic reproaches the same sounds the belch the sigh the dish being washed the same smells sweat breath, inertia has too strong a grip on us, habit too, inertia and habit are almost the same thing, you couldn't distinguish between them, and they are full to overflowing with menaces that fall on those who break with them. At 4:30 A.M. the body of Lt. Castillo leaves the headquarters of the Public Safety Commission, it lies in its solemn casket, all caskets are solemn and mahogany caskets even more so, and in a glass-sided carriage followed by another loaded with flowers and wreaths, they are taking it to the city cemetery to the section that used to be called the civil cemetery, when they secularized the cemeteries they ordered the wall that separated it from the Almudena Cemetery to be torn down, it was a dispute among the living, the dead once they are dead don't care about this question one way or the other, nothing matters any more to the dead, they have no sense, no way of knowing what matters to them and what doesn't matter to them, if they are Catholics they go to heaven or to hell, they take them to heaven or to hell and if they are atheists they go to the atheists' heaven or hell, they take them to the atheists' heaven or hell, their memory and the good or bad use others may make of their memory, the body of Lt. Castillo is escorted by his Assault Guards and the Socialist and Communist militias, the cortege includes officers of the Assault Guard, commissioners for investigation and surveillance, high-level functionaries of the Commission, and people, many people. Foolishness and crime are also a kind of inertia, a kind of habit, almost everything is a kind of inertia, a habit that does not allow the will to breathe, there are spots on the walls that look like strange letters, letters placed there one after the other to produce signs with confused meanings. Matiítas, who is a faggot, is not much of a faggot, that is, he is not altogether a faggot, he lacks joy. There are those who give the name of conscience to the threats that bubble in a lonely man's brain frightening away his tranquility and his joy, you have to be alive for that, yes, maybe it's true, it is the conscience, there are also fools and bitter joyless criminals, fools and criminals whom a little ray of light tells for a few seconds that they are fools and criminals, the sexual organ is like a top that spins and spins, like a waterwheel that turns and turns ceaselessly until suddenly it stops dead and falls over, then everyone steps on it and laughs, Erotyl, eternal youth, recommended for genital asthenia (impotence), the most powerful stimulant and restorative of neuro-spinal-medico-genital activity, available in pharmacies, 21.75 pesetas. No, what for?, try to sleep quietly, count sheep jumping over a gate, or no, don't count anything, there are things that should not be thought about, you also don't like certain things and would like to like them, like certain things and would like not to like them, you know what it's about, all of us have sometimes had a bad conscience and the sexual organ is like a top, like a waterwheel. Matiítas caresses his poor organs to drive away bad thoughts, Matiítas does not masturbate, he really rubs himself unenthusiastically and as though from inertia, it's his habit, it is very late and Matiítas falls asleep with his mouth open like a dead man. Lt. Castillo's body is already crossing the Plaza de Cibeles, an occasional shot is heard in the distance and then four or five in reply and then silence, what is heard closer by is the thump of the watchman's club against the paving and also, monotonous and moribund, the singing of a drunk. Matiítas coughs a little and without quite waking up turns on his other side, now he is facing the wall, Madariaga Syrup, benzo-cinnamic sedative, a pleasant and effective cough remedy. No, do not turn on the light, open the window and look at yourself in the mirror without turning on the light, it is still night, try to see yourself in the half-light that the gas lamps on the street cast into your room, you don't see yourself in the mirror, of course not, all you make out is a faint shadow, a barely visible silhouette, you look like a ghost, do not be proud or suspicious and look at yourself bravely in the mirror, it does not matter that you cannot see, that you cannot make yourself out, the blind do not see either even in the sunlight, they make out nothing and still they neither fuss nor curse, surreptitiously they do curse everything but you can't tell, surreptitiously the blind are very agitated, what happens to them is like what happens to a madman who just got a beating, who is afraid of getting another, what frightens madmen most is the lustful little smile of their executioners (attendants, nurses, nuns, etc.), someone painted a skull on your mirror, maybe it's death which amuses itself by frightening those of you who are going to die, you are not sleepy, you are kept awake by two ideas that you cannot entertain separately, the blood that is being spilled and Toisha naked underneath her nightgown, you entertain the two ideas successively, first one and then the other, together they are too stimulating, almost abject, do not write letters to God to occupy your insomnia, not even in the dark or almost in the dark, do not be foolish or fatuous, never feel yourself to be too important, because you're not, no one is ever too important, in Spain only the dead are important, some of the dead, God knows everything that happens without your having to write him about it, without your being his unnecessary and childish confidant, he knows it better than you and why and what for, he just refrains from interfering in these questions that don't affect him in the slightest, it is true that one can write to God in the dark, if he wants it he can guide your hand in the darkness but if he doesn't want it you will achieve nothing although you pray to him with tears in your eyes and although you dress as a bullfighter or in some other showy disguise, a bishop or a judge or a general of the Hungarian cavalry for example, you will not manage half a line of legible writing, and usually God does not want it, that's what I've been telling you, God takes no part in what we men do, he contemplates us with infinite contempt, with infinite pity, also with infinite sorrow, everything we imagine about God is very strange, most likely he is not a little surprised by our clumsiness, think and do not go to the limit of your capacity for thought, stop before you reach it, there are people who sleep and people who do not sleep, people who die in their sleep and people who wake up to die, death does not exist until it appears with its halo of sticky cruelty, afterward it wipes away your thoughts and then leaves, you see it come but you think it's only hallucination, you don't see it leave, no one sees it leave and that makes for its extraordinary strength, yes, look at yourself in the dark in your closet mirror, in some places it is worn but that does not matter, God, *de potentia absoluta*, is infinitely everything, infinitely good, bad, just, unjust, compassionate, cruel, intelligent, stupid, etc., etc., if he wants it you could see yourself in the mirror even in the dark, but he does not want it, that's what I've been telling you, our image of God is very naive, the theologians have not clarified anything for us but have rather confused the concept of God, it just does not matter to him, he does not even laugh at men, neither does he pity them, you should not be surprised at God's attitudes, so little human, the attitudes of men are frequently inhuman, that's just a way of talking, the attitudes of God are alien to us, it is very difficult, it is impossible to apply finite and earthly measures to infinite and heavenly (also earthly) concepts, man monumentalizes the infinite, he makes it enormous and breathes easily thinking that he has hit on the solution, but he is wrong, the enormous is not infinite, the infinite is something that cannot be measured above or below, a mountain can be very big, Everest, Aconcagua, but it is not infinite, infinitely big, a microbe can be very small, you have to look at it through a microscope, but it is not infinite, infinitely small, man does not know how to name the infinite and settles for closing his eyes and being frightened, even if you open your eyes wide you will not be able to see yourself in the mirror because you are in the dark. Lt. Castillo's body is passing through the Puerta de Alcalá. It is night, you know that it is night, it is still pitch black, a good time to steal to flee to sleep to love to die surreptitiously to die of fear with your head under the pillow, you cannot all do what you would most like to do at night, often you have to be patient and wait for the new day, by day resignation is more bearable, less ridiculous and painful, what good did it do Magdalena to smell of the seven worst smells in the world?, no good, none at all because now she is dead and lying on a marble table, matter that absorbs the disinfecting lye, waiting to be thrown into the common grave, the final bitter brothel of poor men and women, respectable or not but poor, in no whorehouse does the flesh of men and women respectable or not but poor blend more quickly or more thoroughly, don't be alarmed, you have never laughed at the death of the poor nor have you pissed on the common grave, neither have you spat into the alms box for the blessed souls in purgatory, it doesn't matter to Magdalena that they will throw her into a common grave, more than once she thought that she would end up in the common grave, Magdalena Inmaculada Múgica was very stoical, all she wanted was to eat and keep on smelling. General Espartero, on horseback and in bronze, shows the way of the dead with the gesture of a man very much used to being obeyed, sometimes, not now at night, the little birds that pass by dump on him but General Espartero is unmoved, that means nothing, Magdalena would also be unmoved, once when a pigeon dumped on Toisha she broke out crying, afterward you had to take her home to change her clothes, it took her a long time and you got impatient, you have some very nervous impulses. Some of the streetlights don't work and the darkness by the Aguirre school is almost total, *La Safranina* by Professor R. Namias, a new photographic guide for developing in white light, paper covers, 3.50 pesetas. You are not Napoleon Bonaparte, you must not allow yourself to be ill-humored or impatient, people would not tolerate it and Toisha would probably never again let herself be embraced, perhaps she would, perhaps she would embrace you more enthusiastically than ever, you never know, women's susceptibilities lie just beneath the skin and they may react this way or that or not at all, it's very risky to make predictions about the crumbs from the table, take whatever they give you and be satisfied because some are worse off, much worse, just look at King Cyril of England and the way he died. The sisters sleep like a log each one in her bed, in a funeral cortege there is always someone who dozes in the most unlikely position, sleep eventually overcomes even the most enthusiastic. At the Café Pelayo a cat sleeps on the counter, from the front of the Tivoli Theatre the great Angelillo, the hero of *The Black Man with a White Soul*, smiles at the funerals, and a little farther on, on the Calle del General Pardiñas, at the foot of an acacia, a blind young beggar is nursing her child while a stray boy, a boy with a stupid look, probably a stupid boy, and the hair of a sparrow, watches her and masturbates very assiduously, the boy has the face of a fox and his back is arched with lust like a dog's, he's in seventh heaven, there is not a breath of air and people sleep with their windows wide open and half their bodies out from under the covers. Maripi Fuentes is afraid of being pregnant, she doesn't tell anybody but she is very much afraid of being pregnant, have you had sexual congress with a man?, what?, did you go to bed with a man?, no, it was in a box at the Monumental Theatre, that's all the same for our purposes, let's see, have you had any omissions?, what?, have your periods stopped?, well yes, I think so, the fact is I don't really know, I haven't stopped to think about it, well it's a very important piece of information, come on now, think a moment, Dámaso Rioja is not the perpetrator of the mischief, that you know very well, the boxes at the Monumental are comfortable and spacious, if you give the usher a peseta no one bothers you, behind the curtain they have a bench upholstered in velvet and even a clothesrack, many a maidenhead has perished in the boxes at the Monumental, hundreds of maidenheads, it would be interesting to keep track, sometimes you take Lupita and Juani to a box at the Monumental with a friend, Lupita and Juani prefer the Panorama, the boxes at the Monumental make them a little nervous. A watchman reads *Muchas gracias* by the light of a street lamp, sitting on a bench, Sexine, a new aphrodisiac supremely effective against feminine indifference, tasteless and odorless, cannot be detected, soluble in any cold or hot liquid, what people, that's like fishing for trout with dynamite!, one guy is sharper than the next here! José Carlos, Maripi's brother, also goes to the boxes at the Monumental with Conchita and even takes off all her clothes, José Carlos is pretty self-assured about it. Lt. Castillo's body passes by the Calle de Alcántara, where Alcalá, Alcántara, and Hermosilla come together, on the sidewalk in front of the branch post office a drunk is making a hesitating and bombastic and not very intelligible speech. Paquita, or rather Margot, can't sleep and reads *The Naked Virgin* by the Bold Knight, the night did not go well for Margot, or for her colleagues, for two days now people have been sort of withdrawn and reluctant to have anything to do with anyone, Margot has a large enough clientele, not very select but large enough, she just hasn't taken in a cent in two days, neither she nor her colleagues, Margot inherited almost all the regulars of Petra la Grillo, the mulatto who appeared at a picnic ground with her throat slashed, people have very confused premonitions and tendencies and get themselves aroused as best they can, that happens to everybody. Magdalena, that poor evil-smelling slut, was killed by the subway in the Manuel Becerra station, during the day there are usually stands on the street with flowers for the dead, lilacs and dahlias, also yellow carnations, the custom is for the cortege to take its leave at the Plaza de Manuel Becerra, only the family and the closest friends go all the way to the cemetery. Lt. Castillo's body is passing through the Plaza de Manuel Becerra and contrary to custom the cortege does not stop and goes on, in the direction of Las Ventas. The garbage men that are heading for Madrid nod on their carts without getting out of line, their babies sleep in a rope basket or on top of some blankets and between the wheels there trots very submissively the little dog with dirty wool and lively look, the little dog who is their companion in poverty and shares their diet of nutritious filth, the filth that feeds them all, amen and may it never be any worse, people say that there are very rich garbage men who even raise pigs and chickens on the garbage, the fact is it's not worth while to be rich if it means living encrusted in shit, the milkmen inside their portable railings, their four pieces of iron from which they hang their pitchers and their pots, start to distribute the milk groping in the dark, it's a miracle that they manage it but they do, they never make a mistake, in her hut at the Abroñigal Paca sleeps in the arms of Fidel who is very affectionate with her, when Paca eats two days in a row it even seems that her hump turns softer, maybe if she got hot food for a while it would eventually fall off, stranger things have happened, Paca, yes sir Señor Fidel, what's that coming down the road?, I don't know, it seems like it's a lot of cars, this is no time for cars to go by, maybe not . . . , come on, go to sleep, what do we care if there are cars going by, they must know what they're doing, yes sir, Paca holds still to see whether Fidel wants something, but what Fidel wants is to go on sleeping, he'll have another go at her when morning comes, there's no hurry, Paca doesn't want to go to bed with anyone, she doesn't like it and besides she's afraid of getting pregnant, she already got pregnant once and had a lousy time of it, Paca just works with her hands but it's different with Fidel, Fidel is very kind and besides he doesn't make you pregnant, you can see he's not the type, Paca knows that from experience, Paca, yes sir Señor Fidel, the dead are even worse off!, yes sir, where will it all stop!, come on over here, yes sir, Paca allows herself to be loved, resignedly like the slaves of old-time kings, sometimes a sort of shadow of enthusiasm gets into her but it doesn't last long, Paca, yes sir Señor Fidel, move faster, yes sir, sometimes Fidel sends Paca to buy half a pound of lungs and invites her for lunch, Paca is no ingrate, like so many others, Paca, yes sir Señor Fidel, come on go to sleep, yes sir Señor Fidel, asleep Paca looks even smaller than awake, the same thing happens with the garbage men's dogs. The first light of dawn hesitantly breaks over the cemetery walls when Lt. Castillo's body passes through the gate. In his garret Matiítas is sleeping with his mouth agape, like a dead man, he looks like a dead man, anybody could take him for a dead man, maybe he died suddenly and doesn't know it, nobody else knows it either. The doctors are finishing their autopsy on the body of Calvo Sotelo, there were two shots, both inevitably fatal, one of the bullets lodged in the brain, signed Dr. Antonio Piga, this report is never published, people are left with the version of the preliminary report, one shot, not two, the criminal investigation is being carried out by Dr. Blas Aznar, who studies everything, hairs, blood stains and their blood group, bruises on the nose and left leg of the body, etc. Bakers also get up very early but not as early as milkmen, the basket of fresh bread seems like a bathtub or a casket and smells very good and warm, it smells like a respectable woman jumping rope out in the countryside. The noisy coming and going of life throbs in the midst of the silence of the dead, it is a very wise counterpoint that one does not even understand at first, it sounds like Chinese or some other cruel language, the last crickets of the night gradually dim their wounding and almost metallic song and the snails stretch on the luxuriant wild purslane, the kale, and the wild asparagus that suck the nutritious juice of death. Señor Asterio gets up early but not as early as the snails, Señor Asterio is still asleep, also with his mouth open, almost everyone sleeps with his mouth open. In the mysterious empty niches the swallows build their nests and fat, shiny, varnished cockroaches swarm, they have never known the fear of the crushing slipper or the powdered poison, when the niche is about to be occupied by a newly arrived dead man, the grave-digger without taking the cigarette from his lips knocks down the swallows' nests and leaves the cockroaches walled in to grow blind all at once in a few minutes, it must be very enjoyable to produce death while playing with death, everybody does it and even smiles while doing it. Don Máximo spends almost the whole night with the light on drinking coffee, writing in a little notebook and thinking very apprehensively about all that is happening, it hasn't even been half an hour since Don Máximo turned out his light, but he is not asleep. Humidity forms under the old tombstones and hides the beetle and the slug and over an R.I.P. of cracked marble the centipede runs with his rapid stuttering gait. Your Uncle Jerónimo gets up and does breathing exercises for a few minutes, then he goes to the cooler and eats a yogurt and a tomato with a few drops of oil. The grey lizards and the earth-colored toads—the former nervous little busybodies, the latter solemn and almost like abbots—venture their first timid steps of the day. Don Joaquín dreams that he buys an escritoire in very good condition, in a small secret drawer there are thirteen gold doubloons. There are no frogs in the cemetery, it's a pity but that's the way it is, the frogs stayed in the Abroñigal creek, near where Paca and Fidel, who fell asleep in each other's arms, also begin to wake up gradually, Paca and Fidel are in no hurry, nobody's pushing them, it's all the same whether you live slowly looking at the ceiling or die slowly also looking at the ceiling, it takes the same amount of time and nobody knows how long that will be. The dour rats trot shyly and rapidly always escaping from something, and the mice that seem to have quicksilver in their bodies look at the scene of their domestic adventures with their lively little eyes. Virtudes, Victoriano Palomo's wife, is struck by diarrhea, obviously she ate too much for supper, Victoriano, what?, I don't feel well, Victoriano jumps up in bed and turns on the light, hold on a little, I'll go for the midwife, wait till I call your mother, no Victoriano, it's not that, I've just got diarrhea, whew, that's better, some scare you gave me!, well, what do you want me to do about it?, don't you worry, well then go to sleep, oh honey, how grumpy you are! The streetcar workers walk in small groups of three or four with their hands in their pockets and their cigarettes in their mouths they walk sour-faced and in silence, maybe they slept badly or have heartburn. There are many flies in the cemetery but they are ordinary flies and dark grey in color, not green or blue flies like the ones in stables, which sometimes have a ruby-red snout, flies that shine just as though they were made of glass and which you can see right away are poisonous and very brave, no, the flies in the cemetery are like house flies, they are tame ordinary flies, boring and sticky flies. Turquoise knows that she can't run away, she'd like to but she can't, maybe after all it wouldn't really be worth while, the world is full of traps and poison, in some places there is a sign, hunting preserve, no trespassing, caution, traps and poison. The mosquitoes that fly over from the Abroñigal form dense aggressive clouds that attack with no respect for anybody, you can tell that they are fierce mosquitoes of a good breed, disciplined and very bold, maybe they're just hungry, blinded by hunger. If you are afraid to go to the urinal piss behind some tomb, you should not hesitate to piss behind some tomb, you don't do it with any bad intentions or wanting to offend, you just can't hold it in any more, you've been holding it in for a long time which is not good for your health either. Don Olegario Murciego did not invent the telegraph or the submarine that's true, how could he invent them when they were already invented?, is it his fault?, Don Olegario and Gregorio Montes usually win two or three pesetas each when they go to the dog races, Red Arab is some greyhound, you can bet on him with complete confidence, Don Olegario is learning shorthand, Gregorio Montes says that's silly, who would think of such a thing, *Shorthand in Fifteen Lessons*, by A. González Mediano, paperbound 6 pesetas, shorthand will guarantee you a secure and prosperous future, what foolishness! The street sweepers are more respectable than the hose men, the sweepers sweep without bumping into people but the hose men do their watering with bad intentions and jostling people around. In the cypresses the green finch and the blackbird sing and on the marble crosses the lead-colored sparrows, those bold and sociable urchins, play while the swallows chase insects in the air, it's not that the cemetery birds are familiar with death, they just don't know what death is, a band of wild doves flies off toward La Poveda and San Fernando del Jarama and on the other side of the walls, right where the fields begin, the quail trot along among the poppies, hugging the ground, the cemetery watchman raises a dozen and a half chickens that sometimes lift an earthworm in their beaks, they don't usually reach the worms that eat the dead, an occasional hen with bad habits lays her eggs among the graves and later, after not showing her face for twenty-one days, turns up with six or eight round and quick chicks that two or three months later taste delicious fried and in tomato sauce, people call them tomato chickens, it's like saying they're of a certain size. The oxen rule over the bulls and nobody wonders at that, the bulls are braver but the oxen are better versed in regulations and administrative law, you can't deny it, without knowing regulations and administrative law all you can be is a hero, it's all a trade-off, wisdom, heroism, and everything else, in exchange for your testicles knowledge and a place on the public payroll, in exchange for an arm or a leg glory and a little medal to hang on your lapel, people don't call the oxen capons which is what they are, they call them tame and, if they are solemn, wise and worthy, they don't call the lame and the maimed lame or maimed, nobody here speaks plain Spanish any more, they call them heroes and preach to them about the virtue of obedience, Dupont, established 1847, 10 rue Hautefeuille, Paris VI, by appointment manufacturer of every kind of furniture and device for the sick and wounded. You cannot see the worms of the cemetery, they crouch underground or in the niches and you can't even see them, the watchman's chickens can't stuff themselves on worms, they can't eat worms till they explode because they can't reach them no matter how much they scratch, the worms are very well hidden and protected, there must be millions of worms in the cemetery, the cemetery is crawling with worms, every tomb is a nest of worms with its very mysterious rhythm but you cannot see the worms, in the cemetery dissimulation prevails over everything else, men defend themselves by means of disguises, the living disguise the dead, that's well known, and then try not to think, maybe that's healthiest for all, in Spain the living are like the dead but without worms, when you come down to it it's all liturgy. Juanito Mateo is a reporter for *El Heraldo*, a street reporter, his girl, Leonorcita, is photophobically sexy, sexy in the dark, everyone follows his inclinations when and where he wants, nobody can argue with that, keep your hands to yourself Juanito, it'll be dark soon sweetheart. It is 9 A.M. and the cadres of the Socialist unions and the militias of the Communist Party and the United Socialist Youth march past the body of Lt. Castillo. Hold still, I tell you, Juan, later you can take me to the movies at the Carretas. The friends of Calvo Sotelo watch over his body in the chapel of the morgue, the legal proceedings are finished and the doors can be opened and the friends of Calvo Sotelo gather around his body. Earlier you said that it is easy to turn a young man into a murderer, you blow into his brain with a straw and you give him a pistol, the rest comes in due time, the opposite is also easy, to turn him into a dead man, to see how his life spills out through a blood-stained hole, at first the blood flows like water from a spring but soon it dries up, that's when the worry and the flight of ghosts begins, blood calls to blood blood is a good fertilizer for blood, blood breeds blood manufactures blood makes blood which afterward when it dries on the still-tender wound accuses us all even if we close our eyes it will do no good to close your eyes here that would be for Lent and this is a Carnival of blood in which we all wear a mask with splotches of blood, our own or someone else's, it's really all the same, the bad thing is the blood that is spilled outside its courses and that gradually loses its color and its motion, I murder or am murdered you murder or are murdered he murders or is murdered, it doesn't matter much, what's bad is the plural, we murder or are murdered you murder or are murdered they murder or are murdered, people don't usually attach much importance to memory and finally it crashes against a wall of impassive dead men, accusing dead men, stiff and impassive, people usually do not believe that memory acts as a ballast and keeps feelings on an even keel. Don't be so impatient, Juan, honey, don't be tiresome, why don't you behave?, there'll be time for us to love each other, sweetheart. The fritter vendors sell fritters and buns to the passersby and crullers strung on a reed to the housemaids. Gregorio Montes has a mole between his eyebrows and a scar on his chin, identifying marks, hair brown, eyes brown, mole between eyebrows, scar on chin. It's time to shave, now you can look at yourself in the mirror boldly, without dissembling, 44 photographs for private sale, a true motion picture played by lovely young persons against a background worthy of the Marquis de Sade, special printing on flesh-colored paper, this young lady looks like Toisha, she has a more sluttish face and is a little thinner but she looks like Toisha, with Toisha you could also take very good photos for private sale if she'd let you, all men carry in their breast a little bulb of glass which shatters into a thousand pieces at the slightest breath, the egg of giving in is hidden in this fragile bulb, some men give in by murdering, others by taking nude photographs of their girl (alone in artistic pose, man and woman in classic position, tableau of three or more), others by running like rabbits, etc., the lie that is almost true usually produces spots of verdigris on the liar, verdigris is a violent poison that brings about a very cruel death, a pitiless poison that lurks in coins and in kettles for making chocolate or puree of vetch, it's all the same, people lose their minds and are paralyzed from eating puree of vetch, you are quite sure that Toisha would not let herself be photographed in the nude even if you begged her on your knees, that's the limit, it's one thing to get in bed with a man, with one man and always the same one, and quite another to let people take your picture in the buff and leaning against a palm tree, that's indecent. Food stores and yarn shops open at nine more or less, it depends on whether or not the owner had a hard time getting up, but cafés open earlier and begin to serve breakfast while the cleaning women sweep the place in a cloud of dust, people like to dip fritters or crullers in their coffee some have a little glass of anise to settle the stomach, Matías from the commissary always has a glass of anise, if I don't have a little glass of anise in the morning my piss is cloudy, the doctor told me to watch my urine, anise must rinse out the kidneys, well yes, it probably does, anise is very hygienic and good for your health if you don't overdo it, well of course, if you overdo it it can harm you, that happens with anise and with everything, all excess eventually ruins your system, Turquoise's system is ruined, she's good-looking, yes, but she may not last much longer. The tomb of Pablo Iglesias is well cared for and decorated, with fresh flowers in the vase and all its gilding bright and shining, you can see they polish it with Sidol, the tomb of Pi y Margall, on the other hand, is dirty and full of thistles and weeds, it is very neglected and decrepit, Francisco Pi y Margall, April 29, 1824–November 29, 1901. Spain would not have lost her colonial empire had she followed his advice! Turquoise religiously pays her monthly dues to The Sunset, she is horrified by the thought of dying without leaving enough money for the inevitable final expenses. Some officials gather at the cemetery to attend the interment of Lt. Castillo, the Undersecretary of the Interior Mr. Ossorio y Tafall, who is there representing the minister, the Commissioner of Public Safety Mr. Alonso Mallol, the ex-minister Don Indalecio Prieto, the Mayor of Madrid Don Pedro Rico, and numerous deputies from the Popular Front, Muiño, Cordero, etc. Magdalena's system was even more ruined than Turquoise's, if the subway had not killed her she would have died on her own, the fact is she was already half rotten. Lt. Castillo's casket is draped in the red flag of the Provincial Committee of the Communist Party and as it proceeds along the pathways of the cemetery those present salute it with clenched fists. Magdalena's friend from Tangier, Aixa the Moor, the one with her navel tattooed with the solemn Spartacist motto, has a gold tooth and next to it another with a cavity as black as India ink. They bury the body of Lt. Castillo near the grave of Don Nicolás Salmerón, Alhama 1837–Paris 1908. He brought honor and glory to his country and to humanity, Clemenceau. He left office rather than confirm a death sentence. Lt. Col. Mangada, Don Julio Mangada, gives a speech, I swear before history and by my honor that this crime shall not remain unavenged, and the cortege breaks up without incident or fighting, some long-lives and down-withs are heard but there are no incidents. The sisters once raised a real ruckus at the tea dance that the Spinsters' Club gives on Thursdays and Saturdays at the Metropolitano, they couldn't think of a better thing to do than call the author of the club hymn a fairy, a gentleman who parts his hair in the middle and they say touches up his cheeks with a little rouge, the hymn is very beautiful and is sung to the tune of *Los campanilleros*, at the Spinsters' Club dances young folks have a ball, the best people go there, the band's finest of all. It is ten now and starting to get hot, the people are tired and get on the cemetery buses (they are the same as the station buses, the soccer buses, and the bullfight buses), some of them, the most loyal and prominent ones, have spent a sleepless night keeping watch over the body, when people are tired they smell in a special way, the sweat of tired men smells different, Magdalena Inmaculada Múgica did not smell like a tired woman, because she smelled like a dead woman, the one who does smell like a tired woman, a very tired woman, is Turquoise, it's hard to notice but it's true, ladies, you can protect your health with Perleucuterol perfumed douche, the trouble is that the perfume of the douche does not wipe out the treacherous smell of tiredness. In nature nothing is created or destroyed, it only takes on a new disguise, the carbon cycle is also very mysterious and instructive. Engracia gets to the mattress factory late but the manager doesn't say anything, he can imagine where she's been. Maripi has breakfast with her mother and then reads the *ABC*, her father and brother are at the cemetery, this is all going to blow up any minute, dear, no Mama, nothing's going to happen, you'll see, I hope to God you're right, dear, I hope to God you're right! A moving funeral always ends in astonishment, suddenly everything is over and the participants are astonished and quite apprehensive and fearful, things always end too suddenly and people, accustomed to surprises and strong feelings, are surprised that their feelings should vanish like an animal that dies without protesting, there's usually no solution for that, the cattle that die in the slaughterhouse do not protest (only the pigs protest, they scream their heads off) and neither does the bird shot down by the hunter. The aroma of crime is intoxicating but also soporific, criminals act like sleepwalkers who are hypnotized by stripes painted on the wall, not quite parallel stripes and concentric circles, they drew a mustache on the body of King Cyril of England with a charred stick, you would have died laughing, his knights died laughing and some even wet their pants, they would not have dared to draw a mustache on Napoleon Bonaparte with a charred stick even when he was dead, Napoleon Bonaparte was a little fellow but very fierce and did not take any jokes from his knights or from anyone. Miguel Mercader's head aches less now, the doctor ordered him to stay in bed and Miguel Mercader entertains himself by reading novels by Baroja, the trilogy *The Struggle for Life*, that damned Baroja is funny, he's sort of a grouch but he's funny and a good observer. You dream that you drive down the stone stairs of a garden in a small car and with a good-looking showy maid at your side, the maid is scared and holds on to your neck, she hardly lets you breathe, when you get to the bottom the maid is still holding on to you, you tell her, you were afraid and now you're hot, she says yes and you kiss, the maid has more saliva than anybody and you squeeze her and suck up her saliva, when you wake up you've just come, your Uncle Horacio the brother-in-law of your Uncle Jerónimo has his little goings-on with his maid Lola Iglesias who lets herself be petted out of respect and also for money, your Aunt Octavia his wife never dreams of that, the fact is that even if she found them necking she wouldn't believe it, your Aunt Octavia is like a hen stuffed with piety and can't even make out what she sees with her own eyes, there are some very bad people in this world Horacio, just imagine, killing that young officer and that deputy who spoke so well!, well dear, don't you worry, nothing's going to happen to us. They leave Magdalena in the common grave without much fuss and bother, you should have paid for a response for her but the truth is you didn't even find out the time, you were very busy driving the maid around the garden, the dead who go into the common grave are not buried at any special time but in between times when there is a break in the other work, order is a very necessary thing in a cemetery, the car bounces down the stairs and the maid laughs and shouts, not high hysterical shouts but enticing shouts in a low voice, it is very exciting to hear a maid shout with the right kind of voice, your Aunt Octavia thinks that maids are only good for work, your Uncle Horacio has a broader view of the matter. The hills covered with vegetation that stand out against the horizon are velvety black, from the cemetery you do not see hills covered with vegetation but the stark naked plain and in the midst of the plain a peasant riding a donkey, you can hardly make him out, there are two kinds of flowers in the cemetery, some that dry up on the ground and others that rot in bouquets on top of the tombs, they all die but in different ways, some quietly and others in pain, a little stray dog pisses on an R.I.P. and then trots off among the graves, when he stops he lifts one paw and pricks up his ears, no doubt he is heeding the strange signals that you neither see nor hear, dogs see and hear events that men never notice, man is a very clumsy and habit-bound animal that thinks, yes, but that neither sees nor hears, man has a very cruel and melancholy heart that is no good for driving away death, the truth is it's hardly good for anything, the gravediggers usually take off their caps when the priest is reading his responses, if you had paid for a response for Magdalena Inmaculada Múgica the gravedigger would have let you strip her to smell her for the last time, try to weep, and to steal her panties or some other piece of her underwear, but you were negligent, you were embracing the maid in the garden and you were negligent, infidelity has its price. The chapel at the morgue is packed to bursting, as the morning goes on more people keep arriving, some are very well known, the Count de Vallellano, the Count de Rodezno, Goicoechea, Gil Robles, Cid, Fuentes Pila, others are less known. Always stay with Tránsito and always call her Toisha, you have no better defense against loneliness, the lonely die bitterly at last and without a struggle, always call her Toisha, dressed or undressed, today is Tuesday, it's your day to take off her clothes in Merceditas' place, always call her Toisha so as never to feel too lonely. They shroud Calvo Sotelo's body in a Capuchin's robe and put a crucifix on his chest and a rosary between his hands, those accompanying the body recite the rosary and some go out to smoke a cigarette and get some air, a few gesticulate and talk without stopping but the majority stand in silence, in the full sun silence weighs even more heavily than in the shade. At the conclusion of the Evian-Aix-les-Bains stage of the Tour de France, the ranking of the Spanish cyclists is as follows, Mariano Cañardo, 23, Julián Berrendero, 38, Federico Ezquerra, 42, Emiliano Álvarez, 48, and Salvador Molina, 53, things are going pretty well, they've all moved up a little. About 4 P.M. a delegation of the bar association headed by its president Don Melquíades Álvarez arrives at the cemetery, the cigarette man Senén does not go to either of the funerals, he is a republican but he does not go to either of the funerals, what for?, well I don't know, to show solidarity, to protest, to make things clear, what do I know!, you have to live in society, well, I live for myself, nobody gives me something for nothing, if Don Gerardo lays out for my supper it's so I'll dance with Ginesa for him, in this world every man looks out for himself, I've got no reason to go to the cemetery, is that clear, no reason at all, I don't like to see people get killed but then I don't like it either if they get me into a mess, let everybody look out for himself. Three more delegations attend Calvo Sotelo's funeral, from the Academy of Jurisprudence, the Administrative Law Division, and the parliament, the latter consists of the secretary Mr. de la Bandera and the chief clerk Don Luis Sanmartín, who are booed, especially by the ladies, and have to withdraw, their intentions were good but when tempers are aroused it's prudent to avoid arguments, Don Vicente Parreño talks to the Bold Knight, he is a writer he greatly admires and also a brave man capable of going at it cane in hand against anybody, Don Vicente Parreño would gladly be like the Bold Knight but his constitution just won't let him. No, you are not Saint Paul nor the Cid nor Napoleon Bonaparte, but neither are you King Cyril of England or Pepito la Zubiela or Matiítas, you are an ordinary man, more afraid than brave with more aches than health more reluctance than will more memory than talent, pretty much the same is true of Don Vicente, Buffalo Bill was the king of the prairies, neither you nor Don Vicente Parreño could ever have been Buffalo Bill, for the Bold Knight wanting it would have been all it took, disguise your fear as grief, never as wrath, every disguise involves sorrow but the disguise of wrath is also usually spattered with shit spattered with blood, the disguise of wrath is very bitter and polluting, disguise your panic as bitterness, never as pride, and masturbate assiduously in the most mysterious and forgotten, most humid and uninhabitable corner, only thus will you be able to placate the infinite contempt of the gods, man is a contemptible, fearful, and wrathful animal that disguises itself because it is afraid of company, when alone it is more honest. Don Estanislao Montañés the friend of the whore who committed suicide orders a brandy to counteract his fear, coffee?, no thanks, just brandy, a double brandy. In the cemetery, within the cemetery grounds and in the neighborhood, foot and mounted units of the Civil Guard are on duty. Captain Condé is from the Civil Guard, but nevertheless Gutiérrez the waiter at La Granja El Henar feels uneasy, a kind of odd sadness floats in the air and although they keep quiet about it people are afraid, some, very few, disguise their fear as grief, and the rest maybe to build up their courage disguise their fear as wrath (holy wrath, civic wrath, purely external wrath, the wrath of hands, of canes, of firearms, a wrath that attacks and that cannot forgive because fear grows with fear, feeds on fear, burns with fear itself). A little after five the cortege gets under way, it moves very slowly, the body proceeds on the shoulders of Carlist deputies and others from Renovación Española and as it goes by those present salute it with upraised arms. The little eyes of Julianín, Gregorio Montes' cousin, turn lustful when he serves vermouths to the prostitutes, a man's greatest happiness is to look at the rise of a woman's breasts and if he's allowed carefully to run his finger over it so much the better, there's nothing like the skin women have at the rise of their breasts, so soft and slippery, it's a pleasure, but they won't let you, women just look out for themselves and laugh at the poor, they're just wicked sluts that only want to see men spend their money, spend, spend till they're left without a penny and have to walk back home, women just want to be treated to vermouths and amber cigarette holders, then they smile and let themselves be touched, women are always in a hurry, it's as though they were made of water. It takes them at least half an hour to leave Calvo Sotelo's body in the appointed place, section 9, block 2, the leader of Renovación Española Don Antonio Goicoechea gives a speech, I swear before God and by Spain that this crime shall not remain unavenged, people make very solemn and dangerous statements in the cemetery, today is a day of solemn and dangerous burials, the dead are always solemn (the living disguise their fear as solemnity), martyrs are always dangerous (the living disguise their fear by defying danger), it's his mouth that kills the fish and man is gripped and shaken by his own words. Don Gerardo only dances the pasodoble and he doesn't like that much either, the cigarette man Senén is his delegate to dance with Ginesa, it's a good idea to tire women out a little so they'll sweat and grow soft, Don Gerardo thinks women are like goats, creatures that have tough meat, it's a pleasure to see a goat or a woman jump, the bad part is trying to bite into one without further ado, suddenly and without marinating her first, women should be treated very respectfully and considerately and denied nothing, they want to have supper?, well get them a supper, with dessert, vintage wine, coffee, and crème de menthe, it's no good to try to save money here, they want a ring with an aquamarine or a ruby?, well buy them a ring with an aquamarine or a ruby, you say they want a ring with an emerald or a diamond?, then tell them no, they're not in that league and to be still and stop bothering, they want to dance?, make a signal and the cigarette man Senén dances the foxtrot with them and the tango or whatever they play, you have to humor women, you have to be gallant with women and treat them well. In Valladolid Juanita Cruz the lady bullfighter got a warning, it's in the paper, the fact is she had bad luck with the cattle that turned out on the tame side, Amanda Ordóñez likes her better than Enriqueta Palmeño, she's tops!, and the other one Beatriz Santullano, who fights from horseback and rides, God Almighty couldn't do it better, she looks like a centauress, you can't say centauress, well, an amazon, dykes have a wonderful time applauding the mounted bullfighters, Amanda Ordóñez is no dyke let that be clear, she'll go for both fish and fowl, the Assault Guards also ride very well, worse than the bullfighters but very well, they've had a lot of practice, at Las Ventas some Assault Guards are in reserve for what might happen, they seem tranquil but are nervous, there are days when everybody is nervous, days when you light a match and everything goes up in flames, evidently there are some days more combustible than others, perhaps it's the phases of the moon you don't quite know, or strong tides whose effect is felt even far inland, your Uncle Jerónimo says that the rulers are to blame for the nervousness of the ruled, maybe he's right, nerves are as contagious as the itch and the rulers have the obligation not to cough or spit little spiders of mange on the ruled, when the rulers have the itch the whole country winds up scratching. Guillermo Zabalegui caught some king-sized crabs from his Aunt Mimí, she should be ashamed to be so distinguished and such a pig, crabs do not produce disease but they itch as though they did, they itch terribly. There are clashes and skirmishes between the Assault Guards and those who attended the funeral of Calvo Sotelo, near Las Ventas, before you get to the excise tax office, blood was spilled, more blood than necessary, there were dead and wounded, some say one dead and others say four, when people are nervous they kill and die more quickly than when they are calm. Don't put on a special face to look at yourself in the mirror or for your ID photo, keep your natural face and don't twist your mouth as though you'd had a stroke, be natural, above all natural, just as in calisthenics, be natural and keep up the rhythm, no brusque movements, look at yourself in the mirror without grimacing, you know very well that it's hard but you must master it. The worms have not yet begun to tear at the muscles of Magdalena's face, the muscles of her forehead, of her eyes, of the corners of her mouth, to laugh at the grimaces that no one will see, not even they, which are totally blind and totally in the dark, it would be interesting to make a film of the face of the dead, minute by minute, to study their useless and gratuitous grimaces. Look at yourself in the mirror naturally and without making faces and grimaces like the dead and then flee as fast as you can, it doesn't matter if you flee recklessly and aimlessly, you are fleeing the spatters of death, the spatters of blood, the spatters of shit, and it matters little that you crash against the wall, frightened insects also crash against the wall and hardly make a sound, they fall like rapid shadows, flutter a bit and then suddenly are still, alive or not, dead or pretending to be dead, until the wind sweeps them away and takes them where no one keeps evidence of their death or their pretense, the hell of insects is less complicated than that of men, it is more empty but more merciful, man is so naive and proud as to believe that there is no hell other than his, the other animals disappear when they die and for them there is no valley of Jehoshaphat or resurrection of the body, neither for them nor for black dwarfs, who could imagine the valley of Jehoshaphat full of black dwarfs ignorant of regulations?, no, no, for some time now treachery has been appreciated, yes, but not rewarded, that was before, when men could still repent a hundred times and die of old age and in their beds, flee from here before it is too late, every minute you waste is a minute's advantage you give to the world, that hostile poisonous pack, and the world takes enough advantages already on its own, flee from here and don't waste a single moment putting on a special face, no one will smile at you in pity. All of Gabriel Seseña's teeth are loose, pyorrhea is a bad disease that destroys the teeth and causes nausea and bad breath, Turquoise has a strong stomach and is very patient, perhaps the only thing she is is afraid, this is no time to go taking risks and moving around from one place to another, the best thing is to hold still and wait for the storm to die down, no trouble lasts a hundred years, unfortunately there are no men and women that last a hundred years either, well, there are only very few and the few that there are take good care of themselves and lead healthy lives, death is like a gate that blocks the road, it's not very high but neither can you jump over it because when the time comes your legs don't obey you and your heart doesn't react either, women are very superstitious and paralyzed and jump with difficulty and awkwardly, Turquoise prefers to be still and close her eyes, Turquoise does not mind kissing Gabriel Seseña, she even likes it, and moving his teeth with her tongue, they are looser by the day, Turquoise is very submissive and lets herself be loved without any reverence, hunger is worse, and without protesting, Gabriel's gratitude expresses itself in whippings, on her birthday he shit between her tits and made her sleep on the floor for being a slut, a wretch, and a pig, that's what he told her, Turquoise kept quiet and cried to herself, then she fell asleep, come on, come on up here you poor trash, boy, if I didn't love you the way I do!, come on, wipe the shit off on the bedspread, Gabriel Seseña has to go to the dentist, he's been planning to do it for some time, but one thing depends on another and there are lots of faggots loose at La Cigale Parisién and the police could show up any moment and close the place. At 3:30 P.M. people are usually at home listening to the radio or taking a little nap in the rocking chair, some funerals attract a lot of people, today is a day when the cemetery is full of people, first some and then others, at 3:30 P.M. it's hot and people are not out on the street, it's Tuesday and you're waiting for Toisha at the Sevilla subway station, it's 3:30 P.M. and Toisha comes in medium heels, with hardly any makeup on and with her mane of hair pulled back, you don't say a word to each other, she goes ahead with you five or six paces behind her, you start up the Calle de Peligros and when you get to the Calle de la Aduana Toisha turns the corner, you go three or four paces behind her, you catch up with her right at the door, sweetheart, the things you make me do, I'm trembling! no dear . . . , you and Toisha already kiss in the doorway of Merceditas' place and then you spend the afternoon in bed loving each other decorously, Toisha is more decorous than you, in fact Toisha is more decorous than anybody. Don Estanislao Montañés is sort of sad, what's the matter with you?, you look sort of sad, me?, no, nothing's the matter thank you very much, I'm worried that's all, things are starting to look very ugly. La Tropical is on the same block as Merceditas' place, Don Leoncio Romero has a cup of coffee and takes his cough medicine, today the hardware on his leg weighs more than ever, what a nuisance it is to creak like a streetcar when you walk! Government suspends sessions of parliament. Effective this date the sessions of parliament are suspended for a period of one week. El Pardo, July 14, 1936. Manuel Azaña. The Prime Minister, Santiago Casares. Doña María Luisa who manages the house at 3 Naciones in tandem with Doña Margarita suffers from certain female ailments like almost every other woman in the world, some from one cause and some from another, Chaumel ovule capsules with actiol, recommended by leading specialists as the most effective remedy for every kind of irregularity and illness of a woman's special (genital) organs. The city is like a dog and like a hare, it licks the hand that beats it and also shudders openly and in terror at the impulse of both true and false whims, if cities could flee not one city would be left in the world, but cities cannot flee, they don't know how either, cities are like dogs with no sense of smell or like asthmatic and lame hares, sometimes you have thought that cities can at least drag themselves away, but that's wrong, cities do not flee, they suffocate, they devour themselves, they dissolve like lumps of sugar in coffee, but they do not flee, they die stranded in the same place where they were born, at most a little closer to the river or the highway. Don Nicolás Mañes greases and repairs Don Leoncio Romero's orthopedic leg free of charge, you don't charge a friend for such a trifling service, it's not worth while, Don Estanislao Montañés says that Don Nicolás is very generous and correct but that Don Leoncio on the other hand is nothing but an ungrateful and ill-tempered cripple, maybe he's right. Historical figures must be seen from a distance, they lose a lot from close up, about this time, on the Place de la Bastille, Marat, Robespierre, and Victor Hugo give lessons from their portraits to the Parisians who parade with an insignia or a little flag on their lapels, the reason the world gets no better is that people like to parade with their insignias and their little flags, things would improve if the quarrel were between those who are fond of this kind of show and those who aren't, the trouble is that people like parades and hubbub, the only thing they change is the insignias and little flags, you can tell that that gives them more strength or at least so they think, Matiítas would be less afraid if he could walk around with an insignia on his lapel without getting his teeth knocked out, now they knock your teeth out at the slightest slip and Matiítas doesn't want to take any chances and right he is, they knock your teeth out and afterward you get neither thanks nor pay for it. The extreme state of despair is that of the man who fears death so much that he lives scared to death because he doesn't know how and when he is to die, some finally kill themselves in some atrocious way to put an end to this doubt, fear is bad company, painful and bitter company that you can't just leave like an umbrella or a fetus, the extreme state of despair is that of the dying man who would like to have been already dead for many years and can't be because his heart keeps on wetting its wings with its half cynical, half shamefaced rhythm. No, don't turn your face away, it will do you no good, memory is a planet from which no one, not even we ourselves, will ever be able to drive us away, in a moment of decision you can take your life or also in a moment of indecision, but no matter how tiny the memory of you, you will never be able to wipe it from the memory of others or at least from the memory of someone, a sick whore, a most loving mother, a faithless wife, a friend who lent you twenty-five pesetas, your romantic girlfriend, the policeman who always looked at you askance, a beggar who plays the accordion, etc., in the Bible it says that deep calls to deep, one can walk at the edge of the deep but not on a web spun of the deep, take your fill of loving Toisha naked and then when you are again alone close your eyes to feel still alive and touching her, let others be the ones who kill themselves, you don't want to die, you'd like to live forever, you are sick and very thin but you don't want to die, no, not at all, what you want to do is go to bed with Toisha or with whoever will let you and recite verses by Fray Luis and Antonio Machado, you also like to look at people and make strange faces at them so they'll take you for an idiot, it's very relaxing to limp along with one arm pulled up like an idiot, your Uncle Jerónimo does not believe in God but he reads the saints, according to St. Anselm the man who thinks about death does not die suddenly, that's true enough and applies to everything (maybe it doesn't apply to everything), hatred calls to hatred and is suckled by hatred, hatred does not strangle hatred but nourishes and invigorates it, love calls to love and is suckled by love, love does not strangle love but nourishes and invigorates it, the day that men and women will love each other in broad daylight in parks and in the middle of the street many a deep abyss of hatred, lust, and tedium will be closed over, some day they will form the worthy order of whores of charity, who will dedicate their lives to offering to the weak and wounded not resignation and patience but that which no one offers them, kisses on their mouths and a stark naked body on which they can indulge themselves as though they were not sick and crippled, perhaps it will not even take centuries for this to happen, if people believed in the existence of the soul and the equality of souls we would all find it quite reasonable that the blind and the paralyzed and the idiots should also want to sleep in the arms of a naked woman. At the Rosales Jai-Alai they play two games in the afternoon, Lolín and Mirenchu against Filo and Fermina, and Paz and Emil against Angelines and Elena, and another two in the evening, Juanita and Poli against Filo and Concha, and Paquita and Vasquita against Carmenchu and Lolilla, the players are very well built and are agile, young, and strong, on the other hand their boyfriends are rather sickly and extremely carefully combed, it's hard to explain unless it's that they dance very well and play billiards like angels, Toisha is a friend of Mirenchu's and sometimes you go together to the Rosales to see her play, sometimes she wins and others she loses, Toisha would have liked to be a jai-alai player, she's told you that more than once, but she doesn't even dare to tell her father, he'd never go for that. Perhaps it won't be as long as people think before beautiful healthy women go looking for ugly, weak, and deformed men, the liquidation of seducers could happen any time, all that's needed for this liberation of woman is for some obsessions, some habits, to burn, people don't usually connect lust with compassion and that way of thinking is mistaken, the time will come when this will be evident, you can't talk to Toisha about these things because she wouldn't understand them, neither would her friend the ballplayer Mirenchu, women are capable of anything except permitting a change of habits. Engracia and Agustín meet after work as usual, Engracia and Agustín rarely depart from their routine, Engracia looks very bad, she is pale with rings under her eyes, which burn as though she'd been crying, would you like to go to the movies for a while?, no, I'd rather take a walk and get some air, I'm very tired. The body of Juanita Rico is buried behind the tomb of Pablo Iglesias, in a simple grave, Juanita Rico Hernández, June 21, 1934, aged 20 years, you think they killed Juanita Rico on the tenth, you could almost swear to that, but the marker says 21, Juanita Rico was a friend of Engracia's, on Sundays they went to the mountains together and sometimes they also got together in Madrid during the week, the death of Juanita Rico and of her brother, they also killed her brother, made a great impression on Engracia and kept her sleepless, nervous, and feverish for five or six days, since then she tires frequently and gets short of breath as though she were asthmatic, it doesn't last long but she has to go out to get air, the doctor tells her it's nerves and that she'll get over it as soon as she's married, the doctor doesn't know what he's talking about because in the sense that he means it Engracia is already married and more than married, Engracia was a witness to the murder of Juanita Rico, they were coming from the mountains in the same bus and they killed her from a moving car as soon as she stepped on the sidewalk. No one, not even those who commit suicide, chooses his death, but death flies above the heads of everyone striking out blindly, death does not choose those who die either, it's enough for it to point its finger at them even without looking at them, one dead man is the same as the next for death. They didn't kill Miguel Mercader, if they'd hit him a little more accurately they would have killed him, evidently death had not pointed its finger at him, it passed close by him but did not point at him, does your head hurt?, not as much, the doctor says I've got to stay in bed two or three days. After King Cyril of England died they painted the tip of his nose with white lead and his cheeks with tile dust, and they stuck a carrot in his mouth, his knights split their sides laughing and some even wet their pants, some things are really funny, you can't deny that. Juanito Mateo is tireless, if Leonorcita drops her guard for a moment there he is with his hands on her, hold off a little, sweetheart, haven't you had enough?, *The Physical, Intellectual and Moral Education of Children*, by the Abbé Simon, Supervisor of Family Education for the Most Rev. Bishop of Namur (Published with Permission of Superiors), Juanito Mateo is not concerned about the Abbé Simon's sermons or anyone else's, what he wants is to make out with Leonorcita, any time is the right time if she lets him, if I give you the eighty céntimos will you treat me to a vermouth?, all right. Don't get distracted looking at the flies drowning in coffee dregs, flies die all sorts of deaths, some drown in a glass of water, some in a urinal full of piss, some in a cup of broth, if you put them in a vacuum jar they suffocate because they get no air, a bird would suffocate just the same and a mouse and a newborn baby girl, in a sufficiently large vacuum jar you could execute condemned criminals very neatly and cheaply, you deprive them of air and that's that. Napoleon Bonaparte's body was treated with more respect than that of King Cyril of England, no one played any jokes on Napoleon Bonaparte's body, not jokes in bad taste or innocent jokes or jokes of any kind, people stood quietly looking at the body and it never occurred to anyone to play jokes on it, this playing of jokes is something that winds up turning into a bad habit but there are always exceptions, among those who have a bad habit there is a kind of solidarity that no one dares to upset, a chain binds life to death and not a single link of that chain can be dispensed with, all of humanity would crack its collective skull. For 1.70 Juanito Mateo eats soup, a couple of eggs, steak and potatoes, bread, wine, and dessert, La Marina on the Calle del Barco is a very reasonably priced restaurant, when he doesn't have the 1.70 Leonorcita gives it to him, if he contracted for his board it would cost him less than 1.40 but the trouble is he'd have to pay all at one time, life is always more expensive for the poor than for the rich. Don Olegario keeps accounts for Mr. Félix García the charcoal dealer on the Calle de la Cabeza, he does it out of friendship but he accepts the 1.50 and the glass of wine that he gets every Saturday without fail, select oak charcoal four eighty-pound bags at 5 pesetas delivered, 20 pesetas, firewood seven eighty-pound bags at 2.50, 17.50, common slack twelve eighty-pound bags at 3 pesetas, 36 pesetas, retail sales at 25 and 50 céntimos for coal and 10 for slack, coal 12 pesetas, slack 27.80, total barring error 113.30, Don Olegario has a beautiful handwriting and the coal dealer is satisfied with him, he's a gentleman, a real gentleman, he always tells his friends, it's a pleasure to deal with serious people who do dependable work. Gil Robles meets with the members of his party at the CEDA headquarters, on the Calle de Serrano on the right-hand side as you first get to it, some deputies of the Agrarian Party, two or three from Renovación Española, and another couple of independents also take part in the discussions, things are moving very fast and we have to keep a close watch on developments, fifteen or twenty members of the CEDA youth movement provide security. Indalecio Prieto meets with the Socialist deputies in the office of Muiño, the secretary of the House of the People, on the Calle de Piamonte down by Barquillo, several deputies from the Communist Party, the Party of the Republican Left, the Republican Union, and the Catalonian Left are also present, there are well-founded rumors that the Army is preparing for a coup which will perhaps be moved up with the murder of Calvo Sotelo and we must be ready and maintain the solidarity of the Popular Front, a dozen and a half members of the United Socialist Youth provide security. Lerroux's Radicals, Alcalá Zamora's Progressives, and Portela Valladares' Centrists all go about their normal business or meet at a café or at the house of some friend. No one chooses himself, some are lucky in this and others unlucky, Narcissus did not choose himself, he was satisfied with himself and rested his love on that satisfaction, each one of you can become a Narcissus, history is full of Narcissuses, you just have to find yourselves handsome and capable of receiving love, the most pure and disinterested love is that which is felt for himself by a man looking at himself in the mirror, contemplating himself stripped in the mirror, masturbating or committing suicide in front of the mirror, taking a little mirror in his hand (when his family has already begun to weep most respectfully) in order not to miss even the least and last gesture of his own dying. Look at yourself in the mirror and do not smile, stay calm, death has drawn its skull and crossbones on your mirror with its chalk, do not erase them with your breath and a handkerchief or the sleeve of your jacket, it is the sign of those of you who are going to die and it will do you no good to run away, do not close your eyes, contemplate your full and true (or full and false) image in the mirror, take advantage of your being as though hypnotized, just like a chicken into whose eyes you gazed fixedly for a minute or two, a miracle can always be expected from an idiot, the miracle is not likely to occur but you must not give up that hope.

Part Two St. Camillus' Day

To Madrid now go we must;

All of us shall turn to dust.

—Cristóbal de Castillejo,

On the Court's Voyage to Madrid

There are bloodstains on the windshield, on the seats, and on the floor, they cover the three corpses with tarpaulins, the authorities will take off the tarps, two rich boys and a whore accidentally killed in a black Dodge that smashes against a lamppost on Alcalá at the corner of Cibeles across from the Bank of Spain, may they rest in peace and may the autopsy rest lightly upon them, amen. It's 7 A.M., maybe it's not yet 7 A.M. and Don León Rioja is sleeping like a log next to Doña Matilde his paralyzed wife whose butt is cold, you can tell that Don León is already used to it and doesn't even notice, Doña Matilde's butt is always cold, the warmth, 99, 99.1, 99.5, usually goes to her forehead, Doña Matilde's forehead is even colder than her butt, Doña Matilde will never again be able to listen to the record with the holy sacrifice of the mass that her spiritual director gave her, Don León doesn't find out that Doña Matilde has died until eight, Don León wakes up every morning at eight, turns on the radio to listen to the news, shaves, gets dressed, has breakfast, and goes to work, Don León works in a notary's office and is a serious, peaceful, and hard-working man, today he doesn't turn on the radio because when he goes to look at his wife he realizes that her mouth is twisted like a dead woman's, live people's mouths twist in another way, he touches her forehead and it's ice cold, those are the two signs of death, there's no need to listen to her heart. A death close by is a comforting thing, everybody thinks that and some even say it, sometimes the comforted person cries, it's inertia, yes, repentance that appears just a bit before pride, everybody knows that things always get back to normal sooner or later, it's all the same, in the midst of the multitude one can speak to God, you know that it's hard but not impossible, it's God who orders lives and deaths, the devil is more in favor of solitude and among the crowd there are usually many lonely men with a cold butt (not as cold as the women's), with a cold forehead (not as cold as Doña Matilde's or that of other dead people), with a cold heart (the heart should never be satisfied), with a cold cock (beaten down by the years, too), the reasons of the lonely man are useless and poisonous, and his needs and vague whims, his stiffness, are sad. Don León isn't listening to the radio, he's just found out that his wife has slipped quietly away, but the radio is working, it sure is working, Radio Unión gives its first newscast *La Palabra* at eight when almost everybody is asleep, another criminal attack against the Republic has been thwarted . . . part of our Army in Morocco has taken up arms . . . the movement is exclusively limited to a few cities in our Moroccan protectorate and no one in Spain itself, absolutely no one, has joined this absurd undertaking . . . the government is in control of the situation and declares that it will soon be able to announce the reestablishment of normal conditions. Never lose respect for yourself, you're nothing but a poor devil corroded by lust and tuberculosis, some are worse off but that shouldn't comfort you the least bit, if you were surrounded by happy faces your tuberculosis would soon clear up, but no, you're not surrounded by happy faces, lust does not have a happy face because it is the consequence of solitude and sadness, tuberculosis is the corollary of solitude and sadness and not vice versa, it's not true that lust and tuberculosis breed solitude and sadness, solitude and sadness are the feelings that feed lust and tuberculosis, try to get it clear, the solitary and sad man winds up lustful, consumptive, and a poet, but the process doesn't necessarily work in reverse. Don Roque has breakfast in bed: garlic soup, fried bread dunked in hot chocolate, and a little glass of brandy, if he's in the mood he takes a poke at Paulina or Javiera, each week one serves while the other empties the urinals and sweeps up the dust, Paulina and Javiera always have the radio on, they turn it off when the news comes on, it's a bore, Don Roque is a creature of habit and every day with his breakfast he reads *El Debate* and *ABC* and then takes his time getting ready, he gargles with Listerine just so he won't be having bad breath and goes out for a stroll on the Carrera de San Jerónimo and the Paseo del Prado till about eleven-thirty or twelve, when he stops by parliament to see whether there's anything new, from parliament he heads for La Granja El Henar to have a beer or two and get a shoeshine, and before lunch he stops by Lhardy for a cup of broth to get his stomach ready. Women don't have the same color in the morning that they have in the afternoon, they smell different, too, and have different inclinations. The maid who miscarried on the Calle de Mesón de Paredes, that is, Evelina Castellote, maybe nobody said before what her name was, is all right again in no time, by the next day she's scrubbing floors again and within two days she's singing hits from the radio, I'm of the Gypsy race, the race that rules the land, my father was a Gypsy, and royal Gypsy blood runs through my Gypsy hand, and she casts a favorable eye on the milkman, the baker, and the mailman, some women never learn, Evelina got pregnant in her village and came to the capital to miscarry, here it's easier to patch up things that aren't so easy to fix in the village, La Maravilla, natural mineral water from Coslada, not just another laxative, the best, analyzed and recommended by Dr. Ramón y Cajal, they play this commercial on the radio, too, after the pasodoble for Casa Carmena, I'm going to marry a brunette, and from Carmena my coat I'll get, Carmena?, Carmena is the tailor for the upper class, his suits and coats you can't surpass, 4 Duque de Alba and 24 Príncipe, when you miscarry you should have a glass of Carabaña water or La Maravilla water or laxative lemonade, Jesualdo Villegas, who works for the radio, pats Evelina's fanny, he pats her fanny in a refined way and sort of off-handedly, the fact is that patting a maid's fanny doesn't mean anything beyond what you want to make of it, Jesualdo Villegas is awakened by a call from his paper, come over here right away, there's an Army rebellion in Morocco. You'd think a tsetse fly had stung Enriqueta, Enriqueta is on an all-nighter with a gentleman from Ciudad Real who spends the night letting farts that crackle like the snap of a whip (very odd farts in two beats that end with a brief solemn coda), but Enriqueta doesn't even notice, that's the way to be!, deep sleep is the reward of a conscience at peace, you have no reason to doubt it. Yunquera is a town in the district of Ronda in the province of Malaga, the Civil Guard of Yunquera arrests three counterfeiters, Miguel Sánchez Canca, Antonio Gil Díaz, and Juan Rodríguez Díaz, alias Threefoot's Grandson, they were making ten-céntimo pieces that turned out pretty well, they were almost identical to the real thing, people say a mighty lord is Mister Money, the trouble comes when they ask you where you got it. They didn't kill Marujita Expósito for money but out of jealousy and to play tough, a whore's boyfriend will put up with whatever they throw at him till one day he has two drinks too many and feels like an offended gentleman, honor shines with such a showy and violent gleam that it blinds those whom it invades, it's very hard to draw the exact line between honor and a spattering of shit on your self-esteem, man is a peaceful and resigned animal that puts up with the most shameful things and then blows up at a trifle, any excuse is good enough for your own consumption, the trouble is the stream of blood with which the excuses stain consciences and newspapers, Leonardo Álvarez Maderero, Marujita's boyfriend, was no worse than the rest, what happened is that the impulse seized him just at the moment when he had forgotten his peacefulness, if you want a peaceful romance it's not good to be forgetful because you wind up killing yourself in jail. The cripple who sells tobacco (maybe he's a hero of some war) has no name or he doesn't want to tell his name, in the neighborhood they call him Marramáu, which doesn't mean anything either for or against him, when a boy gives him the finger and yells at him, up your ass, Marramáu, the cripple swears out loud and throws stones at him, Marramáu always carries stones in his pockets to defend himself, afterward he mutters may God forgive me and counts his change to keep busy and drive away bad thoughts, every morning his daughter Pilar takes Marramáu to his corner, she's a cleaning woman and could have been a whore but she just didn't want to, she wraps his legs in a blanket, says so long father, good luck, and goes off. Get dressed slowly, imagine that today you're not going to class, maybe it's true that today you're not going to class, it's too bad they don't play tangos on the radio at this time of day, get dressed slowly and without excessive modesty, take off your pajama pants once you're in the bathroom, it's at the far end of the apartment, sit down on the toilet, one, two, three, out, put your pajama pants back on, now take off the top, wash your hands and face, brush your teeth and comb your hair, you have to get rid of the habit of washing with your clothes on like an old man or a heart patient, put on your pajama top and go back to your room, you know, on the other side of the apartment at the end of the hall, then close the door and remain completely naked, you look good in the mirror, a little thin but handsome, if you twist your mouth you look like an idiot, if you stick your tongue between your upper lip and the gum you look like a monkey, if you cross your eyes you get a little headache, they threw Miguel Mercader out of Doña Valentina's whorehouse, it's funny, really, Doña Valentina is very fond of the radio, what she likes best is the soap operas, and then, poor Miguel, what a day he had, they cracked his skull, it doesn't hurt him any more, it's a good thing, now put on your undershirt, it's pretty ridiculous, the shorts should go on first, for you and everybody, it's elegant to wear shorts and no undershirt but not the other way around, a man in an undershirt with no shorts looks odd and silly, if you're alone it doesn't matter, you are alone and it doesn't matter, there's nobody in the mirror, either, except you, the trouble is when you dress or undress in front of a woman or some friend, then you've got to be more orderly, put on your shorts, being sensible isn't being low and modesty is not always perverseness, it doesn't have to be perverseness, now you've got your undershirt and your shorts on. Lupita and Juani probably aren't getting up yet, their TB gives them a good excuse. Dámaso Rioja has breakfast with his mother lying there dead, Don León is grieving and doesn't listen to the radio or shave or get dressed or have breakfast or go to work, Don León is still in his dressing gown, it's a bit old but still good enough, and Dámaso phones the notary's office to say that they shouldn't be surprised by his father's absence from work, our heartfelt sympathy, thank you very much, once Don Feliciano is here we'll drop by your place to express our condolences, thank you very much, what time is the burial?, we don't know yet, we'll be sure to tell you, no, don't worry, again, our most heartfelt sympathy, thank you very much, you're welcome, good-bye, good-bye, Don León's office mates don't listen to the radio in the morning, they get up just in time and get to the office before they've even quite shaken off their sleepiness. The Mediterranean front against Italy is collapsing. First France and now Greece has abrogated the naval agreement with England, well done, yes sir, that's the way, Don Roque is glad because he is pro-Italian and is for Mussolini, a great man and a great patriot who led his country from wretchedness to wealth and empire, hi there, Don Roque, hello, sweetheart, where are you going?, well, you know, to the market, all right, I'm glad . . . listen, let's get together again one of these afternoons for a snack, Evelina laughs a very promising laugh, if she knew how to read and write she could have a career, she really has an instinct, a calling, what Evelina likes best is listening to the radio, if she could she'd even listen to the news, the trouble is the lady she works for won't let her. Now put on your socks and do two or three tango steps, Buenos Aires my home, my beloved, Buenos Aires the queen of the Plata, and put on your shoes, don't polish your shoes with the bedspread but with the dirty socks, today is Saturday and time to put on clean clothes, it never does any harm to be neat and clean. The death of General Balmes, in Las Palmas in the Canary Islands, has no very reasonable explanation, his pistol jammed on the firing range, the general took it by the barrel with his right hand and rested the muzzle on his body while hitting the butt with his other hand, then the shot went off and he fell to the ground, dying like that is more suitable for a rookie than for a general, in a moment of consciousness he was still able to say, damned pistol! Now put on your shirt, you have a very good-looking striped shirt quite well made to measure, of the rest, five in all, three were inherited from your father and altered by Quiteria the seamstress, you can see it in the collars that she can't get quite straight, the woman does all she can, you can't ask any more of her. The commanding general of the Canaries General Franco as soon as he hears of the death of General Balmes, leaves Santa Cruz de Tenerife for Las Palmas in order to preside over the funeral, General Balmes leaves a widow and a seven-year old daughter, he shot himself the day before yesterday, they buried him yesterday, and the papers publish the news today. Few people listen to the radio, and at eight o'clock, fewer still, at that time hardly anybody even thinks of listening to the radio, maybe some servant girl, you have to be a very early riser, the inhabitants of Madrid are not usually very early risers, it's not worth the effort. Now put on your pants, they're well enough ironed, and the suspenders, Guillermo Zabalegui always wears very well-cut suits, you don't dress badly either, you can't complain, this suit of yours looks pretty good, the jacket instead of one handkerchief pocket has two, when you make a jacket over the pocket winds up on the right but that's easily fixed, you give it two pockets. Doña Eduvigis is very much afraid of hell, the cauldrons of flaming pitch really terrify her, all of them full of the damned, actresses, bullfighters, politicians, all victims of despair and shouting useless cries for help, cries that no one listens to, God told us all very clearly that we could choose the path on which we were to walk in this life, one full of thorns and thistles, asthma, constipation, that leads to everlasting glory, blessed be God!, and the other, easy and overflowing with flowers and pleasures, the vanities of this low world, the parties, the cosmetics, which leads to eternal damnation, God deceives no one and laments are no good afterward, each one walks on the path he prefers and in the next life reaps the fruit of his choice. Put on your tie, look at yourself in the mirror one last time and leave the house, try to phone Toisha, maybe she can go out, get your sister to call her, her father can't stand you and always tells you she's not at home, that she's out, Toisha's father is retired and spends all day glued to the radio, what bothers him most is being interrupted. In the Gobelas district on the outskirts of Bilbao an abandoned newborn child has been found in a bramble bush, he was just fine, smiling and in excellent health. Your phone rings, don't call Toisha, you'll call her later. Dámaso has just told you about the death of his mother. States deny their subjects the right to coin money, those who disobey are called counterfeiters and are pursued by the law and the police, Threefoot's Grandson is in jail for minting copper ten-centimo coins, it's an inequitable law, Threefoot's Grandson didn't want to deceive anybody, money was not invented to be saved but to be circulated, with this hand you take it in exchange for something you sell, with the other hand you give it in exchange for something you buy, if people had applied to Threefoot's Grandson's copper pieces the general theory of money, Threefoot's Grandson would not be in jail paying for the faults of others (or for his own faults caused by the lack of confidence of others), in jail they don't listen to the radio, the jailers can but they don't let the prisoners do it, the situation in which Threefoot's Grandson finds himself is not just but ambiguous, on ambiguity you can't base justice but at the most a convenient *raison d'état*. Matiítas, when he's saved up a little change, spends it going to the Price Circus to see the wrestlers, black Siki is very elegant, Mike Brendel the American Tiger is braver than anybody, bald Stresnack looks like the knight Ivanhoe, Karsic the Yugoslavian Panther has truly feline gestures, the Frenchman Pouveroux resembles a young and well-proportioned Apollo like the ones that the students in the school of arts and crafts draw, what men!, Petra la Grillo, the mulatto whose throat was slit, used to go to the circus to feel hot for black Siki, the one Ginesa the Murcian likes is Mike Brendel, Amanda roars when fat Palmers puts a lock on his enemy's neck, Sabina Burguete, who is by now in reserve status, moons over the Yugoslavian Panther, Sabina would have given three fingers of one hand to lay the Yugoslavian Panther, Matiítas likes them all, each one for some detail, some gesture, some muscle, his way of looking, his teeth, etc., the circus is a merciful bottomless bag which will hold every appetite and every false coin of dreams, wrestling matches are very exciting on the radio, too, when Matiítas doesn't have any money he listens to the radio and imagines the scene very realistically, since he knows the wrestlers well it's easy for him, pilgrimages to Lourdes via Saragossa, August 8 to 13, for information contact Pilgrimage Committee, 12 Calle Pi y Margall, Madrid, Doña Matilde would have liked to have gone to Lourdes, she had a lot of faith in Our Lady of Lourdes, it was too late for the poor woman, people get confident and then when they get around to remembering it's too late, Don León wouldn't have been able to pay the round trip for her either, a notary's clerk is in no position to take on expenses, naturally Don Feliciano could have advanced him the money, Don Feliciano is very charitable with his subordinates, very helpful and a true friend, but you should never take too much advantage of the liberality of your superiors, any respectful employee knows that, only a miracle of Our Lady of Lourdes would have saved King Cyril of England from death, and not even that, brain defects are frequently irreversible. Engracia works without any enthusiasm, there are days on which you work better and on the other hand there are sort of lost and painful days when your head feels hollow and your arms heavy and disobedient, something is going to happen, Engracia has not listened to the radio, Engracia lives far off and doesn't have time to listen to the radio, how few people listen to the radio, some servant girl if they let her, some old man, somebody curious, somebody who wants to do exercises . . . !, but she senses that something is going to happen, everybody is looking sidewise and talking loudly, these are confusing symptoms, full of danger, then things happen, things go wrong and nobody straightens them out, into their hole with the dead while the living eat their bread, that's not always the way it is, and often it's into their hole with the dead and the living keep on digging more holes while the bread gets moldy. You have a full twenty-five pesetas in your pocket, five big silver duros worth five pesetas each that tinkle as you walk, your father has been generous with you, maybe you don't even deserve it but your father has been very generous with you, with five duros the world is yours, the fact is you can't ask for more either, Don Roque probably doesn't have five duros on him, maybe at night, for expenses, but in the morning he doesn't have five duros on him, you can bet your life on that, Toisha will be glad, even though today is a bad day, you can't ask for everything, Miguel Mercader doesn't know about Dámaso's mother, you tell him, what you can't tell him are the details, there really aren't any details, Doña Matilde was dead one morning, that's all there's to it, at home none of you listens to the radio in the morning, you read the newspaper, well, you have a look at it when it's available, Miguel Mercader is no radio fan either, but he does like the broadcasts of the soccer games. Don Máximo knows that something is happening, there is no very precise information but something is happening, Don Diego phones him, come on over, is something happening, Don Diego?, you just come on over, haven't you listened to the radio, no sir, well, you have to listen to the radio, you come on over and I'll tell you about it, I'm on my way, I'll be at your place in five minutes, there is news that the Army in Morocco has rebelled, the news is very confusing and contradictory but it's a good idea to be prepared for what may happen, you're the boss, Don Diego, you must know what we have to do, I say we're sitting on a powder keg, you're right, what worries me most is that the powder keg has started to burn, call a meeting of our deputies for an hour from now, everybody is to be there, call Don Felipe Sánchez Román, too, yes sir. Suddenly it's like a powder flash, also like an eclipse, few people listen to the radio but on the other hand rumor flies with incredible speed, it takes a while for it to get under way but then it spreads with a dizzying speed, like a train of gunpowder?, that's it, like a train of gunpowder, in a city with a million inhabitants it's enough for two dozen to listen to the radio, if the rumor springs from a dozen different sources it floods the city in two hours. In the customs academy of Cela's father classes are cancelled at 9:30 A.M., gentlemen, in the light of certain serious official news reports the administration of this academy has decided to cancel today's classes, you should leave in an orderly fashion and await developments in your homes, the situation in Madrid is quiet but one can expect nervous reactions from both sides in which you should under no circumstances participate, that is what the administration of this academy takes the liberty of advising you for your own good, let us trust that order will be reestablished shortly. Eager groups are forming on the streets and at the cafés, one person explains about the radio and the others listen, another brings fresh news from the House of the People, Indalecio Prieto has asked Casares Quiroga to arm the proletariat, but Casares Quiroga refused, how do you know?, I know because I have a way of knowing, what I'm telling you is absolutely true, and what's more, Casares Quiroga told him that he'd have anyone who armed the people without his permission shot, that's an outrage, the Fascists and the Army are armed to the teeth and they're going to make us all run the gauntlet with Casares Quiroga at our head, don't be an alarmist, the rebellion won't get beyond some of our posts in Morocco, maybe by now it's history and the government is once again in control of the machinery of power with the means that the law offers it, it's undemocratic to fight against Fascism with Fascist tactics, well, what I say is that with theories like that by tomorrow or the day after we'll have Sanjurjo as president, you'll see, I'll remind you when we meet in jail. On the Calle de Mendizábal, on the left as you come up from the Paseo de Rosales, lives Domingo Ibarra the Nicaraguan musician, Ibarra doesn't wake up until at least eleven o'clock, then he has a lemon for breakfast, has a mustard footbath, and sits down at the piano to compose suites, waltzes, and symphonies, Luis Enrique doesn't take him seriously but Domingo doesn't mind, your problem is you're an ignoramus, is what he keeps telling him. At midmorning extra editions of *El Socialista* and *Claridad* come out asking for weapons for the people, do you see?, Don Roque's walk and cup of broth are ruined, no, maybe nothing is ruined, not the walk nor the beer at La Granja nor the cup of broth to get his stomach and his palate ready, people get alarmed prematurely, they put on the bandage before they've been slapped, man is like a skittery cat, like a rabbit, the groups of demonstrators heading for the War Ministry are ever bigger and denser, it seems impossible that in the batting of an eye so many can get together like that, the people are asking for weapons, well, no harm in asking, this looks like the taking of the Bastille, doesn't it?, if the government doesn't keep calm this is going to be one fine mess. You must keep calm, retie your umbilical cord with a double knot, you see yourself in the mirror choked by doubt and lack of confidence, all you who are dying are doubters and lack confidence, doubt is a better teacher than wisdom, and also fiercer, and the only noble way of being right is an obvious suspicion of error, it's no use for you to ask the mirror to show you an image other than your own, you have to play your part and the mirror has no choice but to follow you, to portray you with great realism and cruelty, your mirror does not fill up the whole wall, your mirror is, rather, a wretched bit of a mirror but it's up to you to think of it as enormous and powerful, you can even prolong it onto the ceiling and the floor, make it go all around the room, imagine yourself floating like a fish in the fishbowl inside a big container with six parallel reflecting sides, you're dressed and with your tie on but that doesn't make any difference, you can get undressed if you want or you can half close your eyes and imagine yourself getting undressed, you can see your butt and the back of your neck too, you can't manage that with a single mirror, smile, the mirror sends you back your smile, make a face, the mirror also makes the same face, shout or sing a song, the mirror keeps quiet, the dead are quiet but they can move, maybe you are dead but don't even know it and can't say it, close your eyes so as not to see yourself dead and examine your conscience, you are guilty of many abject deeds, none of them solemn, as a matter of fact you're a poor devil with delusions of grandeur, a horny monkey, a not too bright little busybody, would you like to be a count or a marquis?, no, so then what? This is a country of madmen, here nobody knows what's going on and the only thing they want to do is roar and wipe out their neighbor, murder him or shove it up his ass or piss on him, it depends on whether they're more or less criminal, in Spain revolutions always end up as slaughter, you kill your neighbor you shove it up his ass you piss on him you spit in his face you trip him up but the economic and social structure is not revolutionized, when the Spanish people go out into the streets demanding bread and justice they're always in the right, but then within a few hours they stop being right and finally the Civil Guard always steps in. You are at a corner of the world and can't turn your back on the world, it's a pity but it's true, maybe it's not a pity, just true. Catastrophes decimate families and beatitude also decimates families, it seems to be a proven fact that the family is a rather unstable institution, too mobile and artificial, don't turn your back on anything, don't lose sight of the world, maybe it's worth while for you to make an effort, if a man turns his back on dignity he runs too fast, too crazily, the race is full of dangers, that stinking whore after all didn't stink any more or any worse than Don Roque's breath and many other women are fighting over his profitable stink, you can hardly ever draw general conclusions. Don Leopoldo finds out in the office what is happening, may God protect us all!, Don Leopoldo phones his wife, the girls shouldn't go out I'll be home as soon as I can. Don Estanislao catches Radio Unión's broadcast as it reaches the part about how the government is pleased to announce that heroic nuclei of loyal troops are resisting the seditious elements at our military posts in Morocco, defending the honor of the uniform as well as the prestige of the Army and the authority of the Republic, that's bad!, so much solemnity makes Don Estanislao suspicious, they sent Chelo to the first-aid station and then to the morgue with less grandiloquent and well-measured words, almost with no words at all, Madame X's elastic girdles for slenderness, special models for prolapsed uterus, girdles for the new mother, girdles for the well-dressed, ladies, do not forget that there is many an imitation but only one Madame X, Don Estanislao phones his friend Don Sixto Lopera, excuse me for calling you so early, have you been listening to the radio?, yes, I was just going to call you, the situation is extremely critical, that's what I think, too, what are you going to do?, as a first step, get out of Madrid, until things are settled this is like the crater of a volcano, the slightest slip can make it erupt and carry us all off with it, could we get together, of course, go to Negresco, if it's still closed wait for me at the door, Don Estanislao gets dressed and puts the three-hundred-some pesetas that he's got saved up in his pocket, he keeps them in an envelope behind some books by Ricardo León, they don't take up much space, Don Sixto Lopera is a master sergeant of the Army administrative corps on voluntary reserve status, he asked to be put on reserve status so as to be able to look after his auto parts business, much more profitable than his pay in the ministry, Don Sixto is very cross-eyed, one of his eyes almost disappears into his nose, Don Sixto is also fond of visiting the little houses on Alcántara and Naciones Streets, is there anything wrong about a man's wanting to go to bed with a woman? Fewer flies fall into cups of chamomile tea than do into cups of coffee, maybe it's just that there are fewer cups of chamomile, people don't feel so sorry for the flies that drown in a cup of chamomile, probably because they're cleaner and, as it were, less poisoned, neither you nor anyone else can know it and furthermore it makes no difference whatsoever, man becomes cruel and indifferent with the passing birthdays, at first the process is slow but then it becomes very rapid and accelerated, Ceregumil Fernández, a complete vegetarian food product, uniquely suitable for delicate stomachs and intestinal disorders, Fernández & Canivell, Malaga, Don Vicente Parreño does listen to the radio but he doesn't think things will turn out all that tragic, how long did Sanjurjo last with his August 10 coup, and that was Sanjurjo?, well these guys will last even less, Sanjurjo is in Portugal and maybe he won't even show up, the man must have learned his lesson, look, Don Lucio, I'm up to here with this construction strike business, yes sir, people are fed up with strikes and having to put up with all sorts of disorder, what they want to do is live in peace and quiet and get a little piece of ass on Saturdays without big complications, these Army people talk a lot but then they don't do much, all that business about a military rebellion in Morocco is nothing but talk. The flies that drown in a cup of chamomile are almost medicinal flies, they have to be good for curing something, agile flies, athletic, with lots of resistance, sometimes it seems as though an electric current is passing through them just like in Sing Sing, how they kick, what a difference from flies drowned in coffee, they don't even seem like animals of the same species!, all low deeds have their just origin or at least their excuse, even those that are disguised as a happy and suicidal marriage, his wife and children are the hostages with which destiny forces a man to continue behaving badly and abjectly, you don't know that because you are a bachelor but you imagine it, matrimonial flies are in a way creatures of habit and sleepwalking flies, they're not, to be sure, very bright flies, anybody will get tired of contemplating the same domestic navel for a whole lifetime, the nervous system also has its rights and obligations, María Inés' navel is almost a matrimonial navel, with its mole and its meekness, Don Lucio could draw it from memory, Don Vicente could draw it from memory, nobody knows how many men could draw it from memory, there are many, at least a hundred, it's a pity that in brothels they choose their customers with such narrow criteria, mankind should be more flexible and less docile, people take too much advantage of habit, our domestic asthma, our girl's boyfriend (I hope to God his intentions are honorable), a son's fees at the business college. So the people want weapons?, all right, give them weapons, but no ammunition, let them kill each other with sticks and rifle butts and scare each other to death, Casares is absolutely right in not arming the people, Casares is wrong not to arm the people, very wrong, you've got to be very brave to refuse to arm the people, Casares' trouble is he's afraid to arm the people, the bull Civilón was not a noble bull, he was tame, María Inés is not a fierce-naveled woman, there are no more fierce-naveled women, the last two were Joan of Arc and Agustina de Aragón, Enriqueta is a brute-naveled woman, that's something else, a navel like a thistle, they'll be passing out more than a couple of slaps around here, there's going to be plenty for everybody, Don Gerardo is sleeping while the radio screams, Spaniards, stay tuned, do not turn off your radios, the traitors are spreading false rumors, stay tuned!, the cigarette man Senén awakens Don Gerardo, a friend in need is a friend indeed, get out of here, Don Gerardo, the beatings are going to be pouring down around here, they're going to make Ginesa dance by herself, you'll see, Cuprolina Vaginal Douche, sold in all pharmacies, dissolve the contents of the envelope in a liter of water, there are few people but lots of agitation at parliament, all sessions have been canceled and the standing committee isn't working, people shout too much and exchange threats and accusations, people have started to feel itchy and that's a bad sign, Don Diego can't get anyone to listen to him and orders a cup of coffee, black?, with a little milk, Don Máximo prefers a vermouth, the latest reports are even stranger, some are good and others are bad, maybe they're all false, with soda?, yes, it wasn't possible to assemble our deputies, they were all called but almost half of them are missing, Don Diego talks to Don Felipe on the phone, they talk at least twenty minutes, the usual little groups have not formed in the parliament bar, people are talking rapidly and all at the same time and drinking coffee or beer, the only one who's having vermouth is Don Máximo. Senén's only tooth—like a garlic clove or a donkey's tooth—is trembling as he tells Don Gerardo to leave, to get out, here, Senén, here's a hundred pesetas so Ginesa won't get out of training, I'll be back when your friends have cooled off, in Cáceres you can get a piece of ass now and then, too, don't go thinking we're a bunch of hicks in Cáceres, no sir, I don't think anything, in Cáceres and everyplace else. Paquita, well, Margot, finds out about the row when she wakes up, after twelve, she phones Don Joaquín, she plans to disguise her voice and say that the call is from a customer who wants to buy some cornucopias, Don Joaquín has forbidden her to phone, as far as your children are concerned you're dead and besides you don't have to call me for anything, I'll go see you at Villa Milagros if I feel like it, your children don't know who Margot is and they don't care, the phone is always busy and Paquita gets tired of calling, ah, the hell with him, Don Joaquín doesn't think anything will happen, what they have to do is bring in Gil Robles, who stands for the sound part of the country, Azaña will never bring him in because they are enemies, what the Army wants is to be listened to, the only man who can clean up this mess is Gil Robles, the workers have to go back to work, we've had enough of the construction strike, and the Army has to go back to its barracks, everybody in his place, that's it, what we need here is somebody committed to putting things in order. Don Cesáreo leaves by car for San Sebastián, his green hat he leaves on his hat rack in Madrid just in case, Pepito la Zubiela makes a very dignified and useful valet, he is respectful, he knows how to take care of clothes and serve at table, he knows his job well and works with good will and good manners, you can tell that being fired by Isabel because of that business with Don Máximo was just what he needed, there are people who learn their lesson at the first warning and people who never learn their lesson in all their lives, besides, Don Cesáreo has a daughter, Pepuchi, no son, the daughter is in no danger from Pepito la Zubiela, if he had a son things would be different, a valet should not be allowed to lay a hand on people's sons, young boys pick up bad habits right away and go wrong. Asenjo goes to visit Don León as soon as he finds out about the death of his wife, his cousin Don Baltasar Blanco, who works with Don León in Don Feliciano's notary office, told him, my condolences, thank you, my dear Asenjo, thank you very much, my most sincere sympathy, thank you, thank you, and how did it happen?, death sometimes comes without your noticing it, my dear Asenjo, yes, truer words were never spoken, Asenjo's visit lifts Don León's spirits a bit, what's going on out there?, well, you know, people yelling their heads off, this is starting to look bad, friend Rioja, very bad, I think nobody knows what he wants, well, God have mercy on us, it's hot and the window is half open with the blinds closed, you can hear a vague faraway noise outside, you can't understand the roaring of those who are demanding weapons, it's like the coming and going of the sea on the coastal rocks, around the body some ladies of the neighborhood are reciting the rosary, they've gotten to the *virgos* of the Litany, *virgo potens, ora pro nobis . . . , virgo clemens, ora pro nobis . . . , virgo fidelis, ora pro nobis . . .* , no one should have stepped outside the bounds of the law, this may be an act of madness that will cost a lot of blood, sometimes I think that these ups and downs don't come from any wish to patch things up for us Spaniards but from a thirst for adventure, just a thirst for adventure, the passing of poor Matilde has left me pretty confused, here we're all going to wind up with a cracked skull, they've all organized their gangs of toughs, all of them, it's an old story and it's never turned out well but they all keep on with it, this is no time any more for Army coups but we'd be lucky if it just wound up as a coup, no one should step outside the bounds of the law, unfortunately this doesn't look like a coup but like a demolition sale, you'll see, there are a lot of madmen loose out there, the last coup was Sanjurjo's and it didn't work for him, it dissolved like a meringue and made no difference for better or for worse, Mola is more cold-blooded than Sanjurjo, smarter, too, but the country is in no mood for military dictators, sometimes I think, if the Army is going to win, let them win as soon as possible, well, in a word, as you say, friend Asenjo, God have mercy on us! The sparrows are raising a ruckus in the acacias outside, a canary is singing so as not to get too bored in his wire cage, and on the balcony of the ladies on the third floor the parrot Churruca is babbling at the top of his voice proclaiming his nonsense to the passersby, birds feel no particular respect for death. Your Uncle Jerónimo's worries are reflected in his face, we are lost, my boy, we're starting to see people who want to become heroes of Cascorro and that's a bad sign, very bad, every Spaniard is always just a step away from being the hero of Cascorro, it's like a magic formula of repentance for so many centuries of idleness and nonsense, it's a bad sign, heroism, my boy, "Cascorrism," is as contagious as smallpox, what's dangerous is when it becomes an epidemic, an epidemic starts and nobody can escape it, it's true that the Army has rebelled against the government, but so have the workers, each side invokes its martyrs and wants to avenge them, it's a vicious circle that will end up soaking the country in blood, Martínez Barrio is the only man who might resolve the situation, Casares can't come to an agreement with the generals who have rebelled against him, his dignity won't allow it, Casares is played out, even though the Army might not pay any attention to him Don Diego will not arm the people, Casares doesn't want to arm them either but events may get out of control, this business of arming the people is very dangerous because afterward no one gives back the weapons, notice, my boy, that the crowd is not asking for bread or freedom, which is what it always asks for, but weapons, listen to its shouts, weapons, weapons, weapons, with bread and freedom you can eat, yes, and you can breathe easy but you don't rule, you obey, what the people want is political power, anybody who doesn't see that is blind, at this moment in other parts of Spain the people are probably also asking for weapons, some in the name of one set of principles and some in that of its opposite, it's like a surge of waves, or rather like a tide of collective hysteria that the police won't be able to stop, instead of giving the Spaniards weapons it would be more prudent to give them a sedative, this is a very nervous country, fond of miracles and full of dangers. At the crossroads of Robregordo, a little this side of the Somosierra pass, a Hudson sedan avoids a car that is coming in the opposite direction, goes into the ditch and turns two or three somersaults, three persons are killed, the owner Don Cesáreo Murciego, the chauffeur Juan Sánchez Izquierdo, and the valet José González González (that's Pepito la Zubiela), the wife and daughter of Mr. Murciego, who are seriously injured, are taken to Madrid and admitted to Dr. Bastos' clinic, the unfortunate family was on its way to San Sebastián, where it had planned to spend the summer season. Things don't always have their proper rhythm and sometimes they go too fast, the people are asking for weapons, once they have them they will ask for targets, weapons load themselves, some say the devil loads them, anything is possible, in Spain there are more fools than madmen, that happens everywhere, madmen may do the right thing but fools do nothing but foolishness, it's worse when they have a weapon in their hands because then what they do is scatter crimes around without rhyme or reason, this one I want and this one I don't and what I say goes here and you shut up, or else it's I've killed that guy who was bothering you, bothering you by just breathing, don't deny it, why don't you deign to smile at me?, I'd be most grateful, I swear, if you like I'll kill two or three more, all you have to do is point them out to me, fools are a dangerous lot, one slip and they can plunge a country into a deep well of blood, Pepito la Zubiela was never called José González González except on his identification card, Spaniards, stay tuned!, and now in the autopsy papers and the other legal procedures, Pepito la Zubiela is missing out on some very exciting moments, the dead lose interest in everything, in this they give a fine example to the living who are killed by curiosity, who let themselves be killed out of curiosity, who kill out of curiosity while the country sinks into a deep well of blood and shit at the bottom of which dwells the desert of hell (with its stains of dry blood, with its stains of dry shit). Weapons, weapons, weapons, people are asking for weapons, weapons, weapons, there are ever more people asking for weapons, weapons, weapons, the lookers-on don't ask for weapons, weapons, weapons (some of them do) but suddenly they think of themselves with a weapon in their hand, weapons, weapons, weapons, we want weapons, weapons, weapons, the people storm the gunshops but not the barracks, that's a horse of another color, the police always arrive too late, when a convent is burning they also arrive too late, considering what they're paid they do enough, the crowd grows hoarse asking for weapons, weapons, weapons, it's a bad symptom for the people to grow hoarse shouting that they want weapons, weapons, weapons, and nothing but weapons, weapons, weapons, you can't sprinkle the people with oil and set fire to them, they won't burn, a vigorous new shoot will always sprout up, you mustn't treat their foolishness with gunpowder either, a sedative is what they need, that's it, a sedative and also a little justice, the politicians are not just and don't know how to distribute a sedative in time and then things happen, no one knows where so many people are coming from asking for weapons, weapons, weapons, the cars have to go very slowly or make a detour, that's safer, if all the dead in all the cemeteries in Spain suddenly arose they would not outnumber these shouting people asking for weapons, weapons, weapons, that's the only thing that's heard, weapons, weapons, weapons, and off the façades of the buildings (many of the windows are closed) there rebounds a dull echo that always starts with the second syllable, . . . pons, weapons, weapons, weapons . . . , when there are many asking for weapons, weapons, weapons at the same time, the words, the only word that is heard sounds differently and with the stress on the second syllable, . . . weaPONS, weaPONS, weaPONS . . . , musicians are unable to achieve this kind of effect. Don Máximo does not think of himself as a Robespierre or a Marat, weaPONS, weaPONS, weaPONS, revolutions involve a great deal of disorder, what's needed here is to call out the Civil Guard, some militants of the Popular Front parties put on red arm bands and try to direct the revolutionary traffic, people won't put up with that and they're right, revolutions are not organized in any way and least of all by telling people you over here and you over there, revolutions go their own way and then turn out the best way they can, a good way or a bad way but a revolutionary way, what the crowd wants is to shout weaPONS, weaPONS, weaPONS and go from place to place in compact groups, ever more compact, in a short while the city seems like an enormous cooking pan overflowing with soft and movable dough, all revolutions begin the same way, Fidel Ternera does not ask for weaPONS, weaPONS, weaPONS, but he goes to Las Ventas to hear how others ask for them, sometimes he applauds or echoes some long-live or some down-with without putting too much enthusiasm into his voice, all of this that's happening is not all that clear, the fact is that God Almighty wouldn't understand it, Fidel holds Paca by the hand, with so much commotion they'd get lost, don't you let go, no sir, in the assault on a grocery store Fidel gets a can of asparagus, a salami would have been better, wouldn't you say?, well, we can't complain, this stuff is nourishing too, yes, that it is. The widow of Juan Sánchez the chauffeur of Don Cesáreo Murciego doesn't know yet that she's been widowed, what about Juan, oh you know, he's off on a trip. Engracia is no longer at the mattress factory when her boyfriend phones her, and didn't she say where she was going?, no, who knows where she might be!, she must have gone to look for you, thank you very much, don't mention it, Agustín Úbeda found Engracia at home, I was waiting for you, the hour has struck, what hour?, the hour for the people to mete out justice, this is going to end badly Engracia, well don't come if you don't want to, it's not that, not that at all, well what is it?, I don't know, but I'm telling you this is going to end badly. On Hortaleza Street there is an overturned streetcar, some children have their fun spinning its wheels and others cut pieces of upholstery from the seats with a pocketknife, you can make slingshots with the leather, they also enjoy just stabbing it for fun, take that, and that, and pull out its guts, you're going to cut your hand!, no ma'am, we won't, you'll see, some streetcars have leather seats, others have woven straw or wood. When he gets to parliament all Don Roque finds is confusion, Don Diego calls him aside, get out of here, where to?, I don't know, anyplace, get out of Madrid as soon as you can, what's happening here may swamp all of us, take my advice and get out of Madrid, Don Roque thinks it over, all right, all right, if those are your orders, I'm not ordering anything, my dear Barcia, it's not for me to give you orders, I'm just giving you a piece of advice, get out of Madrid before it's too late, tomorrow it may be too late, Don Roque thinks that Madrid is very big and that the fuse has not even been lit in all of Madrid, there are a lot of demonstrators, too many, but there are even more who hope that the police will be able to maintain order, do you think they will be able to?, well, I think so, and will they want to?, ah, that I don't know. Yes, Madrid is very big and it's very hard to fill all of it with shouts, the government refuses to arm people, that's clear, there is no doubt whatsoever that the government refuses to arm people, some say it's fear and nothing but fear, others talk about respect for the law, nobody respects the law any more, the law is like a five-peseta whore at Mardi Gras, and then there are some who speak the word treason, at first in a low voice, the word treason is very scandalous, then almost with confidence and finally in shouts, the government has betrayed the people, come on, do you really think so?, you bet I think so!, the government has sold out to the Army and the reactionaries, don't go talking nonsense!, that's the way it is, the government with Casares Quiroga at the head of it has sold out to the generals, down with the government!, what?, down with the government, can't you hear, long live the social revolution!, what?, long live the social revolution, are you deaf? Toisha phones you at Dámaso's house, I'm scared, no, nothing's going to happen, you'll see, just keep calm, people are stirred up but nothing's going to happen, people are real alarmists, you'll see how nothing happens after all, a dog's bark is always worse than his bite, Africa is very far off and the trouble here, you'll see, will take care of itself or a handful of Civil Guards will take care of it, I'll call you later so we can get together, I'm rich today, I've got five whole duros to spend with you, you hear that?, five whole sparkling duros one next to the other, I'll call you later. On Roberto Castrovido Street, formerly Love of God Street, just opposite Milagritos Moreno's house, wait a minute, you mean her home, yes, that's what I meant, lives the mother of Chelo, the whore who killed herself drinking lye, her name is Mrs. Consuelo Díaz and she's blind and they say she's crazy too, Mrs. Díaz lives off the charity of some of her neighbors, the woman hardly eats anything and isn't much of a bother, she dirties her pants but otherwise she's not much of a bother, Mrs. Díaz doesn't know about her daughter's death, when my daughter comes to see me, she always says, she'll bring me a fan, Mrs. Díaz would like to go to the bullfights wearing a high comb and a mantilla, with a carnation in her hair and carrying a fan, from the time she was widowed until she grew blind Mrs. Díaz worked as a washroom attendant first in a nightclub, the Cuba, and then after she had a fight with them at the Pompeya which is right next door, what was bad were the women who vomited and the pigs who stopped up the toilet with their sanitary napkins, otherwise it was easy work and even well paid. You'll see how finally everybody will say well I wash my hands like Pontius Pilate, ever since Pontius Pilate washed his hands nobody wants to take responsibility for anything, what a way to do things!, is a convent burning?, I wash my hands, is somebody being gunned down?, I wash my hands, not a soul is working here and there's one strike after another?, I wash my hands, the Army is in rebellion?, I wash my hands, the miners in Asturias declare a revolutionary general strike?, I wash my hands, shit, what a clean country!, I'm telling you, what a way to do things! His coworkers from the office come to Don León's house, all of them properly sorrowful, have you heard the one about the nuns' parrot that wanted to screw a hen?, Don León is sad but he hasn't lost his memory, yes I've heard that one, and the one about the seminary student who thought condoms are molds for making sausages?, yes, that one too, well bad luck, all his friends call Don Baltasar Blanco "Ramper" because he's as funny as the comedian, Don Feliciano had to leave Madrid in a hurry, he asked me to convey to you his most sincere sympathy, thank you very much, you're welcome, you're very welcome, it seems to Dámaso that Don Baltasar is a son of a bitch, forget it!, what do you care?, the poor guy has enough with having to stand himself all his life, he's just a friggin' bore whom his wife cheats on with the first guy that rings the doorbell, you think so?, I know so, I know more than one, there's no accounting for tastes!, that's true, but things could always be worse, when powerful is the urge to screw . . . you were going to say even a dead man's ass will do, it's a good thing you stopped in time, interment will be at five, the doctor filled out the death certificate with yesterday's date, the famous Professor Krishna offers his astounding studies of life, love, business, character traits, lucky lottery numbers, and details of his esoteric lore, P. O. Box 93, Valladolid, you will never regret having sought his counsel, Milagritos Moreno turns on the radio at two while she sets the table and prepares a vermouth with gin and a sprig of mint, to avoid the propagation of falsehoods people should know that Radio Ceuta pretending to be Radio Seville is broadcasting news of events supposedly happening in Madrid and the rest of Spain when, as is well known, everything is absolutely normal, shit!, what's going on?, Milagritos would like to know what Don Cesáreo thinks, something's happening here, maybe the fracas has started in some garrison, the fact is things couldn't go on this way either, Maruja!, coming ma'am!, have you heard anything?, anything about what?, about nothing, child, go on, bring the salad, yes ma'am, quickly!, yes ma'am, the tavern El Brasero is on the corner of the Calle de Santa María, of course Milagritos has a telephone but when she calls some gentleman she goes to the tavern to have Luisito pass on the message, a gentleman shouldn't get a call with a woman's voice, that's just common sense, go on call this number and ask for Don Cesáreo, say that it's from the Casino, when he comes on the line I'll take the phone, yes ma'am, Milagritos doesn't notice anything odd in the tavern, but it's an off hour, people are probably home having lunch, there's no answer ma'am, go on, dial again, Milagritos doesn't like it that there's no answer at Don Cesáreo's, there's no answer ma'am, all right hang up. Yesterday was a day of rest in the Tour de France and there's no news today, today they're probably racing along the road again, boy, bicycle racing is a tough sport, what legs and lungs they must have! Railroad connections have been cut, no sir, railroad connections have not been cut, Don Sixto Lopera buys a second-class ticket to Segovia and nobody tells him that railroad connections have been cut, Don Sixto is going to stay with his brother Don Simón, a canon at the cathedral, when people start getting nervous the best thing is to clear out, Don Simón lives comfortably, he'll be very glad to see his brother, Don Simón is worried about the way things have been going, why don't you come to Segovia?, he'd told Don Sixto more than once, in Segovia we live well and quietly, communism and atheism haven't reached there yet, people are good and respectful there and you can work the same as anyplace, besides the cost of living is low, much lower than in Madrid, once you decide all you have to do is show up there, Don Sixto took some time to decide, well the fact is he still hasn't decided, Don Sixto hates to leave his auto accessories business in hired hands, you've got to stay on top of a business and even so, it's the owner's eye that makes it prosper, Don Sixto plans to spend maybe a week in Segovia, no more, eating suckling pig and roast lamb while tempers cool, it's not easy to get Don Sixto away from the whorehouses either and from his regular circle of friends, Don Sixto is a widower and his only daughter went into a convent, no, Don Sixto is not going to Segovia for good, he can't, I'd like to but I assure you I can't, at the door of the Negresco he meets Don Estanislao, what brutes, what a roaring!, don't tell me, friend, don't tell me, if this isn't a true social revolution I'd like to know what is!, what are you going to do?, me?, get out as soon as possible, and you?, me too, things are going to explode any minute, why don't you come with me?, I'm going to Segovia to my brother's place, he's a priest, well, I don't know, I've got my family spending the summer at my in-laws', in Madrigueras, where's that?, in Albacete province, you go by train to La Gineta and then take a bus to Madrigueras, well leave them where they are, they're all right there, you'll see them next week, the point now is to get out of the way until this mob has been taught to behave, Segovia is closer and besides you don't have to change to a bus, that's true. Juani phones you at Dámaso's house, they told me you were there, yes I'm here, Rioja's mother has died, oh dear, give him regards I mean condolences you know listen, do you want to go out afterward?, no, not today, today I'm going to spend the afternoon with Rioja, I have to go to the funeral, oh of course, do you want me to call you tomorrow?, all right call me tomorrow, Juani is easily satisfied, easy to deal with, and very grateful, Lupita is just like Juani, they're both tramps of the respectable sort but they're neither bores nor an embarrassment. Mrs. Blanco suffers from nymphomania, formerly there was no such illness or at least they didn't call it that, Don Baltasar doesn't know the symptoms any too well and confuses them with the charm that oozes from his wife's every pore, my wife is happy as a lark, he always says, my wife's got more charm than anybody, she's not all that good-looking but she's got all the charm in the world, she always has something nice to say to everybody, she's a joy, his friends laugh quietly but hide it, what should they do?, Mrs. Blanco has two regular lovers, she says two respectable lovers, but she doesn't pass up any opportunities either, the delivery boy from the grocery, the bill collector from the gas company, her hometown cousin, the telegram messenger, she's very pleasant and affectionate with her husband, that's her natural character and she doesn't have to make an effort or pretend, she loves her husband too and doesn't allow anyone to crack jokes in poor taste about the cuckold's horns with which she adorns him almost daily, that would be the limit!, she meets Don Wenceslao Bercial in the Buen Gusto Bar, on the Paseo de Santa María de la Cabeza, she gets together with Don Tomás Donato in the Caracolillo Bar, in the Prosperidad district, Mrs. Blanco does not like disorderly places or to be taken for a tramp, these bars away from downtown are very discreet, it's easy to go unnoticed there, Don Wenceslao calls Mrs. Blanco on the phone, if it's not she who answers he asks for Mr. Morales, Don Joaquín Morales, no you've got a wrong number, you've misdialed, I beg your pardon, Mrs. Blanco picks up the phone and coughs before saying hello, that's the signal, Anita it's me, Wences, hello love, hello sweetie, I'm calling to say good-bye, I'm leaving Madrid for a few days, what's up?, are you scared too?, no dear, it's business, I'll only be away two or three days, Mrs. Blanco's voice turns to honey, and what am I going to do without you, sweetheart?, you'll wait for me, honey, I'm telling you, Tuesday or Wednesday at the latest I'll be back, Anita Luque de Blanco is not as distinguished as Mimí, Guillermo Zabalegui's aunt, but she's no less a slut, one's as good as the other. Julianín doesn't understand much of what is happening, people rush in and out at Casa Benito, they order a glass of wine or a vermouth and leave again, some of them without even saying good-bye, at the House of the People they can't keep up with all the orders and commands, Spaniards, stay tuned!, a group of Falangists exchanges rapid fire with men from the House of the People from the corner of Barquillo, there are no casualties but a good deal of running and being scared, a loudspeaker appears at a second-story window, at this very moment the land, sea, and air forces of the Republic that faithfully continue to carry out their duties are proceeding against the rebels in order to suppress this senseless and shameful movement rigorously and energetically, long live the Republic!, didn't you hear me?, I heard you, so why don't you answer?, I?, yes you, long live the Republic!, long live the Republic! At La Granja El Henar the waiter Gutiérrez also advises Don Roque to go, I wouldn't stop to think it over Don Roque, just look for Gil Robles or Don José María Cid in Madrid and you'll see that you won't find them, maybe they're not even in Spain any more, if I were you I'd leave without saying good-bye to anybody and without wasting a single minute, Don Roque mulls it over, yes, maybe you're right, that's what Don Diego says too but what shall I tell you, Gutiérrez, I just can't see running away, I'm no criminal and besides I have parliamentary immunity, I was elected by the people in a free election, the government will eventually restore order, it's bound to, those of us who are honorable people have nothing to fear, a fine mess it would be if honorable people had something to fear!, things can't go on like this, Gutiérrez, tomorrow or the day after everything will be settled, you'll see. In front of the Café Marly, on the Glorieta de Bilbao, a taxi drives up on the sidewalk and kills a blind man who was playing the accordion without bothering anybody, he didn't do it very well but he made a living, people gave him a few centimos or a cigarette or some leftover macaroni or rice and the man managed to live, the driver says his steering malfunctioned, perhaps it did but he should have avoided the blind man and crashed against a lamppost, maybe it all happened so quickly that he couldn't, mishaps usually happen very quickly, almost in a flash, they're like the crack of a whip that you don't see coming, addresses of midwives all over Spain in envelopes, postcards, mailing wrappers, or lists, Alianza Fénix, 2 Calle Ponzano, yes, people rely too much on habit, in matters of parliamentary immunity, of blind men killed by cars, of midwives, of everything, perhaps habit is a second nature, the trouble is that it's false. You're trying not to define situations anew each morning, there are no two situations alike although you try to think there are, just look at King Cyril of England, look at Napoleon Bonaparte, look at Viriathus the Lusitanian shepherd, they all ended up as caricatures of themselves, danger nests within each man, you take the easy road but no one stops to look for the true road, it's cozier to make time with the sisters at the movies or in the park than to try to court them both simultaneously, that would be interesting, no, if people ask for weapons don't ask for weapons, once people stop asking for weapons it'll be another story, then you can ask for them even if they're no good to you, never make common cause with habit, man is an animal killed by habit, also one who kills by habit and not by necessity, nor by whim unless his habits are whimsical, just look at King Cyril of England who was a victim of habit, when you feel too used to yourself vomit yourself out, not in the light of day and in front of the mirror but in the dark and in some corner, only thus will you escape the frightening caricature of yourself, and start all over like the wards of charity whom they give a name that is recorded on a little lead plate, yes, people rely too much on habit, the most noble ideas, the fatherland, liberty, justice, are converted by habit into whitened tombs, people say whitened tombs, it's habit again, the same thing happens to the most ignoble, habit equalizes what life differentiates, Paca is habituated to her hump but she holds on to Fidel's hand when she's afraid of getting lost in the confusion, the trouble with man is that he ends up copying himself perhaps without realizing that he's doing it, Don Gerardo gets out of town and gives Senén a hundred pesetas so the Murcian won't get out of training, Don Roque doesn't, Don Roque stays because he is an honorable person who has nothing to fear, habit is despotic and dangerous, more despotic and dangerous than vice, you know that habit is the larva of suicide, sometimes you thought that but you never dared to say it, refuse to play the follower for nothing, to be cannonfodder, fodder for the whorehouse, fodder for the catechism class, it's hard but not absolutely impossible, say no to obedience, to chastity and to poverty, raise the flag of rebellion and draw into your shell like the turtle, refuse to hear the siren songs, to march in step, to believe in miracles, to ask for weapons that would wind up burning your heart, no, let others take their place in the chorus not you, there is no more bitter and ridiculous tragedy than that of the bit-part actor who feels he has the dramatic lead, or rather, who pretends to feel he has the dramatic lead, King Cyril of England was a faggot but no bit player, history does not remember the bit players, the bit players were the ones who killed him, no one remembers their names, a bit player is capable of sacrificing his conscience for a gesture that is not his either but is copied, on the pyre where the consciences of bit players are burning there also burns the peace of those who just want to live in peace and quiet and get an enjoyable piece of ass on Saturdays with a woman who sighs and is even charitable, who sighs falsely and is falsely even charitable, refuse to play anybody's follower for nothing, it would be bad for you to wind up noticing a little itch on your palate, Evelina Castellote is like a mare in heat, what she likes is drinking barley water and killing chickens by holding them tight between her thighs. Excuse me sir, could you spare a cigarette paper?, Don Roque offers his package to the man who ran out of cigarette paper in the middle of the street, help yourself. Do you remember the flu of '21?, it was milder than the flu of '18 and though it did kill people it didn't decimate whole families, the trouble was the loss of Cuba, Napoleon Bonaparte tried to land in Havana and was thrown back by the rebels, there were no rebels then, by the grandfathers of the rebels, you think Paquito and Alfonso, the two fellows from Salamanca who had come to blow a few pesetas in Madrid, get on the train as soon as they hear the first shouts, maybe nothing will happen but this really isn't any fun, too bad we can't take those two girls to Salamanca, what a sensation that would cause!, the sisters set you right, Paquito and Alfonso miss the train and stay in Madrid. After lunch the cabinet meets at the Buenavista Palace to study the situation, the news from Seville is contradictory, in the morning the Minister of War receives General Don Miguel Núñez de Prado and General Don Virgilio Cabanellas in his office, that's impossible, Cabanellas is in Saragossa, but he could have come, yes, naturally he could have come, the news from the Canary Islands is also contradictory, it seems that Franco has rebelled, the news from Asturias is more reassuring, Aranda is absolutely reliable, it's very hot and half of the demonstrators who were asking for weapons have gone off for their siestas, what's going to happen here?, nothing much dear, it's just that we're going to give those savages a good thrashing, fine, just as long as you're not the ones that get thrashed! When the heat gets worse Marramáu opens an umbrella to protect himself against the sun, he says the solar rays because he's a little affected in his speech, a paralyzed man can be forgiven certain liberties, Marramáu likes to toss compliments to the women who come along the street and also to have the sun on his crotch, Marramáu doesn't harm anybody with his likings, he is obliging and respectful and his compliments are hardly ever coarse but witty. Señor Asterio Cuevillas is worried and sticks to his radio, Lupita and Juani keep quiet so he won't get mad, when Señor Asterio gets mad he won't let Lupita and Juani go out, that is the worst punishment they can receive, if the government doesn't take its measures quickly we'll have Gil Robles as prime minister again, of course, what do you mean of course?, well just that the government ought to take its measures quickly, Lupita and Juani don't feel too revolutionary, what they'd like is to marry a doctor or at least a doctor's assistant and live well in a cute and cheerful little apartment, may we go out, father?, yes girls, don't get home too late. Don Máximo is uneasy but he shores up his spirits by talking about the Sancamilada, all this will amount to is an attempted coup, you'll see, you think so?, sure I do, history will remember this revolt as the Sancamilada, the San Camilo Coup, and won't give it any more importance than the little that it has, we're just too close to it and lack perspective, Don Diego is worried, that's understandable, Don

Diego carries a lot of responsibility and Casares is tottering, but it's one thing to be worried and another to be afraid, worry is patriotic and constructive, when history does not take some event seriously it baptizes it with a name ending in *ada*, Carlistada, Sargentada, Vicalvarada, though the Francesada was more dangerous and, you see, it ended with the victory of the Spanish people over the armies of Napoleon, when besides being trivial and insubstantial the event has a droll and grotesque air about it, people attach the *ada* to the name of the saint of the day, the Sanjuanada for example, this Sancamilada now is going to mean the end for precisely those enemies of the Republic that started it, the Sancamilada makes no sense and just won't work, the news received from all over the country is the same, the forces of reaction are being crushed everywhere and with their own weapons, now the people must show discipline and stop demanding weapons, what do they want them for?, the loyal forces are more than enough to give the rebels what they deserve, Don Máximo orders another vermouth to show that he is calm and confident, and some olives stuffed with anchovies, please, after his Friday diet of fruit Don Máximo feels powerful and sure of himself, the Sancamilada will help to establish the Republic on genuinely democratic principles, you'll see. The undertakers who are to convey Doña Matilde to the cemetery arrive at 4:30, the priests put on their vestments inside the doorway because conditions out on the street are not very favorable, some ladies also step inside a doorway when their garter comes loose, it's more discreet, Don León and Dámaso are very shaken, Doña Matilde was tiresome but good, the marriage had lasted many years, you can't say it came to an end of a sudden because Doña Matilde had already been sick and paralyzed for more than ten years, but just the same, death even though you see it coming from afar always stuns the family, stuns it if nothing else, we're terribly sorry, thank you very much, Don León gives the undertakers five pesetas, here you are, for a glass of wine, thank you very much, we'll drink it to your health, out on the street people don't bother the priests who walk at the end of the procession reciting their prayers, some ladies make the sign of the cross and men raise their hats or caps more out of habit than respect, it's easier to let yourself be carried along by habit than to be respectful, yes that's what I think too, habit is like a kind of inertia, something that moves on its own, for respect on the other hand you have to make distinctions, what happens is that respect is often only habit, it's very hot and on the way to the cemetery, between the Abroñigal creek and the cemetery you hear the song of the crickets, at night what you hear is the frogs, there must be hundreds of frogs, near the bullring some groups of people are talking loudly and very excitedly, they fall silent as the funeral procession passes, some Gypsies sitting on the sidewalk look at what is happening as though the street were the stage of a theater, you can tell it from their faces, from the way they pay attention and also the way they get distracted. At the offices of his paper Jesualdo Villegas writes a headline for the report that will be broadcast on Radio Unión, in Seville where a state of war was seditiously proclaimed by General Queipo de Llano, some Army units have engaged in acts of rebellion that have been repulsed by the forces loyal to the government, it looks bad!, if only it's true!, that Queipo is a megalomaniac who likes to live it up, he's perfectly capable of rebelling just for the fun of it, you bet he is!, well we'll see how it all ends . . . , at this time a cavalry regiment has already entered the city as a reinforcement to shouts of long live the Republic, the rest of Spain remains loyal to the government which is in full control of the situation, it seems to me that if things go on like this Enriqueta can screw her father tonight. The Philippine airmen Arnáiz and Calvo are received as honorary members by the Economic Society of Madrid. Those who accompanied Doña Matilde to the cemetery, fourteen altogether, found it fairly easy to leave her there, it's easy to bury an ordinary dead person, you hire an undertaker, you give some tips, you put on the expression of a grieving relative, you spend a bare couple of hours and that's that, case closed, see you the next time, hope it's not mine, notices in all the papers, well, the *ABC* is enough, Los Tiroleses is a very dependable advertising agency, advertisements in every newspaper in the world, the Emperor of Ethiopia appears in every newspaper in the world and doesn't buy any ads, all he needs is the Italians, advertisements in railway guides, Don Sixto does not buy the railway guide to go to Segovia to his brother the priest's, it wouldn't pay, advertisements on the curtains and in the lobbies of all theaters, Don Vicente Parreño knows them all by heart, he is a great theater-goer, he saw *Perfectly Indecent* the brilliant work by Pauline Singermann at least five times, Doña Eduvigis does not usually go with him because the theater is a permanent incitement to sin, let everyone look out for his conscience and the salvation of his soul, besides the air in the theater is not good for her asthma, Count Casa Redruello also likes the theater, *How Alone You've Left Me!*, you'll die laughing, advertisements on the screens of all cinemas, Doña Patro the Lacemaker advertises her house at 13 Naciones in the movies, Victoriano Palomo and Virtudes often go to the movies, to the matinee, at the Newsreel Theatre they're showing the Schmeling-Joe Louis fight, the Tour de France, and the arrival at Barajas Airport of the glorious Philippine airmen Arnáiz and Calvo, heroes of the fabulous nine-thousand-mile flight from Manila to Madrid, advertisements on walls and partitions, Paca knows a lot about walls, advertisements on streetcars, do you remember when you were a kid and you rode on the bumper of the number 32?, advertisements on the radio, at 8:30, variety concert with Isabel Ballester, soprano, and the Radio Unión sextet, the Socialist unions order their members to begin a general strike of indefinite duration in every city in which the rebels have declared the state of war, advertisements in every new medium, yes, obviously, one must always look toward the future, at the stands by the bullring people are drinking lemonade and lemon fizz, they are once more agitated and shouting, weapons, weapons, weapons, the midday truce is over and the people are asking for weapons, weapons, weapons to defend the Republic, you see more red armbands and some of the demonstrators already carry pistols in their belts and shotguns on their shoulders, weapons, weapons, weapons, groups of people asking for weapons, weapons, weapons come up the Calle de Alcalá from the bullring, they don't bother the young couples at the outdoor cafés, they look at them but they don't bother them. Matiítas has an appointment with a gentleman at the corner of Fuente del Berro and Duque de Sesto, on Saturday afternoons, after he's closed down the condom shop, Matiítas carries on an occasional affair with some reliably discreet gentleman, it all starts out as lofty conversations and sometimes doesn't get beyond the stage of airy declarations of love, fondlings, caresses, a little kiss or two, poems, etc., other times it does, other times it gets serious and Matiítas gets impaled ruthlessly like a dog, Matiítas suffers a great deal but he also enjoys it, some gentlemen are very strange and you have to beat them and spit in their faces, Matiítas doesn't like to beat people or spit in their faces, he likes getting beaten and being spat on and being called a whore and a fairy, the gentleman with whom he has the appointment even beats him with his belt, he's a real man and never tires of beating Matiítas and calling him whore and faggot and low-down slut, they usually meet at the house of Doña Soledad, a widow who supplements her government pension by renting rooms, Doña Soledad accepts male couples and female couples, she doesn't care, everybody knows his own tastes, what she won't accept is threesomes because they wind up wrecking everything and making a lot of noise, Doña Soledad doesn't want to shock the neighbors, from the Calle de Alcalá comes the murmur of people asking for weapons,

weapons, weapons, Don Fausto will be coming any minute, he should be here already, Don Fausto always brings him a present, a little box of toffees or sugar-coated almonds, he's a very well-bred gentleman and from a very good family, Matiítas doesn't know his last name but you can tell right away from his manners that he's from a good family, Matiítas steps into the doorway a bit when he sees people coming, if it's one person or two it doesn't matter, but groups are bad, maybe Don Fausto hasn't been able to come with all these demonstrations, Madrid is in an uproar, Matiítas thinks it's better to wait a little, Don Fausto would never forgive him for not waiting, Doña Soledad has twin daughters, both of them half-wits, they caught meningitis when they were little and lost their wits, now they're already almost thirty, Rogelio Roquero from the dairy stable got them both pregnant on a bet, the son of a bitch, I'll bet you I get both of Doña Sole's half-wits pregnant the same day, how about twenty-five pesetas each?, no, twenty-five for the two of them, if you get one pregnant and not the other, you lose the bet, all right?, you're on, Solita and Conchita are already in their eighth month, it turned out not to be too hard to get them pregnant, Rogelio will collect his twenty-five pesetas soon, Doña Soledad takes loving care of her two daughters, if they weren't a pair of innocents she'd have thrown them both out of the house, she always says, Matiítas sees Solita and Conchita coming up the street, they're holding hands, and he hides behind a soda delivery truck, he's ashamed to have them greet him, you know people gossip and have nasty minds, a boy is pissing behind the truck, Matiítas pinches him on the neck and then marches off to avoid temptation, it's very risky to stop to talk with a boy who is pissing, Matiítas walks ever faster, no, Don Fausto must not have been able to come, obviously he preferred not to go out, Don Fausto is very fastidious and crowds are truly repulsive to him, that's what he always says, Matiítas is sorry because he'd already gotten used to the idea of spending the afternoon at Doña Soledad's romping with Don Fausto, well, man proposes and God disposes. You would like to call every thing by its proper name, surprise for example, you know that it is quite difficult to find the proper name of things, feelings, and situations, whistling is a very worthy consolation, that's well known, but today you must not whistle, Toisha's father will not let her go out and besides Saturday is a bad day, everybody is out on Saturday and today, what with this Army rebellion in Morocco, there are even more, if a plague of crabs fell on the city, a ferocious plague like those of the Old Testament, people instead of scattering would gather in circles just like horses attacked by a wolf, Toisha had never heard the word crab in that sense, you had to explain to her what a crab is, if you put a crab that you could see well in front of Toisha, on a glass for example, she wouldn't have known its name, knowing the name of every thing is a difficult science that almost no one masters, people are asking for weapons, weapons, weapons, but there are also those who aren't asking for them and who even dissemble, Maripi Fuentes doesn't know what a crab is and doesn't ask for weapons, weapons, weapons, nobody at the house of her friends the Aguados is asking for weapons, weapons, weapons, and only half the family knows what a crab is, it's like the ones you eat but small, tiny, and discolored, pale, Dámaso heads home, he is sad and a little tired and would rather be by himself, maybe I'll read a while, you go to visit him and take him a bottle of champagne that you swipe from your father, we can drink it a little at a time without doing any harm to anybody, Don León gets into bed and turns on the radio, he is very depressed, well, a little depressed and the news on the radio helps to distract him, Don León wants to drive La Hebrea's tits out of his mind, no matter how hard he tries he always imagines La Hebrea's tits, round and powerful and with jet-black nipples, he usually goes to see her on Saturdays, that's his habit, if he doesn't go today it's out of respect for appearances, for what's proper and for what people will think, poor Doña Matilde can't care any more, that's what I say, how can she care when she's dead?, it was worse before, Dámaso is sad, that's normal, well, not a movie but if you like we'll take the sisters to the park at the Dehesa de la Villa . . . , you almost slip and that's the second time, it's very hard not to put your foot in it, people can always take offense, you were going to say the park at Skull Fields, I don't know what's the matter with me man, yes I understand, maybe you're right, but look, you're not going to do your mother any good shutting yourself in here. Jesualdo Villegas is very excited and talks about the French Revolution and the mission of the intellectuals in the political struggle, the reporters who cover parliament, six or seven of them, get together in the Gambrinus tavern, Casares is acting as though nothing were happening or as if what's happening were unimportant and that, gentlemen, is not composure or fear either but indecisiveness and what's worse ignorance of the real state of affairs and what it means, of course composure and fear play their part in this indecisiveness, I understand that, the composed man is better at putting up with things than at taking action, and the indecisive man eventually is frightened by the decisiveness of others, Casares doesn't believe in the competence of the Army and that is a seriously mistaken view, I assure you that this uprising is not just another barracks revolt but something that has been in preparation very calmly and I'm afraid also very competently, politics is not a chess game by correspondence but something more like tennis, you have to make instant decisions and furthermore not hold back or get ahead of yourself, Casares is holding back, Radio Unión repeats that the uprising in Seville has been crushed, that means there was an uprising in Seville and nobody told us a thing, Casares insists on not arming the people and it seems Azaña agrees with him, the state of things is turning more serious than either the president of the Republic or the prime minister suspects, the only solution is to arm the people before it's too late and the time for lamentations has come, Jesualdo Villegas speaks very passionately but his colleagues listen to him rather skeptically, another beer, right away sir, and a little beef jerky, yes sir. Fear is a bad counselor because it undoes and overflows everything, Paquito is waiting for his father's death to return his friends' favors, a glass of white, a fried bird, a cheap cigarette, a lay at the house that's upstairs from the Golden Grapes, thank you very much Don Leoncio, God bless you, I'll pay you back when I get my inheritance, it's bound to be some day, yes my boy, don't worry, it'll come some day, Paquito is thin and coughs constantly, that comes from jacking off, Victoriano Palomo always says, that Paquito is a drone who just wants to live it up sponging off respectable people, Paquito gets caught in the turmoil on the Calle de la Montera across from the scorched ruins of the church of St. Louis, weapons, weapons, weapons, people shout ceaselessly and you can already see some rifles, the Socialist unions have distributed six or eight thousand rifles among their members, various decrees are announced over the radio, General Don Virgilio Cabanellas Ferrer is hereby relieved of the command of the First Mixed Division, a screw on Don Leoncio's apparatus gets rusty and Donata fixes it with a nail file and some vaseline, I think that's all right, can you walk?, yes thank you very much, Donata is no child but on the other hand she is very compassionate and her body still looks good, the *ABC* publishes list number 422 of the collection taken in Madrid for the support of the basilica of Our Lady of the Pillar, a pious lady 1 peseta, a Catholic husband and wife 2 pesetas, a grateful Catholic 1 peseta, P.V.E.B. 5 pesetas, the military units whose commanders have defied the lawful authority of the Republic are hereby dissolved, José Sacristán Gutiérrez shit on February 12 in the toilet of the Pleyel Theatre and then went back to Alcázar de San Juan to serve the customers in his mother's yarn shop, José has a subscription to the magazine *Natura* that comes in a sealed unmarked envelope, tomorrow's mass and divine offices are those of the seventh Sunday after Pentecost with semidouble rite and green vestments, all units of the Army that take part in the insurrectionary movement are hereby dissolved, José Carlos Fuentes, Maripi's older brother, is in the company of several young infantry officers affiliated with the Spanish Military League, there are also some civilians there, the only one you know is Guillermo Zabalegui, all we still have to do is wait for orders, it would be too bad if they came too late, I don't think they will, Monday marks the beginning of the solemn triduum to St. Mary Magdalene, sermons by Don Mariano Benedicto, chief vicar of the parish church Our Lady of the Pillar, I don't know, I don't know, but I think we're going to miss out on the sermon, General Francisco Franco Bahamonde is hereby relieved as military commander of the Canary Islands, he's the most dangerous one and very young too, as long as he stays in the Canaries we don't have to worry but if he gets to the mainland it's going to be another story, when Virtudes was chosen Miss Carabanchel the mothers of the other candidates just had to swallow it, Virtudes was by far the best looking, superb German boxers 250 pesetas up, Brigadier General Don Gonzalo González de Lara is hereby relieved of the command of the eleventh infantry brigade, that's in Burgos, the government doesn't say so or says it in a roundabout way but the uprising is taking hold on the mainland, Don Olegario doesn't know that Don Cesáreo was killed in an automobile accident, the two brothers were not on good terms, or rather, they were on no terms, good or bad, but Don Olegario is a man of kind feelings and incapable of resentment, what Don Olegario likes is inventing mechanical appliances and sneaking into the dog races, miraculous discovery, grey hair disappears in one week with Mexicano vegetable oil (aromatic), manufactured by José Beltrami, 566 Avenida del 14 de Abril, Barcelona, General Don Gonzalo Queipo de Llano y Sierra is hereby relieved of the post of inspector general of the Customs Guard, there are many more to come, I mean almost all of them are yet to come, the symptoms indicate that Emilita Tendero will never marry, it's hard to marry off women with a mustache because their boyfriends balk at it, Juventor, created by German science to help the impotent and solve their problem, simply slip over the dormant member, inflate by means of the attached rubber bulb, and that's it!, it's a little ridiculous but it seems to work, Miguel Mercader calls it the blowhard, your Uncle Jerónimo does not agree with Jesualdo Villegas' theories, no, the people should not be armed, hysteria is worse than indecisiveness, Spain is a country of epidemic hysterias, I've always told you so, of collective insanities that are hard to shake off, religious hysteria drives Spaniards to dragging chains in processions and to ask the saints for what they cannot fix on their own or even with the help of the lottery, when it's mixed with the hysteria of fire we get the Inquisition and the burning of convents, the point is to have a fire, the fuel doesn't matter so much and a heretic is as good as a wooden saint, the Inquisition and the burning of convents are only the heads and tails of the same pyromania, the hysteria of blood is like an epileptic drunkenness and few Spaniards escape it, that's the worst of all, my boy, and must be avoided by every means at our disposal, when it begins it spreads like a sea of lava and drowns hundreds and hundreds of Spaniards, there is also an inhibitory hysteria that leads to our doing nothing because we come to think that everything will get better by itself, a gross error!, inhibitory hysteria brought us to the loss of the colonies, the last of them Cuba, when we tried to understand what was going on they'd already kicked us off the island, no son, Jesualdo Villegas is a bright boy but a little hysterical, Casares is right not to arm the people, it's harder for them to kill each other with sticks and fists than with bullets and cannon shells, the government is obliged not to facilitate hysterias, a fine shape we'd be in if it did otherwise! The Socialist unions offer the government three thousand taxis to fight against the rebels, obviously somebody remembered the Battle of Verdun, now it turns out that the crowd does not smell of sweat or feet, which would be normal, but of tranquil breath, that's very paradoxical, of the sweet breath of cattle, it's incomprehensible, do you remember the smell of that unfortunate tart whom the subway killed?, Magdalena stank of death, of grease, and of antiseptic, yes, but her underwear was different, her panties, her bra, her stockings, that handkerchief with which she wiped the sweat from her armpits, her transparent slip, sheep when they have given birth, and cows, and she-wolves smell like the underwear of a dead whore, like the warm breath of the companions of death, you can understand all the twisted ways of odors, nothing ever travels in a very straight line, the newborn lamb and the combative ram who will die with their throats cut, the swaggering bull and the humble ox, the wolf who scents the traces of the mountain goat, people's noses are not well trained, that's why people are slow to feel sexy when a sudden powder flash blinds them, theft is difficult in the cemetery but not impossible, the cemetery is a good place to flash your dick at a young or middle-aged widow, now the crowd turns out not to smell like the troops. Gabriel does not move from the counter of La Cigale, these days you've got to watch things all the time, Turquoise goes on stage wrapped in a pearl-grey tulle cloak, dreams born in the half-light of the cabaret, dreams of pleasure, of a happy day, oh romance born of the dance, treasured memories that will never go away, Turquoise very gradually takes off her cloak until she is naked, with only a daisy over each nipple and a triangle of silver lamé over her crotch, Turquoise stands for a few moments with her arms outstretched and her eyes closed, as though in ecstasy, the audience applauds enthusiastically and Turquoise opens her eyes, lowers her arms and smiles, long live the Republic!, the ovation grows louder, long live the Republic!, long may it live!, the next performer is Lolita Diamante, whose specialty is the light chanson, remember you're a woman, to please men is your duty, it's elegance will let you live and love and flaunt your beauty, people don't like her as well and there are some catcalls. Maripi and her mother have supper by themselves, José Carlos and his father are obviously eating out, turn off the radio dear, it's all so vulgar, yes Mama. Clarita is still at her parents' house, the burns on her butt are better but not quite healed, Sánchez Somoza is a brute, a real brute, there's no excuse for burning your wife's butt with boiling chocolate, a democrat or a civilized person doesn't behave like that, his wife was eating out with somebody else?, well then, let him punch the other fellow in the mouth but not burn anyone's butt with chocolate, that's really savage, an outrage, a real outrage, Clarita's parents care for her very attentively, poor child, what bad luck she's had with her husband!, what agonies the child is going through!, Virgilio Taboada phones her every afternoon, how are you doing?, better, and you?, I'm better too thanks, we'll be well soon and then we can start a new life far away from that brute of a husband of yours, just have confidence in me, yes sweetheart, I do have confidence in you, it's just that I'm really scared by what we're going to do, no sweetie, don't be scared of a thing, I swear to you we won't take a single step that's not perfectly legal, we'll do everything according to the letter of the law, I swear it, you have a clear case for a divorce, I hope to God you're right, dearest, but listen, aren't they going to fire you at *El Debate*?, we can't let that matter to us now, honey, I can work anyplace, I sure want to give you the kind of life you deserve, you know that as well as I do, yes Virgilio, you're so good!, no, not good, just so in love with my Clarita, etc. Every Saturday Manene Chico goes to Timoteo Despedide's tavern on the Calle de Santa Catalina to have a few glasses of wine and to talk about the bullfights with a group of fans, some women bullfighters also go, Maruja Colás the Manchegan and Pepa Manzanedo the Cabra Kid, matadors, and Maruja Onrubia the Widow and Sara Topete Garrafita, who fight from horseback, among others who are less well known, today they're all talking about the old-style bullfight advertised for tonight, maybe the authorities will cancel it in view of what's been happening, Manene Chico has great confidence in the talents of Consuelo Barrera, she is very brave and knows her stuff, if she were a man she'd go far, that's what I said, she reminds me of Marcial Lalanda, Don Braulio Mandueño stares at Manene, that's blasphemy, Manene, Marcial you say?, yes that's what I say, well say what you want, I know you like to pick a fight, Manene smiles, orders another round of drinks, and pats Don Braulio's knee, are we friends or aren't we?, man, what do you think?, do you think I'd put up with you if we weren't friends?, Sara Topete defends the Volunteer, what I say is that if that woman had backers she'd make a clean sweep of all the others, her trouble is she's a respectable woman and doesn't want to split the dough with anybody and even less let the first bum that catches her fancy set himself up as her pimp, what we've got here is a lot of rascals running after all of us, I should know!, if Julita Alcocén had taken up with Tiri by now she wouldn't have enough money to rent an outfit, but she drew the line because she's respectable too and now look at her, I'm not saying she rakes in the money but then she's got everything she needs and two costumes of her own, both of them by Ángel Linares, and she supports her mother and her little brother, the gathering at Despedide's tavern is like an oasis of peace in the midst of the turmoil, all they talk about there is bullfighting and what's happening outside is of no interest, people just like to jive, don't tell me, I'd like to see all these guys asking for weapons out on the firing range, not a soul would ever bet on them! The cabinet meets with the president of the Republic at the palace, Azaña can't make up his mind to arm the people either and in this he agrees with Casares, the government wants to fight the rebels from the *Official Register* and with decrees instead of cannon shots, it's a gentlemanly system but it's sure not to be effective, a man with a rifle in his hand laughs out loud, I mean, he splits his gut laughing at what the *Register* may say, the declaration of the state of war is hereby canceled in every locality of the mainland, Morocco, Balearic Islands, and Canary Islands where it may have been proclaimed, any person contravening this decree will be subject to the most severe penalties of the law, you can see that the Socialists don't read the *Register* either because there are ever more people asking for weapons, shouting for weapons, weapons, weapons, the Puerta del Sol is jam-packed, it's like New Year's Eve, some leaders of the Republican Left go to the Interior Ministry and the crowd cheers them, weapons, weapons, weapons, stay calm, stay calm, stay calm, everything in its due time, just stay calm, Don Alejandro Lerroux goes to Lisbon, he evidently no longer believes in revolutions. Jesualdo is a political and military strategist, suddenly he discovers that his true forte is strategy, Casares is either crazy or a traitor, you can decide for yourselves, in any case he's not the man the Republic needs to fight against the rebels (down with the cabinet!, away with the bull Civilón!), we've got to arm the people (weaPONS, weaPONS, weaPONS . . . !) and keep the troops from leaving their barracks (down with the Army!), it's not me who says that, that's what a prestigious man like General Riquelme said to Casares (long live the generals with honor!), we have to act quickly and efficiently (weaPONS, weaPONS, weaPONS . . . !), there is an eternal right to defend yourself against an enemy, you can read that in the *Law of the Twelve Tables* (silence), we must fight him with every means at our command because the defense of a just cause (long live the Republic!) does not recognize forbidden weapons (weaPONS, weaPONS, weaPONS . . . !), now is the time to risk everything (right you are!), it's democracy or tyranny (long live democracy!), freedom or slavery (long live freedom!), the people must learn to form their own political system (long live the revolution!, long live the proletariat!), the people must have weapons (weaPONS, weaPONS, weaPONS . . . !), so that they can fight in defense of their ideals (long live the Popular Front!, long live the unity of all antifascist organizations!), we must establish the reign of truth by the force of arms (weaPONS, weaPONS, weaPONS . . . !), we're not the ones who have chosen the path of fire and blood (silence), we're not the ones who have shaken the dust from pistols and cannons (right!), we're not the ones who have buried the pipe of peace (that's showing 'em you've got balls!) and unburied the hatchet of war (that's telling 'em!), worse than war itself is the fear of war (weaPONS, weaPONS, weaPONS . . . !), those are the words of Seneca, the wise Seneca (silence), I ask all you antifascists not to desist from your efforts until you have made them give you the weapons (weaPONS, weaPONS, weaPONS . . . !) with which you can win your own freedom (long live freedom!, long live the proletariat!, long live the proletariat!, long live the proletariat!), lock up the Army in its barracks! (down with the Army!), do not allow it to declare the state of war! (silence), bring down the cabinet that refuses to give you weapons! (down with the cabinet!, away with the bull Civilón!, weaPONS, weaPONS, weaPONS . . . !) Jesualdo is out of breath and wipes his forehead with his handkerchief, yes, Jesualdo is a strategist but he's also an effective agitator, he's just proved that, when he gets to Madame Teddy's he orders a beer and a salami sandwich, hurry up Enriqueta, I'm in a big hurry, oh come on, you'd think they'd made you president! The only lights visible at the Montaña Barracks are the ones on the outside, obviously they've either turned everything off or in spite of the heat they've been ordered to keep the shutters closed, the black silhouette of the barracks stands out against the glow from the Paseo de Rosales, a big building that's dark and with no signs of life though we know there's someone, even if it's ghosts, inside is always very mysterious, at the Ideal Rosales people drink brandy and soda and dance with the girls, will you buy me a drink, marquis?, sure sweetheart, order whatever you want, at the Rosales Jai-Alai the lady ballplayers smash into the ball, and at the stands on the other side of the street married couples from the neighborhood drink their peaceful domestic Saturday lemonade, from every open window you hear the music of Radio Unión, sometimes the announcer reads the communiqué of some political organization, the national committees of the Socialist and Communist Parties have given us the following announcement that we broadcast with the full knowledge of the government, the secret intrigues of Spanish Fascism led by Gil Robles and Franco have now borne fruit in the criminal endeavor that has today spread to the mainland with Seville as the center of the rebellion . . . , it is imperative that the working class prepare for combat in the streets . . . , comrades, be prepared for the coming struggle, when the order for combat is given we must fall on them like an avalanche, that's great!, we're going to get the hell beaten out of us here, you wait and see!, Karakú anchovies are advertised with the music for *El Marabú* from the operetta *Doña Francisquita*, Karakú, I want Karakú with my vermou . . . . . . th . . . th. . . that's what I need, Karakú!, then it goes on without music, the best by far in the new glass jar, Don Leopoldo and Doña Bernardina say the rosary with six of their seven children, the third glorious mystery, the descent of the Holy Spirit on the apostles, our Father who art in heaven hallowed be thy name . . . , Enrique is the only one missing and tonight he's not on duty at the first-aid station, his father knows where he is and approves, if he were twenty or twenty-five years younger he wouldn't be here either without lifting a finger, José Carlos Fuentes and Guillermo Zabalegui have also got into the Montaña Barracks, the approaches have not been cut off and nothing unusual is to be seen in the neighborhood, just that the poor hookers around the empty lots by Príncipe Pío have suddenly lost all their customers, Gumersindo accompanies the family, he's sitting next to his girlfriend and prays very devoutly and with his eyes half closed, give us this day our daily bread . . . It's gotten too late to take out the sisters and Dámaso gets into bed, he's bored and would rather get into bed, he doesn't want to listen to the radio either, the idea that Doña Matilde doesn't care any more what he does keeps going around in Don León's head, what difference can it make to the poor woman when she's dead now?, it was worse before, come to think of it it was much worse, at Villa Paca there are more people than any other Saturday, less light too and more quiet, all the johns have a mysterious and sort of sleepwalking air about them, you can see they're worried and their conscience bothers them, you can get rid of your worries (or at least forget them for a while) by going to the whorehouse, having a bad conscience helps a lot, if a man is horny and on top of that his conscience bothers him, what more can he ask?, La Hebrea is busy, it's not unusual for her always to be busy, but Don León is not in any hurry, it doesn't feel so bad to be having a cigarette in the half-light while the world is on flame, Don León, yes Doña Encarna, you can go in now La Hebrea is free now, all right, and like I was saying, my sincere sympathy at the loss of your wife may she rest in peace, thank you very much, La Hebrea is more beautiful than ever and very serious and devoted to her work, you'd say she was a respectable woman who hates and also enjoys what she is doing in a dirtier and more loving way than ever, today La Hebrea is not cheerful but depraved and instead of giving her the usual three pesetas as a tip Don León gives her five, Doña Encarna is glued to the radio, a very good static-free five-tube Selectone, in Seville the lawful authorities are holding the rebels in check, in Pamplona a known Fascist has treacherously murdered the commander of the Civil Guard, the city and province of Santander are absolutely tranquil, Professor Piccard has arrived to give a series of lectures at the summer school, he was received by Professor Don Blas Cabrera and the secretary of the summer school Don Pedro Salinas, Don Ramón Menéndez Pidal has also arrived, at Las Palmas in the Canary Islands the subversive movement continues, the city has been occupied and the provincial administrative buildings, where units of the Civil Guard and the Assault Guard are resisting, are under pressure, a general strike has been declared, Doña Encarna is on edge, she's as nervous as can be, how far is this going to go Don León?, who knows Doña Encarna, let's just hope they can restore order, while she presides over her congregation Doña Encarna keeps following the news, Servetinal, Servetinal, Servetinal, now they're playing commercials, it's hard to believe but believe me it's so, San Mateo's prices are so low low low, the national committee of the Syndicalist Party urges its members to maintain total discipline so that they may rapidly carry out any orders given by the Popular Front thereby achieving the unity that will make it possible to crush those who wish to establish the blackest of dictatorships. Maruja la Valvanera is delighted when she sees Don Roque arrive, really, Don Roque, I thought you weren't going to come!, that's a good one!, and why shouldn't I come?, what does the revolution have to do with a man's liking to stick it to a woman with her tits in their place, can you tell me that?, well you're right there, at this time when democratic liberties are seriously threatened by feverish reactionaries the POUM (Partido Obrero de Unificación Marxista) orders all who belong to its ranks or sympathize with its aims to prepare without delay for an effective defense, Maruja la Valvanera considers it a good omen that Don Roque hasn't lost the itch to fuck, what's going on outside, Don Roque?, nothing Marujita, nervousness, it's just nervousness, tomorrow or the day after at the latest Mola will show up here and kick a little ass and put an end to all this uproar, you'll see, nothing whatsoever is going to happen here, just remember a firm hand is all it takes and you'll see how this is all just a flash in the pan, Don Roque rolls himself a cigarette and changes the subject, let's see now, have you got the Santander girl in there?, yes Don Roque she'll be free in a minute, would you like me to bring you a glass of brandy?, well I'll never pass that up. People say the Montaña Barracks but they're really three barracks, those of the 31st Infantry Regiment, those of the 1st Engineers, and those of the searchlight unit, from the outside the three buildings look like just one, that's a fact. Matías from the commissary, Matías Suárez, goes to the bullring to see the lady bullfighters and for the clowns, he'll visit Amanda later, there's no hurry, at the evening bullfight people have a good time with the antics of the Great Lerín and the Bullfighting Cop, they're very funny and ingenious, at the Zarzuela Theatre Estrellita Castro is singing *My Mare* and *María de la O*, and Tina de Jarque is showing her legs and her chest, everybody does what he can, that happens in the theater and everyplace, Juanito Mateo, for those hours that his girl Leonorcita leaves him free, has a thing going with Irma Hollywood, one of the Rogers Sisters, whose real name is Juana Pagán, she uses the Irma Hollywood when she's working by herself, the Rogers Sisters also perform at the Zarzuela, they sing *No, no, Nanette* and *Hallelujah* and since they're young and luscious people applaud them and they smile thankfully, Juanito Mateo picks Irma up at the door, they won't let him into the theater because one night he laid a couple of punches on the leader of the claque and they had to turn up the lights and interrupt the performance, Irma is wearing a little cretonne suit and a lot of eye shadow, you can see right away that she's an artiste, take me home, stay with me if you like but take me home, any one of these brutes could start hassling us you'll see, those are not brutes Irma, those are proletarians who are fighting for democracy, well you can call them what you want, the Torres Sisters, Mary and Dorix (for the first time in Spain), Alady, Piruletz, Margary and Francis, and as many as fifty new performers are also appearing in the show at the Zarzuela. Don Máximo is tired but he holds on, duty is duty, Don Máximo does not leave Don Diego for a minute, call here, call there, order some sandwiches and beer, order some coffee, phone *El Sol* for the latest news, the rebellion is spreading by the minute and it is necessary to act diligently before it is too late, if the fuse of social revolution is lit at the same time as that of military subversion Spain will burn to cinders, it is necessary not to lose hold of the reins of power, the Republic can be killed by one band of extremists just as well as by the other, the Anarchist unions are right when they remind their members of the agreement to oppose Fascist provocations but also every kind of dictatorship, the survival of liberty is threatened from both sides, if the government loses control of the streets the Republic will be wrecked in a sea of blood, there is still time to compromise, the Army has not yet rebelled in Madrid, the attitude of the labor parties can sink any possible formula for conciliation, Casares is tottering and the Socialists and Communists are maneuvering to succeed him in power and to strangle liberty in the streets, Azaña is very worried by the turn of events all over Spain, what is needed is energetic action to reestablish order, Don Máximo agrees with everything, Don Máximo greatly admires Don Diego, with half a dozen, no, with four men like Don Diego Spain would be France and the Spanish Republic could work as well as the French. At midnight La Pasionaria addresses the nation, workers, antifascists, working masses, all of you on your feet, all of you ready to defend the Republic, the liberties of the people, and the advances of democracy, with the cry, Fascism shall not pass!, the butchers of October shall not pass!, Communists, Socialists, Anarchists, and republicans are destroying the traitorous rebels, the whole country is trembling with indignation at those heartless men who wish to plunge our democratic people's Spain into a hell of terror, they shall not pass!, all Spain is ready for the struggle, long live the Popular Front!, long live the people's Republic! They're hard to count, you can't know exactly because they're very hard to count, but there are probably many families saying the rosary tonight, some out of devoutness, others from inertia, and still others out of fear, when it's thundering people remember St. Barbara more than when it's not, the rosary works for them all, the first glorious mystery the resurrection of Our Lord, Maripi and her mother say the rosary with some people from the neighborhood, it's easier to fight fear when you're not alone, the windows are closed and the curtains drawn, it's hot but it doesn't matter, you can fight the heat with beer and a fan, the radio sounds as though it were tipsy, that must be Radio Seville, people of Seville, Spaniards, the commanding general of the second division Don Gonzalo Queipo de Llano is about to address you, yes that's Radio Seville, be quiet a bit, people of Seville, to arms!, the fatherland is in danger and in order to save it, we, a few men of courage, a few generals, have taken on ourselves the responsibility of leading the movement of national salvation that is triumphing everywhere . . . , I hope to God it is!, there's a guy with balls!, the die is cast and it is pointless for the rabble to resist . . . , the trouble is they're going to resist, you think so?, you better believe it!, anyone disturbing order will be hunted down like a wild beast, well said!, no quarter must be given to these vicious brutes, long live Spain!, long live the Republic!, well he's got to say that, we all know what the Republic is, nothing but chaos and rackets for people with pull, the inhabitants of Madrid who are sleeping now don't count, there are nights when one should not sleep, almost half of those who are not sleeping are saying the rosary and another almost half are demanding weapons, weapons, weapons, the rest don't count for much and no one pays much attention to them, you can remedy a situation by praying or by fighting depending on what it is, you can also complicate it even more, some people believe in the efficacy of the rosary, the second glorious mystery the Ascension of the son of God, some prefer the tangible recourse of a rifle, weapons, weapons, weapons for the revolution or for the counterrevolution, Engracia is demanding weapons, her boyfriend Agustín is at her side but demands weapons less enthusiastically, maybe he's a little tired, and Guillermo Zabalegui and José Carlos Fuentes each with a rifle in his hand are on duty in one of the sentry boxes of the barracks, Guillermo Zabalegui doesn't know why he is where he is, he is a revolutionary who naturally doesn't believe in revolutions of the Right and still joins a revolution of the Right, he can't quite understand who pushed him into it, maybe nobody did, you never understand these things too well, you can get up one morning a Fascist and the next a Marxist, if Christ returned to walk on earth and to live among men he would not preach humility to the powerful but pride to the timid and the humble, it's not good to believe too enthusiastically in anything, adventure is beautiful in itself but what it usually isn't is just, but that's another story, Mimí Ortiz de Amoedo, Willy's aunt, is archaically proud, her pride reeks of the Roman Empire and the Old Testament, Guillermo laughs when he thinks of that but he's also a little afraid, Guillermo Zabalegui and José Carlos Fuentes and all the other sentinels have instructions not to fire come what may until they receive the express order to do so, it will come, there are also some who dream that people will cool off and only the devout will say the rosary (and in a low voice) while weapons rust slowly in their cases, the rosary can help to bring peace to the conscience, you know the third glorious mystery, but also to spur the conscience on until it wants to impose its devotion by force of arms, there is no appropriate mystery for that, not sorrowful, not joyful, not glorious, it depends on what consciences are saying it and with what sort of conscience, weapons never help to bring peace, which usually dwells on other less noisy and less violent paths, the problem does not look the same within the conscience as out in the middle of the street, nor the same within each individual conscience as in the sum of the consciences of all (which is usually a contaminated sum), people abdicate their own consciences and adapt too quickly to the common conscience, the fourth glorious mystery, the assumption of Our Lady, Doña Eduvigis says the whole rosary, the fifteen mysteries one after another, she's already on the fifth and last glorious mystery, the coronation of Our Lady. At 1 A.M. the House of the People addresses its members, this radio is a great invention that lets you get information to people in no time, they also managed before when they didn't have radio, we ask that no worker leave Madrid today, Sunday, his presence may be necessary to fight our enemies, of course, people wouldn't have left Madrid anyway, those who lack enthusiasm are afraid or at least curious, it's hard not to be curious, you usually go off on Sundays to swim in the Jarama River with Luis Enrique Délano, Gregorio Montes, and Miguel Hernández, sometimes somebody else goes too, you take the Arganda train in the Niño Jesús station, on the other side of Retiro Park, Paca the hunchback knows well where it is, and you get off at the Puente station beyond La Poveda, after the bridge and before the sugar factory of Azucarera de Madrid, S.A., well then you weren't going to go tomorrow, the Arganda train goes very slowly, as it passes through the vineyards of Montarco there is time to get off the train, swipe two or three bunches of grapes, and get back on while it's still moving, the girls on the train egg you on and when you catch it they applaud and smile at you, that's living, when it gets to the bridge they have to put on a tiny locomotive so the bridge won't collapse, you can have a good time at the Jarama, you can get in the water and then dance to some phonograph, there are many of them, sometimes you can pick up a girl, it doesn't last but it has its charm, the sun always warms the girls up, the next day they won't pay any attention to you but look, once you've made out you've made out, they can't take that away from you, they're nice people at Telesforo Mateo's tavern and if they know you they'll trust you from one Sunday to the next. Don Roque spends the night at Maruja la Valvanera's, it got a little late and besides who wants to go out on the streets now with so many people yelling and running around, it's not that they'd do you any harm but then just in case. When Don León gets home he finds Dámaso still awake, what are you doing?, just reading a little, Don León would have liked to stay a while chatting with his son but he doesn't dare, for that matter he doesn't have anything to say to him either, good night son, get a good rest, good night father, the same to you, the double bed seems too big to Don León for just himself, obviously he isn't used to this, and it takes him a while to fall asleep, Mrs. Frances Creighton, 38, and her lover and accomplice Everett Appelgate, 36, were electrocuted last night in the prison at Auburn, New York, in execution of the death sentence pronounced against them for the murder by poison of Appelgate's wife in September of last year, one slip and you've had it, these Yankees are really something!, Don León turns out the light on his night table and thinks of Doña Matilde, afterward he thinks of La Hebrea and then he falls asleep, it was about time to fall asleep, the noise outside seems to have stopped a bit. Casares clearly cannot stay in office, the news that reaches Interior and War is not encouraging, the military uprising is catching on simultaneously at various points on the mainland and Las Palmas and Morocco are in the hands of the rebels, in Madrid the Army has not rebelled but all indications are that it could rebel at any moment, in Madrid the Socialist and Communist militias are in command, the Anarchists have forgotten old grievances and have joined them, they all demand weapons which Casares does not want to give them but it's going to be hard to get them to go home, the government lacks the forces needed to maintain order, better said to restore order, at 2 A.M. Casares hands his resignation to the president, as your Uncle Jerónimo says they all killed Casares and he died all on his own, your Uncle Jerónimo knows lots of proverbs and he always uses them opportunely, they say that people with tuberculosis are lyrical and liberal, maybe it's true, their heart is free but their flesh is in chains. Don Olegario lives in a shack on the Vereda de Postas, now called the Calle de Orense, among empty lots full of dead cats (sometimes even fetuses show up there and are eaten by the live cats), mountains of garbage, and flocks of goats that feed on thistles and newspapers, Don Olegario lives by himself and in great poverty, what nobody knows is whether he lives with dignity or without dignity but come to think of it that's the least of it, everyone lives as he can and as circumstances permit, in Don Olegario's den there are at least twenty or twenty-five empty Torres Muñoz bicarbonate boxes full of screws, nails, corks, soda-bottle caps, wires, erasers, pencil stubs, cigarette butts, ball bearings, etc., Don Olegario saves everything he finds, inventors utilize everything, by the light of a candle Don Olegario is talking with his neighbor Cándido Modrego, a harmless nut who used to be a proofreader for a printer and who has written a plan for spelling reform that he doesn't want to show anybody, Modrego was a vegetarian and very leftist until he caught a case of typhoid fever that put him in death's antechamber and he was converted, since then Modrego reads nothing but saints' lives and the speeches of Donoso Cortés, some of them he almost knows by heart, things are turning ugly Don Olegario, we must return to the Inquisition and the torture of our ancestors, there's no other way, you see how the people act up as soon as they get a little confidence, what we need here is a ruthless military dictatorship, what we need is an iron fist in the name of the cross and the sword, anything else is just the way to our downfall, yes maybe, I think you're wrong, I mean, not a hundred percent right, but maybe you are, yes maybe you are right Modrego, who knows, I can't say, maybe they're all right and this really is going to be some mess, Cándido Modrego and Don Olegario smoke butts, there are lots of them in the bicarbonate boxes, there are least three boxes full to overflowing. At 3 A.M. the president charges Martínez Barrio with the mission of forming a cabinet, the news leaks out and the Socialists are waiting to see what will happen, Don Máximo feels important, if Don Diego can't solve this no one can, if Don Diego doesn't put it back in order we can say good-bye to the Republic and its democratic achievements, it's the obligation of every Spaniard to support Don Diego because he is the last hope of our fatherland, now we'll see what the Army says, I trust that common sense will win out at the end and that our principles and institutions will be saved, the Socialists are going to be a harder nut to crack, but then, keep calm, keep very calm, call Don Felipe Sánchez Román and General Miaja, right away Don Diego, beg them in my name to come by here as soon as possible, yes Don Diego, we can't lose a single minute, very well Don Diego, anything else?, nothing else thank you, what will you gain from Eureka shoes?, good humor because they are comfortable, savings because they are durable, elegance because they are stylish, Victoriano wakes up, turns on the light, and dashes out of bed, Virtudes wakes up too, where are you going?, to the bathroom, something must not have agreed with me because I've got something like cramps, I'll be right back, what a scare you gave me, dear!, what do you want, you want me to shit in the bed?, Victoriano has diarrhea, when he comes back from the toilet he feels better, what could it have been?, I don't know, last night it was me and tonight it's you, you didn't eat anything heavy, that's what I say, I thought I wouldn't make it to the bathroom! Don Román Navarro is sitting with his family, nobody seems to be sleepy there, or so you would think because really everybody there is sleepy except the head of the family who is nervous, Don Román is explaining to his wife and children that what is needed in Spain is another General Narváez because as Balmes so well said political passions are evil, well that's what he meant, he certainly said it differently, Don Román's wife and children are dead tired and yawning, what's the matter with you?, it seems you're not interested in what I'm saying, no dear, it's not that, it's just that it's very late, do you know what time it is?, any time is good or bad depending on for what and when, people think the night was made for sleeping and the day for work, they also say all things fade away with time but you can forget about that, time fixes all things and as time passes the memory is like a photograph that's been dipped in fixer and that won't ever fade or won't fade even half-way for at least fifty years or more, in spite of the time Don Román is not sleepy, neither is his family, what's happening with his family is that they're bored, very bored, our capacity for putting up with each other has its limits, some families put up with each other better and others worse, and good will won't solve that, it helps but it won't solve it, on Vereda de Postas King Cyril of England would not have died so bitterly as he did, the tortures of the Holy Office were effective and showy but not very varied, Cándido Modrego has never heard of enemas of molten lead, do you know when they close the Souper Tango?, no sir, I've never been there in my life, the Souper Tango wasn't made for the likes of me, come on now, and why not?, every six months Cándido Modrego goes to the Oriente baths on the Plaza de Isabel II, soaps himself well, puts on clean clothes, pays, and leaves, that's the only luxury he allows himself, hygiene is not incompatible with anything, these baths ought to be a free and compulsory public service, a bath for every Spaniard every six months. Don Diego discusses his plans with President

Azaña, we can't count on Maura, I talked to him on the phone, he's in La Granja, he won't budge from the idea of a republican dictatorship that he developed in his articles in *El Sol*, a national republican dictatorship of supporters of the Republic who would govern for all and undertake the task of rebuilding the state, maybe he's right but I can't admit that, I'm obliged to defend our democratic constitution, it's hard to be president under these circumstances, we ought to try for a grand coalition but it can't be done, the Socialists refuse, Prieto might have compromised but Largo Caballero refuses and without the Socialists on the one side I can't call on the Agrarians and even less on Gil Robles, try to form a cabinet of republicans, in the empty coffee cup a fly is kicking with its last angry energies, one two one two one two, pause, one two one two one two, epileptic pause, one two one two one two, lengthy pause, we need some respected names, it is probable that things are done less by guesswork in the orderly and haphazard kingdom of the flies than in the confused and tiresomely farseeing republic of humans, names that no Spaniard can argue with, yes of course, we have to look for them within the ranks of republicans, the fly does not know what is happening to it, it senses that it's dying but it doesn't know why it's dying when it was feeling so strong and healthy, later we can expand the base and move to a coalition cabinet, in the brandy glass a wanton mosquito is drowning, it's hot and half of the mosquito's body is paralyzed, it kicks with great difficulty, one one one one one one, pause one one one one one one hemiplegic pause, one one one one one one, almost absolute and definitive pause, right now all we seek is harmony, shipwrecked flies doubt everything they hear, Spain has reached the limit of her political tension and beyond this there are only blows and blood and messianic zeal, the fly in the coffee and the mosquito in the brandy are discovering that death has no size, yes I think you're right, that death has no size?, no, that beyond the limit of political tension lurk only chaos and blind chance, we'll see, the point is to be able to achieve harmony, there is no other solution and you know that as well as I do, better than I, it's disgusting but some people finish flies off with their spoon and mosquitoes with their finger, between two fingers, I'll try, thank you very much, also on Vereda de Postas, a little farther down, Dominica Morcillo Fernández, an old hooker who lives on charity, sits by the light of a candle stub while she sings the songs that were already out of fashion when she was at the top of her profession, long live General Serrano, and Topete, long live Prim, as for our queen's fairy husband, up his ass, to hell with him, Dominica Morcillo never goes to bed before sunrise, she's wide awake all night drinking anise and singing popular songs, she sticks out her tongue at politicians, laugh, just laugh at antipornography campaigns, Dominica Morcillo never thought of tomorrow, she doesn't much believe there will be a tomorrow but she still has her memories, her syphilis, her anise, and her songs, the day I was born my mother said, gal, you're the spitting image of your father's best pal, sometimes Dominica Morcillo sings the Royal March, the Virgin Mary is our shield, the Virgin is our spear, with Mary to defend us there is nothing that we fear . . . , shit, you really have to be patient!, in the midst of the struggle the politician carries on without getting bored, tedium is a sublime sentiment but still, that politician is very patriotic, so patriotic that he is ready to be moved at the thought of any fatherland, he is never bored but he never has much fun either, no, on the contrary, he is very politic, he is always ready to forget promises and offenses, being able to stand boredom or at least conceal it is something that's part of the game, of the rules of the game, dice are the devil's molars, you can't be a politician if you feel like resigning, there is no deceit in a resignation (maybe there is), no resignations, they'll throw you out in due time, anything but a resignation, all that business about starting over and a clean slate is not the right attitude for a politician, a politician chops up consciences and behavior and with their splinters he stokes the flames of history, in politics everything is an eraser, everything is a whole lot of little blots, white, pearl grey, dark grey, black, shiny or dull it's all the same, that form something like constellations of little stars, Cassiopeia, Centaurus, Coma Berenices, in politics all accounts are old even though we citizens sometimes come to think they are new, Azaña is tired but he's holding up, it's his duty, lovers also get tired and also hold up, Martínez Barrio is tired but he's holding up, it's his duty, circus wrestlers also get tired and also hold up, the people who are demanding weapons are tired but they're holding up, in this case hope weighs as heavily as duty, the ants in the anthill also get tired and also hold up, the rebellious generals are tired but they're holding up, it's their duty, unfaithful wives also get tired and also hold up, the Carlists in the hills are tired but they're holding up, God our almighty father will reward them for it in the next world, amen, in the midst of a battle a victorious or defeated general cannot say this is quite ridiculous, piss on it all, I'm going home, I wash my hands of it, no, you know that everything is quite ridiculous, that the best thing to do is piss on it all and go home, that you can wash your hands of it and nothing will happen, but you are not a general either victorious or defeated, you are a nobody whom no one takes into account, you are thankful fodder for the whorehouse, neuter fodder for the catechism class, ora pro nobis, ora pro nobis, inspected cannon fodder, next year you'll be called up for service, it wouldn't matter if you pissed on everything, no one would notice, Dominica Morcillo gets tired too and holds up heroically and with a smile on her lips, just yesterday my Bernabé sat by me in the park, he seems all ice but he's very nice and loves petting in the dark, long live Spain!, long live the Republic!, here's the list War General Miaja Petra la Grillo mulatto from Guinea and a loose woman was never avenged nor did anyone have a mass said for her soul Navy Don José Giral what good did it do Magdalena to smell of rotten cheese and burning sulphur what good did it do her if all her deceits and renunciations are now buried? Interior Don Augusto Barcia in his papers Pepito la Zubiela's name is José González González fat lot he cares now when Isabela kicked Pepito la Zubiela out of her house for patting Don Máximo's butt she didn't call him José González González Foreign Affairs Don Justino Azcárate in the morning Doña Matilde's forehead was even colder than her butt and so of course they gave her a Christian burial Education Don Marcelino Domingo Don Cesáreo Murciego was against coeducation it is a seedbed of promiscuity he explained to Don Román Navarro while they were waiting at Milagritos' place an antidote to lust Finance Don Enrique Ramos death comes as it likes with banners fluttering in the breeze or like the wolf in the night Justice Don Manuel Blasco Garzón Engracia wants to be another Juanita Rico but today she won't go on an excursion to the country we must be on the alert Agriculture Don Ramón Feced Don Roque Barcia is no relative of Don Augusto's Don Roque is only an agriculturalist or rather a member of the Agrarian Party the foundation of the Spanish economy is agriculture Communications Don Juan Lluhí the angels play the harp and the trumpet but they don't talk on the phone or write letters or even poetry they shot Calvo Sotelo in the back and the angels neither noticed nor said anything Labor Don Bernardo Giner de los Ríos the angels can live without laboring and without thinking they shot Lt. Castillo in the back and the angels remained dull and dumb Industry and Commerce Don Plácido Álvarez-Buylla the widow of the chauffeur Juan Sánchez does not know that she's a widow if she goes to bed with some neighbor she'll make a cuckold of the dead man because she doesn't know he's dead Public Works Don Antonio Lara just now Rómula has died in the hospital of San Juan de Dios she still lies on the cold marble table of the morgue next to another dead woman who has no name no one will wear mourning for either of the two Minister without portfolio Don Felipe Sánchez Román, would you like some more coffee?, yes thank you we must not go beyond the ranks of the republicans we need respected names names that no one can object to and Prime Minister Don Diego Martínez Barrio of course Don Manuel and Don Diego are very tired but they're holding up it's their duty you can be sworn in early in the morning all right before that I'll talk with Mola on the phone Miaja will call him as Minister of War if necessary I'll call him next everything depends on what he tells us in any case I won't take the responsibility for arming Largo Caballero's legions thank you there's no need to thank me Mr. President in the gardens below the palace the owl whistles and the nightingale sings its melodies those who were demanding arms have gone to bed dead tired and over the city there hangs a kind of strange quiet crossed from time to time by some isolated and distant gunshot if Don Olegario had found an investor for his musical urinal or for his anti-hailstorm balloon he'd be rolling in money by now and could pay for women more for some less for others history marches on as it likes and wishes and it is fruitless to think or act against the grain of history it would be useless empty thought and hollow action before and after drinking Matías López' chocolate delicious chocolates Madrid-El Escorial manufacturers of the world's finest candies and chocolates Don Olegario goes to bed with Chonina when she lets him Chonina is not a lusty girl at least not with Don Olegario but she is compassionate at least with Don Olegario it's sad but look, it'll do, Don Olegario can't be too fussy Pepe the Dog-Man was murdered on the road from Húmera to Pozuelo and the authorities questioned a brother of Chonina's I swear to you that I didn't have anything to do with all of this you can ask Don Olegario that night I was with Don Olegario helping him to glue a mirror and sort at least a hundred screws by their sizes I'm innocent I swear it sir Ginesa also spoke on behalf of Chonina's brother I sent him on an errand and then he told me he was going to see a gentleman who lives on the other side of the sports field of the streetcar company Ricardín is a good boy sir as decent as they come Ricardín couldn't kill a chicken General Miaja makes two calls to General Mola they've made me Minister of War congratulations thank you are you planning to have me shot? that's not why I'm calling you did you get the letter I wrote you? I haven't had time to answer it yet but we can talk whenever you like the situation is confused but Mola's words give no hint of anything the second conversation is clearer is it true that you have ordered the military commandant of Vitoria to proclaim the state of war? yes sir don't you know that the authority to issue such an order rests with the commanding general of the sixth division? I am commanding the sixth division how's that? what about Batet? I've relieved him what? are you crazy? that's outright rebellion yes sir I am in rebellion along with the division you could have told me that! I said as much when I asked you whether you were planning to have me shot well well you are responsible for your actions Victoriano has another attack of diarrhea this time he can't make it to the bathroom and shits on the bed and along the hallway this is too much fine shape I'm in! don't worry dear you'll get over it tomorrow with a little rice and some quince jelly you think so? sure I do that's the best way there's no diarrhea it won't cure go on change your pajama and I'll get some clean sheets Don Máximo falls asleep in an armchair and Rafaela fans him with an ostrich-feather fan like the one used by Miss Dolly the dancer from Gibraltar the princess of the cabarets and queen of the charleston Angelines offers him a crème de menthe and Dulce offers him drags on a Cuban cigar that smells heavenly Victoriano like Rabelais has another attack of diarrhea here we are all surrounded by whores and may we never be worse off the daughter follows in the footsteps of the mother and a spider lays its ten thousand eggs inside a bottle of mineral water if there is an indistinct noise no one should be alarmed it is the spider giving birth Don Máximo wakes up joy lasts but little in the poor man's house Don Diego Don Felipe and General Miaja speak slowly also worriedly Don León has been recently widowed the widow of Don Cesáreo is seriously injured and in her recent widowhood she is treated in Dr. Bastos' clinic the chauffeur's widow doesn't know that she's been recently widowed once she knows it she will dress in strict mourning Pepito la Zubiela leaves no widow General Mola is in rebellion General Queipo de Llano is in rebellion General Franco is in rebellion General Cabanellas has been relieved General Batet is a prisoner General Villegas is nobody knows where General Miaja is confused it's no wonder Don León sleeps like a log with the whole bed for himself you can throw black hookers out of bed when you're through they're used to it but not white hookers because they won't let you and they scratch and insult you with the worst insults lousy john son a bitch pimp discipline is breaking down and good manners no longer count it makes no difference that they're reading the list of the new cabinet on the radio nobody is listening neither those who sleep nor those who are demanding weapons by this time there are fewer people demanding weapons that's natural Paulina and Javiera sleep soundly Paulina tends to fart a little farting women have a certain charm Javiera doesn't then Jesualdo buys a strawberry ice cream for

Evelina who does not make counterfeit ten-centimo pieces that's Three-foot's Grandson and the Civil Guard has already arrested him maybe the cripple who sells tobacco is a hero of some war if a hero of some war gets a bullet in his spine he's paralyzed forever but he gets along selling tobacco Victoriano has another attack of diarrhea it's like the jet of the Artichoke Fountain the cripple who sells tobacco is called Marramáu and keeps his pockets full of stones his daughter has to set him on the toilet as if he were a child your Uncle Jerónimo is a friend of Don Felipe's Don Máximo wakes up Don Diego telephones General Mola we have to form a grand coalition cabinet that can keep order no that's what you think but I tell you only the Army can give Spain back the peace she so badly needs general think about it carefully you and I may be the last chance for peace I offer to make you Minister of War in exchange for your help in establishing peace and keeping all these events from degenerating into a civil war you know that I refuse to arm the people but if you don't accept my point of view I'd be forced to resign and my successor whoever that may be would arm the people we must avoid the spilling of blood Mr. Prime Minister your patriotic sentiments do you honor but I can't turn back any more I'd be dragged through the streets I've already armed the people they'd spit in my face they'd call me a traitor they'd drag me through the streets the die is cast the situation demands solutions that are very different from those that you with all your good will are proposing to me your Uncle Jerónimo is a friend of Don Felipe's if the crisis had come twenty-four hours earlier perhaps we could have saved democracy and the country Mola is a reasonable man after his fashion of course but he is trapped by circumstances so is Don Diego Don Diego is very tired and orders more coffee Azaña is also tired everybody is tired all we can do is wait for news the situation is serious but can become even more so even though you don't want to your only way out is to look at yourself in the mirror in the shape of a parallelepiped you are wounded in the back you have a stab wound in your back no you are not wounded in the back you do not have a stab wound in your back it's a mole you just can't see it in an ordinary mirror in a flat mirror Paquito and Alfonso get in the Montaña Barracks every man knows what he's doing Señor Asterio is sleeping peacefully in the mirror in the shape of a parallelepiped you look like a fish with a stab wound in its back with a mole on its back in the mirror in the shape of a parallelepiped you see yourself a little stooped they don't leave the decision fear/heroism to you I hope to God it all ends as just a Sancamilada they tell you here or there and you obey like a robot Victoriano has another attack of diarrhea his system is out of control you can slit a Chinese hooker's throat like a pigeon's when you're through they're used to it but white hookers you have to pay if Don Olegario had managed to manufacture his little urinal or at least his balloon he'd be a great man by now and a celebrity and he'd be able to pay women according to their assiduity their beauty and their merits General Mola is in rebellion General Queipo de Llano is in rebellion General Franco is in rebellion General Patxot is in rebellion and sorry for it General Llano de la Encomienda is not in rebellion General Martínez Monje is not in rebellion General Sanjurjo is in Estoril General Saliquet they say is also in rebellion General Gómez Caminero is not in rebellion on the fourteenth of April the people of Madrid were shouting oh me oh my, Mola has to die! General Cabanellas is in rebellion this report has not been confirmed General Batet is a prisoner General Villegas Montesinos has disappeared General Miaja is confused General González de Lara is in rebellion this report has not been confirmed General Pozas is not in rebellion General Núñez de Prado is a prisoner General Romerales and General Gómez Morato may be dead General Castelló is not in rebellion General Aranguren is not in rebellion General Riquelme is not in rebellion General López Pinto is in rebellion General Varela escapes from the castle of Santa Catalina General Goded is in rebellion this report has not been confirmed this business with Victoriano has become ridiculous he's spending more time sitting on the toilet than in bed we all want to play our parts but Victoriano's part is very unglamorous ridiculous and painful theology is nothing but a quarrel among dialecticians the gods don't care about theology the Gypsy bullfighter who set a whore on fire after sprinkling her with anise is not concerned about theology either in this he's like the gods to call things by their true and proper names not to call things by their true and proper names dog love bread to curse all things human and divine not to waste time cursing all things human and divine to fight tooth and claw in defense of the lawful republican and democratic system not to fight by any means and least of all with enthusiasm in defense of the lawful republican and democratic system to go to bed with this woman who smells of sweat and food or with that other one who stinks of fried oil and the drugstore and kick her out of bed when you've finished or slit her throat like a pigeon's depending on whether she's black or Chinese or not to go to bed with this woman who smells of sweat and food nor with that other one who reeks of fried oil and the drugstore and not kick her out of bed when you've finished even if she's black nor slit her throat like a pigeon's along the little dark feathers of the throat even if she's Chinese to follow a rebellious general not to follow a rebellious general to go for walks in the parks and the open spaces where couples mistreat each other among howls insults saliva and streams of semen under no circumstances to take walks in the parks and the open spaces where couples mistreat each other just like pigs in love among jealous grunts insults spit and come to play solitaire with the deck of hearts diamonds clubs spades to cheat at solitaire with the deck of hearts diamonds clubs spades to watch with great satisfaction how they beat a child to death not to watch with great satisfaction how they beat a child to death to hunt frogs with a club to hunt frogs with a net to hunt frogs with dynamite or with kerosene to kill a neighbor by surprise and with a poisoned dart while she is undressing in front of the open window to hunt a neighbor down after giving her a warning and not with arrows but with blows of a hoe like the gravediggers to give the finger to the cripple Marramáu not to give the finger to the hero Marramáu hero of some war to demand weapons weapons weapons so as to fight alongside the people blended with the people not to demand weapons weapons weapons weapons weapons weapons in order to fight alongside the people or blended with the people nor for any cause just or unjust to take your life with gas or sleeping pills not to take your life with gas or sleeping pills to feed the hungry to laugh at the hungry and push an old man in the way of the train to give drink to the thirsty to laugh at the thirsty and push two old women walking arm in arm in the way of the bus to squeal to the police to squeal to the wild flowers that the police abuse their power to compose sonnets not to compose sonnets or compose imperfect sonnets to play dominoes to make obscene faces while playing dominoes to murder a schoolmate treacherously to murder a schoolmate distractedly to murder a schoolmate compassionately you are not Napoleon Bonaparte but neither are you King Cyril of England cut off your right hand before it is too late the destiny of tools is very bitter very bitter very bi

Part III The Octave of St. Camillus

What have we done, oh Lord, to kindle thus your ire?

Do not for these our sins plunge Spain into the fire!

—*Poem of Fernán González*, 554 a, b

I

You look at yourself in the mirror with all the attention that you can muster, Julius Caesar was capable of a great deal of attention and astuteness, you seem to be hypnotized like Saint Paul, you don't blink, you don't wink, William Tell dared to shoot his crossbow (it was no crossbow, it was a long bow) at the apple, not the tiniest line in your face is trembling and your eyes seem to be of glass like the eyes of stuffed owls, of stuffed lizards, like the eyes of the dead whose eyes no one has closed, mildew, verdigris, inevitably spreads over them, your eyes hurt (especially your eyeballs) from keeping them fixed on your startled and deformed figure, you are not the Hunchback of Notre Dame but you're far from being a pink marble Apollo, don't move, we all must make some sacrifice, we are all green wood on the sacrificial pyre, warm breath of the mouth of the sacrificial lamb, no one will forgive you the slightest guilt because you smile, your vices, your sinful habits, your inhibitions, King Cyril of England died of burning mockery, or because your figure is startled, deformed, and gangly, people take more kindly to pardoning a triumphant hero than a nobody, you don't hear of any exemplary deeds done by helots, you are who you are and we're all good for something, the lash of the whip, the insult, the oblivion of Saint Helena, people step on an earthworm without any real cruelty with surprising indifference, that's what they always do, step on an earthworm as soon as they see it almost without looking at it, if you don't catch it on a hard surface, a stone, a head, a plate, an old coin, the earthworm doesn't die, it shudders but it doesn't die, you look at yourself very diligently in the mirror because you don't think the phenomena of the reflection of light can any longer be possible and nonetheless you continue to address yourself in a familiar way although less confidently, it all needs to be said, your flat mirror with its splendid frame gilded with patience and with gold leaf no longer does you any good, it reflected various women in their slips and with one tit sticking out (never with both tits sticking out), it began to smell like a corpse and you had to break it in a thousand pieces, somebody probably broke it treacherously some time ago and it's a pity because maybe you could have used it again sometime, one must never lose confidence in the usefulness of things, your mirror in the shape of a parallelepiped with its polished surfaces no longer does you any good, it doesn't do you any good either, it reflected six or seven women in their slips each with her butt sticking out, with their multiplied butts sticking out, it began to smell like a corpse and you had to paint its six polished surfaces with black pitch, you can reasonably suspect that someone corroded by envy painted the six beautiful polished surfaces of your mirror in the shape of a parallelepiped with miserable sticky black pitch some time ago, don't feel bad about it because yes it was a beautiful mirror but a very confusing one, in your mirror in the shape of a parallelepiped you could see your unknown butt, less known than those of your girlfriends, the unknown stab in the back and that mole that sometimes many years ago you tried to tear off with your nails as though it were a tick full of sweet blood, it was funny to see the most unusual images reflected in your mirror in the shape of a parallelepiped but it would never have done you any good, bad examples must be put aside, someone corroded by envy probably painted it with black pitch but you really shouldn't weep over its grave or take it fresh-cut flowers or wax flowers or cloth flowers because it would never have done you any good except to bring you grief, don't take it paper flowers either, you look at yourself in the mirror without any confidence and you address yourself in a familiar way but timidly and also without any confidence, it's not a flat mirror with its glass in better or worse condition and its frame of carved wood or its little molded frame that reflects your bitter and disjointed features, no, nor a multiple mirror either, six mirrors that form a kind of cell in the shape of a parallelepiped in which if you jump up and down you can even see the soles of your feet with their itineraries, no, it's an ovoid mirror that has no floor or ceiling or walls but in which you float in a rare sweetish atmosphere, sweetish to the taste, like a fetus in the womb, in books they always show a fetus floating in the womb, what you can't do is stop, you always move in a very slow rhythm but without letup, like the bump of protoplasm on the yolk of a monstrous swallow's egg, nobody knows it but the world's first king was born of a monstrous swallow's egg, sometimes your legs are long like a stork's or your hands big, your head tiny, your eyes bulging, your penis in the shape of a snail, it depends on which way you look, the best thing would be to close your eyes even if you notice symptoms of nausea, you can take a long time to die but not forever, at breakfast time no one sees cheerful faces in his family, you can tell that we Spaniards sleep badly maybe we eat too much for supper, it is uncharacteristic for the fortunate to shower consolation on the wretched, you know what I'm getting at, Azaña and Martínez Barrio did not sleep last night, neither well nor badly, their sleep would not have alleviated the sleeplessness or the miseries of anyone, Martínez Barrio's cabinet is never sworn in, it is stillborn or depending on how you look at it it is born moribund and dies at once, Mola is on the phone and the people of Madrid are in the streets calling Don Diego a traitor who has sold out and other worse things, your Uncle Jerónimo shows up at your house very early, you're all still in bed, you haven't even had time to shut yourself up in your egg-shaped mirror to feel a little alone and separate and recite your poems and caress your poor salty parts, Don Diego couldn't hold out, it's too bad but he couldn't hold out, above your parents' bed there is a large silver crucifix with its basin for holy water in the shape of a seashell, your Uncle Jerónimo sits down at the foot of your parents' bed and speaks rapidly, you can tell he's nervous, Mola had already armed the people in Navarre, he said so quite clearly on the phone to Don Diego, Don Felipe was there, and he didn't dare to turn back, and he wouldn't have been able to turn back either, your Uncle Jerónimo's hair is tousled, he looks like a porcupine, Casares lost twenty-four precious hours, he thought he was facing an attempted coup like the one in 1932 and no, he wasn't facing an attempted coup like the one in 1932, even so it's a shame that Don Diego has failed, politics is not the art of all or nothing but quite the contrary, in politics you never start with zero, politics is the art of saving what you can and governing Spaniards so they won't hunt each other down, Don Felipe should have served as a guarantee for everyone but nobody wanted to listen to the voice of reason, your Uncle Jerónimo stops and looks at your mother, María, may I have a glass of milk?, Azaña calls in the Socialists, Prieto and Largo Caballero, Don Diego is there while they talk, a compromise is out of the question, it's resist or surrender, shall we surrender?, no, do we resist?, yes, all right then we have to arm the workers, the rebellion is spreading and that's the only choice left to the Republic, to arm the unions, we have to try just once more to form a republican cabinet, will you support it?, yes, and what about the Communists and the Anarchists?, they probably will too, Radio Unión is breaking the news that a new cabinet is being formed that accepts Fascism's declaration of war on the Spanish people and that is prepared to defend our republican constitution, this cabinet has the backing of the unions, the UGT and the CNT, the members of the Socialist and Communist Parties belong to the UGT and the Anarchists belong to the CNT, outside the shouts against Martínez Barrio are gradually dying out, they were calling him a traitor who had sold out and other worse things, you know what, your Uncle Jerónimo drinks his glass of milk very slowly, all nourishment should be well insalivated even the liquids, of course, with Don Diego there goes our last hope that all of this will not wind up as a horrible massacre, go on, let's hope not, I wish I could hope!, María, may I have a slice of buttered toast?, your Uncle Jerónimo doesn't eat much, man is an animal that starts to rot from the belly like a partridge and like almost all the others, it's easier to start to rot from the belly than from the heart, the heart doesn't rot, it bursts into pieces or stops like an old rusty motor, the belly is a treacherous and fragile organ, a tool that spends a lifetime making demands and causing annoyance, the belly is an organ incapable of love or gratitude. Early each morning the silent troop of garbage men descends on Madrid, Giral besides being Prime Minister takes over the Navy Ministry, some garbage men invade the city from the north, Fuencarral, Tetuán de las Victorias, and others from the east, Las Ventas, Canillejas, their direction is the opposite of that of the dead, Ramos continues at Treasury, Blasco Garzón at Justice, and Alvarez-Buylla at Industry and Commerce, the garbage men don't wash much but they eat well and abundantly, good healthy food, pork, lettuce and other vegetables, goat's milk, Giner de los Ríos trades Labor to Don Juan Lluhí for Communications, everybody knows that garbage men are honest and return the silver spoons that accidentally go into the garbage can, that's not the business they're in and they have whole bags full of silver utensils of unknown ownership, they'll speak up once they notice, Barcia leaves Interior and goes to Foreign Affairs, General Pozas replaces him and Don Justino Azcárate steps down, the garbage men's children grow up healthy and ruddy, early rising and fresh air are more powerful than germs, Marcelino Domingo, Feced, and Lara are out at Education, Agriculture, and Public Works, they are succeeded by Don Francisco Barnés, Don Mariano Ruiz Funes, and Don Angel Velao, from the south, Vallecas, Vicálvaro, garbage men also go up toward Madrid, some of the youngest ones sing flamenco tunes but most of them usually don't, General Miaja leaves the War Ministry to General Castelló and Don Felipe leaves the cabinet, they're all republicans those who come those who go and those who stay, the question being debated was compromise or fight, compromise was impossible and a fight can be won but can also be lost, the outcome of a fight except at the circus, you know about that (they say at least somebody knows), is always in doubt like the heads or tails of the flip of a coin, at first everybody thinks he's going to win and what happens afterward is that everybody loses, the winners and the losers, some more, some less, but they all lose, their faith, their hope, their charity, their freedom, their decency, their dreams, their life, your Uncle Jerónimo does not believe much in fights and even less in chance, almost no one asks for a mirror to see himself die and very few kill themselves in front of a mirror, there have been some but few, remember the flu of '18 that decimated families, parents buried their children and servants buried the parents and were left unburied at the foot of the chestnuts and the oaks until an immense wolf carried them off into the hills in its mouth, man is a very histrionic and tragic animal, not very prudent and farseeing, man is an avaricious and needy beast, he is like a weasel puffed full of stinking air, of accusatory air, and assaulted by the mastiffs that nest in its own conscience, that's a bad business so many vulgar paradoxes embroidered on a canvas of criminal absurdities, look at yourself in the mirror without missing a single one of your last moments, take precise note of every detail, make use of an efficient notarial prose, run away from beautiful words, from mortal words, learn algebra in order to die and do not grant yourself a single advantage, there that's right, twist your mouth, turn up your eyes, move your ears rhythmically, make an effort of the will and keep your hair standing on end, there that's right, now smile, smile contemptuously, ask your Uncle Jerónimo for his firm opinion and don't get in the way of the bullets, the flu of '18 has already given at least a hundred performances in Spain, display your modesty and store up strength capable of producing death, always remember that you are a poor man manipulated by others, a poor sick man pitied by others, tolerated by others, place yourself serenely or rather nervously in front of the mirror and look at yourself with excusing eyes, close your ears to the siren songs of family, you have no family and don't need any either, the noise from outside keeps you company but also alarms you, don't think that those who roar are less alone or less alarmed than you, you are still too young and you must strive to form a sporting idea of death, you'll give in eventually if you make it to the last act alive, in the twilight of dawn the distribution of weapons begins, maybe it's true that there were fifty thousand rifles, the bolts are in the Montaña Barracks, there are five barracks in Madrid, Montaña, Saboya, Pacífico, María Cristina, and the tank barracks, there may be more, General Fanjul is at his brother-in-law's home on the Calle Mayor almost across the street from the military headquarters and the first mixed division, he is the one who is to take charge of the first mixed division but he still hasn't received the order to do so, nor does he have enough forces to hold out, nothing is known about General Villegas, he is the chairman of the military junta and his target is the War Ministry, Don Máximo is very depressed, he doesn't want to stay alone and drops by the house on O'Donnell to take a bath and have breakfast, what's going on Don Máximo?, ah if I only knew, Isabelita!, Rafaela and Angelines between them give Don Máximo a bath, Isabel attends the ceremony seated on the toilet bowl, how do you think all this is going to end Don Máximo?, I don't know Isabelita, believe me I don't know, Don Máximo's bath is gloomy and ritual, is the water right?, yes fine, would you like to dry off in bed with us?, no give me a robe, Don Máximo has not slept all night, he can't put on clean clothes either, Isabel sprinkles talcum powder on his girdle and tells them to shine his shoes a little, they're ironing your pants, you'll have them right away, your money I put on the night table, thanks Isabelita, would you like coffee or chocolate?, it's all the same, well, coffee, give me a good strong coffee with a little milk, would you like crullers?, all right, and jam?, no, Rafaela and Angelines are quiet, Rafaela wears a salmon-colored robe that comes down to her bare feet, Angelines is in bra and panties, with very elegant electric blue slippers, Don Máximo drops by Don Diego's house, is Don Diego in?, no sir, he went to Valencia, didn't he leave any message for me?, no sir. You go to mass with your father to Christ church on Ayala Street, your father tells you boy, put on your tie and come to mass with me, and you put on your tie and go to mass with him, your mother stays at home with your little brothers and your Uncle Jerónimo, the church doors are half open and the priest says the ten o'clock mass for five persons, your father, you, and three others, Catholics have suddenly lost the urge to comply with their religious obligations, nobody bothers you as you go in or as you go out, they look at you but they don't bother you, the *ABC* doesn't say anything special, the fact is that nobody knows anything about anything, Don Máximo is right, ah if I knew what was going on, Isabelita! Don Roque wakes up at midmorning at Maruja la Valvanera's place, Consuelito is still lost in blessed sleep, Don Roque gives her a pat on the buttocks and the girl opens one eye, grumbles under her breath and wakes up, what's going on?, nothing, the end of the world, can't you see?, Don Roque takes a sip from the glass of water on the night table, phew, that's like soup!, come on get up and get me some water from the basin, yes, let the faucet run, Consuelito bends over the basin and Don Roque jumps out of bed and impales her just as she is, without any preparations, Maruja la Valvanera prepares breakfasts in the kitchen, the maids are only good for washing the dishes and making the beds, besides they're a bunch of thieves who eat the crullers and the rolls, Don Roque is awake now, don't you hear him?, he's already laid Consuelito again, Don Roque really likes the women's posture when they bend over the basin with their butt sticking out, go on, tell Maruja to get my breakfast ready and bring me the *ABC*, Maruja la Valvanera takes the *ABC* to Don Roque, breakfast is coming right away, fried eggs?, yes, of course, what else should I have, a yogurt?, Don Roque is sitting naked on the bed with the sheet around his belly, is Mola in Madrid yet?, no, well, not as far as I know, Don Roque rolls a cigarette and lights it gingerly, he'll come, tomorrow at the latest, what's the news?, I don't know, God himself wouldn't understand this mess, it seems to me everything is all mixed up, Consuelito combs her hair naked in front of the mirror, Maruja la Valvanera stands there looking at her, what a woman, Don Roque!, have you noticed those tits, that derriere, those hips . . . ?, yes, she's not bad, the truth is I can't complain, not many voices are heard on the Calle de Alcántara, at any rate no more than any other Sunday at that time, Alcántara is a very quiet street, with its cookie factory, its sparrows chirping in the acacias, its children who play their little games, no fair cheating, Paquito can make a top spin on his hand better than anybody, or leapfrog, one said the mule, two said the kick, each according to the season, with its whorehouses and its gentle mystery of dissimulation, Don Roque goes to mass at the church of St. Emmanuel and St. Benedict, the main door is closed and you have to go in through the sacristy, there is hardly anyone in the church, the situation is not as mellow as Don Roque imagined, downtown armed groups of people go along the Calle de Alcalá shouting long live and down with, long live the Republic, long live the social revolution, long live the people's militia, down with Fascism, down with the reactionaries, down with Army traitors, Don Roque thinks all this racket would come to an end with half a dozen well-distributed thrashings, Don Vicente Parreño does not take his wife to mass, no Eduvigis, let's be sensible, all you have to do is see what it's like out there, I wouldn't be a bit surprised if churches started to burn any moment, the prudent thing is to stay at home, if you want to we'll say the rosary, yes Vicente, how good you are!, no dear, like all the rest, Don Vicente goes to bed with María

Inés la Cordobesita but he takes very patient care of Doña Eduvigis, the poor woman's asthma gets worse by the day, the least slip and she'll be gone, the doctor has told him that, Vicente do you think things will have been settled by tomorrow?, I don't know whether tomorrow or three days from now but it can't go on like this, you can be sure of that, I hope to God you're right!, yes, that's what we need. General Villegas gives signs of life and sends a messenger to General Fanjul, I bring the order for you to occupy the first mixed division and take command, no, I wouldn't be able to hold on there, I don't have enough troops to hold on, have you seen how things are out in the streets?, yes sir, well then you've seen enough, if I don't receive an order to the contrary I'll establish the command post of the first division in the Montaña Barracks, tell that to General Villegas from me, yes sir, General Villegas' messenger coincides with those sent from the Montaña Barracks, in view of the hesitation of the chairman of the military junta the garrison of the barracks approaches General Fanjul to offer him the command, yes, now there is no longer the slightest doubt, no orders come from Mola either or from his liaison in Madrid Colonel Galarza, Don Valentín Galarza. Don Leopoldo gives an absolute order to his family, no one is to go out for any reason whatsoever, keep the windows closed and may God help us, the situation is truly difficult and I doubt that the Army will be able to control it, they should have left their barracks by now, now we'll have to wait two or three days, maybe a whole week before order is restored, Doña Bernardina and the children are still, let's say an Our Father for Enrique. Matiítas suddenly finds himself with a rifle in his hand, he didn't want a rifle but they gave him one, he doesn't know who or where, maybe it was on the Plaza de Cibeles, there are a lot of people at Cibeles and they're distributing rifles from two or three trucks, Matiítas gets a rifle with no bolt, so much the better, a rifle with no bolt is decorative and doesn't go off, the best thing would have been to leave it in the lobby of some house under the stairs, there are no lobbies on Cibeles, the bolts are at the Montaña Barracks, well then send for them, long live the Republic!, all right, the crowd is like an enormous soft whale that ends in hundreds of fringes through which it's losing strength, the fringes are ever more distant and the whale moves like the water in a lake, from the bottom up and with ambiguous little ripples on the surface, Matiítas likes being pushed from one side to another, being squeezed on one side and another, almost everybody is carrying a rifle in his hand, countless rifles have been distributed, revolutions evidently always begin with a lot of squeezing, Matiítas would also have liked for his customers from the condom shop to see him and for Don Esteban the blind man, that would be more unlikely Don Esteban's eyes are no good to him, Matiítas is very excited and trembling, it's too bad the customers from the condom shop and Don Esteban can't see him with the rifle, somebody says that there are also bolts stored at the Pacífico Barracks, there could be, General Fanjul in civilian clothes arrives at the Montaña Barracks, wait for me to put on my uniform, gentlemen, before you and at this moment I proclaim myself commanding general of the first mixed division, long live Spain!, the colonel of the regiment Don Moisés Serra is General Fanjul's classmate, the government demanded that he hand over the bolts but he gave an evasive answer, the cadets gathered in the barracks have gone to mass at the church of the Carmelites and come back without incident, it was certainly imprudent, from the barracks General Villegas is notified of General Fanjul's presence and he transfers responsibility for the uprising to the new commander, Fanjul addresses the three units in the barracks and the civilians who have been joining them, we shall conquer or die but in either case with military honor intact, General Fanjul draws up the proclamation of the state of war that ends with three long-live's, long live Spain!, long live the Republic!, long live the Army!, we must move out at precisely 3 P.M., the artillery at Campamento must join us, sir Colonel Castaños says that he awaits orders from General Villegas, I'm the one who's giving orders!, General Villegas is no longer chairman of the junta!, get me Campamento on the phone!, they've cut our phone line sir. At the conclusion of the Digne-Nice stage of the Tour de France, the ranking of the Spanish cyclists is as follows, Mariano Cañardo, 7, Julián Berrendero, 14, Federico Ezquerra, 19, and Emiliano Álvarez, 35, except for Salvador Molina who dropped out they're all moving ahead, Berrendero and Ezquerra think a Spaniard may win today's run, which is very short, only 126 kilometers and with three mountain passes very well suited to their capabilities, Brauss, Sospel, and La Turbie, right now they're probably pounding the pedals, they're tough, bike racing like that must be exhausting, wham, wham, always on the road going uphill and downhill with the sun burning their necks or getting soaked if it's raining, they're tough, Dominica drops by her neighbor Don Olegario's house to ask him for some tobacco, of course, naturally, what are friends for, we have to help each other, that can is full of butts, take as many as you want, do you have paper?, yes paper I have, in the morning Dominica prefers butts of Virginia tobacco, there aren't many but enough for rolling a couple of cigarettes or even three if they're not very thick, may I choose?, of course, I've got them all mixed together, Dominica brings Don Olegario two apricots, they're a little bruised but they're good, thank you very much, Dominica and Don Olegario live as good neighbors, if they were younger they would have shacked up long ago, do we still have a revolution?, yes so it seems, nobody is satisfied here, well, it's their lookout, that's what I say to myself, for all we're going to get out of it!, here everybody looks out for himself and the hell with us poor folks, the trouble with people is they don't feel like working, that's for sure, Dominica lights a cigarette while Don Olegario eats the apricots, it tastes great, yes and so do the apricots, you're always so attentive Domi!, Dominica smiles gratefully and draws deeply on her cigarette, I like Camels better than Lucky Strikes, how about you?, they're all the same to me, I don't smoke virginias, Dominica used to have a very elegant amber cigarette holder but she lost it once when she was drunk, it was too bad because it was very pretty and in good condition, did you look thoroughly all through your place?, of course I looked thoroughly, the first thing I did was turn everything inside out but I didn't find it. Don Roque arrives at his boardinghouse very worried, he finds his landlady worried too in spite of being a strong woman with a lot of presence of mind, Don Roque's landlady's name is Doña Teresa and she is the widow of a captain of artillery who was killed in Africa, Doña Teresa rules her boardinghouse with a tight rein and does not let anyone get out of hand or, even less, leave without paying, Don Roque gets special treatment from her because she admires and respects him, she forgives him the liberties he takes with the maids because they're weaknesses of the flesh, he's a gentleman she always says, Don Roque is a real gentleman, if you could see him like I saw him one afternoon in parliament defending religion, family, and private property!, you can't apply the same rules to men like Don Roque as to other men, sure, sometimes his hand slips when one of the maids goes by, so what?, the flesh is naturally sinful and a man isn't made of stone, these maids are a couple of tramps that spend their whole time leading him on, Don Roque doesn't try anything when he isn't sure, you're looking for it?, well you'll get it, just see how he's always treated me with respect, he's never allowed himself the slightest slip with me, there are reasons for that!, Doña Teresa is worried, I was very worried about your being out Don Roque, I kept on saying to myself, what could have happened to Don Roque that he hasn't come home all night?, Don Roque tries to appear calm, well it's nothing Doña Teresa, nothing happened to me, I just ran into some friends and we made a night of it, I'm not so old yet Doña Teresa, no that you're not Don Roque, it's just that everything is so stirred up, but anyhow, thank God we've got you at home now, I feel sort of safer with you here, what do you think of all this Don Roque?, it's a bad business, what else can I think of it, but this confusion can't go on, Mola is bound to show up here any time, you'll see, it's a matter of hours, and maybe the troops in Madrid will rise up before that, it's odd that they haven't done it yet, they'll get these brutes under control with a few cracks of the whip, you can be sure of that, I hope you're right Don Roque!, they've got me scared, good and scared, cheer up there and don't lose faith, just a few hours and all these wild men will be like lambs, you'll see I'm right. Toisha calls you on the phone, why didn't you call me?, well, I was reading and got distracted, that's not true, no but it sounds good, do you want to go out for a while?, my father won't let me, why not?, come on, why do you suppose, are things quiet over where you live?, yes, nothing's happening here, some shouting, that's all, and over there?, this is a madhouse, more and more people are heading down to the Montaña Barracks, they say they're going to storm the Montaña Barracks, and are you worried about it?, no you know it's all the same to me, Toisha gets you aroused even over the phone, that happens with some women, with others it doesn't, there are women whose voice is very exciting and full of hints and promises, others on the other hand talk like crickets or like toads, women who talk like crickets or like toads should be abandoned in the Gobi Desert, not in the Sahara, so they'd be eaten by repulsive hyenas, now that seems to me a bit too much and besides there aren't any hyenas in the Gobi Desert, well then scorpions, Toisha has the voice of a radio announcer or better yet of a high-class whore, of a whore with an emerald ring, from Malaga the governor reports that enthusiasm is at a fever pitch with all the armed forces on the side of the Republic, when Toisha says to you oh sweetheart, the things you make me do!, you feel like the happiest man in the world and wouldn't trade places with anybody, that is the sin of pride but pride in good fortune is excusable, the unfortunate person does not imagine certain situations, in Asturias the enthusiasm of the people is indescribable and the Republic and the government forces are being cheered everywhere, there is always some poor devil inclined to masturbate while the announcer on the radio says dear listeners you will now hear the pasodoble *The Wildcat*, in Valencia republican feelings are running high as is indignation at the treason of Queipo de Llano, Toisha will die in your arms in some one of her little Tuesday and Wednesday raptures, especially in the little raptures that she bestows on you on Tuesdays and Wednesdays as though you deserved them, drama, pretense, and love have their limits and you won't be able to get rid of her body or say that you don't know her, that you don't know who she might be, that you've never seen her or if you have you don't remember it, loyal forces are attacking Cadiz where the governor with the support of forces of the Civil Guard and the Assault Guard is under siege and resisting heroically, Toisha, what do you want, love?, why don't you come down to the doorway?, you're crazy, don't even think of going out, wait till this is all over, Toisha, what, I just wanted to hear your voice, well now you've heard it, in Huelva the garrison has rejected the mutinous leader Queipo de Llano and is on the side of the government, chance is a fish that always bites the most clumsily baited hook, one afternoon you said so to Toisha in Merceditas' place, Toisha was lying on the bed naked and very cheerful but when you spoke she covered herself with the sheet and started to cry, in Jaén, Granada, and Almería all the troops are on the side of the government, no one should make excessively precise plans for the future, Toisha enjoys making very precise plans for the future and that's her mistake, you don't dare to tell her so when she's naked because you're afraid she'll burst out crying again, in Catalonia the situation is under control, the rebellion of a regiment of infantry and another of artillery has been suppressed with the capture of five pieces of rebel artillery and a number of prisoners, there is no reason whatsoever to be compliant with a woman in love, the trouble with questions of principle is that they become distorted when you try to apply them, their edges and outlines blur, perhaps it would be prudent to be quite compliant with a woman in love, Toisha, what, nothing, I wasn't saying anything, in Madrid the situation is perfectly calm, some seditious radio stations have reported that Madrid is in the hands of the revolutionaries, all reports of an alleged uprising in the capital are false, your egg-shaped mirror is useful for many things but not for predicting the future, Toisha doesn't know that you have an egg-shaped mirror, Don Leopoldo looks at Doña Bernardina, if this is the way things are, that's the end, she has conjunctivitis and her eyes smart, don't say that Leopoldo!, Chonina comes to Don Olegario's place, here, I've got a pistol for you, what do I want that for?, I don't know, in case you have to defend yourself, no, no, take it away, I don't have to defend myself from anybody, Don Olegario thinks a minute, or no, wait, I'm sure I can use it for my inventions, is it loaded?, I don't know, Don Olegario aims the pistol up and pulls the trigger, the pistol is not loaded, leave it there, thanks a lot, I'm sure I can use it for my inventions. At the Montaña Barracks there are four or six sergeants and perhaps two dozen corporals and privates who are Communists, almost all of them are out on pass, one of the leaders of the sergeants' group is the master sergeant of engineers González Lagares, the cells of the lower ranks are under the authority of Corporal Nieto, a very clever and energetic man from the province of Orense, about three thousand men, maybe more, are gathered in the Montaña Barracks, many of them are Fascists—the Falangists, the Carlists, the monarchists, the Civil Guards, the reserve officers who arrived at the last minute—but not all of them, a lot of the enlisted men are antifascists, their leaders are prisoners in the basement. Javiera asks Don Roque, will you take us to the bullfight Don Roque?, Javiera always speaks in the plural, she never forgets to represent the other maid too, Paulina, sure sweetheart it's a fine day for a bullfight!, maybe they'll fight all of us in the Puerta del Sol!, Javiera doesn't argue, what choice does she have, better luck next time, by order of the authorities the bullfight advertised for this afternoon is canceled, six fine young bulls, six, surplus from the renowned herds of Don Celso Cruz del Castillo for Félix Almagro, Raimundo Serrano, and the novice matador Paco Godín, first appearance in this ring, seats one peseta and up, refunds at the box office. General García de la Herrán seems to have taken charge of the Campamento Barracks, the point is not to stay in the barracks, what we have to do is get the troops out on the streets, yes that's easily said, but the point is being able to do it, it's very easy to talk, people talk a lot but then when it's time to stand up and be counted it's another story, some get scared, others get mixed up, and others get in a rush or go too far, it's very hard to hit on just the right time and just the right action, when no one's in charge things start deciding for themselves how they're going to go, General Fanjul can't communicate with Campamento, he sends various messengers but he doesn't know whether they get there or whether they get killed en route, signaling with mirrors doesn't do much good either, the only thing to do is break out, break the siege if possible, declare a state of war, and establish order at gunpoint, the government doesn't control the streets either, that's plain to see, inside the Montaña Barracks the civilians are more spirited than the soldiers, the same thing is happening outside, enthusiasm is probably more effective than discipline, you can't be absolutely sure of that but sometimes it happens, on the Plaza de España and in the vicinity of the barracks a solid and expectant crowd has been gathering, people shout but not a shot is heard, inside the barracks there are very strict orders, no one may act on his own even though many would like to, the order is given not to go out till dawn, the crowd forms a barrier that no one could cross, they're so many they seem like Russians or Japanese, you'd need a force of highly disciplined veterans to make a way through the multitude, the government forces have succeeded in bringing some artillery pieces into the street, General García de la Herrán is able to organize a column and get out of Campamento at 4 A.M., a messenger manages to go and come back, some people have got balls!, General Fanjul gives the order to dig a line of ditches, perhaps he fears a tank attack, they haven't come but they could at any moment, there is no news from the tank regiment, good or bad. Jesualdo Villegas is very pale and pessimistic, maybe he's just very depressed, we republicans will die proclaiming our principles, that is our destiny which we must not try to avoid, in Spain we have to have a French Revolution that will vaccinate us against the Russian Revolution, who knows whether it's already too late to try, no, it's not too late, it's never too late to channel the revolutionary inertia of a people and for the Spanish people every channel has always been blocked, give me another beer, yes sir, and some potato chips, yes sir, the Spaniards ought to reread Ganivet, or rather, they ought to read him since they have never read him, in the *Idearium español* Ganivet talks like a prophet, in the face of Spain's spiritual catastrophe one must replace one's heart with a stone, one must cast a million Spaniards to the wolves so that we may not all have to cast ourselves to the swine, I think I remember it right, the people must storm the Montaña Barracks but remember what I'm telling you, if the people succeed in taking the Montaña Barracks they won't know what to do with the victory, in our country everything starts out as heroism and winds up as farce, it's sad but true, have you read the opinion poll in *The Firecracker* where they ask what should be done with our reverends?, well listen to a couple of samples, it's a jewel, Ramón!, yes sir Don Jesualdo, would you lend me *The Firecracker* for a minute?, yes sir, I'd be glad to, it's really great this time!, the waiter keeps *The Firecracker* in his jacket pocket to read between filling orders, there you are Don Jesualdo, thanks, look here, I'd make a giant firecracker out of all that rabble in black with dumdum bullets and a fuse and finally the Pope as the bomb and when it blew up he wouldn't say boo, do you like that?, here's another answer, hang them from the electric wires, pour gasoline on them, set a match to them, and then make them into sausages for animal feed, now you tell me what we're supposed to do with this shitty country we're stuck with, that's what I'd like to know, you say we have to take the Montaña Barracks if we can and if they don't break out first, and crush the rebellion?, right you are but then what?, Joaquín Costa is still right, what's needed in Spain is schools, we also have to cure Spain of religious superstition, the friars who want to burn heretics are the same kind of brutes as the heretics who want to burn friars, sometimes one side wins and sometimes the other but it's always the country that loses, you can be sure of that, and at the end it all comes to what Larra wrote, here lies half of Spain, it died of the other half, now we've got an Army rebellion, the first thing that's going to burn is democracy no matter who wins . . . , I'm going to drop by Madame Teddy's, there's always room for a little fuck, afterward I'll drop by at the paper. Engracia has a fever but she's holding up, the hour of the revolution has struck, Proletarian Brothers Unite!, long live the people's militia!, that's something you don't have to be eagle-eyed to see, poor Juanita Rico, how she would have liked to witness the triumph of socialism!, they shall not pass!, better to die on your feet than to live on your knees!, the forces of reaction will not stop the people from taking the Montaña Barracks, everyone to the support of the Republic!, for the first time in history Spain is going to have a government of workers and peasants, Lenin predicted it with his revolutionary wisdom, Spain will be the second country in Europe with a proletarian government, Agustín gets Engracia into the café on San Bernardo and makes her drink a cup of black coffee with an aspirin, here, this will keep you going, Agustín had tried to take her home but he had to give it up as impossible, down with Fascism!, all right, come on, drink your coffee and take the aspirin, Engracia looks beautiful now and her enthusiasm puts a strange gleam in her eyes, you've got big rings under your eyes, forget about that, what do I care!, Agustín is quiet, sometimes it's better not even to talk to Engracia. Don Máximo is disoriented, he can't understand how Don Diego could go off to Valencia without saying a word to him, obviously he had to go off in a hurry, Don Máximo goes by the Buffet Italiano, what can I bring you sir?, brandy and soda, hasn't Don Andrés come?, no sir, nobody's come this afternoon, Don Andrés Jiménez went to Cáceres with Don Gerardo, he really could have said good-bye, they left on the last train to leave the Delicias station, death of owner forces urgent sale well-established tailor shop 21 Fuencarral, what did you say?, nothing, what it says here, P. Catalá's antiworm candies will save your children from many an illness, Señor Asterio is bored in the House of the People, suddenly everything has become too quiet, Señora Lupe brings him bread, sausage, and half a bottle of white wine, here you are I've brought you this for a snack, all right leave it there, what are the girls doing?, nothing, they're home, they wanted to go out but I didn't let them, yes it's better they don't go out, they'd get overtired if they did, buy them some veal ribs and two bottles of orangeade, let them at least enjoy that, they're good girls, come on now, nobody says they're bad!, Lupita and Juani are in the attic making out with two boys from the neighborhood Cándido and Tomasín, both fifteen, go on silly, don't be ashamed, do you like looking at my titties?, yes Juani, I like it a lot, they've got to operate on Tomasín for phimosis, his family is putting it off, now just stay like that, don't be ashamed, why are you scared to give me a little kiss on the pussy?, when Lupita and Juani go down to their apartment their mother is already back, where were you?, no place, up on the roof looking at the people on the street, what did father say?, he says you shouldn't go out, that you'd get too tired, yes, maybe . . . Mrs. Díaz the blind woman dirties her pants the same as always but today nobody cleans her up, people have other things to worry about than whether an old woman dirties her pants or doesn't dirty her pants, when my daughter comes she'll bring me a fan with a bullfighter on it, you'll see, my daughter always brings me something when she comes to see me, Rogelio from the dairy stable is hot for Doña Sole's two half-wits, here's the milk, is Doña Sole home?, no, she's gone out, then Rogelio unbuttons his fly, lifts the skirt first of one and then of the other and screws them both on the floor or leaning against the wall, the half-wits laugh and bite on a handkerchief to keep from crying out. Gutiérrez, the waiter at La Granja El Henar, is a veteran of his trade, it's not easy to skip out on him without paying because when he doesn't know a customer he always watches him like a hawk, you've got to be careful with these people you don't know, sir that'll be 2.85, excuse me I hadn't noticed, quite all right, here's your fifteen centimos, you keep it, thanks, you mustn't try to find deep explanations for things, almost everything usually happens without any explanation, Don Roque had always respected Doña Teresa he'd been respecting her for many years, Don Roque is stretched out on his bed reading the paper, it's not wise to go out until the excitement dies down a bit, this seems like the end of the world or the moments before the Flood, Doña Teresa knocks on the door, may I Don Roque?, come in, Don Roque always sits up when he's stretched out on the bed reading the paper and Doña Teresa knocks on the door, today he doesn't, Doña Teresa is still good-looking, may I close the door?, of course, Doña Teresa locks the door and stands looking at Don Roque, don't move, you needn't bother, I wanted to talk to you, all right, I'm all ears, Doña Teresa sits down, she is breathing hard, well, the truth is I don't have anything special to tell you . . . , you've always respected me Don Roque, no more than you deserve Doña Teresa . . . , a dying fly flutters against the window pane, do you think I'm a woman?, Don Roque feels his heart pounding in his chest, don't answer me, a confused sound of voices drifts up from the street, Doña Teresa's nose trembles a little, Doña Teresa sits down on the bed, don't answer me just keep still, Doña Teresa caresses Don Roque's forehead, angels never caressed the forehead of a defeated gladiator with greater tenderness, do you think I'm a slut?, Doña Teresa kisses Don Roque on the mouth, the spirit blows where it wants to, it doesn't have to give prior warning, don't say anything, Roque, let me talk, Doña Teresa takes off her clothes, of course I'm a slut!, don't you realize that?, Doña Teresa and Don Roque make love like two adolescents who are sick or condemned to death, think what you like, Roque, I've been holding down the slut inside me for too many years, Doña Teresa's voice turns hoarse and quiet, do you want me to call Paulina and Javiera so they'll see us in bed?, how awful, what nonsense gets into my head!, Doña Teresa closes her eyes to speak, Roque, what, did you enjoy that?, yes, do you love me?, yes, I love you too, sometimes it doesn't much matter that the world is burning up or perishing from poison. Matiítas heads home with his rifle, he doesn't know whether he's happy or sad at having a rifle, sometimes he's very merry and proud and sometimes he's afraid it might go off on him, on the Plaza de Atocha they gave him a bolt and bullets and wrote his name down in a notebook, his neighbor Carmencita laughs when she sees him coming, where are you going with that cannon, Señor Matías, look out it doesn't go off on you, you look like General Polavieja, Carmencita is very bold, pants makers are usually very fresh and bold. Mrs. Blanco gets a phone call, Anita it's me Tomás, go to the Caracolillo Bar, now?, yes as soon as you can, is something happening?, I'll tell you when I see you, her husband doesn't understand her rush, where are you going?, Anita is worried, what the fuck do you care?, I'm going wherever I want to go, well now, there's no call for all that, at least that's what I think, Anita kisses her husband on his bald spot, I'm sorry Baltasar, I'm very nervous, I'll be right back, it's far to the Caracolillo Bar but Don Tomás Donato waits patiently, what's up?, I just wanted to see you to say good-bye, I'm leaving, where are you going?, I don't know but I'm leaving, they're not going to hunt me down like a rabbit, Anita Luque de Blanco suddenly turns amorous, but darling, are you going to go away just like that and leave me here alone?, come with me if you want to, no, you know that's impossible, you know I have my obligations, all right then don't come, my you're so crabby!, Don Tomás and Anita say farewell in bed at Micaela Crespo's place in the Guindalera district, by the time they leave it's pitch black outside, Don Tomás takes Anita as far as the corner of her house and then leaves, nobody knows where he might have gone because he never reappeared dead or alive. The Communist Party committee of the Saboya regiment, Moret or Infante Don Juan Barracks, has control over more than two hundred corporals and privates, Master Sergeant Alonso Moreno is in charge of the cell and Private Francisco Abad of the committee, the officers don't seem to want to rebel against the Republic, old Taboada, the one from *El Liberal*, goes from one place to another taking notes on sheets of paper and talking to people, street reporters have two enemies, lack of news and excess of news, neither they nor you know which is worse, Raúl Taboada goes by the newspaper office every hour or every hour and a half, if Don Paco Villanueva is there he tells him what he knows and asks him for orders, if he's not there he leaves him his papers on top of the desk and drags himself off again with his tongue hanging out, these bastards could have calmed down by now!, what bastards?, all of them!, Roque Zamora also works in the same building on the Calle de Marqués de Cubas but at *El Heraldo*, under the baton of Don Manolo Fontdevila, Roque Zamora treats Raúl Taboada with real reverence and calls him chief, in return Taboada gives him an occasional cigarette, Roque Zamora doesn't have a fixed salary and lives from day to day, borrowing a peseta here and there and accepting dinner invitations from actors and writers who aren't any model of liberality either. Every evening Raúl Taboada brings a little container of stew or some other dish to eat late at night, he heats it a little on an alcohol burner and enjoys his meal, Roque Zamora knows that when he arrives in the morning a container with a little sauce and half a roll will be waiting for him on the shelf over the basin in the men's room, first he drinks what can be drunk, then he wipes up what's left with the bread, and then he washes the container, dries it inside and out with paper, and puts it on Taboada's desk, he'll pick it up when he comes in the afternoon, Raúl Taboada goes back to the Montaña Barracks to see whether they finally fall or don't fall, people have been jamming the intersections till they form a human barrier that's hard to get through, nerves are taut and nobody here is going to bed, a lovely situation!, some militiamen ask passersby for their papers and sometimes you hear shouts and insults against a background of long-lives and down-withs, Taboada thinks that antifascism is like a contagious disease that can attack a whole multitude in a few hours, there couldn't have been this many antifascists before, if you push me I could even swear that there weren't this many inhabitants before in all Madrid, Victoriano Palomo and Virtudes live on the Calle de Leganitos and from their balcony you can see all that's going on very well, you've got to stay alert here, all hell can break loose at any moment, it's night now but it doesn't seem as though anybody wants to go to sleep, nobody sleeps during a revolution, that doesn't make sense but that's the way it is, in a novel nobody pisses or shits either and everybody thinks it's perfectly natural and asks no questions. There's no way for you to get Toisha out of her house today you can forget about that, you can tell her father won't budge, he's very headstrong and it's no use arguing with him, besides you can't do it because he really loathes you, the fucking old guy is really funny, he's very difficult, once he says no it's no use insisting because it would be a waste of time, he loathes you, maybe he doesn't even loathe you, he won't acknowledge your existence which is worse, Toisha phones you, don't think I've gone crazy, sweetheart, I'm not drunk either, I'm just hot like a bitch in heat, what did you say?, you heard me, hot as a bitch in heat, hotter than ever, I just got off in front of your picture, your voice makes me feel hot again, I don't know what's happening to me, I'm sorry, oh honey, I'm crazy about you!, Toisha speaks with a trembling, almost stuttering voice and suddenly she starts to cry, I'm a big slut, sweetheart!, I'm hanging up, my father's coming, I'll call you later, good-bye, good-bye, this girl has read Catullus there's not the slightest doubt about that, no, this girl doesn't even know who Catullus is, she's just got the itch, remember what Dámaso says about how Juan Ramón never went to a whorehouse in his life, well maybe it's not true, some unusual things are going on here, Toisha is usually well-spoken, she's not like the sisters who say the first thing that comes into their heads, Toisha has never talked to you like this not even in bed, Toisha had never thought out loud, her brute of a father is to blame for all this because he won't let her go out, do you think the devil exists?, no, I don't, well I do, the devil exists, you bet he exists!, and furthermore he has the face of a smiling crocodile, others imagine him with a baboon's face, with a leopard's face, or with the face of a hairy spider, people used to believe he had a goat's face, evidently because of the horns and the little beard, but no, a goat's face he doesn't have, theologians already demonstrated many years ago that he doesn't have a goat's face, your Aunt Mercedes insists that La Pasionaria is the devil, or rather that she's possessed by the devil, all you'd have to do is make the sign of the cross against her and sprinkle her with holy water, Engracia doesn't believe in either God or the devil and she doesn't say that Mola is the devil, not even that he's possessed by the devil, in spite of the aspirin Engracia doesn't feel better, would you like another cup of coffee?, no forget it, Master Sergeant Víctor Gómez is in charge of the cell in the armored regiment, he used to be Engracia's boyfriend and he's a resolute and brave man, very clever and well trained. Doña Sacramento phones her daughter, Victoriano answers, hello, it's me son, your mother-in-law, how's Virtudes?, all right I think she's all right, not the slightest symptom for now, well I'm glad, it's better she waits till this whole row is over, yes that's what I say too, Doña Sacramento doesn't much understand what's going on, she's a hardworking woman who loves order, five young fellows came bursting into her branch on the Calle de las Naciones with weapons and bedded down with her girls, it wasn't enough that they left without paying but they broke a glass cabinet and a bidet, shit on the rug and called a gentleman a Fascist, that's behaving like Bolsheviks, if the authorities don't get around to imposing a little order we're on the road to Bolshevism, there've always been people who leave without paying, anybody can get the urge to fuck when he doesn't have a peseta in his pocket, that's not the trouble, but they used to be more respectful and didn't break anything or shit outside the toilet bowl or insult the customers, what happened now was unheard-of before. Between the pages of her Kempis Doña Bernardina keeps a flower that her husband gave her when they were engaged, it's faded and dead now but it hasn't lost a single petal, Doña Bernardina has forgotten its meaning by now, she keeps it out of inertia, Don Leopoldo offered her the flower as a reminder of their first kiss, here, a reminder of our first kiss is what he said to her, God grant you never lose it as long as you live, it was the day before the wedding twenty-five years ago now, on the feast of Saint James patron saint of Spain they will celebrate their silver wedding, Don Leopoldo plans to give her a silver box that he's ordered from Espuñes Jewelers, that way she'll be able to store it very well and forever, Don Leopoldo is very secretive about it, he wants to surprise her, Saint James' day is the twenty-fifth, by then all this mess will be over, I hope so, I hope to God that we can all celebrate these twenty-five years in peace and good health. Three cars drive down the Calle de Alberto Aguilera at top speed, their windows are down and the passengers are shooting left and right, they must be desperate Fascists, what's beyond doubt is that they've got balls, people run and throw themselves to the ground while the cars drive off always one behind the other in the direction of the Plaza de Santa Bárbara, it all happens in a few seconds and then they're out of sight, when they were distributing weapons if anyone didn't get a rifle it was because he didn't want to, some people even took one without wanting to, they found themselves with a rifle in their hands and then didn't dare to leave it propped up against some light pole, the weapons were just handed out any old way and now everybody makes war on his own, Dominica Morcillo finds a rifle in an empty lot on the Calle de Maudes and takes it home, I'll get something for it, Dominica plans to ask twenty-five pesetas for her rifle and then come down to twenty, not a penny less, La Goya used to sing like an angel when she did that song about I don't want champagne or nothing fine, you just give me soda and red wine, the second part had different words but the same tune, go and see the cabaret, just you go, you will see them dance you know, fox-trot all the way, the last bit is very fast, yes it's sure worth twenty-five, you can't get a rifle for less than that. Lt. Col. Don Julio Mangada is organizing a battalion, at least that's what they say, Don Máximo doesn't understand how half the Army can rebel against the government from one side and the other half from the other, well, maybe Lt. Col. Mangada's example won't spread and the loyal officers will manage to restore order, Don Máximo would like to be able to talk to somebody, but he can't find anybody to talk to, at the lodge on the Calle del Príncipe everybody has lost his head, it's like a madhouse, Don Diego was right to leave Madrid, this is a very hysterical city, it was right on the Second of May that's true but every other time it's been wrong, Don Máximo goes into the Café de Levante, some customers are drinking beer with a rifle leaning against a chair, it doesn't seem very natural but he sees it with his own eyes, the Interior Ministry is right next door, General Pozas has a problem, Don Sebastián is an energetic man of solid judgment but he certainly has a problem, nobody knows what's going on inside the Montaña Barracks, it's odd that they haven't tried to get out, if they stay shut up inside there it's going to be so much the worse for them, there are more and more people around outside, if the troops from Campamento don't join them they're going to have to surrender, but to whom?, General Pozas sure has one big problem, Don Máximo wouldn't have liked to be in his shoes, no, when things act up the best thing is to step aside, nobody's going to untangle this tangle, most probably it'll never be untangled and we'll all die caught in it like in a big spiderweb kicking and cursing and blaming everybody else, if her brother gets a woman pregnant the child is born a half-wit but not if her father gets her pregnant, Don Máximo has supper in the Achuri Restaurant on Príncipe, there's hardly anybody there, with what's going on the customers are obviously losing their appetite, Don Máximo phones Isabel, send me two girls and any young fellow who's not running around with a rifle, I'm at the Achuri, and listen, you come too, right after supper you can go back, I'd like to have somebody to talk to, a quiet supper, you know, no party, Don Roque tells Doña Teresa, don't go in the kitchen, the maids can take care of the guests, I'm inviting you to supper at the Achuri, Doña Teresa feels like the happiest woman in Madrid, won't we create a scandal?, why should we?, well just because I never go out at night . . . , well the fact is I don't much care, I've worn mourning for my husband long enough and respected his memory, when Don Roque and Doña Teresa come into the Achuri Don Máximo's friends have not yet arrived, hello there Barcia, what a pleasure, you don't know how glad I am to see you!, Don Roque and Doña Teresa sit down at a table in back and each orders a vermouth, who's that?, a friend from parliament, a deputy?, yes, an Agrarian?, no he's from Republican Union but a very good man and very decent, do you want to look at the menu?, you choose, I'll eat whatever you do, Don Roque smiles gratefully and squeezes one of Doña Teresa's hands, let's see, how about asparagus with mayonnaise, poached eggs, and veal cutlet?, fine, Don Roque turns to the waiter, that's it, you heard me, bring a little salad with the meat too, lettuce, tomato, a couple of radishes, a little onion, you know, and half a bottle of Valdepeñas, no, not half a bottle, a whole bottle, and Rioja, today is special, dessert we'll think about later, Isabel takes some time getting there, I couldn't find a taxi to save my life, did you come on foot?, no, finally we got a ride with a gentleman who was at the house, well it's a good thing, Isabel comes accompanied by Rafaela and Nati, Angelines was with a customer, don't worry, Nati is very nice too, what I didn't find is a young fellow to come with us, all the better, that way there's more for me, Isabel and her two girls laugh as if they'd heard something very funny, Isabel doesn't know Doña Teresa and of course doesn't greet Don Roque, Doña Teresa doesn't take her eyes off the three women, who are those women?, I don't know, I've never seen them before, to judge by their age I'd say they were his wife and two daughters, Doña Teresa has a sharp instinct, don't you think they're a little overdone, dressed a little too tight?, well yes, maybe, women do overdo it a little these days, you know, it's a matter of fashions, mightn't they be a couple of working girls and their madam?, the things you say!, go on, eat, what do we care who they are?, yes that's true enough . . . , Roque, yes Teresita, how happy I feel when I'm with you!, I never thought I'd live moments like these!, how could we have taken all this time to discover the way we feel?, who knows Teresa, life is always very strange, the ways of love are like an incomprehensible labyrinth, Doña Teresa closes her eyes and feels as though she's floating on a cloud of joyful blessedness. Across from the Montaña Barracks four tanks are on guard, one is stationed at the beginning of the Paseo de San Vicente, another in the little garden of the Piarist nuns, another on the Calle de Ferraz a little farther down, and the last on the corner of Marqués de Urquijo, go on, get out of the way, can't you see you're blocking our target?, come on, a little order, out of the way!, the crowd sings revolutionary songs, gives cheers for the Republic and the people's Army, and applauds the tank crews, it's very hot and some Assault Guards are in their undershirts, with their leather straps on top of their undershirts, Engracia also has straps and a pistol, it's harder to find straps than a pistol or a rifle but Engracia found some, Engracia is wearing overalls and a garrison cap, she looks good in her disguise and she's very serious, the aspirin didn't get rid of Engracia's fever, it doesn't matter, do you feel better?, don't even ask!, sorry, on the grey iron of the tank in the garden of the Piarists Engracia paints two sets of initials, UHP for Proletarian Brothers Unite and JSU for United Socialist Youth, and the hammer and sickle, Agustín holds the can of paint for her, Virtudes and Victoriano get tired of looking out on the street and go to bed, Virtudes sleeps naked and Victoriano in his undershirt and pajama pants, after two hours of sleep Virtudes wakes up her husband, Victoriano, what, well I think the tango's started, what tango?, what do you think, the baby!, Victoriano jumps out of bed, how about that, no electricity, wait till I call your mother and the midwife, Victoriano gropes his way to the telephone, you hold on just a bit, they'll both be here in no time, the telephone isn't working, there's no tone at all, fuck, this thing isn't working!, Victoriano goes back to where his wife is and gives her a kiss on the forehead, Victoriano is a little nervous, wait, I'll try again, the telephone is still mute, it's not usual for a phone to start working again all by itself but that doesn't even occur to Victoriano, you hold on a little, I'm going to get them, you'll see they'll both be here in no time, but are you going to go like that?, what difference does it make, it's not cold, I'll be back with both of them in no time, Victoriano dashes down the stairs and when he gets to the bottom runs out on the street, at the corner of the Calle de Torija they tell him to halt, halt!, halt your ass, you bastard, I'm in no mood for jokes!, halt!, get him, get him, shoot, he's a Fascist!, Victoriano is about to say the fuck I'm a Fascist, I'm going for a midwife for my wife!, but all he can say is the fuck, they don't give him time for more than that either because two shots ring out, first one and then another, and he falls flat on his face on the ground, they hit him in the back and he's dead, the bullet probably got him in the heart and finished him instantly, some people mill around the body, who is it?, a Fascist who was escaping from the barracks, go on now, you think the Fascists escape in their pajamas?, who knows, I guess the Fascists escape any way they can, yes, you're right there, at 123 Ayala, in Doña Sacramento's whorehouse, the night is quiet and without incidents, there's not much business but at least it's peaceful and nobody is making a ruckus. Jesualdo Villegas doesn't stay long at Madame Teddy's, I've got a lot to do, they're waiting for me at the paper, but tomorrow is Monday!,[1] that makes no difference, the country can go up in flames overnight, at *El Sol* everybody thinks something else, there's an opinion to suit every taste, Jesualdo reads the wire reports, the famous Spanish dancer Antonia Mercé, La Argentina, has died of a heart attack in Bayonne, Jesualdo phones Adolfo Salazar, excuse me for bothering you so late, have you heard the news?, no, what's up?, Antonia Mercé has died, how awful!, and how did it happen?, well, just a heart attack, I'm stunned, Villegas, it's an irreparable loss!, my sentiments exactly, did she die in France?, yes in Bayonne, write me a biographical sketch for tomorrow, you can count on it, I'll bring it to you tomorrow. Before midnight the churches start to burn, the glow of the fires soon begins to stand out against the Madrid sky, one, two, three, as many as fifty or more, who knows whether it's more, the relationship between the church and fire gives your Uncle Jerónimo much food for thought, you can be sure, my boy, that inside every Spaniard there dwells a religious arsonist, you just have to give him the right occasion for displaying his talents, the extremes meet, the reactionaries burn heretics and books and the revolutionaries burn churches and images, the point is to burn something, notice my boy that the Spanish people although they're hungry don't burn banks but convents, behind all these flames there is no political motivation and even less an economic one but a religious and magic motivation, maybe the Spaniard confuses politics, economics, religion, and magic, that could be, fire is the great remedy, the universal panacea for all doubts and the Spaniard doubts everything except the eternal fire, the fire of Beelzebub's cauldron that's in the catechism, the only thing you can't burn here is corpses because they say that's a sin, here they burn live people and houses with people inside, the Spaniard has a soul attuned to the bonfires of the Valencian fiesta, the more fire the better, the Army is in rebellion and nobody knows what's going on in the barracks of Madrid but the people instead of marching

1. Until recently Spanish newspapers did not appear on Mondays. The *Hoja del Lunes*, or *Monday Sheet*, was published on Mondays as a collective replacement. Translator's note.

against the Army march against the priests, religious fire has the effect of a miracle on Spaniards, on all Spaniards, nobody escapes here, well, a few escape this burning or being burned, here we want to fix everything with a burning torch, the Spaniard would like to burn his history so that later when nothing is left he can throw himself screaming on the embers, in Spain there are more crazy men than we need, the trouble is we can't tell who they are, this is a country that moves by shouts and to the rhythm of bonfires, I doubt that Spaniards can be convinced that fire should not be allowed outside the kitchen, the bread oven, and the forge, María, may I have a glass of milk?, your Uncle Jerónimo is capable of drinking as many glasses of milk as they give him. Lt. Orad de la Torre succeeds in towing two Schneider 7.5's out on the street with a beer truck, he sets them up opposite the Montaña Barracks, the crowd's enthusiasm grows with the presence of the cannons, General Fanjul can't quite make up his mind to try to move out but he also knows he can't stay in the barracks, the barracks are no bastion and are hard to defend, besides the barracks are not the town, you can't command the town from inside the barracks unless your forces occupy it, any word from Campamento?, no sir, and from General García de la Herrán?, none from him either sir, that is, just what we know already, General Fanjul has to wait till 4 A.M., do not reply to harassing fire, keep the windows closed tight, not a speck of light on the outside, look out for the morale of the troops, reinforce the sentries, stay on the alert and ready to carry out orders, yes sir, Colonel Serra goes hither and yon assigning the men to their posts, no one is to take a single step without orders from the general, yes sir, absolute discipline must be maintained, yes sir, Don Moisés Serra is General Fanjul's right arm, reporting sir, all quiet in the barracks, everything is ready to carry out your orders, thanks Serra, perhaps we should attempt a surprise sortie without waiting for Campamento, the general looks at the colonel, it would be imprudent, you're in command, the enemy has placed machine guns on the rooftops, they won't do them much good if García de la Herrán comes, yes that's true, any news of the other regiments?, no sir, and of the Civil Guard?, none, the danger may lie with the Assault Guard and the Air Force, the civilians aren't dangerous, many of them are armed sir, even so, the civilians will throw away their weapons at the first attack, the danger lies where I say you'll see, the general establishes his command post in the colonel's office, General Fanjul and Colonel Serra have a couple of tomatoes with a little bread for supper, they also drink a little glass of wine apiece, lie down for a while sir, I'll keep watch, no, I'm not tired, we'll both keep watch, within a few hours we're going to risk the fate of the barracks, and our own, yes, ours too and that of all of us, Colonel Serra rolls a cigarette while the machine guns rattle without much enthusiasm, what a long night this is going to be for us!, yes, don't think about it, it's better not to think about it, God help us!, there is firing from some roofs down onto the street, a single shot is generally answered by a hundred, by a regular rifle barrage, shut the windows!, the militia checks the papers of anyone wearing a tie, as they come out of the movie houses people hurry to get into the subway, I'll make you a cup of chocolate at home wives say to their husbands, Major Hidalgo de Cisneros gets a scare when four anarchists stop his car and want to take him prisoner, the major is wearing a spotless uniform and even wears an aristocratic little mustache, he looks like a Fascist, the password is we shall defeat Fascism!, since it's given out loud and hundreds and hundreds of times everyone knows it, some little groups of friars, two or three friars here, four or five there, farther on there one by himself walking with a cane, go by hugging the sides of the buildings and looking at the ground, they're all dressed in street clothes and many get stopped and beaten, if the monks and priests knew the beating they'll get . . . , they don't kill them out on the street, the friars are running from the fire but then they don't know where to head, in some houses they won't let them in, in others they do, the watchman opens the door to two friars who ask for Don Leopoldo, they're wearing pants and a shirt and don't mention that they're friars, we're two cousins of Don Leopoldo's who have just arrived from the village and we don't know where to go, with all this ruckus, at Don Leopoldo's they're all startled when the bell rings, wait I'll answer it, Doña Bernardina has more confidence in herself than in anybody else, Father Rómulo!, quiet please my dear I beg you, is your husband home?, Doña Bernardina closes the door behind the two friars, my companion is Father Sebastián, a true saint, God reward you for your charity toward us, let us trust in God, remember his word transmitted by Saint Matthew, *ubi enim sunt duo vel tres congregati in nomine meo, ibi sum in medio eorum*, wherever two or three are gathered together in my name, there am I in the midst of them, God grant you're right father, Doña Bernardina can't hold back her tears, excuse me it's nerves, it's over now, I'll fix you a little coffee and some cookies, thank you my dear. The neighbor of the Count and Countess Casa Redruello who listens to Radio Seville is called Don Felipe Espinosa and is a real estate agent, his two oldest children Felipe and Alberto are also in the Montaña Barracks, be quiet, when they finish the pasodoble they'll have some news you'll see, Don

Felipe's second marriage is to a very cute though a little dull girl who had been his daughter María Victoria's classmate, Felipe and Alberto always pat their stepmother's butt when they pass her in the hallway, the fact is she doesn't really notice and thinks they bump into her by accident, come on be quiet, there's the bugle now, men and women of Seville!, the Spanish Army faithful guardian of the virtues of our people has triumphed completely, Don Felipe turns around and smiles, pst, hush!, General Queipo de Llano issues the following proclamation, first, every person in possession of weapons must surrender them immediately, anyone bearing arms without the permission of the military authorities is subject to being shot, well done, yes sir!, second, all supporters of law and order must report and offer such assistance as their conscience may dictate, well that's in Seville, third, all inhabitants of the city are put on notice that the shades of all windows must be raised and they are warned that if these instructions are not followed they may suffer disagreeable consequences, here it's the other way around, long live republican Spain!, Don Felipe grimaces, there they go again!, private sources of information assure us that General Mola has entered Madrid, it's always good to exaggerate a little, they say that to raise people's spirits, long live Spain!, long may she live!, when they begin to play the anthem of the Republic Don Felipe snaps the radio off, let's leave that polka for whoever wants to hear it! The clock on top of the Interior Ministry drops the ball that announces the birth of a new day, from a rooftop on the Calle de Carretas Antonio Arévalo, María Victoria's boyfriend, aims his rifle at the ball, fires, and misses, it would have been a good joke to shoot the ball of the ministry clock.

II

There you are again in front of the mirror, looking at yourself in the mirror, you can feel comfortable addressing yourself in a familiar way and even feel brash about it, it doesn't much matter, rams always go where there is green grass, even if you wanted to and no matter how hard you try you can't get free of the flat, parallelepiped, ovoid mirror, like a store window, like a bowl, like an eye, it's just as though you had mange or crabs or tuberculosis, it's the same as if your conscience were troubling you because of some irreparable abject deed, taking it in the ass for money, being a police informer, getting scared in a fight, your conscience doesn't trouble you because you have a poor memory and hardly any pain, sometimes you say you have a good memory and a great deal of pain, the memory of an elephant or a volcanic rock, the pain of a hyena, a pain that respects no one, a pain of an old piano used by three generations of blind men, the johns who wait their turn in provincial whorehouses pay you copper coins so you will amuse them in their idle moments with your base singing, the first one is already unbuttoning his fly in the hall, the johns who wait their turn in the whorehouses of the capital pay you in insults and humiliation, pay no attention but remember that telling lies does not produce pangs of conscience, telling lies is something as innocuous as taking bicarbonate, pissing to leeward, or smiling at a dying girl, each country has different costumes and customs, harmonious costumes or ridiculous reds and blues adorned with spangles, strange customs or foreseeable ones, the droit du seigneur, the letter of exchange, the cream puff, you do have tuberculosis but not mange or crabs, you had mange and it was cured with Mitigal, for external use only, apply gently to the affected parts, you also had crabs and they were cured with English Oil, for external use only, apply gently to the affected parts, tuberculosis is harder to cure, you have to be rich, patient, and a capon or at least chaste and virtuous, medicines are expensive (your father buys them for you), you have to be there stretched out on your back without moving (the fact is you're not losing any sleep over your studies either), you have to tie a knot in your merciful insatiable balls and give up all thought of triumphs (Toisha and the two sisters would take your desertion very badly, women don't want to understand certain abdications of an aesthetic or salutary nature), tuberculosis is good for making death interesting but especially for writing poetry and seeing the good side of things, eternal clouds may cover up the sun, a single moment's heat may dry the sea, the axis of the globe may break like glass, all this may be, I may be shrouded in the crape of death, but nothing can e'er quench my love for thee while I draw breath, the afternoon you recited this poem to Toisha she was more skillful, more amorous, more disciplined, and more of a tramp than ever, she even came to smell bad like a dead woman, you can't get free of your mirror but you don't want to either, no one can get free of his monotonous and violent sexual organ but no one wants to either, monotony is a vice of the lonely, a helpful poultice for the spirits of the lonely, violence is a virtue of the lonely and a vice of the gregarious, an anchor for the salvation of the spirits of the lonely and a burden for the damnation of the spirits of the gregarious, do you remember that copper coin, that nickel coin, that silver coin that can form on the palate?, you are sinfully or virtuously lonely, not hermaphroditically lonely, that's the same thing and depends on the phases of the moon, in your mirror good, evil, and cynicism have the identical faded color, yes, look at yourself in the mirror while the city burns and is stained with blood, moans and is stained with blood, dies and is stained with blood, Virtudes is giving birth by herself, she floods the room with blood, her screams are only answered by a neighbor, her little boy who is just like a mouse comes in through a window and opens the door for her, come in mother, shall I go for the midwife?, no son, go home, your mirror in the shape of a shining egg turns into an immense dull melon, it looks like a cell, into a somewhat deformed rugby ball of matte yellowish-white color, the matte white of a skull, it's better that you can't see yourself in your flat, parallelepiped, ovoid mirror, there are memories that do not deserve to be stored up but to be destroyed, rain ought to wipe out almost all memories, Julius Caesar was fatuous, Napoleon Bonaparte was fatuous, Buffalo Bill was fatuous, King Cyril of England paid a very high price for his fatuousness, it would have been better for you to be blind and deaf, mute and without memory. The Air Force remains on the side of the Republic, the first morning birds, sparrows like amiable, elastic, and independent cats, fly chirping over the Republic's coat of arms, at the Getafe air base Captain Cascón addresses the troops, we must move against the Fascists of the artillery regiment!, long live the Republic!, you must admit that no one keeps a Phrygian cap in his night table, the insignias that can lead a man to heroism and death only serve to adorn his grandchildren's Carnival, as though by chance three groups are improvised under the command of Lieutenants Hernández Franch and Valle and Master Sergeant Sol Aparicio, with them go four dozen civilians from the United Socialist Youth and the Communist Party armed with rifles, romantic and prestigious machines, the artillerymen don't put up much resistance and surrender at the first air attack, storming Campamento is more difficult, the planes from Cuatro Vientos bombard the barracks of the engineers regiment and kill an officer, the situation is confused, General García de la Herrán, Colonel Cañedo, and Lieutenant Colonel Álvarez Rementería study the plan of attack, no, the prudent thing is to place two pieces on the road and two heavier ones on the esplanade, we have to prevent any attack by land and put Cuatro Vientos out of commission, Lieutenant Colonel León Trejo refuses to surrender the air base to the Military Junta, long live the Republic!, we must not attempt to march on Madrid under fire from the air, unhitch!, at the Montaña Barracks the situation is not desperate, long live Spain!, they have not yet been attacked, there is no news of the engineer regiment at Leganés, nor from the other barracks in Madrid, it's still night perhaps it's dawning bit by bit, the attack on Campamento comes as a surprise, where did these clowns get that artillery?, we shouldn't have broken formation, not all the noncoms are with us, we should have seen to it that the enlisted men couldn't talk, to arms!, every man to his place!, long live Spain!, the planes reappear and drop more bombs, we should have advanced on Madrid!, now it's too late for regrets, take cover by that window!, hit the dirt!, let's show those bastards an Army officer knows how to die!, long live Spain!, some of the troops rise up against their commanders, where's the general?, they've killed him, and Major Velasco?, they've taken him prisoner, and Major Castillas?, also a prisoner, well this scum isn't going to catch me alive, I promise you that, I won't give them the pleasure of shooting me!, come and get me, you sons of bitches!, long live Spain!, Lieutenant Seoane fires into his mouth and dies instantly, a bullet in the mouth is something that never fails. A naked Toisha pursues Don Máximo with a whip, Toisha's hair is loose it comes halfway down her back and she's wearing high-heeled shoes very high-heeled Toisha has no makeup on but a lot of perfume on her right hand she wears a heavy ring on every finger each one with a sparkling ruby on her left hand she doesn't even have fingers Toisha's left hand is a repulsive dry stump Toisha's ears are big like a donkey's (not in the shape of a donkey's ears) and mercifully dirty, it's a very funny and worrisome dream also very artistic and rhythmical if you close your eyes you can still keep on dreaming you haven't waked up you've opened your eyes but you are still sound asleep or perhaps not very sound asleep Toisha has become furious and is singing obscene songs that you've never heard from her Toisha spits out great mouthfuls of fire from her eyes and a tireless silky nest of worms wriggles in her armpits Toisha has a blinking green light in her navel and a tiny gentleman dressed in frock coat and top hat is peeking out of her cunt and giving stentorian cheers for the Emperor Francis Joseph and Don Marcelino Menéndez Pelayo Don Máximo runs off terrified and Toisha whips him with the cat-o'-nine-tails each tail is a live and very flexible snake a tireless snake Don Máximo reaches a wall on which the slogan long live the Republic! is written with chalk Don Máximo can't escape any farther he stops turns around and fights with the tiny gentleman in the frock coat who is very brave and energetic he is a dwarf who is all boldness and energy Toisha is panting there is great anxiety in her breathing she holds the tiny gentleman in the frock coat between her thighs and stands there waiting for you with her arms outstretched Don Máximo starts to shrink and shrink and Toisha kills him with her whip and then steps on him, you suddenly wake up, you're coming, now you've come, now it's all the same whether you look at yourself in the mirror or don't look at yourself, the dawn is breaking, out in the country it's probably day already, are you on the Plaza de España during the assault on the barracks?, say so, don't be afraid, you're on the outside dressed in the overalls of the militia and with your rifle ready but without any hand grenades, you don't have much ammunition either or enthusiasm or much cheerfulness, don't be afraid to confess the truth, you're inside the barracks walls dressed as a soldier though without insignia and with your rifle ready, you don't have any hand grenades nor much ammunition, you don't have any boundless enthusiasm nor much cheerfulness, don't be afraid to confess the truth, in Vallecas Lieutenant Colonel Lacalle organizes some armed bands, the colonel of the Saboya regiment told Captain Querejeta quite clearly that he wasn't rebelling, in the Casa de Campo Lieutenant Colonel Mangada is drilling the battalion that he has just formed, his men salute him with clenched fists, the antifascist military salute has just been born, Captain Alcántara can't give General Fanjul any good news of the armored regiment either, Major Fernández Navarro arms the civilians and forms a column to help in the siege of the barracks, Captain Betancourt sees with his own eyes how the besiegers are closing in, Lieutenant Orad de la Torre places his half battery at the foot of the monument to Cervantes, it's not possible to try to get out but it's suicidal to stay shut up in the barracks, the besiegers undermine the morale of the troops with their loudspeakers, it would be better if the goddamned firing started once and for all!, a militiaman fires his pistol just to make his finger happy and the firing spreads, gunpowder is very contagious, the artillery begins to thunder at about six and soon the Air Force arrives, the planes throw down bombs and leaflets, fire at the motor!, aim a little in front of the propeller!, the first bombs wake up Don Roque, there's going to be some scandal in the boardinghouse, Doña Teresa has a sweeter awakening, Doña Teresa is awakened by Don Roque kissing her forehead, Teresa my love, what, I'm going to my room before the maids get up, that will be better, no you stay here, I'll talk to the maids, they're a couple of tramps, I'm in my own house and I sleep with whomever I feel like, all right, I sleep with you because I love you, if they don't like it, they can get out, I can assure you it won't be much of a loss, you stay here with me, I'm the owner and you're the owner's lover, after all, what's happened?, we're not fifteen any more Roque, yes that's true enough, cease fire!, a captain of the Assault Guard gives the order but he has to repeat it several times, cease fire!, nobody shoot until further orders!, cease fire!, an emissary steps out from the republican ranks with a white flag, in the barracks they hold their fire, who's that?, I don't know, they must want to tell them something, inside the barracks they're also wondering, who's that?, I don't know, they must want to tell us something, the guards and the militia don't fire, they have to hold themselves back but they don't fire, neither do the soldiers and the Falangists, the artillery is still, and the planes have gone to their bases to await developments, the emissary is a civilian, no one knows what he tells them, they suppose he urges them to surrender, what is known is what they tell him, no, they won't surrender, they're ready to die trying, a fine stew!, well they're the ones who are going to be stewing, they're bound to lose, the fire resumes with greater violence, the cannons, the rifles, the machine guns on the roofs and in the barracks, the Air Force goes back to bombing, long live the Republic!, they fire mortars from the barracks, long live Spain!, the Red Cross sets up a first-aid station in the vestibule of the Velussia Theatre, Engracia is dead when she arrives there, there's nothing the doctors can do to save her life, she has three chest wounds, you can tell she was caught by a burst of machine-gun fire, Agustín feels guilty for not having taken her home even if it meant dragging her kicking and screaming, no man, how can it be your fault?, it's not your fault at all, the wounded in the barracks are treated in the infirmary, the medics can't keep up, General Fanjul is wounded in the head, I won't surrender!, we'll fight to the death!, some of the men raise a white flag, the besiegers jump from their cover and advance toward the barracks, forward!, let's fight 'em!, long live the Republic!, long live the Popular Front!, they are received with volleys of fire and suffer many casualties, bastards, you want to blast us point-blank!, traitors!, Colonel Serra is also wounded, what's going on?, who raised the white flag?, bombs keep falling from the air and the artillery has found the exact elevation, they don't waste a single shell, almost all the men in the barracks are wounded, a little after 11:30 A.M. the main gate of the barracks gives way before the assault and General Fanjul gives his last orders, we surrender, General Fanjul knows all too well what this means, the attackers burst like a tornado into the courtyard of the barracks and hunt the officers down, it's pure hell and no one hears anyone else, it's a demented and bloody wasteland, with a lump in his throat Jesualdo thinks of Antonio Machado, and this is that part of the planet where wanders the shade of Cain, everyone comes into the world with his destiny marked out, no one can escape what is written, some are born with a little star on their foreheads and always fall on their feet like cats, some are born without a little star on their foreheads and never see old age, in the Montaña Barracks there are men with a little star on their foreheads and men who have none, you are fodder for the catechism class, fodder for the brothel, cannon fodder, you are the unknown soldier, the man on whose forehead no little star shines, a man is like a coin you throw in the air, sometimes it comes down heads and sometimes tails, Colonel Don Moisés Serra is killed in his barracks, General Fanjul and Colonel Fernández de la Quintana are taken as prisoners to police headquarters,[2] some succeeded in jumping over the walls and getting out alive, the list of men with no little star on their foreheads, of men whose little star on the forehead fails them, is long, you know some of them, knew some of them, Pepe Carlos and his father Count Casa Reduello are thrown down from the upper gallery, the maid Conchita had a boyfriend who broke up with her because she was a whore, Conchita

2. Both were condemned to death on August 16 and shot the next day at dawn. "Editor's note" in the original.

won't be able to go to the Gran Peña any more on Sunday afternoons to take off her clothes in front of Don Carlos, Willy Zabalegui dies during the siege, they hit him right in the middle of the forehead and he never knew it, there's no more selling him condoms for Matiítas or smiling at him, Willy Zabalegui spoke French very well, he had a mademoiselle when he was little and afterward he went to the Instituto Escuela, Enrique Garrido the second son of Don Leopoldo and Doña Bernardina shoots himself in the temple, he saw things taking an ugly turn and preferred to shoot himself in the temple, Enrique was nicer than his brother Leopoldo and also braver, Leopoldo is rather sanctimonious and has a nasty disposition, it would have been better if they'd killed Leopoldo and not Enrique, death is not distributed fairly, chance is not always fair, the sisters like highballs and stuffed olives, if Señor Asterio had discovered that Lupita and Juani go out with Fascists he would have killed them, Lupita and Juani don't get involved in politics, what they want is to be taken dancing and to the movies entertainment with petting is more complete than the sporting or artistic kind, at the Forteen they have a very good orchestra and at the Panorama Theatre the arm rests lift up, it's very convenient and the ushers are used to it, Paquito and Alfonso won't get back to Salamanca, they throw them off the gallery the same as Pepe Carlos and his father, when it hits the flagstones a body doesn't ring like a bell but croaks like a cracked bell, Felipe Espinosa they hunt down in the vacant lots near the station, he managed to get out but he didn't run fast enough, a few seconds earlier and he'd have been home free, no one knows where death is, come to think of it death is everywhere, it depends on whether it marks a man or doesn't mark him, you're twenty years old, you'll probably die tomorrow or before another twenty years have passed, his brother Alberto dies in the infirmary, he was already half dead when they finished him off, Felipe and Alberto will never again meet their stepmother in the hallway or pat her butt playing dumb, life feeds on death and enthusiasm devours failure, the poets say that hope is a sweet sickness, well let them say what they want, this is no time for clever sayings or for poems and the men with no little star on their forehead have already lost all hope, you are a friend of Andrés Herrera's, from the University Students Federation in law, and of Pío García Huerta and Lorenzo Sosa, both from the University Students Federation in medicine, sometimes you get together to discuss poetry, last Thursday you spent the afternoon going over *The Reasons of the Heart* by Pedro Salinas and *Offering Songs* by Juan Panero, and also talking about politics, Léon Blum is like Goicoechea only smarter, French politicians all seem to be on the Left and aren't, Spain is better prepared than France for an attempt at revolutionary action and if you don't believe me just wait and see, censorship doesn't work here, it's a nuisance but it doesn't really work, they forbade the article by Lenin about the death of Tolstoy that we published in *El tiempo presente* because you can't talk about Lenin, well we submitted it a second time signed Vladimir Ilich and they approved it, our institutions are rusty, for our revolutionary purposes it's more useful to demolish them than to lubricate them, Andrés Herrera plays rugby on the school of architecture team and reads Remarque and Henri Barbusse, Andrés is heavy and athletic, he doesn't smoke and dreams of a more just and clement humanity, the problem lies in the distribution of consumer goods, we produce enough but it's badly distributed, it's not possible to distribute it any better within the capitalist system, first war was at the service of capital and then capital was at the service of war, it's like one of those little fish they serve with their tail in their mouth, Andrés' girl is called Adela Vaquero and belongs to the United Socialist Youth, Adela Vaquero is a swimming champion and very good-looking, Adela is a foreign language teacher, she speaks English just as well as Spanish, and she believes in birth control and in collective farms, Andrés and Adela fire on the barracks from the roof of a building on the Calle de Luisa Fernanda at the corner of Ferraz, Andrés is hit in the head and pitches forward, Adela tries to hold him but she falls too, the two bodies sound like two sinister harps when they smash against the sidewalk, Pío García is not a very healthy boy, he wears glasses and is very punctual and diligent but he's always kind of thoughtful and sad, Pío García is killed by a mortar shell that bursts where he is taking cover, there were six men behind the sandbags and none was left, Lorenzo Sosa is treated in the Velussia Theatre, he's very badly wounded and dies without regaining consciousness, now you'll have to speak of them all in the past tense, history forgets men who do not cut off heads or whose head is not cut off on the scaffold, that's not what happens with the Montaña Barracks, some day history will say, some day history will probably say, and maybe it won't, that the storming of the Montaña Barracks was something like the battle of Bailén pushed to its ultimate consequences, to a paradoxical caricature of itself, stretched to its limits and even beyond, General Fanjul got the role of Marshal Dupont, the victorious hosts were not even under the command of a modest General Castaños, they weren't under anyone's command, orders were being given but they weren't being obeyed, it was the people who faced the Montaña Barracks, this idea of the people is very imprecise, very changeable, perhaps more than twenty or thirty thousand men, each with his moving little novel stuck to his heart, but not a single historic name, it would be difficult to write the history of the storming of the Montaña Barracks with proper names, the storming of the Montaña Barracks was like hail, hailstones don't have names either, it was an anonymous manifold action like a hailstorm or Lope de Vega's *Fuenteovejuna*. Don Máximo takes the train to Valencia, Don Diego has to give him specific instructions about what must be done, Don Diego shouldn't have left without giving him specific instructions, well if he left he must have had his reasons, Don Máximo doesn't know whether what is happening is good or bad, he's sure it's bad but he wants to hear it from Don Diego, it's not worth it to go first class and Don Máximo goes in second class, second class is perfectly respectable and doesn't bother people so much, you mustn't provoke people, three other persons are in his compartment, a gentleman and two ladies, nobody speaks, the gentleman looks out at the landscape, the fact is there's not much to look at in the landscape, and the ladies keep their eyes closed, it's not likely they're sleeping but they keep their eyes closed, maybe they're nuns, you can't ask them that, at the Ocaña station a young couple with an almost newborn baby comes in, when the train gets under way the mother nurses it covering her breast with a handkerchief, the gentleman who was looking at the landscape gets off in Cuenca, good-bye, have a good trip, thank you good-bye, some militiamen ask to see papers, fuck, a deputy!, yes a deputy of the Popular Front, watch your language, there are ladies present, excuse us please, and what about these two women?, they're my sisters, all right, you can go on, *salud*, have a good trip, thank you *salud*,[3] the two ladies look gratefully at Don Máximo and when the train is once more moving the older one says God bless you sir, the lady is ugly and has a mustache but there is a certain nobility in her glance. Yes, Ezquerra and Berrendero were right, the Nice-Cannes stage was won by Ezquerra, furthermore he was second on the Brauss Pass, first on the Sospel with the same time as Vervaecke and Silver Maes and clear front-runner on La Tourbie, all the Spaniards improve their standing, Mariano Cañardo, 6, Julián Berrendero, 9, Federico Ezquerra, 12, and Emiliano Álvarez, 32, they're going to reach the Pyrenees well placed on the general list. Colonel Carrascosa addresses his troops and tells them that they are going to take part in

3. The revolutionary Left used *salud*, '[your] health,' in place of the traditional greeting *adiós*, meaning both 'hello' and 'good-bye' but literally commending one's interlocutor 'to God' (*a Dios*). Translator's note.

maneuvers, no, what he tells them is to get ready to fight against Mola's rebels in defense of the Republic, long live the Republic!, well none of this makes any difference, Colonel Carrascosa leads his signal regiment out of its barracks at El Pardo but he doesn't march on Madrid, he heads north and crosses the Somosierra pass to Segovia, Colonel Carrascosa is smart and he works fast, one of his soldiers is a son of Largo Caballero, his name is Francisco like his father's. You find Miguel Mercader at the Baviera, he's having a beer, do you realize what a battle is shaping up here?, of course I realize it, between the brass on the one side and the anarchists on the other they're going to screw the country you'll see, poor country, and it would be so easy to make it liveable!, it can't be all that easy I don't think so, God himself doesn't understand what's going on here, what Spaniards like is screwing their neighbor don't you doubt it, the Spaniard would rather throw stones on the ground than raise them, the Spaniard is fonder of fire than of water, I don't know why that might be but that's the way it is, let the historians figure it out if they can, two members of the Anarchist militia come into the Baviera, comrade your papers, here you go, student?, yes, that's what it says there, antifascist?, what a question!, of course I'm antifascist, do you belong to the University Students Federation?, yes, I haven't got my card on me but I belong to the Federation in Philosophy and Letters, all right from now on always carry your card with you, I'll do that yes sir, why are you calling me sir?, well I don't know, out of respect, because you're older, the Anarchist militiaman has a face like that of a wooden saint he looks like Saint Roch, you don't tell him that, *salud!*, *salud!*, the manager of the Baviera invites the two militiamen to a beer, when they leave he comes over to you and Mercader, you're going to get in trouble, us, why?, I know what I'm talking about, the best thing you can do is stay away from here, thanks Mañá, in a revolution people like to walk down the middle of the street, not on the sidewalks, and shout and jump and throw stones at the shop windows, here we fix everything in a jiffy, a man can be a poor wretch who never fucks except in a whorehouse or with some girlfriend who loves him and suddenly, without any time even to think it over, he finds himself turned into a hero, into a martyr, or into a murderer, it's a nuisance, if he wins he's a hero, if he loses he's a martyr, if he doesn't hold back and say no, no, not that, somebody else can do that, I won't, then he's a murderer, the line is hair-thin, some people are so nearsighted that they don't see the hair but there are also some who close their eyes so as not to see it, this is a country of pent-up come, of come under pressure, you think so?, sure I think so, people here fuck little and fuck badly, if Spaniards enjoyed their fucking they wouldn't be such brutes and wouldn't feel so messianic, there'd be fewer heroes and fewer martyrs but there'd also be fewer murderers and maybe things would work, nobody wants to face the fact that that's the way it is, I'm going home before they skin me alive, how about you?, no I'm not going, I'm going to get the sisters, I don't feel like going home, this is all yelling and hoopla, nothing's happening, just look, the movies aren't closed, all right I'm going with you, there'll always be time for beating it, Lupita and Juani wear red kerchiefs around their necks, what kind of novelty is this?, you know, a present from father, people are asked for their papers on the streets but not at the movies, personal identification cards are not enough, student?, yes that's what it says there, class 13, occupation student, one and a half pesetas, you students are all a bunch of fucking rich boys, fat lot you know about it!, do you belong to any party of the Popular Front?, no, not the Popular Front nor the not popular Front, this guy and I are students, it's not a very solid reason but it'll do, the girls don't approve of this stopping people in the middle of the street to ask for their papers, it doesn't matter, Lupita and Juani are hot and obliging any time of the day, that's always an advantage, stop and think things over, Juani has put you in excellent condition for thinking things over, not everybody can say as much just now, some can't either now or ever, some people are very miserable and unlucky, the problem is not looking at yourself or not looking at yourself in your flat, parallelepiped, ovoid mirror, it seems to be a little less ovoid, sort of more spherical, but you couldn't swear to that either, hold still Juani, oh you're so crabby!, nor is the problem whether you have or don't have a flat, parallelepiped, ovoid, almost spherical mirror, or whether it's broken because other people broke it, no, no, the problem, the deep and painful problem is that you no longer believe in your flat, parallelepiped, ovoid, almost spherical mirror, you've had enough of believing and more believing and all for nothing, Juani puts away your handkerchief, tomorrow she'll give it back to you washed and ironed, all for a fleeting image, a shadow, a minimal pleasure, a minimal annoyance, why don't you kiss me?, yes dear, you and Juani kiss, it doesn't pay to believe in flat, parallelepiped, ovoid, almost spherical mirrors, to believe firmly in the existence of treacherous ghosts, in the life and habits of treacherous ghosts, shall we go?, you go if you want to, I don't have any place to go, Juani closes her eyes and is quiet, she's probably crying, at least you like to think she's probably crying, you know it's easier to make a woman who's asking for love cry than to convince her that she doesn't need love, love is easy to feign, it just doesn't pay, nobody ever gets free of his own solitary private domestic dirty deeds, Juani is not the Attic bee but she's got her feelings too, her almost beaten heart. There was a time when decent women declared their surrender by leaving their fan in the hands of their suitor, it cost your grandfather a lot of money but he could have roofed his house with fans, Doña Teresa goes from one side of the boardinghouse to the other, nothing's happened here and if something has it's nobody's business, both Javiera and Paulina take the news of the owner's amour very prudently, what choice do they have and besides Doña Teresa is a jump ahead of them, Paulina has to make a little greater effort, have you seen my fan anywhere?, no ma'am, Doña Teresa feels hot, it really is very hot, a sticky nasty heat that permeates everything, first course hake and salad, second, fried eggs, third, veal cutlet, yes ma'am, for dessert a banana or quince jelly, are you through making up the rooms?, yes ma'am, there was something oily in Don Hilario's urinal, well that's his business, it doesn't concern you, it's probably from some medicine, Doña Teresa doesn't want Don Roque to go out, I'll send for your papers and a beer, there are no papers today, well then, the *Monday Sheet*, you've got no reason to go out, you can be sure of that, we'll see whether people have calmed down by tomorrow, Don Roque feels he's the happiest man in the world, what he needed was precisely what he now has, people will calm down, the waters always return to their courses, Teresita, yes my love, why don't you sit here with me a little?, in a minute, wait till I'm through planning dinner, I can't leave the maids on their own, Don Hilario asks Don Roque for a razor blade, could you lend me a razor blade?, the one I have is half rusty, of course, a pleasure, thank you very much Don Roque, you're always so kind and such a gentleman, listen, would you be interested in a fifty-horsepower Otto-Deutz producer gas motor?, I?, yes sir, I'd let you have it for a good price, no, it's not the price, it's just that what do I want a producer gas motor for?, well what do I know!, it has many industrial uses, I don't doubt that, well let me think about it, just at the moment I can't think of a use, maybe later, we'll see, I'll let you know, whenever you like, may I have the blade?, oh yes, of course, Don Hilario manages to get rid of his crabs with Brujo oil, this medication has the advantage of not staining and at the same time having a most pleasing aroma, it is easy to use and works quickly and surely, instantly killing the parasite and eliminating that annoying itch from the moment it is first applied, manufactured according to the formula of the licensed pharmacist Pérez Giménez in his laboratory in Aguilar de la Frontera, after each application Don Hilario carefully washes the affected parts with vinegar diluted with water, if Doña Teresa had found out she would have kicked him right out for being dirty and careless, just imagine that old wreck with crabs as though he were a youngster!, Don Hilario is a clerk in the provincial government offices, department of roads and public works, and a very serious, even-tempered, and reverential man, the crabs were just a case of bad luck, it can happen to anybody, women are very ignorant, sometimes they become carriers of infection out of mere ignorance, yes that's true. The news that reaches the Garrido household could not be more alarming, the crowd has broken into the Montaña Barracks and slaughtered all its defenders, they didn't even spare General Fanjul, the bodies were left lying in the sun, covered with flies, we ought to go see whether Enrique is there, our poor son!, at least we could bury him, Don Leopoldo knows that Doña Bernardina is right, it's not that he doesn't think Doña Bernardina is right, it's that he doesn't dare to go to the barracks, no, look, I'm sure he managed to get away, some must have managed to get away, why shouldn't Enrique be one of the ones who managed to get away?, the last thing we ought to lose is hope, Bernardina, God will help us, the doorbell could ring any minute, Enrique is no fool, that boy is nobody's fool, Don Leopoldo and Doña Bernardina don't know that when he saw that he couldn't escape Enrique shot himself in the temple. Doña Sacramento can't reach her daughter Virtudes, the phone must not be working, well if they haven't called it must be because there's still nothing, they would have thought of sending word somehow, Virtudes isn't well, why doesn't Victoriano come?, hush dear, he'll be right back, he must have gone for your mother, but how can he be going for my mother since last night?, something bad happened to Victoriano, I'm sure, I just know they killed him, hush, for heaven's sake!, the things you think up!, oh yes, Victoriano could never just not come home and especially not at a time like this, they've killed Victoriano, I'm sure they've killed him, Virtudes breaks out crying, she was crying already, now she cries harder and more disconsolately, Virtudes feels too suddenly alone, God does not give strength to the weak, not even to the weak of good will, he's too distant in that, Virtudes gave birth to a stillborn girl, maybe she was born alive and died because she couldn't breathe, the neighbor puts the baby's body in a shoe box and lays yesterday's *Blanco y Negro* on top of it, the cover has a drawing of a very stylized black woman surrounded by cactuses, it's titled *Just between us cactuses*. . . . , at this time of the year Madrid is full of flies, there are flies everywhere, it's what you call overrun with flies, Virtudes is very circumspect but since she's afraid she thinks piss on shame! and tells the neighbor to go for her mother, don't phone her, it's better for you to go if you'll do me that favor and tell her what's happening, if you phone her she'll get even more scared, I can stay by myself, nothing's going to happen to me because I'm by myself, if she'd felt up to it she would have said, I'm going to tell you a secret, you can trust me, I know, my mother keeps a house with women, that makes no difference to me, but she's half fainted away and keeps quiet, would you bring my mother?, of course dear, of course I will, thank you very much Doña Jesusa, God bless you for it, Virtudes' neighbor is called Doña Jesusa, her husband works for the electric company, I'll send you little Jesusín to keep you company. María Angustias the young wife of Don Felipe the neighbor of the Count and Countess Casa Redruello really loathes the republicans, they're a bunch of infidels and heretics, the best among them is still no good, her stepsons Felipe and Alberto besiege her in the hallway, she's none too bright and lets herself be patted on the butt as though nothing was happening, maybe she doesn't even notice, of course maybe she does notice and the truth is that she's a hot number and is just pretending, oh dear, you might watch where you're going!, excuse me María Angustias I didn't see you, the cook comes in from outside saying that loyal forces have occupied the Montaña Barracks, loyal to whom?, be quiet and get in the kitchen to peel potatoes, that's your business!, have you ever seen such cheek?, Don Felipe is uneasy, what the cook says could be true, the cannons haven't been heard for at least an hour, well it could also be that the troops from Campamento have arrived and everything is settled, the mob doesn't have any efficient leaders and without efficient leaders there's not much it can do, María Angustias, what, go on up to Maripi's and ask them whether they know anything, María Victoria's legs tremble when her boyfriend rings the doorbell, but how can you think of coming here?, you be quiet and let me in, good heavens, what manners!, quiet!, is your father in?, yes, tell him I want to see him, but Antonio, how can you think of talking to my father?, go on, tell him, Don Felipe puts on a look of great composure to receive his daughter's boyfriend, officially Don Felipe doesn't know that his daughter is seeing anybody, what can I do for you young man?, look Mr. Espinosa, I'm a friend of your two sons, my name is Antonio Arévalo, get out of here, all of you, as soon as you can, but what's going on?, calm down young man, I'm calm but listen to what I'm telling you, everything is lost, the Montaña Barracks have fallen into the hands of the militias and they've killed everybody, what did you say?, you heard me, they're right on my heels but I wanted to warn you, and what about my sons?, I don't know, the news couldn't be any worse, if you have anyplace to go, an embassy, what do I know, anyplace, go before it's too late, and what are you going to do?, sleep if I can and then hide, what do you want me to do?, let the countess know, they shouldn't just stay there with crossed arms either, Don Felipe thinks a few moments, I don't doubt that Mola will eventually enter Madrid, the point is for him to come soon enough so we can live to tell about it, María Angustias, yes, bring us a little coffee, all right, and call María Victoria, María Victoria?, yes. Don Tomás Donato must be about forty give or take a little, Anita's a good thing, you bet she is, and besides she's fond of me but first comes my skin, anybody who doesn't look sharp here is going to get crucified, they won't hunt me down like a rabbit, Don Tomás has a snub-barreled nine-millimeter Astra and twenty-five or thirty clips, his weapon is no German howitzer but it'll do for self-defense, Don Tomás plans to pump a bullet point-blank into the first man to ask him for his papers, he would have liked to go to Valladolid but when he comes around to thinking of it the trains are no longer running from the Northern Station, he spends the night under a tree in the Retiro and in the morning he went strolling around Las Ventas and on the Plaza de Manuel Becerra, at the end of the Calle de Lista two militiamen order him to halt, Don Tomás thinks, now's the time!, now or never!, but they must have seen it on his face because before he could get out his pistol they put a bullet in his belly and another in his heart, this happens at approximately half past eleven or a quarter to twelve, today nobody's working in Don Feliciano's notary office, at eleven the chief clerk tells all the others they can go, Don Baltasar Blanco gets home at about half past eleven, takes his wife's clothes off and takes her to bed, maybe it was already a quarter to twelve, Anita never puts up any resistance, do you love me lots?, lots you know that, and you me?, me too, shots are heard all over Madrid, two of them sent Don Tomás to the next world. The cripple who sells tobacco is called Marramáu (maybe he's a hero of some war), Marramáu doesn't want to believe that the people have taken the Montaña Barracks, his daughter Pilar has to push his cart all the way up the Gran Vía so he can see the dead with his own eyes, the cripple Marramáu (maybe he's a hero of some war) has no comment (he's surely a hero of some war). Happiness is just like a worm that nests in some hearts, misery too, happiness and misery are carried inside and sometimes, rarely, they let their little light appear in the eyes, happiness and misery are two very fragile and timid feelings, men, most men, don't know whether they're happy or miserable, maybe they don't even dare to ask themselves when they're alone, men, most men, are usually very much afraid of being alone, if you had a mirror in which to look at yourself alone you wouldn't hesitate to do it, Juani, what, don't cry and don't be silly, open your eyes, Juani obeys and opens her eyes, it turns out she's not crying, why do you want me to open my eyes?, oh just so I can see myself in them, boy are you romantic!, yes I'm very romantic you know that, Juani laughs and you embrace her, you can't see yourself in her eyes because the theater is dark, Miguel Mercader and Lupita also embrace but silently, Mercader is a man of silent epilogues. Don Lorenzo Vallejo Paquito's father is a tailor, he's got his shop on the Plaza del Corrillo as you go up on the left, his friend Don Ildefonso Borrego Alfonso's father is an associate in historical grammar at the College of Letters, Don Ildefonso boasts of being a close friend of Don Miguel de Unamuno's, it must be true, Don Ildefonso has sixteen children, my missis is like a rabbit, he always says, as soon as I leave my pants hanging over the back of my easy chair she's pregnant, now I think she's pregnant again, the way we're going we'll have two dozen, well, as long as we can keep the kitchen fire going, Don Ildefonso lives on Correhuela, in a large old house with the convenience of a garden in back, the garden is a godsend, if it's not raining cats and dogs the missis throws the kids out in the garden to work off their energies, inside the house they'd drive her crazy, neither Don Lorenzo nor Don Ildefonso has any news from the boys, I think they'll manage fine, you'll see, neither of them is a fool and besides it's good they're together, that way they can help each other, I hope to God you're right!, I'm very worried, I can't help it, the situation in Madrid must be disastrous, don't be afraid, my friend, don't be afraid, they won't eat them!, this way they'll learn, here in Salamanca everything was too easy for them, yes that's true, besides this can't last long, inside a couple of days we'll have them here telling us fantastic stories, I hope to God!, you'll see, Don Lorenzo is not as tough as Don Ildefonso, what a comfort it is to me to listen to you Don Ildefonso, I just hope you're right. Consuelito, from Maruja la Valvanera's house, goes to the Café Pelayo to have a vermouth, good morning Consuelito, what'll it be?, good morning Serafín, vermouth, bring me a vermouth, Serafín is the oldest waiter in the café, he's at least sixty, the same faces as always are at the tables, almost the same faces as always, but also new faces, people talk loudly but don't seem to be very frightened, did you hear about the barracks?, what barracks?, the Montaña Barracks, no, what happened?, well just that the ones inside rebelled and were put down by forces loyal to the Republic, well that doesn't mean a thing to me one way or the other, the point is to have peace and for a girl to be able to work without being bothered, Serafín feels esteem for Consuelito, lower your voice, child, shut your mouth!, why?, just because, you just drink your vermouth and keep quiet. The parents and little brothers and sisters of Guillermo Zabalegui are not in Madrid, every year about the twenty-somethingth of June, when the children are through with exams, they go to Lequeitio for the summer, Guillermo had stayed in Madrid to study agricultural entomology, he's been flunking agricultural entomology for three years now, the professor Don Miguel Benlloch is really tough, his Aunt Mimí looks for the body in the morgue, she's a brave woman who's not about to be stopped by anything, she looks gorgeous, she's dressed with very elegant simplicity with low shoes and a little cretonne suit right next to her skin, where are the ones from the Montaña Barracks?, which ones, from inside or from outside?, Mimí aims a glance of infinite contempt at the militiaman at the door, do I look like someone who'd come to ask about the ones from outside?, Mimí identifies Guillermo's body, it's not hard, he has a bullet wound in his forehead, a little hole that doesn't even muss his hair, that's the one, Mimí is startled to see him with his eyes open, poor boy!, the morgue smells sickeningly of death, of filth, and of formaldehyde, it also smells of sweat, of feet, and rancid, in gusts it smells of urine and of shit, all the foul smells of the living and the dead stew together in the morgue, the odd thing is that people don't faint or dash out to breathe fresh air, on the Calle de Santa Isabel there isn't much fresh air either, there are many bodies thrown onto the marble tables and on the floor and a lot of people around the bodies crying and gesticulating, Mimí shows her papers, fills out some forms, signs in two or three places, phones the mortuary on the Calle del Arenal and leaves, if you knew her very well you would have seen that her jaw is slightly tightened, not a single tear slips from her, the militiaman at the door is thunderstruck, fuck, what a woman! Dominica Morcillo and Don Olegario come to the place where it all happened, they're always very formal with each other but they're walking arm in arm, perhaps they're afraid of getting lost, my God, what a mess!, cars loaded with shouting militiamen constantly drive down the street, their rifles stick out the open windows, many cars have initials painted on them, the most frequent ones are UGT, PSOE, CNT, FAI, AIT, PC, POUM, JSU, SRI, UHP,[4] there are certainly more, do you understand this?, well no, the truth is I don't understand a word of it, this is going to end badly Don

4. Unión General de Trabajadores (Socialist labor organization), Partido Socialista Obrero Español (the Socialist Party), Confederación Nacional del Trabajo (Anarchist labor organization), Federación Anarquista Ibérica (the Anarchist party), Asociación Internacional del Trabajo (international labor organization), Partido Comunista (Moscow-line Communists), Partido Obrero de Unificación Marxista (Trotskyist Communists), Juventud Socialista Unificada (joint youth group of the Socialists and Communists), Socorro Rojo Internacional (Communist relief organization), Unión, Hermanos Proletarios ('Proletarian Brothers Unite,' revolutionary slogan). Translator's note.

Olegario!, well there's not much they can take from us, yes that's true, on the Calle de Evaristo San Miguel at the corner of Martín de los Heros they run into Chonina who's coming with a gentleman who could be her father, good morning to you both, good morning dear, where are going?, well you know, just for a walk, Chonina is a little rattled, let me introduce you, this is my papa, these are some friends of mine, pleased to meet you, the pleasure is mine, Chonina's father looks like a village sacristan, I come last night from the village to see my girl and you can see what a ruckus I run into, well yes, you didn't have much luck, did you come from far away?, pretty far, a good thirty miles, I'm from Pezuela de las Torres, beyond Alcalá, over toward Daganzo?, no sir, on the other side, past Corpa, oh yes. Don Roque, since Doña Teresa won't let him go out, listens to the radio, the government has confiscated the newspapers *Ya*, *El Debate*, *Informaciones*, *El Siglo Futuro*, and *ABC*, it's a good thing they're leaving us El Sol!, Teresita, yes love, they've confiscated *ABC*, my!, the situation is under control in San Sebastián where the rebels tried to seize the city, well, we'll see what's true and what's false in all of this, Teresita, yes love, would you give me another beer?, of course, for whom do you think I've brought a whole case?, a case?, yes Roque, one whole case, the rumors about Segovia and Logroño and the canard about a march on Madrid are absolutely false, let's hear you say that tomorrow or the day after, the report that some ministers have fled abroad is also false, listen to this, Teresita!, the government denies it categorically, that's bad!, and is pleased to announce that at this very moment all ministers, absolutely all, are at their posts more dedicated than ever to the rapid achievement of the great task of totally crushing the criminal rebellion provoked by Fascism, long live speech-making!, I wouldn't be a bit surprised if more than a couple were already in France with a trunkful of pesetas! Doña Jesusa timidly rings the bell at 132 Ayala, a single-family house, the garden railing is painted dark green almost black, on its backside it has a metal plate of the same color that reaches almost to its top, it's all very discreet and almost mysterious, Doña Jesusa has to ring again because nobody answers, after a little while an old servant comes out, maybe she's not as old as she looks, with painted eyes, messy hair, and every indication of just having got out of bed, she must be a retired whore who didn't manage to save anything, is Doña Sacramento in?, she's resting, what can I do for you?, I'd like to talk to her, can't you give me the message?, no, it's something very personal, does it concern one of the young ladies?, no, it concerns her daughter Virtudes, the servant's face lights up, has she had the baby already?, yes, well, no, I'd rather explain it to Doña Sacramento, come in, come in, the door opens for Doña Jesusa, the garden has a decadent air that gives it a certain remote and almost sinful charm, six paces, four steps up, and the hall with furniture upholstered in garnet-colored moiré and leaded windows, Sacra!, what do you want?, come on out there's a lady here to see you!, from the depths of the house comes the voice of Doña Sacramento, who the fuck is it at this time in the morning?, the servant answers, also shouting, a lady with news about Virtudes!, let her in!, Doña Sacramento receives Doña Jesusa in bed, please excuse me but here we work till very late, you know, and so naturally I take the chance to get some sleep in the morning, yes I understand, don't worry about me, Doña Sacramento sits up a little and lights a cigarette, would you like one?, no thanks, I don't smoke, Doña Jesusa sits down on a very chic bench, Doña Sacramento smiles as though trying to be nice, let's see, a boy or a girl?, Doña Jesusa clears her throat a bit and swallows, well I'll tell you, a girl, wonderful!, no . . . , excuse me, the baby was born dead, for heaven's sake!, yes, it was a real shame, and how about Virtudes?, well you can imagine, the poor girl's taking it very hard, she sent me to get you, Doña Sacramento gets up and puts on a very elegant electric blue padded robe, my poor child!, well, let's go, Doña Sacramento dresses very quickly and puts the money she had in her night table in her purse, and how about my son-in-law?, Doña Jesusa speaks without looking at Doña Sacramento, your son-in-law was killed last night when he went out for the midwife, he went out in his pajama and running like crazy and they thought he was a Fascist, Virtudes doesn't know it yet, Doña Sacramento turns a little pale, as she goes out she tells the servant, I don't know when I'll be back, if I'm not here at seven lock the door, understand?, don't open for a soul, let 'em fuck their mothers, first things first!, don't you worry Sacra. Paquito is a shit and of course everybody forgets a shit, I'll make it up to everybody when my father dies, Don Leoncio Romero invites him to a lay from time to time, then Paquito's face lights up and he even turns handsome, thanks Don Leoncio, God bless you, I'll make it up to you, you'll see, when my father dies I'll make it up to you, yesterday afternoon, instead of going to the Fountain of the Four Seasons to read detective stories, Paquito got into the Montaña Barracks, Paquito will never again say when my father dies I'll make it up to you, Paquito died before his father, dying a minute before is the same as dying thirty years before, the bad thing is dying before, do you know that rams always go where there's green grass? Toisha doesn't like your dream, I swear to you there's nothing bad about it, you were whipping away at a gentleman, that's all, yes, but I was naked, well tell me, is it my fault you were naked?, another gentleman in a frock coat and top hat was coming out of your pussy making speeches, this was a very tiny gentleman, Toisha is not a bit amused, it's not very prudent of you to tell her your dream, you're quite a joker aren't you?, but sweetheart!, Toisha looks at you almost hatefully and her voice turns hoarse, why don't you dream he's coming out of your mother's cunt, sweetheart?, Dámaso Rioja says Toisha is right, it wasn't prudent to tell her your dream, you know how women are, there are things they don't like, yes so I see, the trouble now is how do I make it all right again, wait till tomorrow, maybe she'll have calmed down by tomorrow, the good thing about women is they don't hold a grudge, don't hold a grudge?, they hold it and then some!, no, no, what you have to do with women is pay a little attention to them and let them do things their own way, believe me, your Uncle Jerónimo maintains the theory that the only ones who have nothing to lose are the dead, people say this guy's dead broke and has nothing to lose, that's why he wants a revolution just in case he gets something when they're dividing up the wealth, your Uncle Jerónimo answers, no, that's not the way it is, it's the other way around, just the other way around, all men can lose their freedom and their life, perhaps death is less terrible than life but man prefers life, better the devil you know than the devil you don't know, between freedom and prison bars man has fewer doubts, people pay no attention to freedom or other people's lives because they're blinded defending their own wealth and distinctions, vanity of vanities!, the only ones who have nothing to lose are the dead because they've already lost it all, a live man no matter how poor he may seem is always rich as long as he can defend his freedom and his life, there are also less weighty riches, health, youth, but the important ones are life and liberty, people make a mistake when they say this guy's dead broke and has nothing to lose, that's why he wants a revolution just in case he gets something when they're dividing up the wealth, no, that's not the way it is, Cándido Modrego isn't dead broke, nobody's dead broke any more, they're all really dead by now, every six months Cándido goes to the Oriente baths and scrubs himself hard with medicinal soap, with a eucalyptus soap, Cándido knows the life of Saint Isidore, patron saint of Madrid, almost by heart, it doesn't do him much good but he knows it almost all and without having to stop, leave the burning lead enemas for those who are debauched because Cándido is a decent fellow, of course our spelling has to be reformed, Don Olegario agrees with him and not just to be polite but because he thinks so too, it's much more logical to write ijo and not hijo, kaballo and not caballo, the way we do now, it sounds the same anyway, Dominica Morcillo doesn't care, what she likes are the butts of Virginia cigarettes, better Camels than Luckies, Camels are more aromatic and more nourishing. At Doña Teresa's boardinghouse the radio is in the dining room, the guests listen to the news but don't say anything, the only one who talks is Don Roque, would you please tell me why you're all scared before there's any reason for it?, nobody answers him and they all pretend he's not talking about them, some smile but unenthusiastically, just out of politeness, Don Lucio Saavedra is a retired employee of the assessor's office, he is a widower and his only son is a missionary in Paraguay, Don Lucio feels very much alone and is grateful if anyone pays him a little attention, he's always very neatly dressed and speaks seriously and with moderation, Don Lucio doesn't eat much and gives even less trouble, he pays very punctually and in advance, if I die toward the beginning of the month you're that much ahead, he tells Doña Teresa, don't even think of that Don Lucio, don't joke about that!, you're still in too good a shape to be thinking about that, Don Lucio has a little income from property in his village, it's not much but look it's better than nothing, Don Lucio has made a will leaving what he has to Doña Teresa, he hasn't told her anything, he'd rather it came to her as a surprise, Don Lucio gets special meals, half a slice of ham and a glass of milk with cookies at midday and a soft-boiled egg and another glass of milk but without cookies at night, his diet agrees with Don Lucio, Don Lucio sits alone at the little table by the window and from time to time he looks out on the street, Don Hilario eats with Don Avelino Folgueras a traveling salesman, Don Hilario tries to sell Don Avelino a fifty-horsepower producer gas motor, he's wasting his time because Don Avelino is a salesman himself and knows every trick of the trade, Don Avelino covers his mouth with his napkin when he belches, it's a touch of politeness that Don Hilario is the first to appreciate, Emilio Arroyo has been preparing himself for ten years to get into the school of highway engineers, his companion Virgilio Ricote is a novice, he's only been at it for six, the two students are always broke and have to resort to a thousand tricks to have a beer or a cup of coffee or a cigarette, their fathers pay Doña Teresa their room and board by postal money order so nothing will be filched along the way, there are still two more guests, Don Demetrio Hoyo Martín and his wife Doña Vicenta Mateos who are only passing through the capital, Don Demetrio is a dentist in La Unión, province of Murcia, they came to Madrid to see one of Doña Vicenta's sisters take the veil, Doña Vicenta's sister is called Herminia and she's a real saint, she was joyful through her six months as a postulant, Doña Teresa and Don Roque eat together, when it comes time for the banana or quince jelly Don Roque signals to Paulina and she brings a bottle of cider for each table, Don Roque gets up and strikes an oratorical pose, Teresa and I have something to share with you . . . , at the morgue Agustín takes care of Engracia's papers, Engracia Martínez Sobrino, age 24, place of birth Madrid . . . , Teresa and I want to share our happiness with you . . . , Señor Ramón has just got out of jail and is weeping by his daughter's body, Agustín, yes Señor Ramón, why didn't you take her home even if you had to drag her kicking and screaming?, because I couldn't Señor Ramón, don't think I didn't try, but Engracia wouldn't even listen to me, she was like possessed, Señor Ramón is short and in the morgue he seems even shorter . . . , Teresa and I are free and unattached . . . , are you her husband or her brother?, no, but her father can sign, sign here Señor Ramón, yes my boy . . . , Teresa and I plan to be joined in an indissoluble bond . . . , once they're outside Señor Ramón leans on Agustín's arm, where do we have to go now? . . . , you sure kept it to yourselves!, no, that's not it, it all happened so suddenly, just in a flash, a real whirlwind romance, please understand that neither Teresa nor I are at an age where we go around hiding such things . . . , Señor Ramón stands there looking at Agustín, why didn't you make her a baby?, Agustín doesn't know what to answer . . . , my, my, what a couple of love birds!, long life to you both and to us all!, Emilio Arroyo shouts long live the happy couple! and everyone joins him . . . , Agustín takes Señor Ramón into the dairy in the Doré alley, eat something, have a glass of milk and a bun, you've got to eat something . . . , the two maids respectfully join the celebration and kiss Doña Teresa, maybe they're not that pleased inside but it doesn't show, after lunch is a very happy moment in Doña Teresa's boarding-house on July 20, Saint Jerome Emilian . . . , never in his life has Señor Ramón gone through such pain and anguish all at one time, not when he was at Tizzi-Azza back when there was the trouble with the Moors, not when there was the typhoid fever, not in jail, not ever . . . , Doña Teresa can't hold back her tears, coffee for everybody!, Paulina, use the good coffee, and brandy or anise for whoever wants it!, Javiera, open a bottle of each, or maybe the lady would rather have Marie Brizard, Doña Vicenta likes everything, no, no, don't bother about me, I'll have anything . . . , now Señor Ramón is weeping more slowly, he's obviously running out of tears . . . , Don Roque stands up and distributes cigars around the tables, two per man, this one for now and this one for later, out of respect for the ladies Don Roque lowers his voice to say, and fuck the radio! . . . ,

Agustín offers his tobacco case to Señor Ramón, how about a cigarette?, all right. The sun streams down directly onto the Plaza de Antón Martín, they call the Bar Zaragoza the Palace of Syphilis, there must be a reason for that, Matiítas is having a cup of coffee by one of the windows that face the Calle de León and that's in the shade, he's holding his rifle between his legs, evidently so it won't get stolen, also he likes to hold it between his legs, with him sits Aixa the Moor with the tattooed navel and the gold tooth and the dead tooth, Aixa is smoking English cigarettes that Ibarra gives her, would you like one?, sure, it's not very important that a fly is drowning in the coffee dregs, it moves as though it were getting fucked and then it drowns, Matiítas is sad, it's as though he had a great worry, are you worried?, no, I don't feel well, I don't know what's the matter with me, has something upset you?, no, nothing, I'm just afraid, afraid of what?, what do I know!, just afraid, I couldn't say why, Matiítas claps twice, I'll treat you to a brandy, thanks, when the waiter comes he tells him bring two brandies, are you going to pay in pesetas?, of course, what do you want me to do, pay in pounds sterling?, no, what I don't want is people paying me with vouchers, this establishment does not accept vouchers, Aixa drinks down her brandy at one gulp, Matiítas doesn't, Matiítas drinks it a little at a time that way you get the flavor of it better, well it depends, it's a matter of taste, Aixa sits with her legs spread apart to get a little air, are you horny?, no, how the fuck am I going to be horny?, I think I'm going to go home, what I am is bored, this time of the day the best thing to do is take a nap, what are you going to do?, I don't know, maybe I'll go home too, I feel kind of sick, like I told you, can I go along?, all right, Matiítas lives on the Costanilla de los Trinitarios at the corner of the Calle de las Huertas, in a garret where it's hot and cold, when it's cold outside it's colder in Matiítas' garret than it is outside, when it's hot outside Matiítas' garret is like a bakery oven, Matiítas is not a careful faggot but a resigned one and his garret is all dirty and disordered, with four urinals hanging each from its nail, a felt mannequin gradually being eaten up by moths, a chest for his clothes, a little statue of the Virgin under a bell jar on top of the chest of drawers, two vases with artificial flowers covered with fly shit, a tin chest, his mother's wedding photo, various photos of athletes and boxers (Jack Dempsey, Jack Sharkey, Max Baer, Paulino Uzcudun, Max Schmeling, Jimmy Braddock, Alf Brown), a radio, Royam brand, with some tubes out, two or three pairs of women's shoes all high-heeled, a lithograph of the discovery of America, a small dining table, three chairs, a rocking chair, the bed, and some glasses and plates, there are also some empty bottles and old newspapers, Matiítas gets home and drops onto the bed, maybe he's tired from all those stairs, Aixa takes off her clothes and sits down on the rocking chair, she's fat and has big drooping tits, Matiítas isn't much impressed but then Aixa isn't there in the altogether to impress him but because she's hot, Aixa takes down a urinal and pisses like a noisy mule with its legs apart, I was pissing in my pants, so I see, Matiítas looks at his rifle, what a good dildo!, it's not thick but it is very hard, it's like a dildo for punishment, why don't you stick it up your ass?, what a brute you are Aixa!, you want to see me with a ruptured ass!, Paca and Fidel wander around the Montaña Barracks, it's very exciting to see the dead and everything in ruins all around, would you have liked to be here?, no sir not me, and you?, not a chance!, me either, among these dead there must surely be some soldier who was a client of Paca's some night in the vacant lots near the Niño Jesús station, do you know any of them?, no sir, the militiamen stand guard and don't let anyone touch the dead, some of the dead have already been taken to the morgue, others await their turn, the morgue is chock-full, it's full to overflowing, when Paca and Fidel get bored they continue their stroll, what a battle can flare up in just a few hours!, that's for sure . . . , two planes fly over the Casa de Campo, you can tell they're the ones from Cuatro Vientos that are keeping watch, Paca and Fidel go down the Cuesta de San Vicente to the Paseo de la Virgen del Puerto, the Manzanares has hardly any water in it, it looks like the Abroñigal creek, under the bridge ten or twelve stark naked urchins are splashing in the water, from the other bank some thirteen-year-old girls are looking on with their heads full of wicked thoughts. Aixa wakes up with a start, she had fallen asleep in the rocking chair but she wakes up with a start when she hears the shot, it sounded as though it were muffled with water or with a pillow, Matiítas is lying on his bed naked and dying, he has the muzzle of the rifle stuck up his ass, he must have pulled the trigger with his toe, the bullet came out his belly, the blood is pouring out his belly and his ass and a sad drop of viscous semen is hanging from his penis, Matiítas looks over at Aixa, smiles, and lets his head drop heavily as though it were made of lead, Matiítas has died, he doesn't say a single word, he just smiles almost gratefully, Aixa closes Matiítas' eyes, you really have to be a faggot to kill yourself with a bullet up the ass!, she gets dressed, shit, when the police find out!, and she leaves, she's got no reason to be mixed up in a mess that doesn't concern her, that doesn't mean a thing to her one way or the other, Aixa goes back to the Bar Zaragoza, she's afraid to go home with all this heat, Don Esteban, Guillermo Zabalegui's blind uncle, would never have believed that Matiítas could kill himself with a bullet up the ass, you've got to be a real faggot, it's really funny, making orgasm and death coincide like that is what poets do, maybe he wanted to purge his sin, that's no purge, it's an enema, just the other way around, you are troubled by what Don Esteban says, he is a very undesirable and cynical blind man, very avaricious and cruel, and Manichaean?, yes also Manichaean, you've never believed much in self-purgings or self-enemas, you obviously have no tendency toward confession or suicide, of course no one can say that until he dies of cancer or in a car crash and then goes to hell for not having received the blessed sacraments, his captains gave King Cyril of England a lead enema, he would have preferred to keep on enjoying life, at the Bar Zaragoza Aixa runs into Petra Soto one of the owners of the cooperative at 23 Calle de la Reina, what's new in your life?, same old story, not much, there's less work with this heat. Don Joaquín has locked up his shop, conditions out there are not likely to make his customers itch for a console or a cornucopia, Don Lucio rings at the small door out front, del Burgo, I've got so I don't know what to do, so have we all Mr. Saavedra, I feel like we Spaniards have all gone nuts all of a sudden, Spain no longer has any government and is just groping her way, the worst of it is that the only place that way leads to is a catastrophe, the end of the road is catastrophe, you'll see, yes I'm afraid you're right, we're all groping our way here and thrashing around with our sticks like blind men, did I say sticks?, guns and cannons, more than one of us is going to get caught in the middle and get his skull cracked, nobody can feel safe and protected under these circumstances, I'm old already and there's not much time left for me my friend but I'm sorry to see so many young men gone mad and with their very lives in danger, well . . . , the second-hand dealer feels a great deal of respect for Don Lucio, how about a little cup of coffee?, thanks but I'd rather not drink anything, at my age the less you make your stomach work the better, just as you like, Don Lucio is still for a few moments, do you know we've got big news at the boardinghouse?, I don't know a thing, what's up?, just that Doña Teresa is getting married on us, well then I've got to congratulate her, and whom is she marrying?, Mr. Barcia, shit, it was about time that old playboy settled down!, and is it so to speak official already?, as official as they come, they've just told us about it at lunch, well how about that, well, I'm very glad, Doña Teresa is still a good-looking woman and she's a real lady, a genuine lady, Doña Teresa deserves being taken care of, now what's needed is for Mr. Barcia to respect her, Mr. Barcia is a fine man I'm sure but a bit of a Don Juan, don't listen to gossip del Burgo,

Mr. Barcia is no better and no worse than you or I, so he's had a little fling here and there, we have to excuse him, Mr. Barcia was under no obligation to be faithful to anybody, from now on it'll be a different story, for a while now Don Joaquín has been thinking about Paquita, that is, Margot, the mother of his children who became a whore because neither of the two, neither he nor she, managed to speak out in time or call things by their right name, excuse me just a minute Mr. Saavedra, I've got to make a phone call, don't let me stop you, just pretend I'm not even here, take care of your business, Don Joaquín dials a number and speaks in a low voice covering the receiver a little with his other hand, is Margot there?, what?, isn't this Villa Milagros?, yes it is, is Margot there, I'd like to talk to her, who's calling?, a friend of hers, wait a minute, I'll see, Don Joaquín looks over at Don Lucio who is very busy leafing through some old magazines, hello, yes, Margot is busy, call again later, all right, I'll call again later, or no, it's better she calls me, would you tell her to call her friend Don Joaquín?, I'll be glad to. Don Fausto is a real man and he just about breaks Matiítas' back with some of the thrashings he gives him, sometimes he even hits him with his belt, Don Fausto goes to visit Doña Soledad, my, Don Fausto, what a pleasure to see you, are you waiting for Matías?, no, I was coming to ask about him, do you know what's become of him?, the store's closed, well no sir I don't know a thing, good heavens, do you know where he lives?, well I don't know that either, I think he lives over by the Plaza de Antón Martín but that's all I know, Doña Soledad smiles with the air of an accomplice, did you want to caress him a little?, if you don't find him I can bring you a very refined young man who left me his phone number, Don Fausto's face shows he's in a foul mood, no, that's not it, what I want to do is kick him to hell and gone for being a faggot and a stool pigeon, heavens!, yes ma'am, just as I said, a faggot and a stool pigeon, that Matías is an ingrate and a bum, you'll see once I find him, what that scoundrel needs is a good licking, in the back room Solita and Conchita, Doña Soledad's two half-wit and pregnant daughters, are playing parcheesi, Rogelio Roquero hasn't come yet with his jar of milk and his village stud's confident step, if Rogelio would go along with it life could again smile on Don Fausto, the trouble is that you can't go to Rogelio with certain propositions, Rogelio is a young fellow with fixed ideas, his views on love are very rigid and inflexible, Herodotus was the first to give us a written account of some small men who live in the middle of Africa, the pygmies, and what does that have to do with Don Fausto's being so furious?, nothing, absolutely nothing, nobody said it did either, they're separate things and some people get furious and then there are some who don't get furious, for example, the position of veterinarian is vacant in Aldea del Rey Nuño, Zorita del Maestrazgo, Bercimuel, and Fresno de Cantespino, well, just tell that to Don Fausto, you'll see how he takes it, Don Fausto is a real man, he leaves, used to leave, Matiítas bleeding from the lashings he gave him with his belt, if he finds him now he's capable of going a little farther and killing him for being a stool pigeon and a faggot, there must be some misunderstanding here, what can Matiítas have squealed about?, there's some misunderstanding here, you can be sure of that, why doesn't the shooting stop?, why this heated and distracted scattering of gunpowder?, when will a relative and cautious silence fall, the habitual sound of the city woven of dreams and delusions, shouts, laments, words of love, pleas, and insults?, the cries of the newborn child disguise the scream of the new mother, the languid abandon of the happy man covers up the panting of the man on his deathbed, there are women who take cocaine and men who grow desperate when they don't find the bicarbonate, Aixa the Moor hasn't seen a thing, she'll die with her secret, nor did she hear more than one shot, one single shot, many shots are heard in Madrid, nobody can distinguish one shot from another, a pianist could but the people who are on the streets at naptime or who are taking their naps are not pianists, they don't have a pianist's ear, Matiítas is an aesthete, was an aesthete ridden by death, Matiítas is dying, died, of thousands of lashes and finally a rifle shot, Matiítas is not a lover, was not a lover but a loved and reprimanded object, Matiítas' face is in his ass, was in his ass and he killed himself by taking advantage of just the right moment of heat, it's very hot, Aixa is sitting naked on the rocking chair and Matiítas is blowing on the muzzle of the rifle, he puts it under his arm and in the sun so it won't be so cold, Aixa falls asleep like a jackal in the desert, Aixa is a jackal in the desert and Matiítas caresses his calamities almost nostalgically, Matiítas is an aesthete, not a good lover but an aesthete, every man is the way God made him, a good lover is never an aesthete, anything will do for him, but it won't for Matiítas, almost nothing would do for him, Don Fausto gives him pleasure, gave him pleasure with whippings and Matiítas in his garret and taking advantage of the fact that it's very hot also dies with pleasure and smiling the smile of the blessed, it's too bad Aixa is asleep. Antonio Arévalo rings the doorbell of Doña Teresa's boardinghouse, Paulina answers, Mr. Barcia please, who may I say is asking for him?, a friend, tell him it's urgent, wait a minute, Don Roque comes out to see who it is, you?, yes, can I talk to you just a minute?, yes of course, come with me, Don Roque takes Arévalo to Doña Teresa's sitting room, let me introduce you, my friend Antonio Arévalo, a future deputy for the Agrarian Party, my fiancée, well I'll be . . . , I had no idea!, well now you do, congratulations, thank you very much, consider yourself invited to the wedding, Don Roque offers his visitor a seat, what can I do for you?, well it's something private, I'd rather talk to you alone, speak freely, I have no secrets from Teresa, all right just as you like, they've broken into our offices on Jorge Juan and carried off the membership lists, I thought I ought to tell you, thank you very much, but that doesn't matter, we can reconstruct them, no, that's not the problem, they plan to use those lists to kill us all, don't exaggerate, Antonio!, no sir, I'm not exaggerating, I'm sure they're going to do it, how do you know that?, I don't know it but I'm sure anyhow, as sure as I can be, what I've come to tell you is that you should hide before they find you, I?, no my boy, I'm no Calvo Sotelo or Gil Robles, I'm nothing but a simple deputy whom nobody knows, and being a deputy gives me parliamentary immunity and besides, what am I going to run from when I don't have anything to hide?, let's keep calm Antonio, the solution for all of this must be just around the corner, maybe by now Mola has already crossed the mountains, hiding would be tantamount to admitting guilt for something we haven't done, what did we do?, no, I'm not hiding, I'm no criminal, I've got my own ideas but I'm no criminal. Margot, when her customer leaves, phones Don Joaquín, Joaquín, it's me, Margot, you called me?, yes, listen Paquita, I wanted to talk to you, can you come by the store?, it'll be locked up, ring at the doorway, Margot is surprised to hear her husband calling her Paquita, it's been years now that her husband never calls her Paquita, yes, I'll be there right away, just as soon as I can get there, it's night by now and the sniper fire begins to sound from the rooftops, they don't usually ask women for their papers, the watchman is surprised to see Margot go out at this time of night, where are you going at this time of night in the middle of all this row?, well just going, some automobiles equipped with a machine gun in front and another in back are crossing Madrid and firing on groups of the militia with the sole aim of inciting terror, that's what Radio Unión says, they usually carry four persons and frequently resort to the trick of changing their license plates, one Fiat Balilla was stopped on the Glorieta de Bilbao by some militiamen who faced it valiantly, inside were four Fascists dressed as women and armed with Parabellum pistols, three were killed and one was able to escape although he is believed to be wounded, Margot does not meet any of these cars on her way, an occasional passerby tosses her a compliment without getting out of line and in the subway her butt gets patted a little but not too much either, that's all, Don Joaquín tries to hide it but you can tell he's afraid, he's wearing his glasses and his sideburns and mustache seem somehow less bold than usual, I was beginning to think you'd never get here!, I got here as soon as I could, I didn't stop anywhere, Don Joaquín kisses his wife, look let's get to the point, I'm getting out of Madrid, I'm going with the kids, where to?, I don't know but I'm getting out of Madrid, to Valencia maybe or to Alicante, I'll stay there till this is all over, you think I'm a bastard but that's not true, I didn't treat you right but you didn't treat me right either, neither one of us did right, I don't treat anybody right, well almost nobody, sometimes I want to but then I don't, I'm not a bastard, I'd give anything not to be a bastard for anybody and least of all for you, besides even if you don't believe it I want you to know I still love you, me?, yes you, we can have supper at Rufino's, over there on Echegaray, then you'll spend the night here, that is if you don't have to go back to Villa Milagros, the kids will be glad to see you, you'll see, if you'll come with us I'll take you, let me think about it, during supper Margot is sad, when they finish she sits there looking at her husband, I'm not going, I'm very grateful to you but I'm not going, I've got things to do at Villa Milagros, we whores have our obligations too, Margot is chubby, dyed blonde, and very affectionate, on her neck she always wears a little silk scarf to cover her old scar.

III

No, it's not a good sign, your mirror is like a bloody jellyfish, no longer is it a flat, parallelepiped, ovoid, almost spherical mirror, now it's a mirror in the shape of a bloody jellyfish, soft like a jellyfish and poisonous, poisonous too, your mirror no longer reflects your shape, who knows whether you have a shape any longer, whether you're like a bread crumb that changes its shape, shrinks and puffs up or wastes away, don't weep for your dead shape, you'll have time for weeping for other sorrows, it's not a good sign, there's too much blood for so little heart, the calendar doesn't tolerate being crushed, Tuesday July 21 Saint Daniel prophet and on the back a riddle or some verses, if you crush it too much the heart explodes into a thousand pieces that wound everybody when they go flying through the air, jellyfish sting like nettles and even worse, there are also mirrors that give you hives just from looking at them, auction off your treasures, the lock of hair, the silk handkerchief, your three love letters, your three rose petals, your three violets, the photograph, they won't do you much good, they won't do you any good, it would be better if pretending not to notice you could just go out on the street naked, but you're just not up to it, what you like is looking at yourself in the mirror dressed and with your tie on, your toothache doesn't show in the mirror, it's a very coarse instrument, very insensitive, your mirror is a useless instrument that need not be broken, you call it a mirror because you want to and nobody forbids it but it's not a mirror, look carefully and you'll see it's not a mirror, it's a bloody jellyfish from which you ought to flee, Toisha still sleeps alone, with a silk bedspread and sheets with her initial in raised embroidery but alone, the curtains are silk too, Toisha tells you that she has your picture standing on her night table, maybe she's telling you the truth, fear makes people incredulous, any day now Toisha will decide not to sleep alone any more, she is being very lovingly patient with you, and all your love will be wiped out of a sudden or who knows but all your love will suddenly grow enormously and suddenly like a sick and gigantic octopus, auction off your most prized treasures, the panties of that whore the subway killed, the dirty handkerchief, your poems, your three half-crowns with the head of the king of England, your newspaper clippings, the book Rafael Alberti dedicated to you, nothing will do you any good any more, don't phone Toisha, she mustn't see you so defeated, take refuge in the relative love of the sisters and try to go down the street shrinking and hugging the walls, your friends hardly know you any more, they no longer want to recognize in you the descendant of Charlemagne, you are a man without history or with very little history, you'd like to believe in concepts, persons, and things like everybody else and suffer and enjoy but your mirror is a vile instrument that betrays you, don't break your mirror like a bloody jellyfish, let others be the ones to do it, let others be the ones to keep spilling blood, you have to believe in something to spill blood, in concepts, in persons, in things, so much blood on the ground is too miraculous, so much belief, you'd like to be a whorehouse fly, we all know it, the whole city knows it, a lecherous fly of the mattresses crushed by disconsolate lust and by disgust, but not a morgue fly, never, an indifferent fly of the sheets that the management pays for in the name of the concepts that govern persons and things, morgue flies do not love each other among lusty bursts of laughter but very chastely and cautiously and in the corners, ask at the morgue for a sheet to cover your mirror like a bloody jellyfish. Antonio Arévalo spends the night on the rooftops like a cat, he's very tired but he'll sleep when and where he can, Doña Teresa asks him to stay in the boardinghouse, why don't you stay in the boardinghouse?, the maids can be trusted, Don Felipe Espinosa his girlfriend's father does not go to the morgue to see whether the bodies of his two sons turn up, he's afraid of three things, that they will turn up, that they won't turn up, or that they'll turn up looking at him contemptuously, that would be the worst, the open eyes of the dead always accuse us, that's why the living are in a hurry to close them, he's also afraid they'll ask him for his papers, you could do a charitable deed, why don't you go by the morgue to see whether Felipe and Alberto are there?, all right I'll go tomorrow morning, María Victoria spends the whole time crying, María Angustias is also very frightened but she's not crying, on the radio they read an official communiqué, Don Roque plans to give Doña Teresa a 1936 Crosley, Imperator model, three wave lengths and colored light on the dial, the sweetest songster of the airwaves, the brand that guarantees you technical excellence and a reliable firm, the Minister of the Interior informs the population of Madrid that small groups of agitators are carrying out searches of domiciles claiming to be militia in the service of the government, be advised that no searches will be made other than those decided on by the authorities for which the militia and loyal forces will be provided with appropriate authorization, Don Roque reassures Doña Teresa, you heard that, the government is taking the reins in its hands, these street rowdies will have to stop stirring up trouble, it had to happen!, Doña Teresa is still a little nervous, would you like another little glass of brandy?, no thanks, let's go to bed, yes love, persons who have just come from Valencia inform us that when the popular church of Saint Valerius caught on fire the neighbors cordoned off the building and detained the arsonist who turned out to be the sacristan of the church, now that's a good one!, the multimillionaire John D. Rockefeller turns ninety-seven, he looks very distinguished but photographs of him show him too thin, he looks like dried codfish, Doña Sacramento is alarmed, Virtudes has a high fever, she's delirious and as soon as she gets up the sheet really stinks, it smells of rotten codfish, John D. Rockefeller is an aromatic codfish not at all rotten, Doña Sacramento looks over at Doña Jesusa, this is as bad as can be, I'm going to call the doctor, Virtudes' phone still doesn't work, do you have a phone?, no ma'am not us, Don Daniel the gentleman on the second floor and his wife Doña Andrea, they have a phone, the trouble is they go to bed early, they're old people, you can phone from the bakery at number 4, I won't leave Virtudes, don't worry you can go, thank you very much, sniper fire and sometimes even dense volleys are heard through the open window, a militiaman sings Andalusian fandangos with a very melodious baritone voice, long live civilian power, down with Mola and Goded, down with foes of our Republic, may we live to see them dead in our country's finest hour! A car comes to a dead stop in front of Doña Teresa's boardinghouse, the brakes screech like the crack of a whip, just like a whip striking the whole block, the doors slam, one, two, three, four, almost at the same time and with a lot of noise, nobody's trying to hide anything here, watchman!, the watchman comes up without rushing it, open this door, where are you going?, that's none of your business, come on, open it and shut up!, you'd better keep quiet, come on now, open the door or we'll open it ourselves!, all right, all right, shit what manners!, the five men don't take the elevator, they walk up the stairs, Pensión Marineda, this is it, the knocks on the door startle the neighbors, Paulina answers buttoning up her dress, what's your rush?, our rush is our business, honey, and none of yours, we're here to get a certain Roque Barcia, he's one of Calvo Sotelo's Fascists, Paulina looks the speaker in the eye and has a flash of inspiration, it could just as well have happened the other way, well you're too late, that gentleman left three days ago, where to?, you're asking me?, you think the guests tell me where they're going?, go on, call the owner, we're going to search the whole place, at this time of night!, well, come in, Paulina heads for Doña Teresa's room and goes in without knocking, don't shout, there are some guys out there looking for Don Roque, they're asking for you, what did you tell them?, that Don Roque left three days ago, they want to search the place, all right delay them a little, tell them I'll be there right away, take them into the dining room and get out a few glasses, ma'am, what, I say Don Roque should get into my bed, your bed?, yes, Doña Teresa looks into Paulina's eyes, you think so?, yes ma'am, I do think so, you'll see, the search begins with the owner's room, Don Roque gets into Paulina's bed and leaves his clothes on the chair, Paulina throws Don Roque's wallet down into the courtyard, there's nothing here, some butts in the ashtray, you smoke a lot, yes too much and dark tobacco too, I've had the habit for many years, Paulina talks to Javiera who is scared, go on, you can get scared later, get a move on!, Javiera goes from room to room and wakes up the guests, Don Roque left three days ago, what?, Don Roque left three days ago, now you know, some are hard to convince, yes, three days ago, and where to?, he didn't tell us that, all right, the guests assemble in the dining room while the militia search the place from top to bottom, they look everywhere but don't disturb the clothes in the closets or the objects on the shelves, everybody's papers are in order, seem to be in order, excuse us for getting you up grandpa, I'm really very sorry, Don Lucio smiles, that doesn't matter, what matters is for you to be sure that we're all peaceful folks and loyal to the government of the Republic, the militiaman turns to the guests, excuse the disturbance but believe us it's necessary, we're looking for a very dangerous individual, a Fascist called Roque Barcia, do you know anything about him?, no, he left two or three days ago as a matter of fact almost without saying good-bye, Paulina sticks close to the one in charge, when they get to her room they find Don Roque in the bed, he seems to be asleep, and what about this one?, he's my boyfriend, keep it quiet because if our boss gets to know about this she's capable of throwing me right out, the militiaman bursts out laughing, shit!, so you spend the night fucking away?, yes, we're going to get married soon . . . , and your roommate here, what does she say about it?, nothing, she turns her face to the wall and says nothing, when her boyfriend comes I do the same, the militiaman faces Don Roque, your name?, José Sánchez Sánchez, occupation?, bank teller, member of the UGT?, of course, your papers?, I haven't got them on me, after all comrade I don't need papers to come lay my girl, that's true enough, where do you live?, Paseo de Santa María de la Cabeza, number 17, third floor, center left, Don Roque lies hurriedly and with a certain consistency, all right you stay right here, we've got to check all of this, you can check it right now, if you want I'll go with you, no, not now, you stay here with this hot tomato and enjoy your meal, watch it comrade!, it's a joke, man, you've got to know how to take a joke, Doña Teresa orders coffee to lift her guests' spirits, that was a close one!, yes, and we made it this time, Antoñito Arévalo was so right!, anyhow . . . , Don Roque looks over to Doña Teresa, listen, bring out a little brandy and a few glasses of nice cold water, would you?, of course I would, Don Roque turns to his fellow guests, I'm sorry to have caused you this bother, no, don't you worry, the main thing is they didn't take you away, Paulina really had her wits about her, I'll say!, Paulina has a Sarah Bernhardt inside her, if it wasn't for her they'd have knocked me off or at the very least locked me up for a while, Paulina, yes sir Don Roque, tomorrow morning you're going to buy yourself the best dress in all of Madrid, I didn't do it for that Don Roque, I know dear, I know that, in Doña Teresa's boardinghouse nobody thinks about sleeping and they all talk without raising their voices but incessantly, at 4 or 4:30 Doña Teresa brings out chocolate, it's as though we were on some bender!, well almost, Don Roque announces that he's leaving at 9 A.M., where to?, I don't know, here I'm endangering everybody and besides I got away once but I don't think I'd get away a second time, around eight the guests go to their rooms, some go back to bed, Don Hilario is frightened, so frightened that he doesn't even speak of his producer gas motor, Don Lucio calls Doña Teresa aside, tomorrow morning, I mean today two or three hours from now I'd like you to go to the notary with me, I have to settle a few things, Doña Teresa doesn't even guess what this might be about, just as you like Don Lucio, you know all you have to do is ask, Don Demetrio and Doña Vicenta plan to lose no time in returning to La Unión, wouldn't it be better to take Herminia along?, yes I think it would, the way things are going it's no time to be taking the veil, Don Avelino doesn't know what to do, I'll phone the company headquarters, the manager is the one to decide, I just follow orders, Emilio Arroyo and Virgilio Ricote, each sitting on his bed, contemplate the black horizon, if we could just go home!, why don't you ask for a plane, maybe they'll lend you one, walking's the only way we're liable to make it, Doña Teresa talks to the two maids, Don Roque is leaving today, he's already left, and I'm going tomorrow or the day after, Don Roque and I have already talked it over, you two will be in charge of the boardinghouse, any profits are for you, when this is over we'll get things back in order, Don Roque didn't want to say good-bye to anyone, he left me five hundred pesetas for each of you and told me that besides you should each go buy yourself a dress, thank you very much Doña Teresa, give our thanks to Don Roque. Sit down on a chair and wait, no kindly hand will bring you a cup of coffee but that doesn't matter, you're mulling over the classical education of the Persians, riding on horseback, telling the truth, and shooting the bow, no one taught you to ride on horseback, as a child you were too sickly to be able to ride on horseback like your cousins, you were brought up to respect truth, for your soul's sake never be ashamed to tell the truth, your grandmother always reminded you of these words of Ecclesiastes when you were little, you never had a bow in your hands or any other weapon, in your family weapons were always a souvenir or at the most decoration for the hall, time perverts men and also things, which is even worse, you still don't ride on horseback or shoot the bow but on the other hand you now lie boldly, you lie to your family and your friends, you lie to yourself when you speak, when you think, and when you are still, this lying is an ugly and useful habit, you think you want some coffee but maybe it's not true that you want some coffee, you don't want any coffee and are lying without realizing it, I want a cup of coffee, I want a cup of coffee, I want a cup of coffee, no, you don't want a cup of coffee but finally you come to believe that you want a cup of coffee and even yearn to drink coffee, you think you love Toisha and maybe it's not true that you love Toisha, you don't love Toisha and are lying without realizing it and out of selfishness, what you want is going to bed with Toisha, I love Toisha, I love Toisha, I love Toisha, agnus Dei qui tollis peccata mundi, parce nobis Domine, agnus Dei qui tollis peccata mundi, exaudi nos Domine, agnus Dei qui tollis peccata mundi, miserere nobis, I love her more than anything else in the world, no, you don't love Toisha but finally you come to believe that you love Toisha and even yearn to go to bed with her, you think you have political ideas, but no, you don't have any political ideas, you're lying without realizing it and to curry favor with someone or with yourself but you don't have any political ideas, maybe you don't have any ideas at all, be careful because that can be the road to crime, you don't think you could turn into a criminal, no criminal thinks that until he commits his first crime, you'd like to believe in three or four truths even if they were lies, the signs of the Zodiac, the seasons of the year, the cardinal points of the compass, the same thing probably happens to many men, a cornered animal is blinded and doesn't distinguish truth from falsehood, truth is the luxury of the strong and man is a weak and cornered animal, you are sitting on your chair and you contemplate the boring spectacle of the world, you could have sat in the armchair but you don't do it, you sit down on the chair, it's not that you prefer to sit on the chair, you just sit on the chair, your mother brings you some coffee, here's a cup of coffee,I've just made some coffee and I thought you'd like to have some fresh coffee, it's sad when they give you coffee when you haven't asked for it, most of the time people don't ask for coffee because they're afraid no one will pay any attention to them, the coffee your mother brings you tastes good, hot and with the right amount of sugar, neither more nor less, just as it should be, when you think that you'd like to ride on horseback or shoot the bow you know you're lying, you would not like either to ride on horseback or to shoot the bow, when you think you'd like always to tell the truth you know you're not lying, you would like always to tell the truth, it's just that you don't do it in an absolute way, at least in an absolute way, you could have died inside the Montaña Barracks next to Guillermo Zabalegui or outside the Montaña Barracks next to Andrés Herrera, neither of them was a better friend of yours than the other and each had his charm and his rifle lent by someone, his perverse dreams and kind disillusionments, his wrath and his saint's halo around his head, yes, it all could have been but it was not, you think that truth is manifold and flexible but that's not true, neither is it true that you think that, obviously truth is a destructive and inhospitable cliff, it's too bad that this is so and that it should destroy us. The doctor is at home but he doesn't want to go out at this time of night, look, Doña Sacra, it's dangerous to be out on the streets at this time of night, I'll come tomorrow morning for sure, let's see, wash her parts with corrosive sublimate, .05 percent, write it down carefully, and apply some permanganate, I'll come tomorrow morning for sure, I'm telling you, you'll see the whole business is not very serious, it happens to a lot of women at childbirth, Doña Sacramento can't find any pharmacy open, she knows a medic at the first-aid station on the Callejón de la Ternera, is Celestino in?, no ma'am, he's off tonight, can I help you?, well yes, I'd like some corrosive sublimate and some permanganate, the medic's face is like a goat's, all that's missing are the horns and the little beard, the medic is a real joker, shit!, are you going to commit suicide?, no, it's for a daughter of mine who's just given birth, can you give it to me or not?, wait and I'll ask, the medic goes in back, after a few minutes he comes out again and says no, it's against regulations, you should look in a pharmacy, the pharmacies are all closed, even the ones that are supposed to be on duty, well that's none of our concern, look in a whorehouse then, the medic is very funny, Doña Sacramento finds the antiseptics at her friend Cándida Hernández's place on the Calle de Veneras, what's the matter with your daughter?, what do I know, she looks bad to me, that sonofabitch doctor wouldn't leave his house, he says this is no time to be out, obviously sickness has its office hours just like a pawnshop, well dear, your girl will get better you'll see, you just wash her well and put the compresses on her and you'll see how she gets better, yes, I hope to God she does, Doña Jesusa is still by Virtudes' bed without leaving it for a single moment, how's she doing?, the same, I think she's the same, neither better nor worse, Doña Sacra kisses her daughter and pushes her hair away from her forehead a little, then she lifts the *Blanco y Negro* and looks at the dead baby, what are we going to do with this?, I don't know, bury it, bury it?, it's going to rot while we fiddle with the paperwork, Doña Sacra goes into the kitchen to boil two kettles of water, she rinses them a little first, the fire doesn't catch right away but it catches, Doña Sacra throws in a couple of scoopfuls of coal, when it's burning well she lifts the lids of the stove and throws the baby's tiny body on the fire box and all, she has to push the box with the scoop because it's a little too big, what are we going to do with this?, this is now the *Blanco y Negro*, throw it in too, then Doña Sacramento sets the two kettles on the stove, they'll boil in a minute you'll see. Children are very fragile and mysterious, it's not true that children are the men of tomorrow, many die first of croup or dysentery, care for your children's sight by seeing to it that their eyes receive no light other than from the sun or from Metal brand superargon lamps with strength marked in decalumens and double spiral filament, some children are born twisted and it takes a lot of effort and money to straighten them out and pump health into them, some are born dead or die right after being born and then their grandmother burns them in the kitchen stove in their shoe box, at first they don't burn well but eventually they disappear, anthracite is rich in energy and consumes all it touches, there are many children in the world, very many, the world won't come to an end. Antonio Arévalo buys himself a Communist Party badge, sticks it on his lapel, and goes over to the morgue to see whether he can find the bodies of Felipe and Alberto his girlfriend's two brothers, *salud*, comrade, *salud*, looking for something special?, no, just having a look, at 9 A.M. there are not yet too many people at the morgue, there are more bodies than visitors, there are at least three bodies per visitor or maybe more, later on the number of visitors grows and the ratio is lower, those are the Fascists from the Montaña Barracks, these other ones are the comrades murdered by the Fascists of the Montaña Barracks, and these over here?, those we don't know about, Antonio doesn't find María Victoria's brothers, what if they didn't die and are in hiding!, that's not probable, they would have given a sign of life by now, maybe they buried them without going through the morgue, on the floor and half propped up against the wall there is a body in an undershirt and pajama pants, shit, Gonococcus!, the cockroaches are fat and shiny and scurry back and forth as bold as can be, the cockroaches of the morgue are championship cockroaches, it's a pleasure to see them so proud and shiny, it's as though they'd been shined with shoe polish, Don Roque heads for El Cocodrilo to kill a little time, no, better someplace they don't know me, Don Roque walks on and goes into La Granja del Carmen for breakfast, it's on the left as you go along, on the Plaza del Ángel, a glass of hot milk please, no, a cup of hot chocolate, a glass of cold milk, and a couple of buns, Don Roque is suddenly seized by hunger, Don Roque thinks better on a full stomach, as soon as it's one I'll go see Maruja la Valvanera, she'll think of something, she's sure to think of something, what I have to do now is get away from here a little, Don Roque leaves with no fixed direction, he reaches the Plaza del Progreso and goes into the first café he finds, this one will do, Antonio Arévalo comes up Santa Isabel, turns into the Calle de la Magdalena, and also goes into the Café Toki-Ona, Don Roque is having a cup of coffee at a table in back, what are you doing here?, killing time, I'm just killing time till it gets to be a little later, it's funny, sometimes we don't have enough time and don't know where to get it, other times we've got too much time and don't know what to do with it, Don Roque is glad to have somebody to talk to, do you know they came for me last night?, no!, you heard me, Don Roque gives Antonio Arévalo a detailed account of his adventure, you escaped by the skin of your teeth!, yes Antoñito, it was a miracle, you were so right, anyhow . . . , for now I'm still here to tell about it and we'll see about tomorrow, the waiter limps toward them, he's old and doesn't seem any too friendly, coffee and a sweet roll, Don Roque lights a stogy, want one?, thanks, they're a little too strong for me, Don Roque looks worn and is unshaven, have you read the paper?, no, well read this, the news is on the front page of *El Sol*, it really is front-page news, on his way to Spain

General Sanjurjo is killed in an airplane accident, the accident took place near Estoril, accident officially confirmed, the plane caught fire and fell in flames, fuck it, that's all we still needed!, Don Roque and Antonio Arévalo sit quietly, how about another cup of coffee?, all right, thanks, all I have is three pesetas, don't worry, I've got money, Don Roque puts his hand in his trousers pocket and pulls out a hundred-peseta bill, there you are, you can give it back to me some day, Antonio puts away the money, thanks, I'll take it because I don't even know where my next meal is coming from, we'll talk about all of this some day, thanks a lot Don Roque, don't mention it my boy, wait for me here I'm going to get a shave, all right, Don Roque goes to Cañamero's barber shop, what'll it be?, shave, a little trim around the neck?, all right, when Don Roque gets back to the café Antonio has already read the whole paper, the news couldn't be worse, the fact is that this whole business is going bust on us, Don Roque looks at his watch, how the time drags!, yes, when you get up early the mornings get to be endless, Antonio Arévalo tells Don Roque about his visit to the morgue, I spent sixty centimos on this badge (he takes off the badge and puts it in his pocket), summoned all the cheek I could, and went to the morgue, admission free, the Espinosas weren't there, at least I didn't see them, I've got to tell their father, the one I did find was Gonococcus, Sacra's son-in-law?, that's the one, the poor guy took two slugs in the back, for heaven's sake!, yes, he must have croaked on the spot, he was wearing an undershirt and pajama pants, maybe they dragged him out of bed and killed him on the stairs or in the doorway, who knows, but wasn't Gonococcus sort of a Socialist?, well there must have been some confusion. General Patxot orders the troops back to the barracks, Don Pedro Herrera lieutenant colonel of infantry doesn't understand why but he obeys, Malaga is in the hands of the Army and the government offices would have fallen at any moment, but an order is an order, Lieutenant Colonel Herrera knows that orders are given to be obeyed, not to be interpreted or even less to be discussed, when the city begins to burn in all four directions and the enlisted men join the civilians in their spree and the first revolutionary excesses begin the wicked thought comes to Lieutenant Colonel Herrera that perhaps it would have been better to disobey, it was only an instant, no, orders must be obeyed blindly, that is the first commandment of the military spirit, Lieutenant Colonel Herrera sits down at the desk in his office and writes a letter to his wife, dear María Luisa, all is lost but I want you to know and to tell our children that I die with a clear conscience and without having disgraced the uniform, take good care of María Luisa,

Perico, and Andrés, he is the one who worries me the most because of his revolutionary ideas but he is a fine boy and good at heart, he will himself recognize his mistakes, I forgive him for what he has made me suffer and I ask him to forgive me my reprimands of him, pray to God for me because I shall need it, a kiss from your husband who loves you very much and loved you all his life, your Pedro, Lieutenant Colonel Herrera folds the letter, puts it in the envelope with the photos of his wife and children that he always has with him, seals it and writes the address, Don Pedro also puts the three hundred pesetas that he keeps in his wallet inside the envelope, with them he could have made it to the end of the month, Lieutenant Colonel Herrera stands at attention, puts his pistol to his head, fires, and falls to the floor dead, his son Andrés also dies of a bullet in the head and also falls, but from a rooftop on the Calle de Ferraz facing the Montaña Barracks. According to the paper yesterday was a day of rest in the Tour de France, the cyclists will attack the difficult stages in the Pyrenees with renewed energy, this bicycle racing must be an exhausting sport, what's strange is that they don't all wind up with tuberculosis and spitting blood. Dominica Morcillo goes to visit Don Olegario, I've got a melon for you, it's not very big but it seems ripe, thank you very much, you're always so kind and generous, well I do what I can, Dominica stands there looking at a pistol lying on top of the table, you too?, I too what, what are you talking about?, what could I be talking about, that little pup you've got lying there, oh, don't pay any attention to that, it's a present from Chonina, you bring me a melon, she brings me a pistol . . . and that's the way I live and may I never live any worse, I've always had good luck with women, Don Olegario smiles and puts the pistol in the drawer, don't be scared, it's not loaded, the fact is I don't need it for a damned thing, I think I'll be able to use it for my inventions, could be, Dominica sits down on the chair by where the pistol was, do you remember that ring that I pawned?, yes I remember, why?, well pretty soon I'll be wearing it again on this finger of mine, well congratulations!, and how is that?, well they're handing back everything that was pawned, are you sure?, of course I am, I heard it from Marujita the Sergeant, the one from the tripe shop, she was telling it to some customer I don't know, well I'm glad, I hope it's true, you're going to be showing off like a fashion model, there'll be no talking to you! Dámaso Rioja doesn't know about the death of Andrés Herrera, that can't be!, since the death of his mother Dámaso Rioja has become very skeptical and suspicious, you'd better believe it can be!, he's in the morgue, Andrés was shooting from a rooftop, he got hit and bang, down he came head first, like Garcilaso?, that's it, the same as Garcilaso, he would have liked knowing he was to die like that, as he was falling he no doubt remembered the poet, well maybe as he was falling he was already dead, Dámaso is deeply impressed by the news, have you seen Adelita?, no, that is yes, Adelita is at the morgue too, they died together, when there is a moment of silence Spaniards say an angel is passing by, the English don't, the English say a poor man is being born, Don León has not gone to the notary office, Don Feliciano has disappeared, nobody knows where he is and the chief clerk has told all the employees not to come to the office until further notice, an old servant takes care of Don León and Dámaso, Eusebia, who calls Dámaso and all his friends by their first names, do you want coffee?, yes, Eusebia rules the Rioja home with an iron fist, with Doña Matilde's prolonged illness she became powerful, ever more powerful, and if the home is functioning it's thanks to her, that's a fact, Eusebia is generous with coffee but stingy with sugar, all right, that's enough, Eusebia likes coffee without sugar, she drinks at least six or eight cups a day without sugar, Don León wanders around the house like a lost soul, without Matilde, without the office, and without daring to go out Don León doesn't know what to do, Don León listens to the radio, rolls cigarettes, walks up and down, and reads Galdós, now he's into *King Joseph's Baggage*, that Boozer Joe was a real bum!, Don León joins Dámaso and you, what's new out there?, well you know, chaos and enthusiasm, if the enthusiasm could keep up and the chaos gradually die down maybe the country would get back in order, I don't think so but then, stranger things have happened, Eusebia brings two cups of coffee and Don León stares at her, what about me?, coffee doesn't agree with you, afterward you can't sleep, you had one this morning already and good and strong, if you want I'll bring you a glass of wine, Don León settles for that, the fact is he doesn't have any choice either, all right bring me a glass of wine, Dámaso is talking to his father, do you remember Andrés Herrera, that friend of mine who used to play rugby?, a tall boy, a law student?, that's the one, yes I remember, what about him?, well he got killed at the Montaña Barracks, how awful, poor kid!, but what an idea, what business did he have in the Montaña Barracks?, no, he wasn't inside, he didn't get killed inside, he got killed outside, he was among the attackers, for heaven's sake!, did he have family in Madrid?, no, his father is in the Army and is stationed I don't know where, Don León is quiet and Dámaso and you also keep still, the fact is you don't have anything to say either, another angel obviously flew by, perhaps the angels are disoriented with so much commotion and so much uncertainty, the almost athletic footsteps of Eusebia are heard in the hallway as she comes with the glass of wine for Don León, I've brought you some hazelnuts too, the buffet is closed now till lunchtime, Don León takes a sip of his wine, what a brute that woman is!, but then she has her good side too, Dámaso doesn't remember Pío García or Lorenzo Sosa, the ones I don't remember are those other two, I just can't place them, you will, you've seen them with me more than once. Gabriel Seseña's teeth are all loose, his teeth are really in ruins and his breath smells of shit but it doesn't matter to Turquoise, every morning Gabriel goes to chat a while with the manager of Sirvent's candy shop, they're from the same town and have known each other since childhood, the manager's name is Jacinto Rueda and he's very clever but tends to stutter, meanwhile Turquoise does the shopping and starts to fix lunch, how many did you lay while you were out, bitch?, Turquoise didn't lay anybody while she was out but she doesn't say a word, all Turquoise does is buy staples cheap but when she gets back home she doesn't open her mouth, she knows that if she talks she gets slapped, two other regular visitors at the candy shop are a master sergeant of the Civil Guard by the name of Don Heliodoro and a young priest who is assigned to Holy Cross parish and is called Don Enrique, neither of them shows up today, Don Heliodoro is restricted to barracks and obviously Don Enrique doesn't want to be out in the middle of all this church burning, he said so clearly enough to the manager of the candy shop, the less they see of me the better, I'll come out of my hole once tempers have cooled off, Jacinto is afraid his store will be attacked, I doubt that, you're up to date with your taxes and besides you don't mess with anybody, don't depend on that, once somebody decides he wants to eat candy free of charge we can close shop, for the time being they haven't come with vouchers but they can start showing up at any moment, stuffing yourself with free goodies is a pretty appetizing idea, Gabriel carries *El Socialista* in his pocket, it says it right out here, read this, union clubs and organizations are strictly forbidden to attempt to obtain articles of merchandise from commercial establishments with vouchers, isn't this a commercial establishment?, well yes, of course it is, and isn't candy an article of merchandise?, well yes, of course it's an article of merchandise, well then?, then we're right back where we started, what I say is that if a guy comes in the door feeling like eating candy he'll take it with vouchers or without vouchers, believe me I have no reason to risk my neck for a couple of pounds of candy more or less, for the time being it hasn't occurred to them, but if a bunch of guys slip into your La Cigale each holding his gun and out to live it up a little without shelling out any dough, what are you going to do about it? At the Toki-Ona, which is next door, Don Roque and Antonio are still talking, Antonio got hold of a rifle and thirty or forty clips when they were passing out weapons and has been on the rooftops for two nights firing volleys and harassing the militia, and where do you keep the rifle?, under some boards on one of the rooftops, I'll be fine as long as they don't discover it, the trouble will come the day they find it because then all they'll have to do is lie in wait for me, I don't think I can take two more nights, if I'm still alive the day after tomorrow I'm quitting and getting out of here, where to?, that I don't know, we'll see, wherever I can, do you really think Mola could show up here any moment?, what shall I say, I think so, if he doesn't we're sunk, if this goes on for two weeks there's not one of us is going to be left, no, two weeks I don't think it'll last, neither do I but it's not a bad idea to start thinking that maybe it will, don't even say that Don Roque!, how can this go on for two weeks?, what do I know, my boy, what do I know! Don Leoncio Romero's orthopedic leg has broken down again, I'm going to have to chuck this goddamned leg, I can't go on like this, better a wheelchair, believe me it's no life always to be the slave of whether the hinges are or aren't working, Don Nicolás Mañes tries to console him, don't be like that, it's no good taking things to heart like that, you know I'm always ready to repair your prosthesis just as often as you need it and without charging you for my services, a new artificial leg would cost you a lot of money, it's not worth your while, the one you have will still do if you take a little care of it, it's not good but it'll do, my advice is that as long as you can walk you stay away from expenses, you can always replace it once there's no other way. On the Calle del Carmen you run into Mirenchu the ballplayer from the Rosales Jai-Alai, where are you going?, no place, I went out for a walk because I was going stir-crazy in the boardinghouse, how about you?, same thing, I'm not going any place either, one place or another is all the same to me, Mirenchu is good-looking, very well-built, and you can see right away that she's an athlete and very strong, if she slapped you she'd knock you to the ground, I'll buy you a beer, thanks, Mirenchu and you go into the Bar Central, on the Calle de Tetuán, two beers, gimme two beers!, do you want some squid?, sure, and two orders of fried squid, gimme two fries!, Mirenchu is not frightened, I can live anywhere and besides I live well, I'm not worried about that, but if this is going to go on I'd rather go back to Bilbao, they've shut down the jai-alai and it's anybody's guess whether they'll reopen, I think they will but what if they don't?, to set up as a whore you've got to be practically illiterate or really desperate, I'm no good for that, but we'll see, are you still going out with Tránsito?, yes, well I haven't seen her for a couple of days, her father won't let her go out, and besides I think she's kind of teed-off with me because of a dream I had, come on!, what did you dream?, not much, just that a dwarf in a top hat was coming out of her pussy, what an idea!, and you told her?, well yes, why shouldn't I have told her?, what's so bad about it?, well, maybe there's nothing all that bad about it, but it sure is a little ridiculous, yes that it is, Mirenchu bursts out laughing, what an idea!, Mirenchu eats the squid two pieces at a time, she doesn't spear them with a toothpick but grabs them with her fingers, these squid are delicious, yes really delicious, Mirenchu is a couple of years older than you, do you want me to call her as though it was my idea?, all right, but don't tell her you're with me, of course not, you think I'm that dumb?, Mirenchu goes to the phone which is in back on the left and dials Toisha's number, Miss Tránsito please, yes, who's calling?, Miss Mirenchu, wait a minute please I'll tell her, Mirenchu and Toisha talk for quite a while, sometimes Mirenchu is the only one talking, when she comes back she's smiling, you've got her more in love with you than ever, shit!, I mean it, you've got her crazy over you, she says that at 3:30 today you're to go to the usual place, I guess you know where, she'll think of something with her father. Juanito Mateo feels like an American-style journalist, it's a pity that at *El Heraldo* they don't publish everything he writes, well the truth is they don't publish a tenth part of it, Leonorcita is astonished at how active Juanito Mateo is, Juanito do you love me lots?, lots sweetheart, but at the right time, duty is duty, Juanito writes in the Café Lisboa, duty first, Juanito writes with his right hand, of course, while with his left he feels up Leonorcita, don't distract me, but I'm not saying a word, honey!, well I know what I'm talking about, you just hold still, they're going to see us, honey!, Juanito Mateo puts on the face of a general in the midst of a campaign, hold still, damn it!, just sit still, don't distract me!, Leonorcita speaks with a thin little voice, I'm sorry . . . , Leonorcita lets Juanito Mateo's left hand wander how and where it likes, Leonorcita sits still and puts up with it, sometimes it tickles but she sits still and puts up with it, Leonorcita tries not to distract her boyfriend from his work, the waiter stands looking at the couple, a little more restraint, young folks, a little more restraint!, Juanito takes away his hand but doesn't raise his eyes from his papers, when the waiter goes away Leonorcita takes Juanito Mateo's left hand and puts it back between her thighs, Leonorcita wears a full skirt, go on honey, with a full skirt it's a pleasure, everything is much easier. Don Roque goes to the Calle de Alcántara to see Maruja la Valvanera, there's no major cause for alarm along the way, in a revolution the mornings are usually quieter than the afternoons and nights, madam is not home, what do you mean she's not home, no sir, she spent the night at the other house, on Ayala?, yes sir, Don Roque rings the bell at 130 Ayala, madam is not up yet, well that doesn't matter, I'm in no rush, I'll wait for her to get up, as you wish, I think she'll be asking for breakfast pretty soon, well when she does tell her I'm here, that I want to see her, yes sir, the window is half open with the blinds down and a kind of quiet and very protective and discreet penumbra is floating in the room where Don Roque waits, how pleasant this is!, Don Roque makes himself comfortable in his chair and loosens his belt a little, would you like me to wake up one of the young ladies to keep you company?, no thank you, let them sleep, after about a quarter of an hour Maruja asks for her breakfast, Don Roque is out there waiting, he wants to see you, heavens, why didn't you wake me up?, tell him to come in if he doesn't mind, yes ma'am, Maruja straightens the covers a little and pats down the bedspread, may I?, come in Don Roque, to what do I owe the honor of seeing you here at this time of day?, Don Roque looks for a place to sit down, sit wherever you like and make yourself comfortable, sit here, Maruja la Valvanera points to an ottoman upholstered in very elegant satin, thank you Marujita, Don Roque waits for the maid to come with breakfast, after she's closed the door he still remains silent for a few moments, Maruja, yes Don Roque, the time has come for you to prove your friendship to me, you know you have it, I do, I need you to do me a favor, whatever you say Don Roque, look, what I need, how shall I put it, well, what I need is for you to hide me for a few days, you?, yes me, but what's going on, aren't things getting back in order?, no Marujita, the truth is that things are getting worse and worse, can you hide me?, of course I can, why shouldn't I?, right here, no not here, in a place where nobody except you knows about it, let me think, think all you like, there's no hurry, Don Roque would like a cup of coffee, would you order me some coffee?, yes of course, Don Roque tells about his engagement, you sure kept it to yourself!, and his adventure of the night before, you were lucky!, yes that's for sure, very lucky, Maruja thinks they ought to hide Doña Teresa too, that's what I wanted to tell you, under these circumstances I shouldn't leave Teresa, and there's no reason why you should Don Roque, wait while I think some more, on the top floor there's a room that's not used for anything, it's unfurnished but that's easy to fix, the maids are reliable and furthermore there's no need to give them any big explanations, the girls don't even have to find out and besides they're all veterans here, do you want me to go for Doña Teresa?, no need to, I can phone her, no, phone her if you like but don't give her the address, tell her to go in about an hour to the Café La Rotonda on Alcalá corner of Hermosilla, I'll go pick her up there, tell her too that I'll be carrying a red purse, Doña Teresa says good-bye to her guests one by one, wish me luck the same as I wish you, she leaves the maids five hundred pesetas to get started, this is more than enough for you to get started, yes ma'am, I began with less than that, the two maids kiss Doña Teresa, good-bye ma'am, we'll take care of everything, we know what's good for us, Javiera lets slip two tears, not Paulina, Paulina has more presence of mind, Doña Teresa stops by the Banco Español de Crédito, takes out the seven thousand pesetas she has saved, and goes to the Café La Rotonda to meet Maruja la Valvanera, in her forty-three years Doña Teresa had never in her life exchanged a single word with the manager of a whorehouse. Gregorio Montes has a mole between his eyebrows, Lupita says it gives him a very sexy look, almost everything there is seems sexy to Lupita, the same thing happens with her sister Juani, sexy women see everything as sexy, frigid women with mustaches see everything as sinful, this is a general rule with few exceptions, sexiness is an inclination and is certainly also a result of hormones, of their being healthy and in their place and the right ones, it's hard to train a woman to be sexy if her nature is not the right kind and doesn't respond in the right way, the proper proportion of hormones makes a woman beautiful, besides having more or less correct features her face lights up and her eyes shine with good nature and intelligence, a woman with correctly distributed hormones is usually beautiful and sexy, both at the same time, it's true that there are also sexy ugly women but they're a minority and can be thought of as a quirk of nature, when her hormones are down then a woman is usually ugly and uncomfortable and very hard to bear because her head is empty or full of false ideas which is even worse, your Aunt Octavia is a good example, Lupita and Juani see everything as sexy because they are sexy, Cándido and Tomasín the two boys from the neighborhood know that Lupita and Juani are very sexy, they know it from experience, when they tell their friends about it nobody believes it, worse luck!, with men something similar happens as with women, when the hormones aren't right their voice turns fluty and they talk only administrative nonsense, men with a womanish voice are criminals and very dangerous, they are capable of the worst outrages because they never feel sexy, they go about their business and save energy and money, men with a womanish voice are very treacherous and base and never look at women with the right expression, God looks with little benevolence on ugly men and ugly women and he punishes them all, the women by giving them a mustache in place of their tits, and the men by making their voices fluty, they enjoy other consequences but the truth is they're not worth it, Gregorio Montes has a very sexy mole between his eyebrows, once they threw him out of the Príncipe Alfonso Theatre for making improper advances to a lady who was sitting next to him, on his way to the door he said to the two ushers who were dragging him by the arms that he'd piss on their whole families, it was a waste of time because they answered him that all right, that was his business, your Uncle Horacio makes good use of the maid, Lola Iglesias, who is a world-class slut, and his wife, your Aunt Octavia, doesn't even notice, it's not that your Uncle Horacio dissembles in any way, no, it's just that she doesn't notice, your Aunt Octavia thinks that maids are only good for work, not for fucking, your Uncle Horacio lays his hands on the maid quite openly but your Aunt Octavia doesn't even see it, that way anybody could do it, the cigarette man Senén treats Ginesa to a meat sandwich, all right, long live the rich and handsome!, the cigarette man Senén who is cross-eyed and only has one tooth stops and looks at Ginesa, thanks for the compliment!, and Ginesa bursts out laughing and very politely lets herself be pawed, the cigarette man Senén is funny but sometimes he's got sort of a short fuse, do you want to go out tonight and dance to Don Gerardo's health?, all right, I'll go wherever they take me, to be sure, have you heard anything from Don Gerardo?, no, why should I? At 3:30 Toisha arrives at Merceditas' place, at exactly 3:30 as if she were English, I don't know how I can even look you in the face, don't be silly, Toisha and you kiss in the doorway as usual, I'm so scared, darling, no dear, you'll see how common sense will win out in the end, no, it's not that, it's because any day now my father's going to find out everything, it gets harder and harder for me to get out of the house, I can't stay long today, Mirenchu and Angelines came for me, I told my father we were going to Mirenchu's to look at some fabrics, I said I'd drop by her house at five, well, we have more than an hour, Toisha is affectionate as always but more uneasy, I would have liked to see you at the Montaña Barracks, don't say that!, yes, inside or outside but at the Montaña Barracks, will you stop it?, no I won't, I would have liked to see you at the Montaña Barracks, better outside, the things you say!, yes sweetheart, pardon me, you're pardoned, there's nothing to pardon, I swear to you I didn't even find out about the barracks until it was all over, Toisha smiles with a very distant bitterness, what does it all matter darling!, do you love me lots?, of course I love you lots, you're not ashamed of seeing me naked like a tramp in a whorehouse?, don't talk nonsense!, it's not nonsense, sweetheart, it's the plain truth, Toisha yields herself languidly and breaks into tears, you cover her face with the pillow and possess her with less enthusiasm than on other afternoons, afterward you talk to her, you looked as though you'd been beheaded, how you mistreat me darling, you almost smothered me, I thought of it for a moment there, I won't deny that, then I let you live because I love you too much, Toisha stares into the air, yes, I love you too much in spite of the gentleman in the frock coat, what gentleman in a frock coat?, the one who was coming out of your pussy giving speeches, Toisha laughs very sweetly and then breaks into tears again, pardon me again darling, I'm just acting silly today I don't know what's the matter with me, you close your eyes because this situation bores you, with your eyes closed you can't look at yourself in the mirror nor in the windows of the jewelry stores and the delicatessens, in the bedroom at Merceditas' place there is a very large mirror in a frame covered in sky blue velvet that reflects Toisha naked and with her eyes full of tears, your eyes are not full of tears, you wish they were, your eyes are closed and you don't see Toisha naked in the mirror and with her eyes full of tears, the mirror is flat, not parallelepiped, nor ovoid, nor almost spherical, nor in the shape of a bloody jellyfish and it reflects the body of a naked woman, what a slut you've made of me sweetheart!, no dear, be still, you don't open your eyes to speak, if your eyes were open maybe you'd say something different, it's harder to think with closed eyes and you don't find words, forget about flat, parallelepiped, ovoid, or almost spherical mirrors or mirrors in the shape of a bloody jellyfish, they're all bad and leave you compromised, mirrors in whorehouses behave too discreetly, with very sinful discretion, perhaps they're tired of seeing women in the buff, humiliated or glorious but in the buff, mirrors in elevators are like sweet historic guillotines, you wouldn't be at all surprised if you had your head cut off in some elevator while looking at yourself in the mirror and straightening your tie a little, Toisha doesn't understand a thing, all she does is cry and look at herself naked and full length in the mirror, Toisha is very humble and untruthful, she'll probably die young, forget about mirrors and other exemplary forms of modesty, the mirror of good and evil, the mirror of life and death, the mirror of virtue and sin, Roland was a shining knight, shining like a mirror, etc., and be satisfied with watching your shadow's progress on the wall, your shadow's reverential movements on the wall, it's almost five, and what do I care?, I've got to go, well go, Toisha embraces you violently and you make love again, do you love me like this?, yes, like this and any other way too, I can't help it, Toisha gets up, washes, combs her hair a little, gets dressed, and leaves, good-bye sweetheart, you answer her with an ooooo without opening your mouth, it's hard to say ooooo without opening your mouth, and you make a gesture toward her that means nothing, you turn over on your side and almost instantly fall into a pleasant sleep, when you wake up your head aches, it can't be your digestion, it's probably joy, then you get up, piss, wash, comb your hair a little, get dressed, ask for bicarbonate, let loose a good belch, roll a cigarette, and leave, good-bye Merceditas, good-bye my boy, see you soon. Antonio Arévalo goes to see Don Felipe Espinosa but nobody answers the door, he rings again and nothing happens, they don't open, the concierge hasn't seen them go out, I was gone about half an hour or three quarters, the toilet in the second left got stopped up, at the Muñozes', and I had to go for the plumber, the phones around here only work when they feel like it, unless they left then . . . , it's odd that not even the maids should be there, did you ring right?, of course, I rang two or three times, it's odd!, Don Felipe Espinosa and María Angustias have invented a code for ringing the doorbell, one long, two short, and then tataratta ta ta, if the bell doesn't ring according to the code they don't open the door, Antonio Arévalo is undecided, he doesn't know whether to leave or ring one last time, why don't you look through the courtyard window?, you think I should?, look I don't think one way or the other, from the courtyard maybe you'll see somebody in the kitchen, the maids or the lady of the house, I really feel they've got to be home, if I were you I'd look through the courtyard window, there's a window out on the courtyard on the stairs between landings, Antonio Arévalo looks through the courtyard window and sees María Angustias in the kitchen, she's fixing herself an orangeade, he hisses at her and makes signs for her to open the door, María Angustias disappears and comes back with Don Felipe, I'll open in a minute, good, Don Felipe explains his precautions, we have to be prepared and on the alert, at least we need time to hide or think of something, the tataratta ta ta is María Angustias' idea, and a very good one, María Angustias smiles, come in, thank you, sit down, thank you, Antonio Arévalo sits down and looks at Don Felipe, I've been at the morgue, there's not the slightest trace of Felipe or Alberto, I can guarantee you that, so?, I have no idea, since they haven't turned up dead I have no idea, Don Felipe holds on to conjectures as to a burning nail, you think they might be alive?, look, I don't think anything, I don't dare to think anything, the only thing I can guarantee you is that they're not at the morgue, I'll put my hand in the fire for that, Don Felipe lowers his head, my poor boys!, María Angustias asks Antonio whether he wants some orangeade, would you like a little orangeade?, all right thanks, but don't bother for my sake, it's no bother, thanks a lot, María Victoria is pale and her eyes look as though she'd been crying, I'm sure they killed them both, if they were alive they'd have called by now, or maybe not, the phones are all mucked up, yes that's true, but they would have got word to us somehow, Papa doesn't want to accept the idea but I'm sure they've killed them both, María Victoria is wrong, her father is convinced that his two sons have died, he's just pretending because he prefers not to believe it, he prefers to pretend, yes, it's better to pretend, Don Felipe doesn't think that, but he feels it, my poor boys! Antonio Arévalo presses Don Felipe to get out, look, I told you yesterday and I'm repeating it today, get out of here as soon as you can, get out before they come for you, do you know whom they came for last night?, no, well Don Roque Barcia the Agrarian deputy, how awful!, and did they take him away?, no, they didn't take him away because he was lucky but now he's in hiding, where?, that I don't know, I ran into him just by chance and he told me about his adventure and also that he'd decided to go into hiding, what he didn't tell me is where, and I didn't want to ask him either, you did right, I think you ought to leave here as soon as possible, let the countess know, she has to come to a decision too, it seems to me you don't realize what's going on, Don Felipe does realize what's going on, he just doesn't quite come to a decision, but how are we just going to abandon our house?, Arévalo can't think of any more arguments, what do I know!, just leave it. For three days now an endless flood of hungry people has been falling on Madrid, men and women nobody knows, children nobody knows, sometimes the children get lost and seek the company of other children who also got lost, they form bands of six or eight and throw stones at the birds in the Retiro, they drink from the fountains and shit on the sidewalks of the Paseo del Prado or Recoletos, it's hot and you can sleep in any doorway or under some tree on the Plaza de Santa Ana, these vagabond children gulp down an onion, an apricot, the leftovers from the garbage cans, if it doesn't kill you it'll fatten you up, they have to chase away the cats, some children find their way home but there's nobody there, the house is empty and the doors stand open, there are houses that have no door but a little curtain of burlap or colored cloth, the doors are wood, some are covered with tin, those are stronger and don't let the rain through, the men and women nobody knows have hungry faces, they're very thin and nervous but their eyes shine, maybe not from health, they go from place to place and shout and break store windows, María Angustias and Maripi and your Aunt Octavia don't understand what these shouting people want, it's an odd attitude in people who are already used to living like that, they don't have any cause for complaint, they shouldn't complain, they don't have feelings like other people and don't notice hunger and thirst as much as other people, hunger for potatoes, thirst for water, and hunger and thirst for justice, and suddenly they rise up and fall on Madrid, walking down the middle of the street, shouting all the time, and getting everything dirty, where's the police?, Don Felipe Espinosa does understand it but he doesn't feel guilty, the government is guilty, the government that let go the reins of power, what are they waiting for before they bring out the police?, no, it wouldn't be possible any more, the police don't obey the government, they do what they want and let the mob keep roaring, Don Roque can imagine what's going on and is frightened, Don Roque does not feel altogether guilty but he does feel a little guilty, the guilt lies with all of us and we'll all wind up paying for it, we haven't managed to progress in time here, nobody here ever looked sideways, here we've always kept our neighbor at a distance, the flood of hungry people can turn into an avalanche of blood, maybe it's on the verge of turning into an avalanche of blood, there are even worse swamps in which blood rots and stinks, a country can also die of foul puerperal fever, Doña Sacramento is afraid her daughter Virtudes will end up dying of foul puerperal fever, the men and women nobody knows disguise themselves to die, shout to die, dishevel their hair to die, they also despair to die, it may be that they don't want to go on living, there are symptoms of their preferring death or not being much used to life, suddenly everyone is fighting for his life without giving any notice, holding on to life with nails and teeth and without giving any notice and wanting to exchange his life, some exchange it for life and others for death. Don Estanislao Montañés has very little confidence in lame people and even less in Don Leoncio Romero, I assure you that that Don Leoncio Romero is nothing but a nasty fucking cripple capable of anything, if we had a revolution in Spain the cripple Romero would sign up as executioner, come on now, aren't you exaggerating just a little?, not the least bit, you can believe me, if we had a revolution in Spain the cripple Romero would become famous, Robespierre is nothing in comparison, the cripple Romero is a hyena that's just waiting for its chance, I don't know, I still think you're exaggerating, the cripple Romero is just one more poor bastard, poor bastard you say?, don't kid yourself!, when he found out that Chelo had drunk a whole bottle of lye, do you know what he said?, no, well he said he was glad, that we've got more than enough whores in Spain, are you sure he said that?, you bet I am!, Mañes told me and he's somebody you can trust, don't be too sure, maybe he just wanted to pull your leg, well just in case I don't want to have any more to do with him, I'll just stick to greeting him, good afternoon, good afternoon, and that's it, I don't have anything to say to him, in the restroom at the nightclub Pompeya Mrs. Díaz, this was several years ago by now, found a fifty-peseta bill and a little note pinned to it that said so you'll have seven masses said for my soul and spend the other fifteen on wine, Mrs. Díaz ordered the masses at Saint Martin's, for whom? I don't know, for somebody who didn't want to give his name, Mrs. Díaz spent a week going to mass and then spent the other fifteen pesetas on wine and carnations, she would have liked to go to the bullfight but she respected the wishes of the departed, Don Baltasar Blanco knows another condom joke but he doesn't have anybody to tell it to, his wife is acting kind of strange and doesn't laugh at his jokes any more, she used to laugh at his jokes before, Doña María Luisa the manager at 3 Naciones insists that Don Lucio Martínez Morales has a talent for drawing, María Inés la Cordobesita can testify to that, Don Lucio draws masterfully and also paints in watercolor, he did a nude of María Inés that only lacks speech to seem alive, this man could make a good living doing portraits and caricatures in the cafés, it's a pleasure to deal with gentlemen like Don Lucio, Doña María Luisa's health has improved, the ovule capsules seem to have done her good, Doña María Luisa always wears a lot of perfume and keeps her grey hair freshly dyed, she's no youngster any more you can't say any more that she's a youngster, but she knows how to take care of herself and is always well groomed and elegant, Don Lucio gave her a little framed sketch that shows a rooster mounting a hen, Doña María Luisa has it hanging on the parlor wall. Gutiérrez the waiter at La Granja El Henar is feeling unsociable and looking annoyed and grim, Gutiérrez would have liked to know something about Don Roque but he doesn't think it would be discreet to go over to the boardinghouse to ask about him, people are very uneasy and see danger everywhere, Don Roque is a fine person and a true republican, he's certainly no rowdy, at any moment he might come in through the door and say to Gutiérrez, would you get me some paper and pen and ink?, why of course, shoeshine, some paper and pen and ink for Don Roque!, here's your usual beer Don Roque, thanks Gutiérrez, you always take care of everything, don't mention it Don Roque, just tell me what you need, an elegant figure, radioactive Aldira helps you to lose weight safely, clear, absolute, guaranteed results. At Eulalia's tripe shop they give Paca a pound of heart on credit, it's for Señor Fidel, that's all right dear nobody's asked you for the money, at Marujita the Sergeant's tripe shop they give Chonina a pound of innards for cash, your change, Chonina picks up her change and leaves, Dominica and Chonina plan to invite Don Olegario and Don Cándido for supper, Chonina is supplying the materials and Dominica the art, she turns out a liver with onions that'll have you licking your fingers, Don Olegario and Don Cándido treat them very well and they have to return the favor, Don Olegario reads an official notice in the paper, a report of unknown origin has been circulating in Madrid to the effect that pawn shops are returning all pawned objects, those concerned and the general public are hereby notified that this report is totally erroneous, Don Olegario doesn't say anything to Dominica, it's better for her to keep on dreaming of her ruby ring, Fidel also treats Paca very well, he talks to her, sometimes he feeds her, and he never mistreats her by word or deed, he doesn't insult her or kick her or slap her around, around Las Ventas they've gotten used to her and don't even look at her hump any more, some stretches of time are better than others and now she's in a good one, if only it will last, Don Olegario also reads in the paper the list of donations for the wounded and the families of the fallen of the Popular Front, the advisory committee of urban real estate associations 10,000 pesetas, the association of fish dealers 5,000 pesetas, the commercial and industrial savings association of Madrid 5,000 pesetas, the coal industry employers' association 1,000 pesetas, a mortgage company 1,000 pesetas, the urban real estate association 20,000 pesetas, what a fucking country this is!, over the little coal stove the liver with onions is cooking, it smells very good and the aroma spreads through the whole shack impregnating the walls with its blessing, Don Olegario and Don Cándido have a little glass of wine while they're waiting, Dominica and Chonina can have some later, right now they're very busy with the cooking, Chonina bought Dominica four Camels at the subway station, how nice of you!, I don't know how to thank you, Dominica is smoking one of them, the other three she leaves for after supper, this is a great day Chonina, today we're like counts and dukes!, heart can also be made into a very tasty dish, it depends on the loving care it gets, Paca doesn't even know how to fry an egg (Paca never ate a fried egg) but Fidel has a real knack for cooking, you can eat heart fried and sliced in filets or stewed, it's good either way and very nourishing, vitamins and calories from animals are healthier than the ones they sell in pharmacies, medicines are all right, no one denies that, but hot food is even better, fried or stewed heart, pig's feet, boiled lamb's brains with a little oil and vinegar, tongue with garlic and parsley sauce, liver with onions, tripe with hot peppers and paprika, if people ate the vitamins and calories of animals they would always be healthy and would even die healthy, they'd only die of boredom, of vexation, hit by a train or a truck, or shot like wolves or like rabbits, some people get shot and die like a wolf, and some people get shot and die like a rabbit, you can't tell ahead of time, man is a very strange and changeable animal, very contradictory and undecided, the following announcement is read on the radio, our newsroom has received word of the annoyance felt by the valiant militia of Madrid upon noticing that the radios of private homes in the Salamanca district are not playing as they usually do, we call the uneasiness that this behavior is producing to the attention of the residents requesting at the same time that they put their loudspeakers in service for the proper information of the public, there take that!, a bunch of jokers too!, Don Felipe Espinosa is confused, sometimes he's afraid and sometimes he thinks he's dreaming and then he is very brave and gives orders to his wife, his daughter, and the maids, sometimes he plans to flee and sometimes not, what for?, it's not worth while, this rabble is in retreat, these are the dying spasms, or rather the opposite, there's no way out, the time has come not to offer a resistance that will of necessity be useless, sometimes he thinks more hurriedly and also more confusedly, sometimes he thinks of fleeing and not fleeing at the same time, those are the worst moments, the moments in which his throat goes dry, María Angustias, what, give me another orangeade, right away, from Toledo General Riquelme reports that he has succeeded in crushing the rebels who in their flight have taken refuge in the infantry academy, the Alcázar, neither Don Olegario nor Don Cándido are particularly fond of the radio, Dominica and Chonina even less, a radio is intriguing but it's not worth the bother, a receiver is expensive and it's complicated to set it up, besides it uses up electricity, two artillery batteries from Madrid have been set up facing the Alcázar, four truckloads of armed militia and two armored cars have also arrived, the attack will begin at dawn, Don Olegario and Don Cándido don't live in the Salamanca district either but in Vereda de Postas where the breeze always blows in the late afternoon, Don Olegario and Don Cándido drink their little glass of wine, smell the bubbling of the liver with onions and slowly smoke the delightful tobacco of expectation, from time to time they speak and even laugh when something funny jumps up in their memory, do you remember Garibaldi when he was giving speeches?, he was kind of a friend of mine and more than once I bought him a glass of wine, he was a good man and very loyal and grateful, people used to be more loyal and grateful than now, well I don't know about that, I think there's always been all kinds, Don Olegario and Don Cándido are not two men of action, they are two skeptics, Don Olegario more so than Don Cándido, they both believe in immediate pleasures, smoking a cigarette, drinking a glass of Valdepeñas, licking their chops after liver with onions and mopping it up with bread, going to bed with Chonina, Don Cándido also goes to bed with Chonina, etc., Don Olegario would have liked to have invented the heliograph and the semaphore, to have invented a new code for them totally different from Morse's and that could also have been used for the gongs of the Chinese, the tom-toms of the blacks, and the smoke signals of the redskins, Don Cándido prefers messenger pigeons, come on, time to eat, supper's ready, the endless flood of men and women nobody knows has been falling on Madrid for three or four days now, look at yourself in your mirror that's what you have it for, your flat, parallelepiped, ovoid, or slightly spherical mirror or mirror in the shape of a mortally wounded jellyfish, of a sick and dying jellyfish, flee through your mirror, don't worry about breaking it or breaking with everything, forgetfulness sleeps on the other side of your mirror and who knows but perhaps a smile too in its camera obscura populated by silhouettes, they are the hungry and the thirsty who used to be quiet, who used to live quietly until suddenly they preferred to die speaking, singing, shouting, killing, after eating liver with onions people's spirits are somehow more lively and sociable, Chonina says, would you like me to show you a tit? and they all answer yes, Don Olegario, Don Cándido, and Dominica, it's the government's fault for not bringing out the police, where are the police (Don Felipe), no, you can't play on both sides, you have to know how to win and lose, it's not the government's fault nor the police's, we are all guilty, some more and others less, here we've always kept our neighbor at a distance and confined (Don Roque), distance is a bad system because sometimes it burns, Dominica caresses the naked Chonina while the flies gorge themselves on the dirty plates, Don Olegario and Don Cándido talk about Garibaldi, the time for doing homage will come to them also, people proceed by conditioned reflexes, you tell people x-x-x and people believe it or don't believe it, if they believe it they wipe out whatever stands in their way, Don Olegario cannot signal to the world with his heliograph, here we have a naked young woman, she's very beautiful and knowing and she gives us food, Don Cándido cannot send messenger pigeons to the world with the thoughts of Donoso Cortés, he who loves if he loves well must seem to be going mad, and love to be infinite must seem to be infinite madness, it is dangerous to give in to conditioned reflexes, wherever you hear the word culture shoot, or the other way, wherever you hear the word bourgeoisie shoot, because people shoot, the joy of revolution is dulled with the obligations of revolution, after his triumph the revolutionary puts on his dress suit but there's always still somebody who dreams of another revolution, people act according to their feelings, your Uncle Jerónimo thinks feelings are like an eggshell inside which crouch conditioned reflexes, it doesn't seem like that but that's the way it is, people fight more determinedly for a feeling than for an idea, Don Cándido goes to bed with Chonina while Don Olegario and Dominica sit in the fresh air at the door and play checkers, the trouble is that those who fight for a feeling usually die first, they are bolder and more foolish and die first, Engracia died full of love and Agustín is struck by the idea that he hadn't known how to return it, a feeling is a very jealous selfishness, grand lamas and high priests have ideas, heroes who are going to die should have the ideas wiped from their heads and feelings infused in their hearts, Don Olegario has the whole night ahead of him for loving Chonina, his guests are going to leave any moment now, a feeling is like a drug that is absorbed very rapidly, its effects are also very rapid and don't last long but long enough for death to come, Fidel tells Paca all right go on to sleep now and Paca, pressing her hump against the wall, keeps quiet.

IV

There must be a dead cat in the attic, it stinks to high heaven, how about you going up to the attic?, yes ma'am, there must be a dead cat, it smells dead, and I didn't even notice it!, well then you can go have your nose operated on, the living and the dead march past tumultuously and out of step, no one here keeps in step, the dying too and those who are healthy and do not expect death but die anyway and Julius Caesar and the inquisitor Torquemada and the fetuses who never walked and die floating and Saint Peter and Saint Paul and Saint Cecilia and the cemeteries that retain their physical and mental faculties until the last moment and appear in the newspaper and Charlemagne and Charles V and the mummies of nuns who died in odor of sanctity and of monks who have been working miracles for a long long time and Joan of Arc and King Cyril of England both of whom died by burning but with different degrees of honor and the skeletons (some of them very proud and illustrious) who are tired of being tossed around on the marble tables of the school of medicine (at some point one of their bones gets lost never to reappear) and Viriathus and the martyred Seven Evangelizers of Spain and the souls of the innocent who go to Limbo and Miguel Servet, the souls of the blessed and Caupolicán I, the souls of the damned and Caupolicán II, the souls in Purgatory and Caupolicán IV, the antifascists, the antimarxists and Espronceda and Lord Byron, the wives who did not consummate their marriage to a black husband and Hernán Cortés and Abraham Lincoln, the boy struck dumb with fear and his mother who is struck dumb and the animals with names from the fish to the higher vertebrate mammals and a few more and no one more, this must be the Day of Judgment, any moment the trumpets could begin to sound, pay close attention and forget about petty interests because your life which is a petty interest is at stake, at the last judgment there can be no favoritism but there can be dissimulation, in your family no one devotes himself to science or commerce, the Cid did not devote himself to science or commerce either, in your family they're all farmers and every year they slaughter their pig, your parents never learned to read or write and had no need of either and were able to save themselves from the eternal fire and from the fire of men, your family is not Persian but it's almost Persian, it could have been Persian, Napoleon Bonaparte is not Persian either, I'm sure there's a dead cat in the attic, that stench can only come from a dead cat, Aixa doesn't say anything to her friend Petra Soto about the dead cat, what does she care?, by force of whippings Aixa learned to be discreet, what happens to your neighbor doesn't matter, it doesn't matter to anybody, your neighbor is worth something as long as he pays something and that's always a matter between just two, free lays don't count because that's also between just two, free lays are a secret of the bedchamber, they're like a habit, Aixa knows that anything goes in bed, a dead cat in the attic?, well they'll find out when they look that it's not a dead cat, it's a dead faggot, dead cats and dead faggots smell the same, how about you going up to the attic?, yes ma'am, the concierge thinks there's no reason for her to go up to the attic, so it smells of dead cat?, well let it smell, she doesn't care, in every attic there's always a dead cat and people put up with it, there are some oversensitive and ridiculous ladies who spend their lives discovering odors and running their fingers over the furniture to see whether it's dusty, you don't care about that, nor does the sweet smell of death displease you (it's not a good idea to say this), the civilized smell of death, the nose is a two-way street and the sense of smell behaves like what it is, a spherical sense, all smells are like balls that roll in their not entirely circular but rather somewhat elliptical orbits, with a dead cat or a dead faggot in an attic you can make a poem, paint a picture, or compose a symphony, it depends on whether charity is or is not infinite, without infinite charity you cannot crush the sense of smell or make a truly artistic poem, painting, or symphony, most artists are frauds and immediately want to pass damaged goods, a cat is good but a hare is better,[5] venison is better, the ghosts of dead cats in an attic do not even wander over the mirrors of whorehouses, they slip in through the skylight and then can't get out and starve to death, they meow for a few days in the hope that someone will hear them and open the door for them but then they get tired of it and eventually die in silence, it is more dignified but also more painful to die in silence than screaming, knights

5. The expression *dar gato por liebre*, 'to pass cat off as hare,' means to attempt to deceive. Translator's note.

die in silence because they do not fear death, they even long for it, they are so tired of playing their role as knights that they even long for death, the ghosts of live cats do not walk across your mirror, of Angora cats, Persian cats, Siamese cats, nor do the ghosts of dead cats in attics, of black cats, black and white cats, striped cats, across your flat mirror with its plate corroded by humidity, across your parallelepiped mirror in which you can lick the wound on your back, across your ovoid mirror that always reflects you in fetal position, across your almost spherical mirror that makes you dizzy, across your mirror in the shape of a bloody jellyfish, each arm of the jellyfish ends in a contagious cancer, across your mirror in the eyes of tuberculous Juani or tuberculous Lupita who understand nothing, this crowded and endless parade is not easy to understand, it is probably the Day of Judgment, over the rooftops you can already hear the sharp-voiced clarions summoning to the last judgment, no one cares whether you are alive or dead, the living forget the dead and the dead remember neither the living nor the dead but the clarions call all the living and all the dead, no one alive or dead escapes the judgment, at the last judgment favoritism does not count and dissimulation cannot be maintained, it breaks like a dry reed at the least slip, at the slightest negligence, it is not possible to remain always attentive and alert when the clarions deafen the world with their agonizing metallic voices, it will do you no good to lie on judgment day, the laughter of the angels is very sarcastic and cruel and the weeping of the devils can only console you in hell, resign yourself to everything and curse everything, mount the donkey of the condemned to death and someone will be sure to hang the robe on you, whistle away feigning a contempt you are very far from feeling and smile, always smile, smile to the powerful and to the defeated, both are playing a fraudulent game, they can lose their lives or win glory but both play a fraudulent game in which they won't let you take part, if you don't find the way to the sea sail on the river, not all rivers end in the sea, there are rivers that vanish in the sand or under the foundations of the walls of the city, full of bones and coins, the doctor fills out the death certificate, puerperal fever, then he smiles and says my sincerest sympathy, that'll be ten pesetas, Doña Sacra fishes for two duros in her purse, thank you very much ma'am good afternoon, Doña Sacra doesn't even answer him, it's very monotonous, the smell of the dead cat in the attic is very monotonous, it always smells the same, Gabriel Seseña's breath smells of dead cat, maybe there's a dead cat in Gabriel Seseña's belly, Turquoise doesn't smell the dead cat that the punk Gabriel Seseña has in his belly, and I don't even notice it!, for heaven's sake, what's the matter with your nose?, Turquoise lives on Pernod, Pernod gives her the strength to live with Gabriel Seseña, you just stick to your position, you'll change it soon enough when you start forgetting it, at the end everything is dissolved in the air of the dead, the air breathed by the living always belongs to the dead, Agustina de Aragón was a heroine, she was a woman with hard tits and a soft heart, Doña Sacra forgets her son-in-law, burns her granddaughter, and buries her daughter, when she was chosen Miss Carabanchel Doña Sacra's daughter shone just like a diamond, that was two years ago by now, Doña Sacra is a very strong and brave woman, with women like that history could have been written without early-rising ideas, Doña Sacra does not give in to grief, grief is cured by grief, Doña Jesusa is astonished at seeing her so brave and clear-headed, inside it's another story, when she gets back to 132 Ayala Doña Sacra shuts herself in her bedroom and sits down on the sofa, if she could cry she would certainly feel better but she doesn't want to cry, each installment must be paid slowly and in due time, in the house next door Don Roque and Doña Teresa try to be quiet in their hidden dovecote (the air doesn't smell of dead cat) and not give any trouble, I'm telling you there's got to be a dead cat in the attic, the smell is dead cat, nobody pays any attention to me and then things happen, what good does it do you to look at yourself in the mirror, sir, to spend your whole life looking at yourself in the mirror if afterward you can't even sleep because of the way that cat smells?, don't listen to such foolish words and look at yourself in the mirror even if not confidently, look at yourself in the mirror with infinite misgiving, Napoleon Bonaparte and King Cyril of England wound up stinking of dead cat, ask yourself no questions about your behavior so as not to be ashamed, what desert would it lead to for you to become your own accuser?, Magdalena smelled rancid, she smelled of grease and cologne, now she smells of dead cat, she probably smells of dead cat, you assume that but you can't verify it, dead flies do not smell, clearly they don't have much consistency, sometimes they smell of cold coffee and of the armpits of horny poor lovers, it's not up to you to solve any problem or to help the cripple Marramáu (hero of some war), you have enough to do with giving the cripple the finger and not paying him for the cigarettes you buy from him, the three cigarettes you steal from him, Domingo the musician upbraids you and from Toisha you conceal it carefully, let other people be the ones to found religions and try to straighten out the world, no, no, you just explain to Toisha that you're signing up to be a bum who survives sadness, that you don't have enough feeling in your soul to consider yourself the scapegoat for the world's squalid sins, Aixa agrees with you and her navel shines like a glowworm, let ideas flee from your head like frogs or grasshoppers but don't allow feeling to invade your soul and your heart, rather tear out your soul and heart and throw them to the dead faggots, maybe you are dead and don't know it, maybe you are a dead faggot and people don't know it, what people like is to applaud at the foot of the scaffold, Don León smells the crotch of La Hebrea because the law does not allow him to smell the crotch of the deceased Doña Matilde, Dámaso excuses it because Doña Matilde was sick and resignedly capricious for more than ten years, your parents never learned to read or write but they did know how to assist at mass, pay tithes, and train magpies and starlings, you could be dubbed a knight at any moment because the blood of the heroes who are in the history books runs through your veins, what does it matter to you that you're not a Persian if you don't believe in education either?, be kind to the unsatisfied sexy sisters but bare your head respectfully before the poetic epitaphs of the Jews, Dámaso and you go with the sisters to the Panorama Theatre and you feel transported to the most weightless planet, you must never fret about a bloodstain more or a bloodstain less on the windshield, there are always bloodstains on all the windshields in the world, Don Roque no longer breakfasts on garlic soup, fried bread dunked in hot chocolate, and a little glass of brandy, now he has to settle for the sparse coffee of his hiding place, life demands certain salutary concessions, Lieutenant Colonel Mangada and Major Barceló hand out death sentences at the Casa de Campo, blood calls to blood, breeds blood, makes blood flow, all of you heard in school that blood is the engine of history, that's not true, blood is the brake of history, what happens is that it's easier to spill it than to channel it, blood is not an indelible ink but smudgy, pages written in blood soon grow very hard to read, as soon as the first rains fall they become very hard to read, why do you insist on calling Señor Asterio Señor Ricardo?, don't you think there's enough confusion already?, Evelina Castellote is strong as an ox and tireless, all men will do for her, some more and others less but they'll all do, Evelina hears with gaping eyes about Threefoot's Grandson and his counterfeiting, it was too bad the Civil Guard found him out because ten centimos at a time he would have taken over the whole country, shit what a guy!, Jesualdo Villegas is sorry about the death of Apeles Mestres, we ought to get somebody to write an article, whom?, I don't know, somebody, your Uncle Jerónimo was a friend of Apeles Mestres', he was an odd character, very much the Catalonian, his passing is a great loss for Catalonia and for all of Spain, María, may I have a glass of milk?, your Uncle Jerónimo has moved into your house, he really doesn't bother anybody, all he does is spend the whole day drinking glasses of milk, he told your mother don't worry María I'll pay for the milk, all the milk that's used in this house as long as I'm here with you, you know it's no strain on my budget, military bands are marching around Madrid playing marches and pasodobles, people applaud and shout long live the Republic, Chonina wakes up late, Don Olegario has already been at his inventions for two hours, this girl has really changed from the time she was emptying urinals in the place on Espíritu Santo, she's like another woman now, her father is staying at the Golden Lion Inn from where the buses leave for Valdeolivos via Alcalá, she paid for his room for two nights, Chonina is a friend of Isidoro Galindo the regular driver for Villaconejos, Chonina really shines now and she's even put on some weight, it's a pleasure to see how good-looking she's become, don't deny that you had something to do with her, admit that it was she who got tired of you, some Fascists disguised as sailors fire on the loyal forces from a truck, several members of the militia are wounded, Don Felipe Espinosa is taken from his house and shows up dead on the Dehesa de la Villa behind the Giner de los Ríos school, Antonio Arévalo was right, you don't admit that it was the cripple Romero who denounced him, Amanda Ordóñez tells you that, cross my heart I swear it but even so you don't believe it, no, Don Leoncio Romero talks a lot but he's incapable of denouncing anybody, María Angustias and María Victoria don't stop crying, Antonio Arévalo goes for them and takes them to the Chilean embassy, let them carry off the furniture, haven't you lost more than that already?, the scar of the wife of the master sergeant of the Customs Guard whose face Amanda burned in the little café in San Ginés alley won't fade, obviously the coffee was very hot and right on target, her husband is sent back to Alcalá de Henares, this time to fight against the rebel forces, his truck turns over on the other side of Torrejón de Ardoz and the sergeant is crushed to death, being crushed by a truck is a bad way to die, his wife doesn't know it yet it'll be more than a week before she finds out, Miguel Mercader has not gone back to Doña Valentina's he's learned his lesson and he's right, why don't we call Lupita and Juani?, all right, Lupita and Juani get up late, since they've got tuberculosis they get up late everything has its advantages, we'll call them later, all right, Fidel prepares a very fancy breakfast by boiling the cleaning rags from the Los Angeles Bar or the tavern of the widow of Ciriaco Benito, he filters the slops through a handkerchief and sip by sip drinks at least half a gallon, it's not a very nutritious drink but it's hot and tones up the system, Paca likes Fidel's breakfast a great deal, if you want to dip some bread in it take some, there must be bread over there, Don León turns the radio on full blast, he doesn't need any trouble, Dámaso and Don León have to shout when they want to say something to each other, do you think a miracle of Our Lady of Lourdes could have saved King Cyril of England?, you ask Dámaso, I don't know, I don't think so, he answers you, since the death of his mother Dámaso has lost his sense of humor, Don Leopoldo and Doña Bernardina have six children left, they picked up the other one at the morgue, wrapped his body in a sheet, and buried him, Don Leopoldo puts on strict mourning and goes to his office, duty is sacred, grief must never keep us from fulfilling our duty, Don Vicente Parreño is a friend of Don Leopoldo's, or rather an acquaintance, Don Leopoldo is a homebody and man of sound habits and Don Vicente on the other hand is a whoremonger and a bit nutty, a very nice man but rather a whoremonger, he never misses a Saturday at Doña María Luisa and Doña Margarita's place, he gets there, sits in the dining room for a while with the managers or with one of the young ladies who is not currently engaged, gets laid, pays, and leaves, Don Vicente is very methodical and goes to the whorehouse as a prophylaxis, strictly as a prophylaxis, not from any wanton appetite, Julianín is thinner and weaker by the day, Madame Teddy's whores usually stop at Casa Benito for a vermouth on their way to work, they wear dresses with a very low neckline and you can see the rise of their tits, Julianín jacks off like a horny monkey, he doesn't lack for inspiration, we're going to have to get this one a rifle, he's old enough to hold a rifle, shit leave him alone, can't you tell he's not all there?, at Madame Teddy's the march of culture goes on for Bergamín as for any Christian earthly life is only the path to communion with God, for André Gide the path lies in present society and the end, or the beginning, in communion with the world, with man, why don't you all wake up and pay attention to what's going on here?, Jesualdo doesn't even look at the speaker, he just tells him shut the fuck up, Jesualdo pushes Enriqueta's hands aside, don't be impatient Enriqueta there's time for everything, just be a little patient, it has been officially confirmed that in San Roque the militia have slaughtered eighty-some Moors who had landed at Algeciras, well what do I care?, that kind of news shouldn't even be published, the issue is something else even if people don't realize it, Domingo has his lemon for breakfast and takes his foot bath with Colman's mustard, the keyboard is more limber when the feet are rested, it's too bad that hearts can't be bathed with Colman's mustard to make them lighter, Captain

Sampil bombs Saragossa, the government confiscates all private planes and thanks LAPE[6] for its cooperation, José Sacristán Gutiérrez comes back to the men's room at the Pleyel Theatre, yes, here's what I wrote, they haven't erased it, it's nice to see your tracks still there, those who shit in public restrooms have an inclination to permanence, more than five months have gone by and there's what I wrote just the way it was, some day the medic at the first-aid station on Castelló is going to get his nose punched, Don Estanislao was on the verge of doing it back when there was the business with Chelo, so you're reading Alberto Insúa?, well if you don't watch out you'll get novels up your ass you jerk!, you just keep on mistreating the dead and you'll pay for it, don't you worry, you just keep mistreating the taxpayers, sure, that's what you're getting paid for, they'll settle your account when you least expect it, then you'll be crawling on the floor like some pathetic bum but somebody'll kick your ass upright again, don't you worry, don't you count your chickens till they're hatched, Gregorio Montes eggs Don Estanislao on, why don't you crack his skull?, if you want I'll help you, that guy deserves to have his skull cracked against the radiator and be left there like a dead cat, there's more than one would be happy if we cracked his skull, Gregorio Montes is still friends with Mireya the Frenchwoman, but he doesn't do any more experimenting, he's learned his lesson and then some, Don Estanislao spends his time glued to the radio, please don't distract me because now comes the good part, Don Estanislao believes in miracles and also believes that miracles are announced in official communiqués, Ismaelito, Isabel's son who became a Marist brother, is going around dressed in overalls and carrying a rifle and asking passersby for their papers, that Ismaelito is a bum with no conscience and besides he hates priests, he sure kept it to himself as long as he was a Marist brother but now he's got no reason to hide it, the priests are responsible for the cultural backwardness of Spain, come on now, maybe they are, but it does sound a little odd coming from you, shit, why is that?, what do I know, no special reason, Ismaelito is a scatterbrain going on scoundrel who just wants to live without working, I'm telling you there's a dead cat in the attic, why don't we go look?, leave me alone, you think I haven't got anything better to do than run around attics looking for dead cats?, the character of women can be discovered by studying the form of their navels, men's too though that's harder, a woman's navel can be gentle or fierce, domestic or brutal, flowery or fruited, obsequi-

6. Líneas Aéreas Postales Españolas (Spanish Postal Air Lines). "Editor's note" in the original.

ous or oblong or phosphorescent or dull, all navels can be included in one or another of these classes, Toisha's navel is obsequious or phosphorescent depending on whether she is or is not in heat, this duality is not infrequent and is often found in very amorous women, Joan of Arc was a wildcat with a fierce navel, maybe she was rather barren, María Inés is a little turtledove with a gentle navel, Don Sixto Lopera really likes to hear her oh how you hurt me sweetheart!, Don Sixto Lopera was always very conceited, Enriqueta is a lioness with a fierce navel, hold still goddammit!, Evelina too, Doña Bernardina is a rabbit with a domestic navel, coitus with Doña Bernardina must be very boring and not at all exciting, women with domestic navels find it easy not to commit adultery, Doña Teresa is a cat whose navel has just flowered, how happy I am with you darling!, me too sweetheart, but what a lousy moment we've picked to fall in love!, what's that to us darling, the main thing is being able to stay together, Ginesa is a donkey with a fruited navel, couldn't it be an umbilical hernia?, could be, Baldomera Hidalgo is a goat with an oblong navel, Baldomera Hidalgo's navel is like her cunt only headed the other way, Paca is a sparrow with a dull navel and so on, some women show a mischievous navel but that is usually a trick, Aixa the Moor for example has a motto around hers, a mischievous navel is not always the product of a trick, Mimí Ortiz de Amoedo has two identical moles one above and one below the navel and they are natural, the blind man Don Esteban is surprised that Matiítas hasn't come to read him novels, that bum must have thought that the hour of emancipation has struck, how wrong he is!, the deputy Sánchez Somoza has breakfast at the coffee shop Las Navas, he doesn't care in the least that the customers are looking at him apprehensively and is ready to give the first one to allow himself the slightest liberty another hip-bath in chocolate, you've got to keep one jump ahead of people and anybody who's got any business with me only has to speak up, is that clear, yes sir, very clear, the deputy Sánchez Somoza carries a cane, you can tell from his look that he's ready to take up the cudgels with anybody, Roquito Zamora wants no truck with the deputy, he just wants to be left in peace, he's got enough on his hands with just making a living, Roquito Zamora is a friend of the cigarette man Senén's, come on Senén show your dick to this gentleman who won't believe that it reaches down to your knee, no not now, this is no time to be showing dicks to anybody, that's at night, come on man, don't be like that!, it's a bet, don't let me down, well let's go inside, the three men go into the men's room and Senén pulls out his dick, so now, does it or doesn't it reach down to his knee?, well yes, you're right, my God, what a dick!, all right you win, here's your three pesetas, Senén laughs like a simple athlete who has just triumphed in the stadium, when he laughs his only tooth trembles with excitement, it won't be obligatory to keep in step at the parade of the judgment day, loyal forces capture Alcalá de Henares and Guadalajara and are in control of the situation in Ciudad Real, Albacete, and Almería, the lines are becoming clear and the triumph of the Republic cannot be far off, William Tell and his bow and Buffalo Bill and his revolver give a public demonstration of their skills, there really is a dead cat in the attic?, that's something that will come out sooner or later, things can't remain hidden for all eternity, it's too bad that no dead cats stroll across your mirror, caravans of silent dead cats, it's too noisy in Madrid, the clamor is like an impatience that is overflowing little by little and flooding everything from the bottom up, it begins with the sewers and the subway, it continues through the cellars, flows out onto the street and climbs up to the rooftops of the houses, the dead cats will soon begin to float on the surface of the waters, then you'll be able to shed all doubt and give your assent to whoever is right, can it be true that the poet Juan Ramón never in his life went to a whorehouse?, you can't say that of every poet, you can't say that of Paul Verlaine or Rubén Darío, Juan Ramón is only interested in his verses, he is a very hysterical and withdrawn poet, others are faggots, there are a lot of faggots among poets, writing poems obviously turns people into faggots, Gregorio Montes declares that in Gerardo Diego's anthology there are six definite faggots and two or three doubtful cases, that's certainly an exaggeration, Gregorio Montes sees faggots everywhere, when Don Joaquín remembers Petra la Grillo the Guinean mulatto whose throat he slit on the Dehesa de la Villa he starts to turn around and around in his bed and can't sleep, he doesn't remember every night but when he does remember he can't sleep, Don Joaquín leaves for Valencia with his children but Margot stays in Madrid at Villa Milagros, she still remembers her husband's words, for your children you are dead, then why the fuck was he calling her now?, she doesn't tell her husband at that time why the fuck are you calling me now, she prefers to keep still, no, for my children I'm dead, I'm staying in Madrid and going to bed with whoever pays, by now my children are old enough that they wouldn't understand my resurrection, it's not bad making your living as a whore, it's the same as making your living any other way, you get used to everything and sometimes you can discover a generous heart in a john's look, the heart is the pump of life, it rises and falls, it contracts and expands beating with the rhythm of life, if the heart bursts life spills out like coffee from a broken cup, if the heart suddenly stops life is extinguished like the coffee in a cup that was getting cold without anyone's noticing it, man has never really understood the mystery of his own heart, scientists have succeeded in getting a heart to beat inside a jar by means of electric currents, that is not life but a rough simulation of life, very rough, Rómula is still in San Juan de Dios, she's sad and bored now but before she used to be very cheerful and she even laughed while she was fucking, some gentlemen didn't care for that at all, one night Rómula and Don Roque broke a spring mattress, Don Roque paid for the damage and that was the end of that, Asenjo and his cousin Don Baltasar Blanco go to keep Don León company for a while, Don Baltasar says to him I know two really funny new ones, one about mothers-in-law and the other about druggists, do you want to hear them?, all right, the ladies of the neighborhood no longer say the rosary or they say it quietly because you can't hear them, do you understand what's going on?, well, really understand it, no, not much, what should I say, Manene Chico has his shoes shined every morning on the Calle de Sevilla, people don't say *adiós* any more, now the custom is to say *salud*, they're very strict about it as though it were very important, your Uncle Jerónimo tells you time and again, do you see?, the liturgy!, this is a liturgical country, what happens is that nobody wants to say so, now people are very busy competing with Cascorro but this is a liturgical country, the proper forms must be observed, what has to be saved are appearances, sometimes my boy I think my head isn't working right, there's a phrase that's been running through my head for two or three days now and I can't quite see what it means, breast I don't understand it, what does breast I don't understand it mean?, you don't know either and you can't clear up your Uncle Jerónimo's doubts, you'd like to but you can't, breast I don't understand it, no, you don't know what it means either, a blinding light threw Saint Paul from his horse, could somebody give me a cup of coffee?, that's what you think but you don't say it out loud, you're not brave enough to say it out loud, the least little slip and they might bring you a cup of coffee and then it would be foolish not to drink it, people drink a lot of coffee in a revolution, coffee makes people relatively brave but you know that coffee is a concession, mother, may I have some coffee?, yes son, I'll bring you some right away, can you imagine Buffalo Bill in the circus tracing the silhouette of the crucified corpse of Magdalena with bullets?, you are fodder for the circus, fodder for the catechism class, fodder for the brothel, fodder for prison, fodder for the gallows, fodder for the common grave, the mirror tells you that with laconic impassivity, the time for first-class burials is over with their mahogany coffins, their six plumed horses, and their six family men dressed up in the style of Frederick the Great with their dress coats, their wigs, their horns, and their stomach ulcers, private property has been abolished and King Cyril of England shudders in the midst of his troubled musings, Magdalena is in the common grave and you'll all be following her now or when God pleases, it will be a pity that you won't be able to distinguish among yourselves in the procession, you'll be able to recognize the Cid by his wild goat's smell and Robespierre and the Misses Aguado will be in a deep trunk right next to the band, all the players in the band are mangy and each one has next to him a bare-assed poor boy to scratch him while he blows the pasodoble, the conductor is very tall and has no head or if he has one it has a conical shape, when they get to the cemetery he hides behind a tomb, lowers his pants, and shits very copiously and with a great sense of relief, what do you suppose became of the heroic Philippine airmen Arnáiz and Calvo?, Agustín Úbeda does not want to go to Toledo to face the rebels shut up in the Alcázar, Agustín Úbeda feels defeated, it's not fair Engracia should have died the way she did, she was sick when she got killed, Isabelita Nájera triumphs in the musical *Bring Her to Me!*, and Amparito Sara makes the public roar with *The Eager Ones*, public notice, by decision of the executive committee for public entertainment the program is limited to a select and light but not pornographic show, yes, yes, just as your Uncle Jerónimo says, the liturgy, Agustín wonders whether it wouldn't be better to open a tavern with private rooms and a little flamenco, he's been thinking about that for some time, well we'll see once this is all over, Leopoldo keeps on cramming mortgage law into his head, that's something you can't set aside for even a single day because you get out of the habit, they'll announce the examinations eventually, there's no hurry, the main thing is to know mortgage law very thoroughly and by heart and not to lose the habit of studying, they'll announce the examinations eventually, it's just a question of waiting a little, Mr. Simón Tendero is still in the Retiro, nobody has messed with the guards in the Retiro, at least for now, knock on wood, nothing's been known of his son Raúl for several days now, maybe something is known but they don't want to tell it, people have become very reserved and mysterious, not even a miracle could get Emilita Tendero married, it really is bad luck that that truck killed Alfonsito!, Emilita's two kids are doing all right without any major problems, at least that's something, you are forgetting the cat in the attic, and not because I haven't reminded you, Mrs. Díaz is waiting to see her daughter arrive any moment, waiting to see is a figure of speech because Mrs. Díaz can't see, she's blind, I'm sure she'll bring me a fan, Chelo is very affectionate and always tells me mother I'm going to bring you a fan, with flowers?, no, even better, with a bullfighter, my poor daughter, what a good heart she has and how much she respects me!, your Aunt Octavia is convinced this is the end of the world, the Reverend Mother Ráfols says so in her prophecies, your Uncle Jerónimo listens to her without contradicting her, well don't talk about it with anybody, just with us, there are many crude people who wouldn't understand you, yes that's true enough, Turquoise has not missed a single day from work at La Cigale, people laugh a lot at that song about Balbine, poor Balbine, she don't take no aspirin, Turquoise has a strong sense of responsibility and knows very well that you've got to stick it out, Gabriel Seseña goes through moments when he's half scared but Turquoise encourages him not to desert, as long as people are applauding we're saved and for now they're applauding, yes that's true, Lolita Diamante is less successful, there are always some boos when she performs, you've got to move more, Lola, you've got to make use of your butt and do a little shaking, see what I mean?, what people want is movement and a little spice, the marimba number needs more movement, you just use your butt and you'll see how you'll have the audience eating out of your hand, the audience wants to applaud, all they ask is for us to make them feel a little sexy, that's what we're here for, Lolita Diamante is a light chanteuse, she does refined numbers and maybe she needs a few more pounds on her, the customers at La Cigale like them rather well packed and curvaceous, your curves are there to be seen, not to be hidden, people don't want concealment but meat in the right places, crime is a worm that reproduces by parthenogenesis and a hundred crimes can come to fruit from one crime and then the second batch are already a million crimes, can you imagine the world burned by the blood of so many crimes?, the blood that is sweetest in the veins turns acid when it is spilled and corrodes all it touches, the blood of a virgin who plays the harp (to cite an extreme case) turns into chloride when it is spilled, Miguel Mercader has an ice cream, ever since he got hit on the head he's become capricious, Don Wifredo thinks it wouldn't be a bad idea to spend an afternoon in bed with Leonorcita, playing with Leonorcita, how about it, are you still going with that girl?, the question surprises Juanito Mateo, yes, why?, no reason, just curiosity, plain curiosity, it's getting to be strange but for two or three days now Aixa and the Nicaraguan have had their coffee full of flies, the flies seem stupefied, it must be the heat, another fly, now another fly's fallen in my coffee, so many fucking flies!, order another one, no man no, it's not worth the bother, we're not going to spend the whole afternoon ordering coffees, listen David, what's happening with the flies?, the waiter doesn't know, what the fuck do I know what's happening with the flies?, nothing, nothing's happening with them, what should be happening with them?, remember that the dead cat Matiítas would have liked to be a fly on the crotch of a one-armed man, that's called wanting to play with an advantage, that's called wanting always to win, Chato Getafe and Hipólita plan to get married in church and by the book, the bequest is nothing to let slip away, two hundred thousand plus pesetas are a lot of pesetas, it's not easy now to get married in church and by the book, the priests have been swallowed up by the earth and they'll have to wait till everything gets back to normal, Matías Suárez from the commissary goes into the Bar Zaragoza, brandy, at the next table Aixa the Moor smokes two of the Nicaraguan's Capstans, Matías Tajuelo from La Cigale stares at him, excuse me, are you by chance from Requena, no, I'm sorry, I confused you with somebody from Requena, that's all right, Aixa the Moor and the Nicaraguan go off for a nap, it's very hot, well what do we care?, it's hot everywhere, you throw yourself on your bed to take a nap, you take off your shoes and pants and lie there in your shorts and shirt, after a while you feel hot and take the shorts and shirt off too, little beams of light slip through the cracks in the blind, Amanda's ribs still hurt from when the corporal of the Customs Guard smashed them with a bench, they no longer hurt the way they did but they still hurt, nine flies have lighted on your mirror, you count nine flies, leave them alone, as long as they're on the mirror they won't bother you, Virgilio Taboada from *El Debate* has been fired, when the 370 pesetas he's saved up run out he doesn't know what the shit he's going to do, Virgilio Taboada's butt is still scalded, maybe Doña Ramona will let him have some credit, Doña Ramona is kind, Clarita is better but her butt is also still in tatters, boiling chocolate can really burn!, her mother cares for her very tenderly and applies Hazelina ointment on her buttocks, do you feel better dear?, yes Mama, I feel almost all well now, you've been forgetting Toisha a little, piss on Toisha and all her nonsense, what you want to do is sleep while the sacrificial lambs butt angrily against everything that stands in their way, if you close your eyes the little beams of light that slip through the cracks in the blind don't bother your eyes, most probably a maid is jacking off an eleven-year old boy in the house across the street, maybe not but with this heat it's very probably true, a custom is a custom, nobody should contravene custom, no one can contravene custom, if anyone tries to he is immediately rejected by families, would you have liked to be a Rudyard Kipling character?, of course I would, who wouldn't?, it is all over with Rikki-tikki, we must sing his death-song, valiant Rikki-tikki is dead!, you have dreamt more than once of becoming a Rudyard Kipling hero, the recognition that this is no longer possible is painful, for there to be Rudyard Kipling heroes there must be a great deal of order, there would have to be another Queen Victoria, you know, the rich very rich, very well-bred and cultured, the poor very poor, very resigned and literary, otherwise it doesn't work, Manene Chico and Maruja Onrubia the Widow meet at Timoteo Despedide's tavern, have you heard anything about Don Braulio?, no, they don't know anything at his house either, I phoned there and they don't know anything, he hasn't been by his house for two days, maybe he's in the sack with La Mancheguita, could be, I hope he's in the sack with La Mancheguita but I couldn't swear to it, maybe they've shot him and he's lying in some ditch, Don Braulio really likes to argue and disagree with people, Don Braulio is no shrinking violet and people don't go for that, I hope he's in the sack with La Mancheguita or with whomever, we'll hear eventually, there are village idiots who have sweet eyes and there are also murderers who tremble, murderers who are terribly afraid when they are about to commit a murder, it is the custom in slaughterhouses to cut off the balls of recently killed rams and throw them up against the ceiling so they'll stick there, it's very funny and people laugh a lot when the slaughterer succeeds and they say *olé* and you've got balls, then the slaughterer smiles, salutes by raising his cap, and goes on stabbing at the sheep, the young servant girls start feeling sexy and let themselves be touched on the butt and the tits, the poor have begun to forget resignation and that way there can be no Rudyard Kipling heroes, the law of the jungle punishes with death those who kill at a watering hole, if Don Braulio is in the sack with a woman we ought to leave him alone, the Volga is a very long river but not endless, the Danube is a very long river but not endless, there no longer are any endless rivers that was in the Old Testament, Toisha has very delicate feelings and does not bear it patiently when pigeons do their business on her, King Cyril of England and other subtle coprophagists are a lasting example for her, you know that Toisha has become capricious and despotic, all you can do is regret it and take advantage of the situation, everything has its good side but also its intolerable side, its bitter shadow, Doña Encarna always tells Don León you can go on in La Hebrea is free now, with every day that passes La Hebrea is more impressive and outstanding, also more solemn, women who know their limitations are more affectionate but man is very impatient and hungry and is no longer looking for affection, that was before, now he looks for La Hebrea and other women who like La Hebrea are always with a customer, you can go on in, only one man hears that, the rest have to be patient and reread the exciting history of the death of King Cyril the Shitty Orchid of England, you must not laugh at the death of kings, you must hold back your laughter, you have never laughed at the death of the disinherited the fools the cripples nor have you played the shitting pigeon flying over the as yet unclosed caskets, you have not vomited your loathing and your contempt on the alms box from which the sacristan steals, you have always shown respect for custom, we shall see whether your behavior is enough to placate the unleashed violent wrath of the gods, Juana Pagán tells Juanito Mateo you go ahead and do what you want with me but don't muss up my hair because today I was at the beauty shop, Juanito Mateo can't believe there can be a woman with the good parts of Juana Pagán and the good parts of Leonorcita, well, it is possible but very unlikely, Mrs. Appelgate dies poisoned but sowing death, you discuss it with Gregorio Montes and Miguel Hernández at Telesforo Mateo's tavern on the shore of the Jarama, Telesforo Mateo is Juanito's uncle but he won't let him run up a tab, not Gregorio either, he does let you and Miguel run up a tab, everybody does that for whomever he feels like and there's no reason why he has to give any explanations to anybody, Don Cándido Modrego smokes almost all of Don Olegario's butts, face it what we need here is an iron fist, people are out of control and just bungle around, the first thing we must aim for is to maintain order which is the basis of society, what we need here is a General Narváez, a general of the old school, Spain is on the road to ruin and only another General Narváez could save her from that, Don Román is never sleepy but his family is too bored, Don Román can't think of anything to keep his family from getting bored, he'd really like to think of something that would keep his family from getting so bored, Dominica Morcillo lets Don Cándido talk, what does she care what he says?, Dominica agrees with Don Olegario more than with Don Cándido, what a difference between the two!, Don Olegario is more gallant with women and he also knows how to catch bats with a palm leaf, on Palm Sunday when people throw out their old palm leaves Dominica takes two or three old palm leaves to Don Olegario so he can catch bats, Turquoise would certainly like to run off, she knows she has no place to run to and besides she's afraid they'd catch her with a palm leaf like a bat, it's better to stick with the devil she knows and keep on smelling Gabriel Seseña, you can kill mosquitoes with an olive branch by hitting them hard against the wall, Paca knows that and on Palm Sunday, when people throw out their old olive branches, she takes two or three old olive branches to Fidel so he can kill mosquitoes, some nights Paca kills mosquitoes for Fidel with an olive branch so he can sleep peacefully, it's not the same thing to piss behind a tomb as an irreverent prank as out of necessity, real necessity, Don Olegario is studying shorthand so as to be able to express his thoughts even as they flow, ordinary writing is usually a hindrance to thought, Miss Dolly from Gibraltar comes out on stage stark naked and screening herself with a peacock feather fan, when she fans herself she always shows something and people are very attentive and quiet, it's just for a second but she always shows something, Miss Dolly performs at The Red Owl, they advertise her as the international superstar princess of the cabarets and queen of the charleston, her real name is Dorotea Ibáñez and she was married to Pantaleón Calero alias Strongarm a picador from San Roque, Miss Dolly is not widowed but divorced, Strongarm got tired of her eccentricities and sent her packing, nobody has to be Napoleon Bonaparte or even Frégoli, Pantaleón Calero had been patient long enough and you can't ask any more of him, you go out without much conviction, the Nicaraguan tells you Toisha is at his place waiting for you, she certainly wants to talk to you, no, she certainly doesn't want to talk to you, Toisha is very nervous and demanding, this situation is uncomfortable, there are five hand grenades in that package, take them where you're told and don't ask any questions, obey blindly, that's the way it was before when we were underground, we're always underground, do you think you can make hand grenades in broad daylight?, you can't help being surprised that Toisha should tell you these things about hand grenades, she wears luxurious underwear of good quality and the tip of the lace that borders her slip peeks out from under her skirt, the hand grenades are in that package, don't ask any questions, why are you talking to me with your clothes on?, excuse me I'll take them off right away, why do you smell of carbide?, I don't know and besides what's it to you?, who are you to ask me what I smell of?, you just obey, you know very well that we tramps all smell of carbide, the Nicaraguan is playing the piano in the next room, do you think Chopin waltzes are revolutionary music?, I don't know, I was the one who told him to play Chopin waltzes, the grenades can blow up at any moment, you men are very limited and don't usually understand a word of what's going on, Toisha caresses the back of your neck and kisses you on the mouth and eyes, why do you suppose I fell in love with you?, you tell me, why don't you get a haircut?, I don't want a haircut and besides I plan to grow a mustache, Toisha starts to cry and you make use of the occasion to hit her hard in the face, I'll take the grenades, you wait for me here till I get back, the Assault Guards never rode as well as the lady bullfighters, some difference!, nobody rides as well as the lady bullfighters, no matter what happens Amanda Ordóñez wouldn't miss a performance by the lady bullfighters, it's a pleasure to see them in their outfits with the pants tight over the butt and thighs, Amanda Ordóñez enjoys herself imagining mysterious fights between johns and two lady bullfighters in the bullring and herself in a ringside seat in the shade drinking anise and tossing kisses and carnations to them, the cripple Romero is no good for a fight, the veterinarians of the bullring would reject him, the cripple Romero is only good for asking for bicarbonate and grumbling, he's very rude when he asks for the bicarbonate, the cripple Romero is more unbearable by the day, if his character doesn't improve and he becomes more pleasant I won't grease the hinges on his bum leg any more, if I grease them it's because I want to, not because I have to, ballplayers have strong and flexible legs, the cripple Romero couldn't be a lady ballplayer, Mirenchu, Carmenchu, Begoña, Angelines, Vasquita, they all have agile and flexible legs, the cripple Romero is a shit, if he died it wouldn't be any loss, have pity on the cripple Romero and blind him by blowing bicarbonate in his eyes, the cripple Romero does not deserve pity, you must be inexorable with him, the smart thing would be to go after the cripple Romero with a stick, corner him in some empty lot, subdue him with your stick while blowing bicarbonate in his eyes, and shut him up in a dungeon on bread and water, a memorable example must be made of the cripple Romero, why of the cripple Romero?, come on, you've got to pick somebody!, a microscope enlarges objects, a microbe, a fly's leg, and a telescope brings them closer, the surface of the moon with its craters, the butt of the neighbor who's getting dressed in front of her wide open window, there ought to be a laboratory instrument that would make things smaller and move them farther away, until they invent one you can use opera glasses backward, the cripple Romero seen with very powerful opera glasses backward looks like a fly that can hardly walk, a sick or old fly that is barely alive, the fly Romero can fall into a cup of coffee or of broth, into a glass of water, into a bowl of soup, into a urinal, but he doesn't die, he kicks nervously and then stays still obviously to gather his strength but he doesn't die, a Marist brother with the salmon-colored face of a mental defective stands looking at the fly Romero and says that's really something, that fly has nine lives like a cat, the crowd throws stones at him for his foolishness and the Marist brother runs off terrified and holding up his skirts so as to run faster, people laugh at his fear, look at that, what a coward!, tuberculous Lupita trips him up and the Marist brother smashes against a wall with an advertisement for Ladillol, completely eradicates pubic infestation, Orzán Laboratories, Inc., La Coruña, you feel very sorry for the Marist brother and look away while a swarm of parrots, red and green like the Portuguese flag, devours his remains, may the unfortunate Marist brother rest in peace, the cripple Romero takes advantage of the momentary confusion to fly away, don't get distracted thinking about foolish things, what are the habits of parrots that feed on dead Marist brothers to you?, that's something that doesn't matter to you one way or the other, the Progressives of Alcalá Zamora, the Centrists of Portela Valladares, and the Radicals of Lerroux cross the stage with their tails between their legs, their fate is dramatic and they only know that they have to die and be eaten by the red and green parrots that shatter the air with their confused strident croaking, neither you nor anybody ever renounces the hope of going on living, you look at yourself in the mirror with envy, you don't know of what but you look at yourself in the mirror with envy, Julius Caesar, Saint Paul, and Napoleon Bonaparte were very envious, all great men have their weaknesses and ruling vices, your flat mirror gives you back a prematurely aged image, no, that's not you, that's Pepito la Zubiela killed in an automobile accident, notice his dyed grey hair and his dirty fingernails, look at his butt in your parallelepiped mirror with polished surfaces and count up the seven boils of his constellation, distinguishing marks seven boils forming a constellation around the sphincter of the anus, look at yourself in the ovoid mirror with envy, there's no possibility of fraud here, your ovoid mirror gives you back the image of a little animal in fetal position, a lion cub, a little lamb, a little snake in fetal position, no, no, that's not you either that's King Cyril of England, sometimes he adopts such studied poses that you confuse him with William Tell, you tell Toisha quite clearly, no, I'm not going to take the grenades anyplace, don't insist, I don't want to become the bearer of anything or anyone's mailman, and you're not the czar either, that's what you'd like to be, the czar!, and I'm not Michael Strogoff either, you don't have to wait for me, you can get dressed, I'm horribly disgusted with you naked, Toisha's expression grows hard and she whips you across the face with her bra, you and Toisha are very violent, very impatient, you're always in a hurry, look at yourself in your slightly spherical mirror with envy, there's not much light and you can't make out the image it gives you back, perhaps it's Robinson Crusoe covering his shame with a panther skin, where did Robinson Crusoe get his panther skin?, your slightly spherical mirror lies and exaggerates, the devil is probably behind all this farce, there is no worse beast than an ingrate and the devil is the archetype of ingratitude, you must not blame Toisha for your bad humor or your fear, not for her anger or her lasciviousness either, Toisha is only a naked woman who wants to send somebody some grenades, you ought to understand or at least try to understand your neighbor's reasons, refuse to look at yourself in the mirror in the shape of a bloody jellyfish, you will never store up enough envy in your heart, the slaves who have passed into history are few, Aesop, Spartacus, Uncle Tom, but that is not their fault but history's, Rafaela and Angelines will not pass into history either in spite of their having bathed Don Máximo on Sunday July 19, St. Vincent de Paul celestial patron of charitable organizations, 1936, history is not a charitable science but a heartless cunning, it is useless to try to change it, Doña Eduvigis doesn't know a word of history and doesn't need to either, what she would need is a good cure for asthma and love, lots of love, above all love, should we say the rosary Vicente?, all right, Don Vicente treats Doña Eduvigis well, and La Cordobesita, and everybody, there are people for whom it's easy to treat others well, for other people it's the opposite, Jesualdo Villegas has just come back from the Sierra de Guadarrama where the loyal forces are pursuing the rebels, Largo Caballero visits the war front, this is a war, we must impose discipline, enthusiasm must be channeled with discipline to make it effective, Cándido and Tomasín are in the attic with Lupita and Juani, go on silly don't be ashamed, they change Mrs. Díaz' clothes, the woman has been dirtying herself for two days, good Lord, Mrs. Díaz, the state you're in!, Carmencita smells a dead cat and tells the concierge, you too?, what a finicky houseful of people we've suddenly got here!, attics have always smelled of dead cat, where do you think cats go to die?, come on, tell me, you who know it all, where do cats go to die, to the Red Cross hospital?, no dear, no, cats have been dying in attics all my life, I'm not saying it's a good thing, to me it's all the same, as far as I'm concerned all the cats in the world could be dying, rascals that they are, maybe there is a dead cat in the attic, and maybe there isn't, the attic door is closed, nobody knows what happens behind closed doors, I don't want to be oversuspicious, Micaela Crespo phones Anita, excuse me for bothering you, your friend forgot his undershirt, Don Baltasar is very clever at preparing orangeades, he knows how to mix in just the right amount of sugar, who was that?, nobody, some fellow who wanted the undertaker's, on the shelf over the men's room basin Roque Zamora finds Raúl Taboada's container, inside there is only a sip of gazpacho and rancid at that, well today he can goddamn well wash his own container!, Anita always tells Don Baltasar that his orangeade turned out very well, today she's in a bad mood and forgets, do you like the orangeade?, yes, I sure do, it turned out very well, very refreshing, Don Leopoldo goes by the jeweler's shop to ask about the silver box he plans to give his wife, we'll do all we can but I can't guarantee anything, the help is all in an uproar and we're behind in all our work, you've got to understand that it's not our fault, of course I realize that, if you could just push it along a little, Father Rómulo and Father Sebastián are two cousins of Don Leopoldo's who recently came from their village and whom events overtook in Madrid, the concierge is a good fellow and believes it, Father Rómulo is very clever and helps him fix the elevator, Antonio Arévalo is still on the run, he is determined and he's had good luck, the point is for it to last, Paulina asks Don Hilario to keep the accounts of the boardinghouse for her, it's so we'll know what we're spending, you know what I mean?, yes dear, of course I know what you mean, the expenses over here, the receipts over here, what's left over is the profit, it's best not to touch the capital if we have less well we'll just make do with less, when Doña Teresa gets back she'll be surprised at how well everything's gone, you'll see, from now on you and Javiera are the firm, I mean you don't have to collect your wages any more, Paulina understands what Don Hilario means, Javiera has to have it explained several times and she doesn't ever seem to be quite convinced, all right, all right, if you say so it must be true, Doña Jesusa doesn't let Jesusín out on the street, everything is all mixed up and this kid is always into trouble, hold still boy, boy you're going to burn yourself, turn off the faucet boy, how I'd like to see this all over with!, Doña Jesusa spends the whole day scurrying up and down, Jesusín is a real terror and can't hold still a single minute, if you sit nice and quiet on a chair the whole morning reading a comic book I'll give you twenty-five centimos, twenty-five?, yes son, all of twenty-five just for you and for keeps, Don Feliciano has still not shown up at the notary office, it's odd that he hasn't phoned or sent a message with somebody, do we know anything about Don Feliciano?, well no, not a word, by now I'm a little worried about it, well we'll just have to wait, that's all we can do, our obligation is to keep on working as though Don Feliciano were in his office, yes that's true enough, Serafin goes on serving vermouths and snow cones to the customers, what's going to happen here, Serafín?, do you know, Don Fernando?, no, well neither do I, I'm not happy seeing so many rifles out on the streets, the trouble with weapons is that sooner or later they're always fired, I hope I'm wrong, your Uncle Jerónimo is no trouble at all, he makes his bed, dusts his room, and helps your mother in the kitchen, María, why don't you give your husband yogurt?, don't come to me now with yogurts, Jerónimo, don't you think we've got enough problems already?, your Uncle Jerónimo keeps quiet, sorry, Don Hilario forgets his crabs and even his producer gas motor and Don Cándido lets his new rules of Spanish spelling sleep in peace, something very imprecise is happening, they keep on giving Don Lucio his ham and his cookies, his diet is cheaper than that of the other guests and besides we owe him respect, Paulina feels very protected with Don Hilario's advice, well of course we owe him respect, that goes without saying, Don Avelino Folgueras can't reach his bosses in Barcelona, if this situation lasts I don't know what I'm going to do, don't worry about that Folgueras something will turn up you'll see, you are a resourceful man, your business experience will let you adapt to any situation, I know what I'm talking about, yes, all right, the trouble is going to be if my cash runs out, don't think bad thoughts my friend you have credit, have you put in your call to Barcelona?, in Matiítas' garret it smells of dead cat, the heat and flies make the body rot all the faster and burst the bladders of hidden and foul odors, Aixa is the only person who knows the secret of the dead cat and she keeps it to herself, Matiítas' mother in her bridal gown and the boxers in the photographs are silent witnesses to the stupor of the dead cat, there must be a dead cat in the attic, it stinks of dead cat from a mile off, damn it shut up!, I'm sick and tired of all this smelling of dead cat, smelling of dead cat!, as if I didn't have anything better to do than go smelling dead cats!, when somebody is really mad people say he's madder than a wildcat, well Matiítas' concierge is madder than a wildcat from hearing so much about how it smells of dead cat, it smells of dead cat, I'm sick and tired of all this babbling about a dead cat!, why don't you go to the police about it, come on, why?, want me to tell you?, well it's because you're ashamed to go there and tell the officer listen, in the attic of my house it smells of dead cat, you know they'd kick you right down the stairs, so it smells of dead cat?, well let it, it'll stop smelling when the rains come, in the men's room at the Bar Zaragoza it smells of Zotal, everywhere it smells of something, people miss the urinal and there's a dark amber puddle on the floor that smells of ammonia, the smell is no doubt good for cases of drunkenness, fastidious people piss from the door, some squeeze their dicks to make it go farther, the cake of Zotal is like a cricket in its cage, it gradually gets used up by contact with the air, Zotal is a very powerful germicidal disinfectant, its hygienic smell penetrates everywhere, in Matiítas' garret it smells of dead cat, people have their obsessions, in the attics of Madrid there must be many dead cats, dozens, hundreds of dead cats, Don Fausto has a sharp smell of dead cat in his nose, Solita and Conchita are half-wits and pregnant, all right, but they don't have any trouble telling one smell from another, this one is dead cat, this one is blind woman who shits in her pants, this one is corduroy trousers, this one is chocolate, etc., Rogelio always wears corduroy trousers, summer and winter, Rogelio isn't bothered by the smell of dead cat, he is a country boy who doesn't go for sissy ways, he does his bit by delivering milk and winning bets, Solita and Conchita are half-wits, yes, but they sure like to fuck, they're not half-wits in that respect, a lot of people are called half-wits who aren't, everybody attends to his business and there are certainly fewer half-wits than people think, so Solita and Conchita drool?, well so what?, everybody drools if he leaves his mouth open, Margot doesn't drool but she stays in Villa Milagros servicing the johns and covering the scar on her throat with a silk scarf, is that all that smart?, sell your treasure chest to whoever gives you 2.50 for the lot, maybe it would interest Don Joaquín the scared-shitless secondhand dealer, what do you want souvenirs of Toisha the despot for?, what good are they to you?, what do you need them for?, for nothing, you don't want them or have any use for them or need them for a thing, there are people who pay decent, acceptable prices for used objects no matter how useless they may seem, authenticity is highly prized, a lock of hair that is real hair, a silk handkerchief that has dried a half-dozen tears, three handwritten love letters with some expressions with possible double meaning, three rose petals that still look like three rose petals, three violets (they must have their stems) and a photograph dedicated to my dearest . . . with all my love and many kisses from your own . . . , it's too bad you can't augment the lot with the silk bedspread with a T embroidered on the cover, the panties that the dead slut wore at the moment of her death, the handkerchief for wiping off sweat, the poems, three silver half crowns, the clippings from the literary supplements of *El Sol*, the drawing Federico García Lorca gave you, no, 2.50 is too little, ask for more, ask Don Joaquín the cuckold secondhand dealer for at least five, keep on dissembling, keep on hunched over and hugging the wall, when you're a little hunched over you can run faster and with your back to the wall they can only hit you from the front, it's always easier to defend yourself that way, you shouldn't have thrown your collection of butterflies on pins into the garbage nor the fetus of your great-uncle Ricardo in its little jar of alcohol, there are moments when everything has some value, some more some less but everything has some value, the morgue is inhabited by loneliness, you leave fear at the door like an umbrella and the visitor does not feel even the company of fear, José Sánchez Sánchez, bank employee and member of the UGT, residing at 19, no not 19, 17 Paseo de Santa María de la Cabeza, third floor center left no longer spends the night with Paulina while Javiera turns her face to the wall, Don Demetrio and Doña Vicenta have brought Herminia to live with them, we're leaving for La Unión as soon as we can, if we could have we'd have left already, we've got no business here, I wish we'd never started this trip!, nobody gives either Emilio Arroyo or Virgilio Ricote a cup of coffee, but you get one, all you have to do is ask for it don't tell me you don't want to, your mother brings you a cup of coffee without your asking for it, the truth is you didn't dare to ask for coffee for fear of not being listened to, it's very humiliating to ask for coffee and not to get any, you should have married your mother, no, that wouldn't have been right, there is a big age difference, twenty years is too much, a wife should not be twenty years older than her husband, people would always be saying you married for money, Antonio Arévalo kisses María Victoria and suddenly, without knowing how, he finds himself in bed with María Angustias and María Victoria, María Victoria is a virgin and the two women cry, when María Victoria loses her virginity the three of them cry and then fall asleep in each other's arms, it's very hot and the three of them sweat, the name of the medic at the first-aid station on the Callejón de la Ternera is Celestino and he's a very decent man, he's always ready to do a favor and to help his neighbor, the one with the goat face is another story, the one with the goat face does not have decent feelings and tries to hurt the wounded when he changes their position or takes off a bandage or plaster, fuck you brother, you've got to be tough here!, no charge for service!, some fine day somebody's going to stick the medic with the goat face, it would serve him right for a son of a bitch, the medic with the goat face tells Celestino last night somebody was here asking for you, who?, I don't know she didn't give me her name, a lady who wanted corrosive sublimate and permanganate, I told her politely to shove it up her ass, when Chonina wakes up she lights the fire and fixes breakfast for Don Olegario, is there any sugar left?, yes sir a little, well it's for you, no sir I drink my coffee without sugar, Eusebia Don León Rioja's servant also drinks coffee without sugar, many women have that habit, more women than men, would you like some bread?, is there any left?, yes sir a little, all right give me a little bread, Chonina takes Don Olegario his breakfast in bed, what a pity you're such a slut, Chonina!, really, and why is that?, no reason, Don Olegario really likes to have breakfast in bed, who wouldn't, Don León is sitting in the dining room of his house reading *King Joseph's Baggage*, Eusebia brings him a little glass of wine and some almonds, that's the last of the almonds, I'll get some more today, all right, Eusebia knocks at the door of Dámaso's bedroom, come in, would you like some coffee?, all right, Eusebia is very fond of coffee and spends the whole day drinking coffee, Jacinto Rueda stutters more than usual, clearly the danger threatening the candy shop is stimulating his stuttering, I'm not risking my skin for a pound more or less, it's not worth it, I don't think they'll want to take the whole stock, that would be something else, that really would be robbery with or without vouchers, up to now no one has come to confiscate the stock, this is not a basic commodity like bread or oil, I have a stick here under the counter just in case, you can't trust people, that's for sure!, Jacinto Rueda stutters more than ever and on top of that is spraying spit and talking mush-mouthed, his countryman Gabriel Seseña stands off at a distance so he won't spatter on him, the cripple Romero buys a pound of candy as a present for Don Nicolás Mañes, hard or soft?, almond brittle, do you have almond brittle?, yes sir, top-grade brittle made of select almonds, how much can I get for you?, give me a pound please, Don Nicolás is very generous with the cripple Romero, now he has to make it up to him, whorehouse mirrors always present a good face to the customer, they are very professional and well-bred mirrors, whorehouse mirrors never grow tired of reflecting young ladies in the altogether and lascivious bureaucrats in their fifties, sometimes it even makes a man ashamed to look at himself in whorehouse mirrors, according to Max Planck's theory of wave mechanics the images that the whorehouse mirrors once reflected are still out there someplace in space, are you sure that that's Max Planck's theory of wave mechanics?, no, sure I'm not, maybe it's the theory of the Prince de Broglie, well the truth is that most probably neither of them has said anything about mirrors, I mean as mirrors, but you don't know the first thing about that don't interrupt me, sorry, the day they invent a device capable of reconstructing images that have once existed there are going to be a lot of surprises, can you imagine Don Cándido Nocedal mounting his countrywoman Carolina Otero?, Don Cándido must have died before La Otero was in circulation, well then his son Don Ramón, what difference does it make?, can you imagine General Polavieja making out with Bella Tortajada?, the theory of wave mechanics could be a seedbed of trouble, if you're ashamed to look at yourself in whorehouse mirrors don't do it, it's not elegant to blush for nothing and Toisha will understand perfectly, the way things are going it may be that you and many others will be ashamed to look at yourselves in whorehouse mirrors or in any mirror even if it doesn't present such a good face to you, don't make an effort for anything, no, don't look at yourself in the mirror at Merceditas' place nor in any other, it's not worth while, consider the fact that all is lost and turn your back to the mirror at Merceditas' place and all mirrors, it would be better for you to break them into a thousand pieces that no one could use, escape from the mirror, from mirrors, flee in terror in the opposite direction, you don't want to admit it because you are stubborn and obstinate but you never had a mirror in which to look at yourself, what a shame at your age to have to be always looking at yourself in your neighbor's mirror and in the windows of jewelry shops and pastry shops, in your mother's mirror, in the hall mirror, in the mirror of the maids' bathroom!, break them, break them, no, you never had your own mirror, a mirror for you alone and blind for all others, neither a flat mirror with its pane spotted by humidity, nor a parallelepiped mirror inclined to multiply, nor an ovoid and monotonously fetal rugby-ball mirror, nor an almost spherical and anesthetic and licentious mirror, nor a mirror in the shape of a bleeding jellyfish with a sickness in each silken tassel, no, close your eyes and proclaim the truth with your hand over your heart, declare that you neither have nor have ever had a mirror, may you die if you're not telling the truth, you have never had a mirror, you have never had a mirror, you have never had a mirror, sit down in the ditch by the side of the road to watch death coming, you have never had a mirror, take your pulse to notice how you are losing your pulse, you have never had a mirror, stretch out your legs in the sun so the lizards may trace their paths through your veins, you have never had a mirror, not a flat mirror, nor a parallelepiped mirror, nor an ovoid mirror, nor a slightly spherical mirror, nor a mirror in the shape of a bloody jellyfish, nor any goddamned mirror at all, you are caught in a deep well of darkness, who knows whether you are blind and do not know it, it would be better to be blind and know it, at least you would believe in something, the five cardinal points, the nine signs of the Zodiac, the five seasons of the year, the two works of mercy, the three rights of man, the three theological virtues, above all the battered theological virtues.

Epilogue

Beware of your own Spain, oh Spain!

—César Vallejo, *Spain, Let this Cup Pass from Me*, XV, 1.

Your Uncle Jerónimo believes in the three theological virtues, yes my boy, I have faith in life, hope in death, and charity toward man who sure needs it, I also have charity toward Spain although it doesn't always deserve it, in spite of everything it's necessary to be a patriot, notice, my boy, that I didn't say nationalist, *la patria*, the fatherland, is more permanent than the nation, also more natural and flexible, fatherlands were invented by the Creator, nations are made by men, fatherlands have a voice with which to sing and trees and rivers, nations have a voice in order to promulgate decrees and they also have institutions with which to shackle man and machine guns for defending the institutions, I see you not believing in anything, my boy, and I don't like that, one has to believe in something in order not to feel too much like an orphan, why don't you believe in the three theological virtues?, I assure you they are the only brazier we Spaniards have to keep others from freezing our hearts, do you remember those verses by Machado, God keep you, little Spaniard at your life's start, one of the two Spains is sure to freeze your heart?, you are twenty years old, my boy, it's a crime to freeze the heart of twenty-year-old boys, you should all resist, you should raise the banner of rebellion and warm your own hearts, think about what I'm telling you, your Uncle Jerónimo speaks with an opaque and emotion-laden voice, sometimes your Uncle Jerónimo is very sentimental, search your conscience, sit down at the foot of your bed and search your conscience, you have been losing your faith, your hope, and your charity, you never had much faith, much hope, or much charity, but now you have even less, it's been hard work for you to live a whole twenty years, it's taken a lot of effort, you started to die within a few days of being born but you haven't died yet, your attitude is very brave, very exhausting, perhaps you haven't had any other possibility, death is not a possibility, it is a certainty that can be hastened but it's not a possibility, life on the other hand is a possibility, only a possibility and not a certainty, life is possible but never certain, it can be strangled at any moment and even not come into being, ask Toisha, male pheasants and partridges peck at eggs and break them so that the female will not stop being in heat, you are convinced that when you see your first grey hair (maybe you'll die before you see your first grey hair) you ought to put a bullet in your head or jump off a cliff on your country's coast, it's an absolutely logical idea that doesn't worry you too much, you also admit the possibility that when that moment comes you'll laugh and dye your grey hair, it depends on a number of factors all of them beyond your control, we Spaniards must beware of the Spaniard we bear within ourselves, Ganivet says that we Spaniards live in a perpetual state of civil war, Dámaso Rioja is an assiduous reader of Ganivet, he knows him by heart, Ganivet is right but you dare to go even further, we Spaniards live in a permanent state of civil wars, in the plural, all against all, but also in an inhospitable civil war against ourselves and with our wounded and suffering hearts as battlefields, we Spaniards must beware of the Spaniard we bear within ourselves so that he won't slit our throat while we're sleeping and he's awake like a wolf lying in ambush, your Uncle Jerónimo does not believe in fire, in this respect he does not seem Spanish, yes my boy, the Spaniard is a pyromaniac because he wants to wipe away every trace of his past, every account of his present, and every hope for his future, every account of his present and every hope for his future too?, yes, maybe even more than every trace of his past, the Spaniard is ashamed of his past but fears his present and pays no attention to his future, the Spaniard also is ashamed of his present and knows that he would wind up being ashamed of his future, that's why he believes in fire above all things and bears a Torquemada in his heart, the Spaniard does not believe in God, he believes in fire, he believes in God only insofar as he gives him reasons and permission to light the fire, Torquemada didn't believe in God either, my boy, although people usually admit he did, my friend the poet Manolo Sandoval says very clearly in the last two verses of his sonnet *To an Intransigent* that those who govern Spain always have a burning torch in one hand, with Phrygian cap or monk's hood Torquemada is always part of the government, in government and outside government what the Spaniard likes is setting fire to Spain and to Spaniards, the first thing we Spaniards have to do is not catch fire, then we'll see, you must have faith in life, my boy, and hope in death, faith and hope are two virtues that reciprocally condition each other, remember the words of Unamuno, we only believe what we hope for and we only hope for what we believe, the Spaniard's head must be turned inside out like a sock, if we don't believe in life, why are we awaiting death?, if we don't await death, understand what I'm trying to say, if we don't await death with hope, how are we going to believe in life?, begin by believing in something, my boy, and you'll feel more comforted, it's too easy a crime to freeze the hearts and heads of twenty-year-old boys, all you have to do is forbid them all that might be enjoyable in life, all you have to do is empty their heads or blow them full of messianic ideas, that's the same thing, you twenty-year-old boys really want to be frozen, everything weighs too heavily on you, life, your head, and your heart weigh too heavily on you, you are not yet skilled in the arts of resistance of the flesh and the spirit and you see death as what it is not, a liberation, refuse to live the life of others, my boy, refuse to die the death of others and do not throw fuel on the destructive pyre of others or blow on its embers, I am old and very worn and lonely but I march on the road of death with the hope that death will at last refute all the Torquemadas in Phrygian caps or monastic hoods, yes my boy, I believe because it is absurd said Saint Augustine, life is also absurd and there it is, it's absurd but we still believe in it, death is absurd too, as absurd as life, and yet none of us is denied hope in death, desire can only be strangled with hope, your Uncle Jerónimo speaks sorrowfully, he's probably always spoken sorrowfully and you've never noticed till now, your Uncle Jerónimo had a mistress in Cuarenta Fanegas, maybe he still does and you don't know it, mistress, it's a very confusing word, it would be better to say lover, your Uncle Jerónimo had a lover in Cuarenta Fanegas, maybe he still has a lover in Cuarenta Fanegas and nobody knows it, your Uncle Jerónimo's lover is the mother of six children and very good-looking and healthy, every time she has a child she lets your Uncle Jerónimo suck her breasts, woman's milk is the fountain of life, your Uncle Jerónimo is no doubt right, your Uncle Jerónimo sits down in a rocking chair and rests his head on its back, his lover stands next to him, unbuttons her blouse, and nurses him while she rocks him very softly and with very quiet tenderness, your Uncle Jerónimo's lover is called Cecilia and she is married to a municipal employee in Chamartín de la Rosa, Cecilia's breasts are large and dark and her children are also beautiful and healthy, would you ask your mother for a glass of milk for me?, yes uncle, do you remember those verses by Lope de Vega my boy?, today I'm in the mood for reciting verses from memory, we old people have a very good memory for things we learned in our youth, oh sweet beloved land, stepmother to your true-born brood, and yet, so strangely bland, a kindly mother to an alien blood!, I think they're from his *Arcadia* but don't pay any attention, that I don't remember well, your Uncle Jerónimo looks tired and he closes his eyes, we have to love Spain, my boy, we have to love her very tenderly, very prudently, very cautiously, Spain can die in our hands any day, Spain's blood is poisoned and we have to make her breathe pure air, what I don't know is where we ought to start, do you know?, no, you don't know and you keep quiet, you and I understand very well why you're keeping quiet, does anybody know?, no, and that's the tragedy, nobody knows where we Spaniards ought to start, it could be that we have to start at the beginning and very slowly, Spain always had too many excessively patient Spaniards and too many excessively impatient Spaniards, I don't know what happens elsewhere but I can assure you that elsewhere lies are not usually so forgetful, people here lie with too much forgetting of the truth and even of the lie, of the last lie, unknown dangers are terrible because they are unknown, when we draw near them they are less terrible and frequently they're not even dangers, I don't know whether you understand what I'm trying to tell you, the worst and most terrible dangers are usually nesting in our own breast, our learned young Ortega y Gasset says that we Spaniards offer life a heart armored with rancor, until we open our hearts so the rancor can flee things will never change for us, the passions have been let loose, all you have to do is stand by the window and hear their bellowing, passion can be the cradle of love but also the cradle of death, caskets are the cradles of death, passion should be shown a broad and easy-to-walk path, fuel should go to meet fire so that only the fuel will burn, Unamuno already pointed out the danger, it is easier for the fire to find fuel than for the fuel to find fire, excuse me if I'm boring you my boy, when you're twenty years old it's enough to defend your heart against ice, make an effort to believe in something other than history, that great fallacy, believe in the theological virtues and in love, in life and in death, you see I'm not asking too much of you, love is never a torment and anyhow it's always love, I assure you that contrary to what people think love is never a tyrant and is always a companion for our uncertain voyage through life, life is a tunnel through which we walk sowing and reaping love or striking out blindly and being struck, there is no other possibility, open the doors of your soul wide and let love dwell in you, invade you like a tide, do not struggle against love biting and shooting, surrender without reservations, turn yourself into the food of love, the food of life and the food of death has already been assigned to you by the law of the universe, only your becoming or not becoming the food of love depends on you yourself and your inner law, phone whatever girl you have and invite her to go to bed with you, give love a free rein mounting the first girl that will let you, don't even greet the others, at twenty you have to be generous with love, my boy, love is not a storable commodity, you'll never be able to recover the love you don't offer or receive today, tomorrow's love is something else, love is an open sea unlike hatred which is a shut-up cloister, leave me alone with my old age and with my boredom and phone some loving girl, any girl who is wanting to love and be loved, there must be many because fortunately nature is still producing more love than hate, don't pay too much attention to me but go before it's too late and others get ahead of you, I assure you that if I were your age I wouldn't be here drinking glasses of milk, I'd like to introduce you to Cecilia (now it becomes clear to you that your Uncle Jerónimo still loves), it would be worth your while to know Cecilia, she's a very healthy and decent woman who believes in love and the fountains of life, Cecilia has a daughter your age, blonde, with big breasts, with deep laughing eyes, very cheerful, I'd like for you and Cecilia's daughter to love each other like two athletic puppies, Cecilia and I would really like to contemplate you and applaud you enthusiastically, if your mother finds out about this conversation she'll throw me out, we mustn't blame her, the poor woman never had time to think things over, tomorrow or the day after I'll take you to Cecilia's house to meet her, her daughter's name is Basilia, that shouldn't matter to you, she's much prettier than her name, her family calls her Basi, she wears her hair short like a boy's, you'll see her, it's too bad her father is full of preconceived ideas, it's the same with him as with your mother, he didn't have time either to think things over, he spends the whole day at his office, morning and afternoon, and so there's no chance, you know, I excuse him because it's not his fault that he's obtuse and full of obsessions, with no time to think things over, what can you do?, go on away now, all right don't go if you don't want to, anyhow I'm grateful to you for keeping me company, you'll go later, there's always time for everything, yes, open the doorway of your soul and let love consume you and turn you into ashes and smoke, renounce all you have except love and life, live to love and love to keep on living, be humble in everything and with everyone, also with yourself, don't take what I'm saying as advice, I'm nobody to be giving advice to anybody, I just think out loud in your presence, I'd never allow myself to give advice to anyone least of all a young person, Buddha and Saint Francis of Assisi renounced everything and begged for the piece of bread that they put in their mouths, their families turned against them angrily and wrathfully but Buddha and Saint Francis continued on their way pitying the world and loving even their families, woman's milk is the fountain of life, I live thanks to the fact that a woman lets me nurse at her breast, if it weren't so I would already have died of disgust, love and humility are the two fountains of good, be loving and humble like Buddha and like Saint Francis but don't ever stop feeling sexy, my boy, feeling sexy doesn't depend on a tender age and hard potency, no, feeling sexy is a habit, a tradition, a culture, Buddha and Saint Francis only lacked feeling sexy to reach perfection, if some day man follows in the footsteps of Buddha and Saint Francis and renounces the false wealth of material goods and fortifies his spirit in humility without despising his phallus, that day humanity will be saved and will laugh at wars and revolutions, at the police and the law, at bureaucrats, regulations, and patrons of the arts, what I don't know is whether that blessed day will ever come, we must look at the future with the eyes of hope, no one can take away our hope, people don't want to say so but hope is like a little bell that frightens death away, like a magic flute that drives death away, let us fight with couched pricks against the myths that oppress man, the flags the hymns the medals the numbers the insignia the institution of marriage the regional cuisine the public records office, you and I are obliged to fight against the artifices that adulterate man, that give his existence the color of death and his conscience the dryness of straw, it's possible that no one will listen to us but that should not lessen our holy wrath, our humility, our renunciation of harmful material riches, and our proclamation of the phallus promenading in triumph throughout the wide world, no one is important, my boy, and the dead even less, if you like I'll say it another way, all men are important and equal in their importance, the foolish threads of history are only good for weaving shrouds and the stupidity of the forces of conservatism is only comparable to the stupidity of the forces of revolution, which are also forces in the service of reaction though with the opposite sign, the forces of revolution do not fight against the flags the hymns and the medals but in defense of other flags other hymns and other medals, this is where theory breaks down and the authenticity of man grows numb, numbers keep on staining man, insignias decorate his lapel, marriage appears as a devouring pincers, and regional cuisine and the public records office go on just the same, I have to introduce you to Cecilia's daughter so you can experience for yourself the noble beauty of love and life holding up humility and goodness like two strong columns, Cecilia and I promise to applaud you, Cecilia is a very warm and vital woman, you'll meet her, Buddha and Saint Francis yes but perfected, excuse me, would you get me a glass of milk?, when you come back with the glass of milk your Uncle Jerónimo is looking out the window, night has fallen and the servant girls let themselves be kissed leaning against the lampposts, have you noticed that the world is full of people we don't know?, if you say for example that the Belgian Congo or immense China is populated by many blacks or Chinese who can't be counted because they're all the same, you know you're lying, blacks are not all the same and neither are Chinese, they're just all equally unknown, there are many blacks and they die of leprosy or eaten by lions, there are many Chinese and they die of hunger and of cholera, you can't count them if you didn't know them first and we don't know them, the world is full of people we don't know but they're all different, I assure you they're all different, each one has his pain and his joy, sometimes very small, and when he is born or dies nothing happens, that's true, but a hope and a disillusionment are born or die, no my boy, the blacks in the Congo and the Chinese in China are not all the same and they can be counted, the thing is we don't know how, you just save your three theological virtues and think that there's no great reason to deny the blacks and the Chinese theirs because of a greater or lesser reckoning, a greater or lesser census, never be cruel, my boy, I used to be cruel but I stopped some years ago, when I was cruel I used to accost people on the street and say let's see, what phase of the moon are we in?, now I'm asking you, not out of cruelty but just as a test, let's see, what phase of the moon are we in?, you don't know, don't worry, nobody knows and if somebody does know it's not because he's looked at the moon, you can be sure, it's because he's read it in the papers or on a calendar, your Uncle Jerónimo laughs and steps away from the window, when the history of these events is written it will be said that Madrid found itself suddenly populated by a flood of men and women all the same and uncountable, that will be a lie too, no two are the same and they can be counted with patience and a little order, the hard thing is to know where to start, Cecilia, who is very witty, you'll meet her, says that you can get to know men's ideas, ideas in general, religious moral social political, from the way they behave in bed, I don't know to what degree she's right or wrong but at any rate her method deserves attention, with women the diagnosis may be more difficult, there are few women who don't turn into masks in bed, Messalina, Saint Theresa of Avila, a chameleon, a bouquet of artificial flowers, etc., women have a great capacity for pretense and are not usually very humble, in bed the mother of a family is always a dramatic actress oozing pride or a comic actress, almost a clown, but who also oozes pride, trace yourself a path of faith, of hope, and of charity and don't depart from it no matter what happens, the fire of inquisitorial pyres is extinguished with semen, they burned Miguel Servet at the stake because Calvinists also don't fuck or ever did fuck enjoyably or enough, Calvinists are more inclined toward the procedural code than toward love, don't let anyone freeze the mysterious crannies of your heart, my boy, rebel against death, the epidemic of death, don't listen to me, I'm not alive to be listened to but to serve as an example, but don't listen to the others either, it's been hard work for you to live twenty years, don't squander your twenty years in the service of anybody, I assure you that your sacrifice would be sterile and what's even worse stupid, no my boy, no, your girls are waiting for you in bed, lessen their pride and proclaim your love of this lousy life which is still more habitable than a lousy death, a few shots are heard resounding almost languidly over the rooftops, nothing is more boring and monotonous than the inertia of gunpowder, you must try to see to it that your first grey hair does not sprout to the accompaniment of gunfire, look out for the Spaniard you carry inside you, who knows but he may have a head full of grey hairs to overcome his disgust with the scabby coin on his palate, the rusty coin that wounds his tongue and palate, no my boy, even though you think this is the end of the world it's not, if you like I'll swear it to you in the most histrionic and ridiculous position, whichever one you pick because it doesn't matter one bit to me as you can imagine, this is only a purgation of the world, a preventive and bloody purgation but not an apocalyptic one, the end of the world will be announced with very clear and unequivocal signs: children will poison their mothers in the womb with the most innocent poisons, a brew of savin leaves, a glass of arsenic tea, the most illustrious and reverential trees, the cypress, the walnut, the oak, will turn into opaque hard sponges, and the sun, instead of rising from the horizon, will rise from the bitter mirrors of wakes, from mirrors tired of portraying the trembling funereal candles of useless disconsolateness, for the time being no sign is observed, we can go calmly to bed, it must be very late already, I assure you that suffering is less important than behavior, let's go to bed, it must be very late already and the heart grows tired with so much foolishness.

Palma de Mallorca, in the octave of St. Camillus of 1969

A List of Characters and Other Matters of Interest

The purpose of this list is to help the reader keep track of reappearing characters and to explain who or what some of the possibly less familiar persons and things may be. It is arranged alphabetically; but to avoid the complexities of Spanish names, persons are usually listed by their first names, with a few cross-references made necessary by the text of the novel. Titles such as Don, Doña, Señor, General, are omitted. Thus, to find Don Roque Barcia the reader should look under the letter R. Characters fully identified by the context in which they appear or that appear only once are not listed. Persons with Spanish names are Spanish unless otherwise indicated. The names of those who are historical are followed by an asterisk. Many of the politicians and military officers who appear in the novel and are not listed here are known to the translator to be historical.

A reminder about pronunciation. Spanish vowels have approximately the values that the vowels have in the English words in parentheses: *a* (art), *e* (let), *i* (tea), *o* (fort), *u* (soup), except that *u* is silent in the combinations *gue* and *gui*. *Qu* sounds like 'k.' The letter *j*, and a *g* before *e* or *i*, have the guttural sound of German 'ach' or Scottish 'loch,' or, for our purposes, simply a strongly aspirated 'h.' Z, and *c* before *e* or *i*, sound like 'th' in 'thin.' Ñ is similar to 'ny' in 'canyon.' Double *l*, as in *Calle*, resembles 'lli' in 'million' or just 'y.' H is silent. These explanations would not do in Spanish 1, but they will suffice for the present purpose. Spanish words bearing a written accent are stressed on the accented syllable; if there is none, the stress falls on the next-to-last syllable if the word ends in a vowel, *n*, or *s*, otherwise the stress falls on the final syllable.

ABC: monarchist newspaper
Aguados: party-giving friends of Maripi Fuentes
Agustín Úbeda Martínez: Engracia's boyfriend
*Agustina de Aragón**: heroine of the defense of Saragossa against the French in 1808
Aixa the Moor: prostitute from Tangier with a tattoo around her navel
Alberto: son of Don Felipe Espinosa
*Alberto Insúa**: twentieth-century novelist
Albiñana Sanz, José María*: rightist deputy from Burgos
Alcalá Zamora, Niceto*: president of the Spanish Republic, 1931–1936, a Catholic and leader of the centrist Progressive Party
Alfonso: young man from Salamanca who goes out with the sisters
*Alonso Zamora Vicente**: classmate of the narrator, scholar

Álvarez Quintero brothers,* Joaquín and Serafín: twentieth-century playwrights
Amanda Ortiz: scar-faced whore involved in a café row
"_and this is that part of the planet where wanders the shade of Cain_": conclusion of the poem _Por tierras de España_ from Antonio Machado's _Campos de Castilla_. The reference is to Spain.
Anual: location of a disastrous Spanish defeat in the protectorate of Morocco in 1921
Andrés Herrera: law student, friend of the narrator
Anita Luque de Blanco: adulterous wife of Don Baltasar Blanco
Antonio Arévalo: boyfriend of María Victoria Espinosa
Antonio Machado*: poet, died 1939
Aparisi Guijarro,* Antonio: conservative political writer of the nineteenth century
Apeles Mestres*: artist
Appelgate,* Mrs.: see Frances Creighton
Arturo Serrano Plaja*: scholar
Assault Guard (Guardia de Asalto): special paramilitary constabulary of "storm troops" created by the Republic and recruited among adherents of the Left
Asterio Cuevilla: father of Juani and Lupita, "the sisters." The fact that he is called "Señor Asterio," with the title before his first name, indicates a social rank lower than that of characters whose first name is preceded by Don.
Asturias: province in northern Spain, scene of a leftist revolution in 1934, suppressed by the Army of the Republic commanded by General Francisco Franco
Ateneo de Madrid: a club for persons interested in literary and intellectual matters
Attic bee*: the Greek historian Xenophon, so called for the elegance of his writing
Avelino Folgueras: traveling salesman in Doña Teresa's boardinghouse
Azaña*: see _Manuel Azaña_
Azorín*: pseudonym of José Martínez Ruiz, twentieth-century essayist and novelist
Bailén, battle of: spectacular defeat of a Napoleonic army by a mixed force of Spanish troops and civilians, 1808
Baldomera Hidalgo Ibáñez: manager of a cooperative brothel
Balmes,* Jaime: nineteenth-century Catholic philosopher
Baltasar Blanco: colleague of Don León Rioja, cuckolded husband of Anita
Barberán and Collar*: military aviators who flew from Seville to Cuba in 1933 and were then lost off the coast of Mexico
Baroja,* Pío: novelist, died 1956
Bella Otero*: see _Carolina_
Bella Tortajada,* Consuelo Tortajada: dancer, born in the late nineteenth century
Bergamín,* José: twentieth-century playwright, essayist, poet
Bernardina Pacheco: wife of Don Leopoldo Garrido Manzanares
Bold Knight,* José María Carretero: journalist and novelist who used the pen name El Caballero Audaz
Boozer Joe: see _Galdós_
Braulio Mandueño: bullfight aficionado, friend of Manene Chico
Calvo Sotelo,* José: deputy of the monarchist party Renovación Española, murdered on July 13, 1936, by Assault Guards and others
Cándido Modrego: former leftist who has turned reactionary, friend of Don Olegario Murciego
Cándido Nocedal*: conservative politician of the nineteenth century
Carabanchel: a lower-class suburb of Madrid
Carlistada, Sargentada, Vicalvarada, Francesada, Sanjuanada: various violent incidents of modern Spanish history: the civil wars fought against the Carlists in the nine-

teenth century, the rebellion of a group of sergeants against Isabel II in 1866, the liberal military coup of 1854, the war against the French (1808–1814), an unsuccessful coup attempt against the dictator Miguel Primo de Rivera planned for St. John's Day, June 24, 1926

Carlists: a politically and religiously traditionalist movement of the nineteenth and twentieth centuries

Carlos Fuentes, Count Casa Redruello: father of Maripi and José Carlos

Carmencita: Matiítas' neighbor

*Carolina Rodríguez**: called "la Bella Otero," Spanish dancer, died 1965

Casa Redruello, Count, Don Carlos Fuentes: father of José Carlos and Maripi

Casares Quiroga, Santiago*: politician of the Republican Left party, prime minister at the outbreak of the Civil War

Cascorro: town in Cuba where, in 1896, during the Cuban insurrection against Spanish rule, the Spanish soldier Eloy Gonzalo García distinguished himself by an act of suicidal heroism. His statue adorns Madrid's Plaza de Cascorro, at the upper end of the Rastro or flea market.

Castillo, José*: lieutenant of the Assault Guard, murdered by four Falangists on July 12, 1936

*Caupolicán**: chief of the Araucanian Indians in Chile, killed by the Spaniards in the sixteenth century

CEDA, Confederación Española de Derechas Autónomas (Spanish Confederation of the Autonomous Right), Catholic political grouping led by Gil Robles

*César Vallejo**: twentieth-century Peruvian poet

Cesáreo Murciego: monarchist, wearer of a green hat

Chelo: whore who committed suicide drinking lye

Chonina: former maid, former lover of the narrator, now whore

Cid, Rodrigo Díaz de Vivar*: known as the Cid Campeador, Castilian hero, died 1099

Cid Ruiz-Zorrilla, José María*: republican politician, leader of the Agrarian Party

Civil Guard (Guardia Civil): paramilitary national police force

*Civilón**: a bull that showed fighting spirit when tested but subsequently grew tame. In a bullfight in the spring of 1936, he behaved nobly but also came obediently when called by those who raised him, and the crowd asked that his life be spared, which it was.

Clarita: wife of Sánchez Somoza, caught out with Virgilio Taboada

CNT, Confederación Nacional del Trabajo: Anarchist labor organization

Comuneros: a popular movement against the authority of the new king Charles I (the Emperor Charles V), crushed in 1521

*Concepción Arenal**: nineteenth-century social reformer

Conchita: maid in the house of the Count and Countess Casa Redruello, and part-time whore

Conchita Garrido: daughter of Don Leopoldo

Consuelito: whore at Maruja's

Consuelo Díaz: see *Díaz*

Cordobesita, María Inés la: former painter's model, now whore

*Cristóbal de Castillejo**: sixteenth-century poet

Croix de Feu: French Fascist movement

Customs Guard, (Carabineros): paramilitary customs service

Cyril: a king of England apparently invented by Cela, but whose murder resembles that of Edward II in 1327. The name may be related to *cirio* 'candle,' a vulgar term for 'phallus', according to Pierre L. Ullman, "Sobre la recitificación del espejo emblemático en *San Camilo, 1936* de Cela," *Neophilologus* 66 (1982): 381.

Dámaso Rioja: classmate of the narrator

Dehesa de la Villa: park in Madrid

Díaz, Mrs.: blind old mother of Chelo, the whore who killed herself drinking lye

*Diego ("Don Diego") Martínez Barrio**: leader of the leftist Republican Union Party

Domingo Ibarra: Nicaraguan musician, friend of the narrator

Dominica Morcillo Fernández: a former whore, friend and neighbor of Don Olegario Murciego

Donata: a prostitute

Donoso Cortés, Juan*: Catholic and monarchist essayist of the nineteenth century

Dulce: one of Don Máximo's repertoire of whores

Eduvigis Olmedillo: asthmatic wife of Don Vicente Parreño

El Debate: Catholic newspaper

El Siglo Futuro: Carlist newspaper

El Sol: a distinguished liberal newspaper

Emilio Arroyo and Virgilio Ricote: perpetual students, boarders at Doña Teresa's

Emilita: daughter of Simón Tendero, an unwed mother

Emilito: son of Señor Asterio and Señora Lupe, drowned in childhood

Encarna: madam

Engracia Martínez Sobrino: enthusiastic young Socialist

Enrique: physician, son of Don Leopoldo Garrido Manzanares

*Enrique Gil y Carrasco**: nineteenth-century Romantic poet and novelist

Enriqueta: a prostitute at Madame Teddy's

Espartero, Baldomero*: nineteenth-century general whose equestrian statue stands on the Calle de Alcalá, on the way to the Eastern Cemetery

Espronceda, José de*: Romantic poet

Estanislao Montañés Sainz: client of Chelo who inquires after her at the first-aid station

Esteban: blind man for whom Matiítas reads, uncle of Guillermo Zabalegui

"eternal clouds may cover up the sun . . .": verses by Gustavo Adolfo Bécquer, nineteenth-century late Romantic poet

Evelina Castellote: maid who miscarries in the street

Eyes, Miss: whore at Milagritos' place, whose sister, Marta, is also a whore

Falange Española: Fascist party or "movement" founded in 1933 by José Antonio Primo de Rivera

Fausto: sadistic lover of Matiítas

Feliciano: notary, Don León Rioja's boss

Felipe: son of Don Felipe Espinosa

Felipe Espinosa: neighbor of the Count Casa Redruello

*Felipe Sánchez Román**: liberal professor of law

*Ferdinand VII**: king of Spain 1808–1833, who repeatedly sought to reverse movement toward constitutionalism and democracy even after having sworn to support it

*Fernán Cruz**: witness to the murder of Lt. Castillo

Fernando: a café customer, mentioned only once

Fidel Ternera: alias Vicar, a poor man, Paca's friend

Fourteenth of April: anniversary of the proclamation of the second Spanish Republic on April 14, 1931

*Frances Creighton**: "Mrs. Mary Frances Creighton, 38-year-old housewife, and Everett Appelgate, 36-year-old former American Legion official, were executed at Sing Sing Prison shortly after 11 o'clock tonight [September 16, 1936] for the poisoning of Appelgate's wife, Ada, at Baldwin, L.I., last Sept. 27." (*New York Times*, July 17, 1936, p. 1) Sing Sing Prison is at Ossining, New York, nowhere near Auburn.

*Francisco Pi y Margall**: federalist politician, president of the first Spanish Republic in 1873

Free Educational Institute (Institución Libre de Enseñanza): an independent liberal educational establishment outside the universities, associated with the followers of Krause

Frégoli, Leopoldo Fregoli*: an Italian actor of the late nineteenth and early twentieth centuries, a volunteer in East Africa and subsequently famous for his ability to play several characters of the same play or skit

Gabriel Seseña: nightclub manager, lover of Turquoise

*Gabriela Mistral**: Chilean poet, Nobel Prize winner

Galdós, Benito Pérez*: 1843–1920, Spain's greatest novelist after Cervantes. Two of his novels are referred to in *San Camilo, 1936*: *Fortunata and Jacinta*, generally considered his masterpiece, quoted in the epigraph to Part I, and one of his historical *Episodios Nacionales, King Joseph's Baggage*, which Don León Rioja reads. Joseph Bonaparte, brother of Napoleon and king of Spain as Joseph I, was accused by his enemies of being a drunkard and called Pepe Botellas, 'Boozer Joe.'

Ganivet, Angel*: late nineteenth-century essayist, novelist, and poet

*Garcilaso de la Vega**: Spanish soldier and poet of the sixteenth century, who died of wounds received as he fell while scaling a fortress wall in southern France

*Gerardo Diego**: twentieth-century poet, published an influential anthology of contemporary poetry in 1932

Gerardo Sanemeterio: rich provincial, Ginesa's customer

Gil Robles, José María*: leader of the Catholic political grouping CEDA (Spanish Confederation of the Autonomous Right)

Giner de los Ríos, Francisco*: a leading intellectual associated with the liberal Institución Libre de Enseñanza, died in 1915; not to be confused with Bernardo Giner de los Ríos, member of the Martínez Barrio cabinet

Ginesa: whore from Murcia, friend of Don Gerardo and Senén

Goded Llopis, General Manuel*: leader of the insurgency in Barcelona, captured, tried, and executed in 1936

Goicoechea, Antonio*: leader of the monarchist party Renovación Española

Gonococcus: nickname of Victoriano Palomo Valdés, expectant husband of Virtudes

Gregorio Montes: friend of the narrator who has an unfortunate experience with Mireya

Guillermo Zabalegui: friend of the narrator

Gumersindo López Lahoz: fiancé of Conchita Garrido, daughter of Don Leopoldo

*Henri Barbusse**: twentieth-century French novelist

Herminia: sister of Doña Vicenta, planning to take the veil

Hilario: boarder at Doña Teresa's

Hipólita: woman whose lover leaves her money on condition she marry

Hungerford, Margaret Hamilton Wolfe Argles*: Irish novelist, died 1897. The title given in Spanish, *Por amor y por bondad*, does not correspond to any I have seen in library catalogs, unless it be the short story *Sweet Is True Love*, which I have been unable to examine.

Ibarra: see *Domingo Ibarra*

*Ildefonso Manolo (i.e., Manuel) Gil**: twentieth-century poet

*Indalecio Prieto**: Socialist politician

Inmaculada Múgica: rancid-smelling whore, eventually killed by subway
Instituto Escuela: a school affiliated with the Free Educational Institute (see above)
*Isaac Peral**: nineteenth-century inventor of a submarine, construction of which had to be abandoned
Isabel: brothel manager
James, Saint*: patron saint of Spain, whose feast is July 25
Javiera: maid in Doña Teresa's boardinghouse
Jesualdo Villegas: reporter, former avant-garde poet
Jesusa: neighbor of Virtudes and Victoriano
*Joaquín Costa**: sociologist, historian, and advocate of reform, died 1911
Joaquín del Burgo: secondhand dealer, husband of Paquita (Margot)
*José Antonio Primo de Rivera**: son of the dictator Miguel Primo de Rivera and founder of Falange Española, a Fascist party or "movement"
*José Canalejas**: prime minister murdered by an anarchist in 1912
José Carlos Fuentes: brother of Maripi, son of Count Casa Redruello
*José María Cid**: see Cid
José Sánchez Sánchez: false name given by Don Roque
Jovellanos, Gaspar Melchor de*: leading figure of the Enlightenment in late eighteenth-century Spain
*Juan Panero**: twentieth-century poet
*Juan Ramón Jiménez**: poet, Nobel Prize winner in 1956
Juan Sánchez: chauffeur of Don Cesáreo Murciego, killed in an accident
Juana Pagán: alias Irma Hollywood and one of the Rogers Sisters, singer
Juani: one of the tuberculous sisters
*Juanita Rico**: took part in the mutilation of the corpse of a Falangist killed by the Socialists on June 10, 1932, and was killed a few days later in a Falangist reprisal
Juanito Mateo: reporter for *El Heraldo*, a man of revolutionary ideas and wandering hands
Julianín: Gregorio Montes' half-wit cousin
*Julián Marías**: contemporary philosopher
*Karel Hynek Mácha**: Czech Romantic poet, 1810–1836
Kempis, Thomas à*: fifteenth-century German mystic, author of *The Imitation of Christ*
Krause, Karl Christian Friedrich*: German philosopher of the early nineteenth century whose thought inspired a liberal movement in late nineteenth-century Spain
La Hebrea: Jewish whore in Doña Encarna's establishment
Largo Caballero, Francisco*: left-wing Socialist leader, prime minister in 1936 and 1937
Larra, Mariano José de*: essayist of the Romantic period
La Tierra: Communist newspaper
Law of the Twelve Tables: ancient Roman legal code
*Léon Blum**: French Socialist politician
León Rioja: father of Dámaso, and husband of Doña Matilde
Leoncio Romero: man with a crippled leg, a Treasury employee
Leonorcita: Juanito Mateo's girl
Leopoldo: son of Don Leopoldo Garrido Manzanares
Leopoldo Garrido Manzanares: father of seven children
Lerroux, Alejandro*: leader of the centrist Radical Party
*Lope de Vega**: playwright, poet, and novelist of the seventeenth century; his *Fuenteovejuna* is a play about a popular uprising after which the villagers declare themselves collectively responsible for killing their lord
Lucio Martínez Morales: brothel client

Lucio Saavedra: dieting boarder at Doña Teresa's
Luis de León,* Fray: Spanish poet of the sixteenth century
*Luis Enrique Délano**: Chilean novelist who lived in Madrid in the mid-thirties
*Luis Felipe Vivanco**: twentieth-century poet
Lupe: wife of Señor Asterio and mother of Juani and Lupita, the tuberculous sisters
Lupita: one of the tuberculous sisters
Macías Picavea,* *Ricardo*: nineteenth-century novelist and political writer
Magdalena: real name of Inmaculada Múgica
Mahogany: former whore and then mistress of important men
Manene Chico: a *banderillero* with the bullfighter Rafael el Gallo. Manene Chico was the nickname of the *banderillero* Rafael Martínez, called 'Manny Junior' after his brother Manuel Martínez, alias Manene; but this Manene Chico died in 1900.
*Manolo (Manuel de) Sandoval**: twentieth-century poet and member of the Royal Spanish Academy
*Manuel ("Don Manuel") Azaña**: leader of the Republican Left party and president of the Spanish Republic
*Manuel Bartolomé Cossío**: liberal educator and art historian, died 1935
*Manuel García Morente**: twentieth-century philosopher
*Marañón**, *Gregorio*: twentieth-century physician and essayist
*Marcelino Menéndez Pelayo**: conservative historian of Spanish literature and culture, 1856–1912
Margarita: brothel manager
Margot: whore, formerly Paquita, wife of Don Joaquín del Burgo
María Angustias: young second wife of Don Felipe Espinosa
María Luisa: brothel manager who suffers from a female ailment
María Victoria: daughter of Don Felipe Espinosa
*María Zambrano**: philosopher and essayist, born 1904
Maripi Fuentes: youngest daughter of the Count and Countess Casa Redruello
Marramáu: a cripple who sells tobacco on the street
*Martínez Barrio**: see *Diego*
Maruja la Valvanera: madam, perhaps named after Our Lady of Valvanera, an image venerated in the province of Logroño. Maruja is a nickname for María.
*Maruja Mallo**: twentieth-century surrealist painter
Maruja Onrubia: woman bullfighter
Marujita Expósito: murdered whore
Matías from the commissary: Matías Suárez, client of Amanda
Matiítas (diminutive of Matías, 'Matty'): homosexual clerk in a condom shop, reads for Don Esteban
Matilde Brocas: invalid wife of Don León Rioja, mother of Dámaso Rioja
*Max Aub**: twentieth-century Spanish novelist
Máximo: deputy of Don Diego Martínez Barrio's party
Merceditas: owner of a house of assignation
Micaela Crespo: owner of a house of assignation
Michael Strogoff: heroic courier of the czar in the nineteenth-century adventure novel *Michel Strogoff* by Jules Verne
*Miguel de Unamuno**: essayist, novelist, poet, playwright, professor and rector of the University of Salamanca, died 1936
*Miguel Hernández**: poet who died in captivity after the Civil War
Miguel Mercader: friend of the narrator, hurt in a scuffle
*Miguel Servet**: Spanish heretical theologian and physician burned at the stake in Geneva in 1553

Milagritos Moreno: madam, known as Socorrito
Mimí Ortiz de Amoedo: aunt of Guillermo Zabalegui
Mirenchu: female jai-alai player and friend of Toisha's
Mireya: French whore
Mola, General Emilio*: one of the leaders of the uprising against the Republic, killed in an airplane crash in 1937
Murcian, Ginesa the: whore, friend of Don Gerardo
Narváez, General Ramón*: conservative strong man of the mid-nineteenth century
Nicaraguan, Domingo Ibarra: musician, friend of the narrator
Nicolás Mañes: orthopedist who fixes Don Leoncio's "hardware"
*Nicolás Salmerón**: republican politician of the nineteenth century
October ("the butchers of October"): see *Asturias*
Olegario Murciego: Don Cesáreo's poor brother, an inventor
Ortega y Gasset, José*: twentieth-century philosopher
*Pablo Iglesias**: early leader of the Spanish Socialist Party
*Pablo Neruda**: Chilean poet, Nobel Prize winner
Paca: hunchbacked whore specializing in masturbation
Paquita Pineda: madam, also owner of a house of assignation
Paquito: impecunious aristocrat waiting for his father to die, nephew of Don Leopoldo and Doña Bernardina
Paquito: young man from Salamanca who goes out with the sisters
Pasionaria, Dolores Ibarruri*: Communist politician
*Paul Verlaine**: nineteenth-century French poet
Paulina: maid in Doña Teresa's boardinghouse
*Pedro Mata**: twentieth-century novelist
*Pedro Salinas**: twentieth-century poet
People's Olympics: organized in 1936 as an alternative to the official games in Berlin
Pepe Carlos, José Carlos Fuentes: son of Count Casa Redruello
Pepita: a teacher, daughter of Don Leopoldo Garrido
Pepito la Zubiela: homosexual, former brothel employee, then valet to Don Cesáreo
Pérez de Ayala, Ramón*: twentieth-century novelist, essayist, poet
*Pérez Galdós**: see *Galdós*
Perico: assassin of Lt. Castillo
Petra la Grillo: mulatto whore murdered by Don Joaquín; *grillo* means 'cricket,' but is also a slang term for a venereal disease
Petra Soto Coscoja: manager of a cooperative brothel
Plus Ultra: an airplane, piloted by Ramón Franco (brother of Francisco) on a record-breaking transatlantic flight in 1926
Poem of Fernán González: anonymous narrative poem of the thirteenth century
Polavieja, Camilo García de*: conservative general who served in Cuba and the Philippines and as minister of war
Ponson du Terrail, Viscount Pierre Alexis*: French author of popular novels in the nineteenth century, among them *Turquoise la Pécheresse (Turquoise the Sinner)*
Popular Front: victorious alliance of the parties of the Left in the elections of February 1936
POUM, *Partido Obrero de Unificación Marxista (Workers' Party of Marxist Unity)*: a Trotskyist party
Prieto, Indalecio*: Socialist politician
Prim, General Juan*: hero of African war of 1859 and leader of the revolution against Isabel II in 1868, assassinated in 1870

Primo de Rivera, Miguel*: military dictator from 1923 to 1930
Puerta del Sol: square in central Madrid
P.V.E.B.: initials of a contributor who wants to protect his or her privacy
Quevedo, Francisco de*: poet and novelist of the seventeenth century
*Rafael Alberti**: twentieth-century poet
*Rafael Pérez Delgado**: twentieth-century historian and critic
*Ráfols, María**: 1781–1853, nun, heroine of the siege of Saragossa in 1808, founder of an order, author of spiritual writings
Ramón: father of Engracia
*Ramón Nocedal**: reactionary politician, son of Cándido Nocedal, died in 1907
Ramón y Cajal, Santiago*: physician, Nobel Prize winner in 1906 for his research in histology
Ramona: Virgilio Taboada's landlady
*Ramper**: a very popular comedian of the early twentieth century whose real name was Ramón Pérez
Raúl T. Ortiz de Ojuel: society veterinarian, son of Simón Tendero
Raúl Taboada: journalist
Remarque, Erich Maria*: twentieth-century German novelist
Renovación Española: monarchist party
*Ricardo León**: twentieth-century poet and novelist
Rikki-tikki-tavi: the brave mongoose in Kipling's *The Jungle Book*
Rogelio Roquero: milkman who got Doña Soledad's half-wit twins pregnant
Román Navarro: brothel client
Romero, Don Leoncio: a man with a crippled leg
Rómula: whore formerly at Maruja's, hospitalized
Roque Barcia: deputy of the rightist Agrarian Party, not to be confused with
*Roque Barcia**: antireligious and antimonarchist politician and writer of the nineteenth century, leader of a movement to establish the city of Cartagena as an autonomous "canton," and author of *Diccionario general etimológico de la lengua española*
Roque Zamora: impecunious journalist
*Rubén Darío**: Nicaraguan poet, 1867–1916
Ruiz Zorrilla, Manuel*: republican politician of the nineteenth century
Sabina Burguete González: manager of a cooperative brothel
Sacramento (Doña Sacra): madam, mother of Virtudes
Sánchez Somoza: deputy, catches his wife out with Virgilio Taboada
Sanjurjo, General José*: leader of an unsuccessful coup against the Republic on August 10, 1932
Sanz del Río, Julián*: nineteenth-century philosopher who brought the philosophy of Krause into Spain
sapienti est ordinare: 'the wise man's task is to classify'; *itinerarium mentis ad Deum*, 'the mind's journey to God'
*Sarah Bernhardt**: famous French actress, died 1923
Second of May: uprising of the people of Madrid against occupying French troops on May 2, 1808
Senén: cigarette seller befriended by Don Gerardo
Sert, José María*: twentieth-century painter
Seven Evangelizers: seven disciples of Sts. Peter and Paul who, according to tradition, were ordained as bishops and sent to bring Christianity to Spain, where they eventually met martyrdom

*Silverio Lanza**: a writer of fiction, died 1912
Simón Tendero: park guard, father of Raúl T. Ortiz de Ojuel
Sixto Lopera: businessman with a brother in Segovia, friend of Don Estanislao Montañés
Skull Fields (Campo de las Calaveras): an open space in Madrid, former site of a cemetery
Socorrito: fictional name of the madam Milagritos Moreno
Soledad: a widow who rents rooms for sexual trysts
Solita and Conchita: pregnant half-wit twin daughters of Doña Soledad
Spanish Military League (Unión Militar Española): an organization of military officers conspiring against the Republic
Syndicalist Party: Anarchists
Teddy: madam of a very cultured brothel
Teresa: Don Roque Barcia's landlady
Tetuan: city in the Spanish protectorate in Morocco, also the name of a street and a district in Madrid
Tizzi-Azza, Tizza: scene of a bloody battle near Melilla, in Spanish Morocco, in 1921
Toisha: the narrator's girl
Tomás Donato: lover of Anita Luque de Blanco
Tragic Week of Barcelona: labor unrest and anticlerical violence of July 1909
Tránsito: Toisha
Turquoise: chanteuse, cousin of Ginesa the Murcian, lover of Gabriel Seseña
UGT, Unión General de Trabajadores: Socialist labor organization
*Unamuno**: see *Miguel*
Valencian fiesta: on St. Joseph's Day, March 19, large figures similar to the floats of some American parades are burned in the streets and squares of Valencia
Valentina: madam who expels Miguel Mercader
*Velázquez**: the painter
Verdun, Battle of: taxis were used by the French to rush troops to the defense of Verdun (1916), where General Pétain had proclaimed, "They shall not pass"
Vicenta: provincial lady who with her husband is staying at Doña Teresa's to attend her sister's taking the veil
Vicente Parreño: brothel client
Victoriano Palomo Valdés: alias Gonococcus, husband of Virtudes, son-in-law of Doña Sacra
Virgilio Taboada: journalist, caught with Clarita by her husband Sánchez Somoza and bathed in hot chocolate
*Viriathus**: leader of a rebellion of the Lusitanians, in what is now Portugal, against Roman rule, eventually assassinated, second century B.C.
Virtudes: daughter of Doña Sacra and pregnant wife of Victoriano
Vivre libre ou mourir: 'Live free or die,' motto on Aixa's belly
Wifredo: managing editor of Juanito Mateo's paper
Willy: nickname of Guillermo Zabalegui
works of mercy: traditionally seven in number for the corporal works of mercy (to feed the hungry, to give drink to the thirsty, etc.) and seven for the spiritual works of mercy
Ya: Catholic newspaper

Bibliography

The bibliography on Camilo José Cela is extensive and likely to grow with the award of the Nobel Prize. What follows makes no pretense at completeness. I list only those studies available in English; for further information, the reader should consult one of the listed bibliographies.

Bibliographies

Abad Contreras, Pedro. "Bibliografía de Camilo José Cela." *Insula* 45.518/519 (February-March 1990): I-VIII [green pages separately numbered in Roman numerals].

Huarte Morton, Fernando. "Camilo José Cela: Bibliografía." *Revista Hispánica Moderna* 38 (1962): 210–20.

General Studies on Camilo José Cela [Note that the date of most of these precludes their dealing with *San Camilo, 1936*.]

Foster, David William. *Forms of the Novel in the Works of Camilo José Cela*. Columbia: University of Missouri Press, 1967.

Ilie, Paul. *The Novels of Camilo José Cela*. Dissertation Brown University. Ann Arbor: University Microfilms, 1959. A revised and more up to date version in Spanish is the author's *La novelística de Camilo José Cela*. 3a. edición. Madrid: Gredos, 1978.

Kirsner, Robert. "Cela's Quest for a Tragic Sense of Life." *Kentucky Romance Quarterly* 17 (1970): 259–66.

———. *The Novels and Travels of Camilo José Cela*. University of North Carolina Studies in the Romance Languages and Literatures 43. Chapel Hill: University of North Carolina Press, 1963.

McPheeters, D. W. *Camilo José Cela*. New York: Twayne, 1969.

Studies of *San Camilo, 1936*

Bernstein, J. S. "Confession and Inaction in *San Camilo*." *Hispanófila* 51 (1974): 47–63.

Díaz, Janet W. "Techniques of Alienation in Recent Spanish Novels." *Journal of Spanish Studies: Twentieth Century* 3 (1975): 5–16.

Ilie, Paul. "The Politics of Obscenity in *San Camilo, 1936*." *Anales de la Novela de Posguerra* 1 (1976): 25–63.

Pérez, Janet. "Historical Circumstance and Thematic Motifs in *San Camilo, 1936*." *Review of Contemporary Fiction* 4.3 (Fall 1984): 67–80.

Polt, J. H. R. "Cela's *San Camilo, 1936* as Anti-History." *Anales de Literatura Española* 6 (1988): 443–55.

San Camilo, 1936, in Spanish Editions

Vísperas, festividad y octava de San Camilo del año 1936 en Madrid. [Short title on the cover: *San Camilo, 1936.*] Madrid and Barcelona: Alfaguara, 1969.
Vísperas, festividad y octava de San Camilo del año 1936 en Madrid. [Short title on the cover: *San Camilo 1936.*] Madrid: Alianza Editorial and Alfaguara, 1974. Paperback edition, several reprints.

Books by Camilo José Cela Translated into English

The Hive. Translated by J. M. Cohen. London: Victor Gollancz, and New York: Farrar, Strauss and Young, 1953. Subsequent reissues.
Journey to the Alcarria. Translated by Frances M. López-Morillas. Madison: University of Wisconsin Press, 1964.
Mrs. Caldwell Speaks to Her Son. Translated by J. S. Bernstein. Ithaca: Cornell University Press, 1968.
Pascual Duarte's Family. Translated by John Marks. London: Eyre & Spottiswoode, 1946. Also translated as *The Family of Pascual Duarte* by Anthony Kerrigan. Boston: Little, Brown, 1964. Reissued 1966 and 1972 by Avon (New York), and 1990 by Little, Brown. Also translated by Herma Briffault. New York: Las Américas, 1965.
Rest Home. Translated by Herma Briffault. New York: Las Américas, 1961.

Histories of the Spanish Civil War and Related Matters

Bolloten, Burnett. *The Spanish Civil War: Revolution and Counterrevolution.* Chapel Hill: University of North Carolina Press, 1991.
Brenan, Gerald. *The Spanish Labyrinth.* Cambridge: Cambridge University Press, 1943.
Jackson, Gabriel. *The Spanish Republic and the Civil War, 1931–1939.* Princeton: Princeton University Press, 1965.
Thomas, Hugh. *The Spanish Civil War.* New York: Harper & Row, 1961.

John H. R. Polt graduated from Princeton University and received a Ph.D. in Romance Languages and Literature from the University of California, Berkeley, in whose Department of Spanish and Portuguese he has taught since 1956. Along with editions and studies of modern Spanish and Spanish American authors (Forner, Jovellanos, Mallea, Meléndez Valdés), he has published a translation of Governor Juan Bautista Alvarado's *Vignettes of Early California*. The American Philosophical Society, the American Council of Learned Societies, and the John Simon Guggenheim Momorial Foundation have awarded him fellowships.

Library of Congress Cataloging-in-Publication Data
Cela, Camilo José, 1916–
[Vísperas, festividad y octava de San Camilo sel año 1936 en Madrid. English]
San Camilo, 1936 : the Eve, Feast, and Octave of St. Camillus of the year 1936 in Madrid / Camilo José Cela : Translated by J. H. R. Polt.
Translation of: Vísperas, festividad y octava de San Camilo sel año 1936 en Madrid
ISBN 0-8223-1179-8. — ISBN 0-8223-1196-8 (pbk.)
I. Title.
PQ6605.E44V5413 1991
863'.62 — dc20 91-13388 CIP